Author's Note: The characters and events in this book are fi
tional. While some names of places are real and some of the
events are historically accurate, the story is a product of the
author's imagination.

Scripture quotations: New American Standard Bible
copyright: Creation House, Inc., 1960, 1962, 1963, 1971, 1972,
1973

ISBN-13:978-1542880862
ISBN-10:1542880866

Available from: amazon.com

Cover design: thecovercounts.com

Without A Doubt

Accident or Murder

DEDICATION

For my husband;
whose love, support and encouragement kept me going.

For my MacLaren Clan relatives;
whose names I borrowed with no similarity to the character.

For my Grandpa Low and my mother;
who taught me what it meant to be Scottish.

Special thanks to my Oregon Christian Writers critique group who
spurred me on to learn and develop my voice in the writing craft.

Set in Scotland a century ago, this mystery provides intriguing twists and turns as Maggie Richards struggles for answers in a foreign land from a family she never knew. With artful descriptions, the author created a wholesome tale with authentic scenes filled with suspense, romance and touches of humor. A thumbs up to "Without A Doubt."

—John Lawe, author

Maggie Richards knows, from her mother's letters, that the woman was supremely happy with her marriage to a Scottish Lord. Shocked at the news of her mother's sudden death, Maggie disagrees with a verdict of 'accident.' Determined to learn the truth, Maggie and two friends journey to Scotland. There,they meet interesting villagers and discover the Lord of the manor is missing. His son romances Maggie. Surprises move the story along in a gripping way. A GOOD read. 4+stars

—Geni J. I. White
Author of FigLeaf Mystery, Anders Village, and
Ho, Ho, Ha: Merry Heart Medicine

Donna Hues' debut novel, "Without a Doubt," is a well-written historical set in Scotland near the turn of the 19th century. A young woman journeys from America with two friends. Maggie seeks to discover if her mother's death was not an accident, but murder, and if murder, bring her mother's killer to justice. A good, clean entertaining story with elements of mystery, light romance, and characters you will love.

—Lorna Woods
Author of the Southeast Alaska series

Contact Donna at: https://donnahues.com or
donnahues@hotmail.com

Without A Doubt

Accident or Murder

MNM Mystery Series
Book 1

MNM Mystery Series is based on the adventures of three
friends: Maggie Richards, Nellie Cox and Max Sullivan

Donna Hues

You shall know the truth and the truth shall set you free.
—*Jesus Christ*—

For here we are not afraid to follow truth wherever it may lead.
—*Thomas Jefferson*—

Chapter 1

No time for a change of plans or second thoughts for Margaret Richards. With her cheek pressed against the carriage's cold glass window and eyes closed, she listened as each hoofbeat transported her closer to Stuart Hall. Her face pulsated from the vibrations on the glass.

Scotland seemed a bleak country. The fog lay heavy on the moors while a canopy of mist prevented the sun from warming the carriage. A wool tartan blanket, courtesy of the coachman, lay over Maggie's lap to ward off the chill. Her two companions didn't seem to mind the coolness.

Maggie, to her friends, lowered a window and craned her neck to peer beyond the black steed. As the trees whizzed by, the minutes ticked away before she would stand face-to-face with the man whom the court had found innocent. She, however, had judged him guilty of the death of her mother. A fierce determination to change the judge's decision bored its way deep into her being.

With one hand on her hat, she jerked her head inside. "That brisk wind froze my cheeks." She forced the window closed, then removed her hat and slid the hat-pin into the brim.

"Nellie, Max, thank you for coming to Scotland with me. I covet your skills, not to mention your moral support."

"Maggie, a friend never lets another friend down." Nellie moved a disheveled curl back in its place behind Maggie's shoulder. "Besides, if there was mystery surrounding my mother's death, I'd want you and Max right beside me to uncover the truth."

Maggie rested her head on the seat back. "How I long to be in the States. The warm colors of spring filled me with new hope. Here, one dreariness seems to follow another."

"Use your artistic imagination! Visualize an artist's brush soaked with each pigment from the palette and fling them into the air." Nellie Cox inhaled, her shoulders raised, eyes closed. "At home, you could smell the blossoming cherry trees and beautiful roses. Doesn't seem to happen here," Nellie sighed. "That's why imagination is so important."

"It wasn't my imagination digging a chasm that ripped my mom and I apart." Maggie slammed her fists on the seat. "We were opposites, and now it's too late." Maggie snapped her head to the side. A tear dripped down her cheek.

"Do you remember when we first met?" Maggie slouched. "A few months after I moved to Chicago from Portland, your publisher suggested we meet. I still remember that cute little café. The homemade food was delicious." She wiped the tear from her cheek. The corners of her mouth raised.

"Yes, I remember. You had soup and half of a ham sandwich. I opted for salad and a fresh roll," Nellie said. "But more amazing was your art work. I couldn't get over how perfectly it illustrated a story I had finished."

"And I'm still amazed at how well we bonded in a short time. Being an only child, I'd always wanted a sister. You were perfect for the role. And still are, I might add."

Maggie removed a tiny crocheted purse from her handbag and gently pried the wrapped loop off the button closure. She shut her eyes and bit her lower lip. Maggie unfolded the crumpled telegram and flattened it on her lap. The words glared back at her. Tears puddled at the edge of her eyes. Through blurred vision she forced the words to clarity, yet it was unnecessary since she'd memorized the brief message.

"Claire Ferguson MacLaren dead - STOP - Horse riding accident - STOP - Buried Rolen Presbyterian Church, Scotland."

A babbling stream joined with the rhythm of the horse's hooves. Maggie allowed the cadence to calm her jittery nerves. She blotted her eyes with her gloves, then glanced at Max Sullivan.

"How are you doing, Maggie?" Max leaned forward and gazed into her eyes.

"One minute I feel strong. The next I'm ready to crumble." Maggie rubbed her hands. "I'm trusting in your support should I collapse when we meet Mr. MacLaren."

"Nellie and I promise to catch you whenever you need it," Max said. "If that means falling into my arms, well," he paused, "it will be my pleasure."

Maggie's cheeks warmed. She had never heard Max express a romantic interest in her. The hint of a relationship beyond friends surprised her.

She had forgotten his masculine attraction. Dapper in his three-piece suit, a silver watch fob chain glistened across his vest. His undone coat button exposed his muscular physique with a starched collar and gray tie, creating a frame for his handsome face. Stories of hikes, and evening swims in the lake at his ten secluded acres in Oregon entranced her.

Several years ago, Max had tried to entice Maggie to visit him. She considered the offer, hoping the peacefulness of Eden Lake would be the tonic she needed to bring purpose to her life. Maggie thrived on classic literature and Max had assured her, "You'll not go wanting at my cabin. I stocked my shelves with more classics than the local library." Maggie wondered if he ever experienced the loneliness that often engulfed her.

The sun's rays penetrated the windows and warmed the coach. No need for the blanket now. Maggie folded and placed it on the seat beside her.

"You know, I'd rather be curled up with a good book than embarking on this journey into the unknown."

This could be a glorious day for an afternoon ride in the country, yet it would be no ordinary day. Nor a nice afternoon jaunt. Her hands trembled at the thought of meeting her mother's murderer.

"I still can't believe we're here, so far from home." Maggie opened her purse and retrieved a handkerchief. Anything to keep her hands busy.

"Not knowing what lies ahead places us in a precarious situation." Max glanced out the window. "We're about to tread the unknown."

"But don't worry, my dear Maggie," Nellie interjected. "Max and I are ready to meet this villain head on. We promised you a month of our time and I'm eager to discover the truth about your mother's death. Whether by accident or this man's cruel hand, we will uncover the truth."

How could Maggie have made it this far without her closest friend? Even though a mere five years separated the two in age, Maggie knew Nellie would become the wiser voice when needed. She knew her to be a trustworthy friend and the keenest of observers.

Maggie loved Nellie's choice of traveling attire. The white blouse with a bow tied at the collar brought out a matronly quality. Nellie had confided in Maggie that she chose the dress and matching jacket not only because of the flattering cut but also for their ability to conceal some extra pounds she always intended to lose.

She envied Nellie's wavy dark brown hair. Why did hers have to be so straight? Yet, Nellie had expressed to Maggie her desire for straight hair. *Seems we're never satisfied.*

Nellie had enthralled Maggie with her tales of criminal cases and investigations and tried not to show jealousy over her friends' chosen profession. While Nellie spent her day in activity, Maggie felt chained to a drawing table designing playbills and story illustrations. She longed for something outdoors to break up the monotony.

"From my mother's letters, it's so obvious that this man killed her, yet the judge exonerated him." Max and Nellie frowned. Maggie added, "Yes, I know. I will remind myself that Master Laurence MacLaren is innocent until proven guilty. This may be a most formidable task."

She watched the landscape pass by and longed for home. If she could erase lost time and recapture five years of life not well spent, the ache in her heart might mend. She realized all too late how preoccupied she had become with self. Had she repented and reconnected with her mother, the outcome may have been different. Her friend's words, "Let it go, Maggie," echoed in her head and yet, she could not surrender to their advice. Until satisfied beyond any doubt that she had misjudged the cause of her mother's death, she would continue on this path.

Maggie scooted forward in her seat. "This reminds me of meeting a producer about designing their playbill. I was always afraid of rejection. Did I choose the right outfit?"

"You definitely chose the right outfit." Nellie brushed a piece of lint off Maggie's emerald green skirt. "It's the perfect color to set off your coiffed red hair. And the ruffles on your white blouse accent your abundant femininity. You're a picture to behold. And the heirloom brooch from your grandmother is stunning in the lapel."

Maggie turned sideways.

"You look perfect, Maggie, like a proper American lady. Except for those scuffed boots." Nellie cupped her chin with her hand. "However, the more I ponder this, they show a love of the outdoors and long walks. I've changed my mind. They portray the real you. Max, what about you? Any opinion?"

"I wouldn't change a thing, Maggie," Max said. "You're a picture of loveliness."

"This is it, Sir. Stuart Hall." The driver called through a small open door on the roof.

Maggie trusted the coachman not to reveal their deliberate falsehood. The arrival at Stuart Hall must appear as happenstance. The coach veered off the main road.

A decisive moment had arrived. They still had time to turn around and go back since the road to the manor extended another quarter mile. Maggie glanced at her friends one more time, but no sign of hesitancy showed on their faces. They were still of one mind and continued in silence.

The coach rounded the last corner. A break in the trees afforded Maggie her first glimpse of the two-story stone structure. Awestruck at such an impressive edifice, Maggie clutched her chest and gasped.

"Can you two see this? It's immense. Nellie, what do you remember about the original owners?" Maggie knew how important it was to fix this information in her mind.

"Now, let me think," Nellie said, and scratched her head. "Mr. and Mrs. William Cheshire bought the estate after it fell in disarray when the previous owners became financially ruined. I remember they built in the late 1600s and encompassed about 300 acres." Nellie peeked through the open window. "I've seen nothing so architecturally pleasing. That must be the family crest on the flag waving from the cupola."

"I wonder if the servants' quarters are even half as elegant as this." Max craned his neck to spy the edifice. "I wouldn't mind life in an expansive estate for a while. Just for a while, mind you. I still prefer my little cabin by the lake."

As they drew closer, Maggie's attention switched to a lovely gazebo. At the center of a well-maintained flower garden, the pavilion became a focal point. A rose covered trellis marked the entrance to the garden with fruit trees in full bloom on each side.

"Max, you studied the family's history. Can you refresh our memories? I'm so nervous, I may forget my name." Maggie wiped her palms with a hankie.

Max removed a small notebook from his jacket pocket. "From my research at the Inverness library, I discovered that Mr. and Mrs. Cheshire had three sons who left home and never returned. They also had one daughter, Gwen. After her husband's death, Mrs. Cheshire bequeathed the manor to her daughter who married a Ramsay MacLaren. They were Laurence's parents."

"That must have been quite a blow for Mrs. Cheshire, to never hear from her sons again." Nellie shook her head. "Almost like a slap in the face, saying, 'Thank you very much, but no thanks.' The poor dear must have been distraught."

"And what happened to Gwen?" Maggie asked.

"She died of an undisclosed illness." Max held his finger on the note page. "I'm confident we'll learn the rest from the manor's staff and residents of Rolen. Then, of course, there's Laurence himself."

"Thank you, Max."

Maggie wrung her hands and pushed in the pin to secure her hat. She brushed her shoulders and jacket front, then inhaled a deep breath. She sat up tall, stretched her neck, and shoved her shoulders back. With muscles relaxed, she squeezed Nellie and Max's hands for a last reaffirmation. They were ready to meet Mr. MacLaren.

Chapter 2

As the coach drew near the main house, Maggie noted the immaculate grounds. Even uncontrollable ivy remained intertwined up the four columns on the veranda and kept from spreading to other parts of the Hall. A chain-supported swing and assorted porch chairs invited guests to enjoy an evening sunset or a cool summer breeze. She spotted a silver tray with a pitcher and two glasses on a round table in one corner. There were no barking dogs to greet them, only a faint whinny from behind the manor.

The large front door of the Hall opened. A bent over gentleman lumbered down the steps. He halted close to the coach and peered toward the driver.

"Guid afternoon. Fàilte tae Stuart Hall. Kin ah be o' some a hawn?"

Maggie studied this Scotsman. From his heavy brogue, well-pressed jacket and pants to the polished black shoes, his appearance matched her image of a butler.

"I wonder if you could assist us with some directions," the driver responded. "We left Rolen this morning on our way to Covenshire. I seem to have taken a wrong turn, or perhaps not traveled far enough. I thought I was familiar with this area, but it's been a while. Things tend to change over time."

"Noo laddie. Ye hae tae turn aroon back tae the lane. Ye need aboot twa hours frae here." The butler wrinkled his brow. "Dae ye nae ken whaur ye'r gaun, Laddie?"

Max called to the coachman. "What did he say?"

"He said we have to turn back to the lane, and it's another two hours from here. He's also confused that I don't know the way."

"Max," Maggie sat straight, "ask him if it might be possible for us to rest on the veranda."

Max leaned out the window. "May we stretch our legs a spell on the veranda and allow the horse some water before we continue?"

"Aye laddie. Please, come in." He opened the coach door, then gave directions to the driver for the stables and fresh water.

Maggie waited for Max to exit the coach and assist the women down the steps. She felt like a butterfly, forced out of a safe cocoon into the harshness of an unfriendly world. The warm breeze calmed her as they followed the butler to the shade of the veranda.

"My name is James. I'll let Master MacLaren know ye are here. Wid ye care for a cup of tea?"

"Thank you very much, James. We'd be most appreciative of a cup of tea," Maggie said.

As they waited for Mr. MacLaren, they captured impressions of the surroundings; the garden, the veranda, and while they tried not to be obvious, the rooms on the other side of each window. Idle chitchat filled the air. How good to stretch and move again.

"Master MacLaren asked me tae invite ye into the foyer. He will be wi ye in a short while. Will ye follow me, please?"

The three travelers accompanied James into the Hall.

"Please wait here." He disappeared through a door at the back of the foyer.

The foyer had a round marble topped walnut table in the center, graced with a large indigo and white designed vase filled with red and violet flowers. The architectural focal point drew Maggie's attention; a beautiful winding staircase with a small carved basket of wooden apples, pears, and peaches on the bottom newels. An ivy vine enwrapped both newel posts starting under the basket and cascading down to the first stair step. Apple, pear, and peach motifs graced the edges of the stair rug, vibrant with red, green and gold threads.

Large double doors on each side of the foyer suggested four rooms. Glass windowed doors at the back, under the staircase, gave some light to the area. The stained glass windows above the front door permitted the afternoon sun to stream into the room.

The butler carried a tray with three English china tea cups and saucers. Steam emitted from an elegant matching teapot and added a sweet fragrance to the air. He placed the tray on the round table.

"Allow me tae fill yer cups," James said as he poured the hot beverage.

"Thank you so much. This smells wonderful." Maggie received her cup and saucer.

"Thank ye for the compliment. Now if ye will excuse me."

James left the friends alone once more.

"Maggie, did you see the portraits on the walls?" Max asked. "Look at the detail and facial expressions. This last one, however, has a unique style compared to the first two. Perhaps a different artist painted this one."

"These paintings drew my attention when we first entered the foyer," Maggie said. "With what we know about the Cheshire and MacLaren families, I would surmise the portrait on the left is Mr. and Mrs. William Cheshire, their three sons and daughter, Gwen. The artist did an extraordinary job with the boys' appearance. They seem to be the age when boys dream of adulthood and awaiting adventures. You can almost read their minds. The girl looks about sixteen. I suspect the black Labrador at her feet is her pet, or maybe the family dog."

Maggie regretted her lack of attentiveness during the study of Scottish painters. To recall artist's names was just not her forte. As she studied the second portrait, she observed a couple with a young boy and another, or perhaps the same black Lab, at his feet.

"They look so content by the piano. There seems to be a resemblance between the young girl in the first painting and this one. Nellie, Max, do you agree that this is the same girl, and that it may be Gwen? If that is true, that would be Ramsay MacLaren beside her and Laurence at their feet." She glimpsed the culprit for the first time. Maggie's eyes glued on him.

Maggie sipped her tea and sensed Nellie's eyes riveted on her. She returned Nellie's gaze and followed her friend's nod toward the third painting. Maggie understood what Nellie surmised.

The butler reentered the foyer and interrupted her inspection. He opened the doors to one room.

"Mr. MacLaren requested ye tae wait in the library. He'll be wi ye shortly. I'll place the tea tray in the room wi' ye."

A bright and cheerful room, the full afternoon sun streamed through the lace curtains. A pleasant smell of pipe tobacco hung heavy in the air. This room had a masculine feel, decorated with warm red painted walls, natural cherry wainscoting, dark brown leather furniture and leaf green accents in a large round rug. Landscape paintings graced the walls.

"I could get lost in here for weeks," Max said. "No, make that months. I've never seen so many books in one room. Good thing there's a ladder to reach the upper shelves. I wonder..." Max scanned the titles.

A large glass chandelier hung in the center of the room over a rectangular table. The repeated motifs of apples, pears and peaches had been included in the lace table runner. A large leather-bound book occupied the center, perhaps the family Bible. One enormous fern rested on a wrought iron stand in the far corner by the window. The atmosphere lured visitors in to search for a good book, find a favorite corner and read the day away.

"Max, I can visualize you as lord of the manor. A cozy chair, book in hand, even a pipe dangling from your mouth. Perhaps a remodel of your cabin ..." Maggie stopped mid-sentence. Footsteps in the foyer. Maggie's heart raced. She scooted to the window, then inhaled a few times to compose herself.

Maggie's shoulders raised to her ears. She forced them down and noticed her hands shook. Wiping her palms on her hankie, she tried to concentrate on the beautiful weeping willow tree outside. The cascading branches seemed to cry out in sympathy for this tragic family.

Chapter 3

"Good afternoon. I'm Laurence MacLaren," the tall, handsome man said as he entered the library. "Sorry, I wasn't here to greet you when you arrived. I had returned from a ride and was brushing down my horse."

He stepped toward Max. "James tells me your driver has lost his way. Seems strange for a coachman not to know his directions. I hope you paid little for his services." He held out his hand to Max, who responded.

Maggie pivoted toward him; her first glimpse of her mother's stepson.

"Not at all, Mr. MacLaren. I'm Max Sullivan, and this is Miss Cox and Miss Richards."

Maggie knew her hankie would crumble if she wiped her hands one more time. She focused on slow breaths as Laurence greeted Nellie. Then he sauntered across the room and held her hand longer than she would have liked. She tried hard to keep her emotions in check. She may be face-to-face with an unconvicted murderer. Be cordial, Maggie. You must be cordial!

"I'm so thankful to your butler, and yourself, for inviting us in for a stretch and cup of tea." Maggie cleared her throat. "We've been on the road since early morning. I am also obliged that your butler allowed our coachman the use of your stable to cool his horse before we continue our journey."

Maggie stepped toward Nellie. "Neither we, nor our driver, anticipated such a long trip. Yet we've enjoyed brief stops from time to time and admired the breathtaking beauty along the way."

Maggie did not know where all those words came from. A simple thank you, or nice to meet you, would have sufficed. "Your home is beautiful and a welcome respite." Maggie hoped to make their trip to Stuart Hall seem a natural departure for wayward travelers.

"Please, rest as long as you like. We get few visitors, so guests are a pleasant diversion from daily tasks. Especially visitors from another country. America, I presume?" Laurence's eyes sparkled.

"Yes, we are from the United States." Maggie placed her moist hankie in her pocket and searched for a clean, dry replacement.

"We rented a flat in Inverness," Max said. "Interested in local history, a monastery built in the 1500s sparked our attention. We came down last evening to Rolen for an overnight trip. Time got away from us today. The hour is late, so we must return to the inn."

"Which inn are you staying at?"

"The Creag an Tuirc," Maggie answered. "Are you familiar with the proprietors?"

"No, I've not been to that hamlet in quite some time," Laurence said. "Why did you lodge there?" He picked up a pipe and checked for burnt tobacco remnants, then knocked them into a small dish.

"We were told in Inverness that the quaint town of Rolen had an interesting history and scenic bypasses." Max moved closer to Maggie. "We're interested in local folklore and history of small towns and magnificent manors such as your own. Since it appeared to be about a day's journey to Covenshire and the monastery, we felt it would be a good choice."

"But you must have had a map to consult?" Laurence laid the pipe down on a small tray.

"No, we didn't," Nellie said, and set her tea cup and saucer on the table. "Our driver assured us that if we stayed on the main road, all would go well. However, since there were so many enticing side trips into the natural scenic beauty and many roads appeared to be the main road, he veered off our intended course. I don't regret it though, as the journey has been most delightful."

Maggie was eager to maintain a cordial conversation. She grew uncomfortable with the direction Laurence's inquiries might take.

"Miss Richards, if you'll excuse Mr. Sullivan and myself, we'll check on our driver and inquire whether he's ready to return to Rolen."

"Yes, of course, Miss Cox. I'll wait for you on the veranda."

"Thank you so much, Mr. MacLaren, for your kind hospitality to Mr. Sullivan and myself. The change of situations was most appreciated." Nellie pulled on the hem of her jacket.

Awkwardness set in for Maggie alone with Laurence. The urgency to leave the library pressed on her. She faced Laurence and feigned a smile.

"I, too, must take my leave of your kindness. You've been most gracious to wayward strangers."

She extended her hand and thanked Laurence. As she left the library, she felt Laurence's eyes inspect every detail of her body. Being outdoors couldn't come soon enough to suit her.

Maggie exchanged goodbye nods with James, who opened the front door. Once on the porch, Laurence assisted her down the steps.

"Since your coach is not in sight," Laurence said, "may I show you my garden before you leave?"

"That would be very nice." Maggie strained to see any signs of her friends. Seeing none, she accompanied Laurence to the garden.

"This is lovely, Mr. MacLaren. Your gardener's expertise at landscaping is to be admired."

"Thank you very much, Miss Richards. Each tree has a story to tell, as well as this rose trellis. If you could stay longer, I would enjoy sharing the tale with you." He paused. "I don't want to appear forward, Miss Richards, but I would like to place Stuart Hall at you and your friends' disposal."

Laurence faced the back woods. "There are some beautiful scenic paths right here in my backyard. If you desire lessons on folklore, I'm sure James would be a wealth of knowledge. He grew up in this area and has been with me since I was a small boy. Would you consider spending a few days with us?"

"That's a very tempting invitation, Mr. MacLaren. It would be delightful to see more of this area and learn of the folklore. My traveling companions interests are like mine. Mr. Sullivan craves information about local history. Miss Cox is an aspiring writer and I'm an artist. Together we travel off the beaten path, hoping to find a story waiting to be written and illustrated." Maggie moved a few steps toward the Hall. "But we've secured lodging in Inverness and must return."

She saw Nellie and Max accompany the carriage to the front of the Hall. Maggie walked toward them, with Laurence by her side.

"I don't want to seem presumptuous, but might I inquire when you'll have more time to explore?" Laurence asked.

"No, not at all. We plan to return in a week or two for intensive research."

"Splendid. I have no plans and the manor has plenty of rooms." Laurence waved his arm toward Stuart Hall. "This is the perfect place to meet all your needs. May I invite you and your companions to spend it here at Stuart? I'm sure James would enjoy sharing the local history with Mr. Sullivan. Miss Cox could have some quiet time compiling the information. Then there's the architectural wonders of Stuart and the surrounding woods that would make interesting subjects for your drawings. It would honor my staff and I to have you as guests."

Maggie blinked and stepped back. "I'm overwhelmed by your generosity. You warmly accepted us for a brief rest and now you've extended us the honor of more time at your manor. I'll discuss this with my companions and drop a note in the post as to our decision."

Laurence drew close beside Maggie. "I look forward to your return in a couple of weeks, then."

Maggie found Laurence had wrapped her hand around his arm before she could blink. He escorted her to the carriage, then waited while Max assisted Nellie inside. Maggie held Laurence's hand, climbed the step, and sat next to Nellie.

"Thank you again for your hospitality and use of the stables," Max said as he entered the carriage.

Laurence closed the door. "See you in two weeks."

Chapter 4

As the carriage ambled back to the Creag an Tuirc, Maggie and her friends shared little about the visit. They reserved their conversation for dinnertime. Few townsfolk wandered the streets as the coach pulled up to the hotel's front door. The smell of stew and sweet desserts filled the air as they entered. Maggie spied a corner table.

"I don't know about you ladies, but whatever Mr. and Mrs. Wellington have fixed for dinner smells delicious." Max awaited a hearty meal.

Maggie scanned the room and noticed steaming kettles in the center of many tables.

"And did ye all hae an eventful day?"

Maggie flinched. "Mrs. Wellington, you're so quiet. I didn't hear you."

"Yes, we did," Max said, licking his lips. "Now, what do you recommend for this evening's meal?"

"My homemade stew and fresh baked bread are popular tonight. Shall I bring ye a kettle?"

"Sounds delicious. Nellie? Max? Is that all right with you?" Maggie asked.

"It's perfect!" Nellie and Max said in unison.

With dinner ordered, they reviewed the day's events.

"Max, why don't you start? What was your impression of Stuart Hall and Mr. MacLaren?" Maggie leaned back in her chair.

"The library contained many of the classics and some contemporary works, but I'm bewildered, as it seemed remiss of any law volumes. Mr. Ramsay MacLaren should have collected an extensive reference library. I understood he had a very successful practice as a local solicitor and guest lecturer at the university."

"What might you surmise from that observation?" asked Maggie.

"Not sure. Almost as if young Laurence doesn't expect his father to return to the manor anytime soon, if at all, and removed all his father's books. I would like to know if he departed a short time after his wife's death, or much later," Max responded.

"Death or murder?" Maggie paused for a moment, gazed at her companions, and apologized. "There I go again. Deciding murder would better fit the situation. I need to sort out the facts before I judge Laurence."

Max continued. "I spoke with a few of the locals. They felt the elder Mr. MacLaren's departure was not just unexpected, but under mysterious circumstances. Some suggested he might have had suffered a nervous breakdown. Whatever happened, no one has seen him for quite some time. The stable hand, Walter, has worked at Stuart since Laurence was twelve years old. When I asked about the elder Mr. MacLaren's absence from the estate, he thought his master was traveling abroad and fidgeted with a harness."

Max paused for a sip of water. "He stated the shock of his second wife's death devastated Mr. MacLaren and he had left the manor about a week after her funeral. Walter knows nothing about a possible nervous breakdown, or at least, does not want to talk about it."

"Seems incredible to me that Walter would still think Mr. MacLaren is 'traveling abroad' almost a year after his wife's death, with no mention of any correspondence. I sensed he knows much more. Perhaps on another visit he'll open up."

Mrs. Wellington set the kettle of stew and a basket of bread on the table. Maggie ladled the hearty meal into individual bowls while Nellie buttered thick slices of bread.

"What about you, Nellie? Did you talk with anyone else?" Maggie asked.

"I saw the gardener as he left the shed. He carried a bucket filled with hand tools. I approached him and struck up a conversation, expressing an interest in the grounds. His name is Leach, and he was eager and proud to show off his handiwork." Nellie placed the slices of buttered bread on plates and passed them to Maggie and Max.

"He was told that Mrs. William Cheshire had three sons and one daughter. She requested the gardener plant fruit trees for each son; two pear trees, two peach trees and two apple trees. The rose trellis was for her only daughter, Gwen, who became the first Mrs. MacLaren. I asked if Mrs. MacLaren enjoyed yard work. He said that she often strolled in the garden and rested on the bench under the oak tree at the far end to read or write in her journal. He emphasized that everything he told me was concerning the first Mrs. MacLaren. When I asked about the second Mrs. MacLaren, your mother, Maggie, his head fell to his chest, he turned and sauntered away."

"Thank you, Nellie. Time to lay your notebook down and enjoy your stew before it gets cold." Maggie passed the bowls to Max and Nellie.

With the main course consumed, the innkeeper cleared the table and brought a dessert plate of pastries and fresh fruit. Maggie chose a blueberry scone while Max reached for the warm apple dessert with a dollop of hand-churned ice cream.

"I can never get enough chocolate." Nellie licked her lips and anticipated the flavor of the moist chocolate cake.

Maggie gazed at her two friends.

"Is something wrong, Maggie?" asked Nellie.

Maggie leaned back in the chair with a sigh of complete satisfaction for a delicious meal. She wiped her face with her serviette and swallowed a small drink of water. Maggie cleared her throat, leaned toward her friends and rested her elbows on the table, her fingers interlocked under her chin.

"My dear friends, we have a big job ahead of us. Investigations need to be made before we return to unravel the threads that bind Mr. Laurence MacLaren's story together. Thank you for all the information you gathered in such a brief period. We've made a good start. Tomorrow we'll speak with the village folk. Let's try to glean some in-depth information about the manor and Mr. Laurence MacLaren. I'm content that our first meeting was amiable and believe the connections that we made today with the gardener, the stable man, and Mr. MacLaren will prove beneficial on our next visit."

Maggie's friends remained motionless as they listened. She rubbed the back of her neck. Then twisted her head from side to side.

"I have too much stuff in this brain tonight to think straight." Maggie closed her eyes. "I suggest we all turn in and get a fresh-start in the morning. Let's come to breakfast with a game plan. Our train leaves for Inverness at four o'clock. Is that correct?"

"Yes, four o'clock," Nellie responded. "Sleep sounds wonderful. All that fresh air today, the beauty of the countryside and this delicious meal will lull me into a good night's rest. How about you, Max?"

"Yes, indeed. A good book, a glass of wine, and a down comforter have all the makings of wonderful dreams. I'll see you lovely ladies in the morning."

With their "good nights" said, the three left the table, thanked the innkeepers, and climbed the stairs to their rooms. Maggie's head buzzed from her brief encounter with Laurence MacLaren. Would she have a good night? She must. Tomorrow, inquiries would fill the day and her mind needed to be clear.

Chapter 5

Max rose with the sun. He loved early morning quiet time. The town's gathering spot, the M-G Store & Cafe', would be his first stop. By reputation, they had the best breakfast rolls and coffee in town.

As Max entered, he noticed a group of men gathered around the potbelly stove, devouring pastry and slurping steaming coffee. He slid into a corner table with the local paper under his arm. After he ordered breakfast, Max opened the paper to conceal his presence. More men moseyed in. Some joined the pot belly stove group, others found tables.

"Guid-morning to all of ye," a lady said. She wore a red apron tied around her waist. Her hair formed a bun at the base of her head and a pencil stuck out behind her ear.

"Guid-morning, Mabel," many of the men responded.

"Laddies, after serving your breakfast for the past thirty years or more, I can predict your order. Unless there are any changes, George has coffee ready and I'll get your breakfast started."

Max liked this Mabel. After all those years in Rolen, she and her husband could be a wealth of information. He listened carefully and patiently waited.

A man wearing an apron sauntered in with two pots of coffee. Max admired the man's ability to pour without spilling a drop. He assumed this must be George, who greeted the customers. "Looks like we may have a pleasant, warm day today." He glanced out the window. "The sun is glowing over the trees and the sky looks clear from here to Elk Mountain. I bet the big one's up there calling Ernest."

"If you can guarantee agreeable weather, I'll hang my wash outside and make sun tea for this afternoon," Mabel said as she carried in breakfast plates.

"We have no guarantees on anything," another customer said as he entered the cafe'. "God is in charge of it all. Now, how about some of your melt-in-the-mouth cinnamon rolls and a cup a coffee, if you please?"

Max peeked around the edge of the paper. He caught sight of a husky man meandering past the stove. From the plaid shirt, scruffy dungarees and heavy hiking boots, his attire spoke of an abundance of time spent outdoors.

Mabel carried a plate of cinnamon rolls to the table where the man had plopped, then stoked up the fire. The Scotsman held his cup in the air for George to fill with coffee.

Max listened to the customers' conversations. He enjoyed the strange sounds of the Scottish brogue, but strained to understand what they said, almost like a foreign language. To join their conversation might take longer than he thought.

Then, a break occurred and Max seized his opportunity. "I hear there's some great fishing around here."

He lowered the newspaper, smiled, raised his cup, and nodded. Mabel hurried to Max's table with another tray of pastries.

"I'm so sorry, laddie. I forgot we had a stranger in our midst. You looking to fish? Well, if you don't mind waiting a spell for a nibble and are comfortable on a horse, there's some fine lake fishing near to here. Why, t'was only last week that Ernest said he hooked the grandpappy of them all." Her head nodded toward the husky man. "But the call of a bull elk frightened the fish clean off his line. Least-wise, that's what he said."

The room filled with laughter as the men shared slaps on each other's backs. The robust man with the plaid shirt approached Max, coffee cup and pastry in hand.

"I'm Ernest McIntyre, the brunt of jokes from this group of locals. May I join you?"

"Sure, Ernest." Max rose and extended his hand. "My name is Max Sullivan. Would you join me?"

"Thank ye. I'd like that." Ernest settled into the chair across from Max. "Don't pay them no mind. At least, I don't. They never believe me. One of these days I'm going to bring in both the granddaddy fish and the elk. Then they'll have to eat their words. At the very least, buy me breakfast." He glared at the men across the room, then chuckled loud and hearty. Max foresaw an imminent fishing trip.

"Be careful what he tells ye."

"Sift fact from fiction if ye can." The jovial men cautioned.

"If you need a knowledgeable guide, Ernest is the one." One elderly customer pointed his pipe at Ernest.

Max accepted a coffee refill from Mabel. The other customers rose from their tables.

After the men exchanged "Guid-mor'ings," "Hae a great day," and "Don't believe everything Ernest tells ye," they departed into the warm sun.

"How about I buy you another cup of coffee and Mabel's delicious pastry?" Max offered.

"No thanks," said Ernest. "I'm grateful and all that, but I keep my eye out for some fetching young lassie. Gotta watch my waistline." He let out another hearty laugh and slapped his robust stomach. Max laughed also, not at, but with this man who had lived so much of his life in this village and didn't mind when jokes came his way. He seemed to relish it.

"You're not from around here, now, are ye? Not that I mind sharing what I know with strangers." Ernest removed his hat and set it on the empty chair beside him.

"Now, let me see. There's fishing, and then there's fishing, if you get my meaning. Do you want some citified fishing hole that's easy to walk to in about an hour's time and will give you ample sized trout? Or perhaps you're looking for adventure that will take several hours on horseback, but give you the excitement real anglers dream about. I could go with you as your guide. No charge for my services and I wouldn't take no credit for the fish ye caught. My reward is giving credence to my story that a granddaddy fish waits for the right bait."

A twinkle in his eye and excitement in his voice, Ernest leaned forward, mouth gaped. The man resembled St. Nick himself.

"To answer your first question, no, I'm here from the U.S. for a brief holiday. I'll be leaving this afternoon for Inverness, but plan to return in no more than a couple of weeks. If I can fit in a day of fishing, it would be my pleasure to accept your offer as my personal guide. I haven't ridden a horse in several years, but I'm sure with your able assistance I could manage."

The sparkle left Ernest's face.

"Ernest, have you been fishing all your life?"

"Aye, sir." Ernest slouched to the back of his seat, interlaced fingers rested on his ample belly. "I've been fishing since a wee lad, but work at the paper got in my way. I love talking, as you can tell. On fishing days, we talk only on the trail to the lake. Once there, it's silence until lunch time or we'll disturb the fish."

"That sounds delightful, Ernest. Lake fishing is my favorite. You mentioned you worked on the paper. Is that the local newspaper?" Max asked.

"Aye, Laddie. I reported on all the events from here to Covenshire north and Perth south. My mind still remembers things that happened twenty, thirty years ago. Ye see, when you're in the news business, you've got to investigate every piece of evidence before a story goes to print. Don't want anyone calling you a liar and suing you. I guess that's why I'd like to take you to my lake. Maybe you could catch Ol' Moses, that's what I call him. Then I could print the story because of your corroboration. Wouldn't that be great!" A clinched fist slammed down on the table.

"I'd be the talk of the town." Ernest glanced at the ceiling. He raised his right arm. His index finger pointed upward while his left hand flung across his chest. "Why, they might even erect a statue of me in the town square, like Bonnie Prince Charlie."

"You seem like you'd be spendid company on a fishing trip and I'm a newspaper man myself. Although I don't write stories for papers. I write books and articles about the history of local communities. So I like to get the facts correct too. It's important we know and understand the truth. Don't you agree?"

"Aye," Ernest said. "Makes no sense to print half-truths. Gets too many people riled up and then they believe nothing else you write later. A good investigator who receives respect from his readers is more important to me than the pay."

Max wanted to ply Ernest for information about the MacLaren's, but he might seem too inquisitive if he focused on one family. He'd need to develop an alternate approach. One that involved horses.

"Ernest, you mentioned I'd need to ride a horse to get to the lake. Do most people ride horses for necessity or pleasure around here?"

"It may start out as pleasure, but you soon learn it's for sheer necessity. We're on horseback as wee lads and lassies and by the time we've grown, we're accomplished riders. When we have our local fair in the fall, there's an actual competition for the best rider."

Ernest scratched his head. "Why, I remember a few years back, we placed bets on who would win. There were four or five favorites, so the odds were split. Well sir, if the horse I bet on didn't look good all the way around the track, with a fine looking bay and a roan right on his heels. I thought sure I would bring some extra cash home with me. Then what do ye think happened?"

Max opened his mouth to respond, but Ernest gasped a quick breath before he had time to fire out the answer.

"Well now, I'll just tell ye. My horse came round the last turn and the crowd went wild. Then out of nowhere, here comes this other black, ridden by a young upstart kid. That horse's nostrils flared wide like he came out of you know where, and gaining on Ol' Blue with every stride. I started yelling, trying to spur Ol' Blue on with my shouts of encouragement and hitting my leg as if I was the rider and not Johnny Short. Anyway, what do you think happened?"

Max shrugged his shoulders.

"Well, I'll tell ye! That other horse got alongside Ol' Blue, looked him in the eye and then, well, us Scots have a saying, 'A nod's as guid as a wink tae a blind horse.' And Ol' Blue must have been blind. He let that black pass him by as if he were standing still. I couldn't believe it! Ol' Blue was so flabbergasted that he even let the bay and roan go by him. Fourth place wasn't so bad, but first would hae been a mite better."

"Was the winning rider from Rolen?" Max asked.

"He came from up near Covenshire. No one had seen him ride his horse at full bore. After he received the winner's trophy, he pranced around the rest of the day like he owned all of Scotland. He hasn't entered a fair race since."

Ernest sipped his coffee.

"There's talk about getting a group to go to his place at Stuart Hall and find out if he'll race this year. We don't even know if he still has the horse. He doesn't come to town much."

"He must be one of the best riders around," Max said. "Do you know his name? Perhaps I could interview him for local history?"

"Sure, Max. His name is Laurence MacLaren, but he keeps to himself. All family is gone, but he has servants to keep the place up. When you get ready to go, you best ask someone for directions as the roads wind through the countryside and it's easy for a stranger to get lost. Only one of them will lead to Stuart Hall."

"Thanks, Ernest. I will." Max paused. "Ernest, I don't want to keep you from your day, but I'm curious. With so many people riding horses, your doctor must have patients with broken arms and legs. That must be a precarious position up so high in the saddle." Max placed his mug by the edge of the table as Mabel came by for refills.

"Max, I'll tell ye. We have had very few accidents, but always need a doc for the other ailments. You're right though, a few broken bones now and then, from a first time rider. Don't you worry none about that. I'll be sure you hae a slow moving nag when we go fishing. Don't want any of my friends falling off, especially if they're going to validate Ol' Moses' existence." Ernest grabbed Max's arm. "I'll take special care of you. Don't you worry none about that."

Max sensed Ernest became fidgety to be on his way. He hoped an opportunity would present itself another day.

"Hey, Mabel, got my lunch ready yet?" Ernest faced the kitchen as Mabel came out with an overstuffed bag.

"I get lunch to go, so I've got something to eat when my stomach chatters. Great talking with you. Look me up when you're ready to get on that horse and do some serious fishing." Ernest scooted off his chair.

Max shook Ernest's hand. With his hat plopped back on his head, Ernest met Mabel at the counter.

"Thank ye very much, Mabel. See ye tomorrow. And nice to visit with ye, Max." Ernest gathered his sack and headed out the door.

"I've been fixing him lunch every day since he retired," Mabel said. "Hope he didn't bend your ear too much. Old Ernest loves telling tales about the old days, especially his fishing and riding horses."

Max finished his coffee as Mabel wiped down tables and gathered mugs and plates left behind by the early morning breakfast group. Max folded the newspaper and pondered Ernest's words; "His name is Laurence MacLaren, but he keeps to himself."

Maybe Stuart Hall has become a prison for MacLaren. Seems like no one ventures to the mansion and sounds like he seldom goes out. Max determined to follow this path of inquiry and expected a grand fishing adventure with Ernest.

Chapter 6

Pots and pans rattled and disturbed the silence in the empty cafe'. Max flung the local paper wide and skimmed for interesting articles. His eyes scanned for the keywords: MacLaren, Stuart Hall.

"Is there anything else I can get you?" Mabel dabbed her hands on her apron. "We keep the store stocked with about everything this little hamlet needs, from stamps to peppermint sticks."

"No, thanks." Max rubbed his stomach. "I'm fully satisfied. Your rolls and coffee were incredible." He wiped his mouth on his serviette. "Could I ask you one more question about Rolen?"

"Go right ahead. I've lived here all my life, so I know everyone." Mabel swept crumbs off the table, then plopped in a chair. "If it's historical stuff you want, I may have the answer. Ye see, I overheard your conversation with Ernest."

Max cleared his throat. "If everyone rides horses, I'm wondering if there have been any fatalities. Anything more serious than broken legs and arms? I promised Ernest I'd go fishing with him when I return, but I haven't ridden for years." Max scratched his head. "Come to think of it, I haven't been on a horse since I was a young boy."

Mabel let out a hearty laugh, which startled Max. He fell to the back of his chair, eyes wide. George ran out from the kitchen.

"What's going on here, Mabel? Your laugh frightened me and I almost dropped our pot of porridge. No one has told me a good story all month. Let me in on it." He grabbed a chair to join them.

Mabel held her sides. Her head bobbed toward the table. Then she straightened and sucked in a deep breath of air.

"Oh, George," Mabel said as a tear ran down her cheek. "Max here's afraid of riding a horse with Ernest. He asked if anyone ever died from a fall. That brought to mind the time widow Grubbs rode into town still in her nightgown." Her chuckles rumbled again. "The whole town heard her yell and scream that some critter had gotten into her chicken coop. Remember her description?" Mabel rose to her feet and used hand gestures. "Big as a bear, two huge yellow eyes that glared right through her, and the animal tore the whole coop apart?"

Max smiled at Mabel's animation. Her grins and laughter became childlike. A deep breath for composure, then she continued.

"What a sight to behold." Mabel sat down, leaned toward Max. "That widow woman. Her hair flew every which way, nightgown tangled up above her knees and gardening boots on her feet. And that poor horse." Mabel slapped her knee. "Why she tugged the reins so many directions, the poor critter couldn't decide which way to turn."

By now, Max had joined in the laughter. His focus shifted from Mabel to George and back again. They were on the verge of hysteria.

"She brought that poor beast to a screeching halt right in front of the store. But the stop was so abrupt," Mabel's animation continued, "she flew out of the saddle, up in the air and landed beside me on our porch. I held a cup of fresh hot coffee. The impact jostled the liquid, but nary a drop spilt. When she came to her senses, she peered at me, then at the coffee cup and said, 'Do you have something a mite stronger, Lassie?'" Mabel guffawed. "Even as hard as she fell, not one bone broke. We Scots are a hardy folk."

George bent over in laughter. "I remember like it happened yesterday. What a picture. Her nightgown almost over her head and those oversized garden boots on her twisted feet." He grasped his wife's hand, and they chuckled together.

From Mabel's retelling, Max felt he had witnessed it first hand. He waited for the laughter to subside. Mabel tapped a tear on her cheek with her apron corner.

"Did you ever find out what got into her hen house?"

"Some men from the town loaded their guns and rode back to her little farm ready to meet this ferocious bear." George proceeded with the story. "Instead, they found a large mangy black dog cowering in the only corner of what remained of the chicken coop." George swiped a drop of moisture from his cheek. "That poor dog. It seemed disoriented and scared. Once quieted with food, water and gentle handling, she relaxed like a newborn pup. Widow Grubbs adopted that squalid critter, named her Calamity, and they've been inseparable ever since."

"So, back to my original question." Max rested his forearms on the table. "As far as you remember, no one has ever died falling off a horse."

Mabel and George exchanged glances and paused longer than seemed necessary. Their expressions altered. The seriousness concerned Max. Mabel closed her eyes and remained motionless. George squeezed her hand, then spoke.

"Yes, Max." He paused and bowed his head. "We've had one fatality in all the years we've lived here. Mabel won't talk about the accident since she considered the lassie a close friend."

Mabel excused herself, wiped her eyes on her apron, and made her way outside.

"It happened, oh my, several months ago. No wait, as I think about it, it might have been close to a year now." George retrieved a hankie from his back pocket and blew his nose.

"At my age, you lose track of time. You might have traveled by Stuart Hall, just north of town, on your way to Covenshire. That's where it happened." George slid into the seat across from Max. "There's been nothing but sadness since the Cheshire's purchased that decaying manor. Their only heir, a daughter, married Mac-Laren. But passed before her time. We hoped, with the second Mrs. MacLaren, gaiety and laughter might fill the manor once more. I won't go into the details now." He stroked his gnarled fingers.

"Anyway, Mrs. MacLaren was riding with her stepson when, according to him, her horse veered too close to the cliff and a snake, or something, spooked it. Her mount jolted, which sent poor Mrs. MacLaren over the edge."

"It's a deep gully." George cleared his throat. "Some people, like Mabel, think it wasn't an accident. The judge listened to the evidence and concluded there was no other explanation." George nodded his head toward the porch. "Poor Mabel. Whenever young MacLaren comes in, which is rare, she prays that she'll not harbor ill feelings. She's still grieving. We best not talk about it anymore."

Max could tell that George hurt. Maybe more for Mabel than himself, but he appeared shaken.

"Please excuse me now. I want to comfort my wife." George left for the porch.

Max waited by the counter. When they returned, George had his arm wrapped around Mabel's shoulder.

"I want to apologize if I dredged up unwelcome memories. That was not my intent." Max clasped George's hand and touched Mabel's arm. "Thank you for your hospitality. I left my money on the table."

When he reached the doorway, Max surveyed the quiet hamlet. How could such sadness invade this idyllic community? He ambled down the street in the hopes the blacksmith could shed more light on the junior MacLaren.

Chapter 7

The aromas of freshly baked scones, hot porridge, and steeping tea tantalized Maggie as she and Nellie entered the dining room. Mr. and Mrs. Wellington added a tray of fresh fruit to the already ample breakfast buffet. Maggie scanned the sideboard, overwhelmed with even more choices: tatties, bangers, sauted mushrooms, fruit-sauces, four jams, two marmalades, toast, black pudding and fresh rich cream.

"I don't know about you, Nellie, but I'm going to try the Scottish porridge with brown sugar and fruit-sauce, a hot cup of tea, and one of those scones." Maggie picked up the top plate from the stack.

Mrs. Wellington entered with another tray, baffling the ladies with still more choices.

"Good morning, Lassies. Help yourself. Most things are straight off my stove. Mr. Wellington milked our cow this morning and ladled the cream for your porridge. It can't get fresher than that."

Maggie and Nellie dished up breakfast, poured a cup of tea, and found a table in the corner. Since their train left for Inverness in the afternoon, they used the wait time to plan their itinerary.

"Max left me a note." Maggie pushed her hand into her skirt pocket and retrieved a folded paper. "He's heading for the M-G Store & Cafe' this morning to mingle with the locals. I trust he'll learn something of interest." She laid the paper beside Nellie.

"Thought I'd walk down to the church. Not knowing the Pastor's office hours, I'm taking a chance he'll be there. I understand several small communities share one pastor, so he may be out of town. Still a nice day for a walk before our train ride to Inverness. What are your plans, Nellie?"

After one last bite of breakfast roll and a sip of tea, Nellie responded. "I remember reading many well-to-do families wore handmade clothes. Perhaps one, or both, Mrs. MacLarens solicited the town's seamstress. I'll start there and see where it leads. If she has time, I may have her measure me for a new dress. One great way to enter conversation."

"An excellent idea. You always had a keen sense for gleaning information." Maggie finished her tea and added, "Let's meet back here about two o'clock. We should have plenty of time to pack and walk to the train station."

They complemented the Wellingtons on an excellent breakfast. The sunlight immersed them in its morning glow. Nellie and Maggie bid adieu and headed to their separate destinations.

✳✳✳

The bright dress shop sign made it easy to spot. A tinkling bell announced Nellie's arrival as she opened the door.

"Guid mor'ing Miss, and such a beautiful day it is. Don't you agree?" A jovial woman with an amiable smile and engaging manner greeted her. She wore a red dress with a pattern of tiny flower clusters. A green apron with large front pockets which held scissors, pin cushion and a tape measure protected the front of her dress. Her shop displayed an array of fabric bolts, thread, and other sewing notions.

Overwhelmed with a veritable kaleidoscope of color, each bolt of fabric beckoned for Nellie's touch. She imagined a new frock especially tailored for her.

"Oh, my yes," responded Nellie. "If an enchanting summer's day ever existed, it's today. I'm Nellie Cox. I passed by your shop last evening. Your window display caught my attention, and I wondered who made that exquisite green dress."

The seamstress blushed and placed her hand over her mouth to muffle a giggle. "I take full blame for that frock. Pleased to make your acquaintance, Miss Cox. My name is Mary Beth." She extended a hand to Nellie.

"Thank you for your compliment. I must admit it's one of my favorite creations. I sometimes special order my fabric, but this bolt arrived by mistake from my Edinburgh supplier. Since the return postage would be beyond my budget, I came up with a solution. I informed them of the oversight, made a dress and sent the sale money to my supplier. Well, I don't mind telling you, I've made four dresses from that bolt. Can't keep them in the store. Like you, lassies walk by, see the beautiful fabric and pray the dress is their size. And my supplier? They said to not worry. 'Consider it a gift for your loyal patronage.' This gift from heaven blessed me and I'm passing the blessing on to others." Mary Beth straightened several bolts of fabric.

"You should see the smiles as lassies walk out with a new frock. Oh, I know what you're going to say. Most women don't enjoy wearing the same dress as other women. But, I change the pattern for each dress. Give each a different trim, or sleeve style, or neckline, or something to make the frock unique. Even though I use the same fabric, they're not the same dress. It satisfies the lassies, and the dress lifts their spirits." She paused for a moment. "Miss Cox, would you like to try it on?"

Nellie moved her fingers over the fabric with light touches. "While this dress is beautiful, my needs are more practical. Side pockets are a must and I prefer long straight sleeves, no shoulder puffs."

"Why don't you peruse *The Delineator* while I make us a pot of tea? There are several copies over there on the magazine table. I have it mailed from London and love the new Butterick styles. A new dress decision always comes easier with a spot o' tea." Mary Beth disappeared, leaving Nellie to daydream about her new dress.

Nellie scanned the magazine, fascinated with the designs and articles for women. Several caught Nellie's attention. She marked them with strips of paper Mary Beth provided, then glanced at the alluring bolts of fabric. So many enticed her. Drawn to green and blue tones narrowed the decision.

Mary Beth ambled back into the shop carrying a tray with a teapot, cups and saucers, sugar, creamer and a plate of scones. She placed them on a corner table.

"Now while the tea brews, show me the patterns you like. And, please help yourself to the scones. Homemade, you know."

"Thank you," replied Nellie. "I'm still full from breakfast, but I seldom turn down a cup of tea." She handed Mary Beth *The Delineator*. "There are several patterns I like, but this one suits my needs best." She laid the magazine flat at her first choice. "I picked out several bolts of fabric and would value your expert input."

Mary Beth studied the pattern, then examined each bolt of fabric.

"Any of these fabrics would make an excellent dress. It's a hard decision." She held several bolts up to Nellie's face. "My preference would be this green fabric. Your brown hair has a slight hint of red. Complementary colors brighten a room." Mary Beth set the fabric down. "Who knows? You may develop some new admirers. My schedule is pretty open right now and I do have that pattern in my sewing room. If the pattern is your size, I could have it finished for you next week."

"That's very thoughtful, but I'll be leaving this afternoon for Inverness and return within two weeks. If you agree, I could give you partial payment now and the rest when I return."

"Well then, let's measure." Mary Beth pulled out her measuring tape and order pad. This was the perfect time for Nellie to ask her questions.

"How long have you lived in Rolen?"

"Well, Nellie, I've lived here all my life. Learned how to sew sitting beside my mother, bless her heart. She went home to be with the Lord almost ten years ago. To my way of thinking, she was too young, but then none of us know when our time on earth will end. She would say, 'Mary Beth, my dear, you must understand all of us are just camping out down here. The Lord can take our tent down anytime He wants, take our hands and lead us home.'" She removed a kerchief from her apron pocket and dabbed her eye.

"When I sew, I still think of her and thank God for a talented mother who not only taught me to be a seamstress but also to make this business my livelihood.

"This community is my home and I've made clothes for entire families. I've even made men's work clothes and dress shirts. Some of the little ones call me Grandma Mary Beth, even though I am not old enough to be a Grandma. Why, I've never even married and had children. Yet that's what they say and it makes me feel special."

"You have a marvelous life. You live in a small village, you have work to keep your hands busy, and the joy of watching families grow."

"My yes, Nellie. I've attended weddings, baptisms, and way too many funerals. Rolen is a great place to live and ideal for raising a family." She poured two cups of tea, opened her tape measure, and wrote Nellie's measurements, one at a time.

"My friends and I passed a manor outside of town yesterday and wondered if anyone lived there. We thought the manor might be pleasant to rent for a month. A sign by the road read Stuart Hall." Nellie stretched her arms wide for Mary Beth.

"The old MacLaren place. More accurately, the Cheshire's place. They were the original owners. My mother made dresses for Mrs. Cheshire and her daughter, Gwen. Mrs Cheshire, bless her soul, loved her children with an unending love. The story around town is that the boys left home when they were in their late teens or early twenties. Never heard from again. Sweet Gwen married, had one son and cared for her mother in the manor until the day Mrs. Cheshire died." She rechecked her measurements.

"There, all done. Let's sit down and have our tea. No sense letting an entire pot get cold."

"Does Gwen still live there with her husband and son?" Nellie's query continued as she recognized Mary Beth's talkative mood and knowledge of the family.

"No. Gwen died too young and her husband married again years later. Their son, Laurence, never seemed to warm up to his new stepmother. Her name was Claire, and she tried everything to gain his acceptance. She played the piano beautifully, rode horses well, showed an interest in his studies at the university, but he would have nothing to do with her."

Nellie placed a scone on her serviette and sipped her tea.

"I remember one day Claire came in to pick up a dress. I asked if things were better between them. She forced a smile, and said 'fine', then broke down in tears. I helped her into my kitchen, placed the closed sign in the window, and locked the front door. I had never seen her so distraught. She poured out her heart over the difficulty of engaging Laurence in a conversation. Claire was a gentle, sweet spirit. A high priority for her was to connect with her stepson on some level. She mentioned an estranged daughter and hoped this relationship with her stepson would not end the same way. Claire loved his father and desired the family to create memories for a lifetime. I let her talk and kept pouring the tea. Oh, my, ours is getting cold, isn't it? Can I pour you more?"

Nellie extended her cup to Mary Beth, who filled it to the brim, placed the teapot on the table and continued as if she had never stopped.

"I became worried as her demeanor changed. The more she shared the things Laurence would do when they were alone, the more fright showed in her eyes. I asked if she feared for her life. She seemed shocked that I would ask. Quicker than a grasshopper in front of a brush fire, she gulped her last spot of tea, jumped up, grabbed her dress bag and purse. She opened the door as if escaping a prison cell, thanked me, and scurried outside. I caught her arm and apologized if I upset her, then suggested she visit Dr. Shane, our local minister. I told her I would pray for her and Laurence. Her eyes filled with tears as she thanked me and pressed my hand in hers. I watched as she hurried down the walk, placed her packages in the buggy, and headed back to the manor. I never saw her again."

By the look on Mary Beth's face, retelling this encounter, dredged up old memories. Nellie hoped for sensitivity to the situation and discernment when to stop.

"Do you mind if I ask why you never saw her again? Did the family move?"

"Oh, no. Laurence still lives there. Mr. MacLaren has gone away, but no one seems to know much about that. Poor Claire died two weeks later. Almost the entire town attended her funeral, held right up the street at the Presbyterian Kirk. I never found out if she talked with Dr. Shane, but prayed she was at peace with the Lord and ready to be with Him." She lowered her head a moment, then gazed at Nellie.

"I'm sorry for going on so long. My goodness, you only asked if the manor was available to rent and I gave you the family's history. Please forgive me. I've thought little about Claire until you brought her to mind. You also reminded me I've forgotten to pray for Laurence."

She rose, placed the teapot, cups, and plates on the tray. After she completed the calculations for the dress and totaled the items, she handed the paper to Nellie.

"Will this be within your budget? I can trim a couple of items if needed."

"Oh, Mary Beth, that's very reasonable. Thank you for the tea and information about the manor. I'm sorry for your loss. You had a close friendship with Mrs. MacLaren."

Nellie desired to ask Mary Beth how Claire died, but discerned the seamstress didn't want to talk anymore. She removed enough money from her bag for half the cost of the dress and handed it to Mary Beth.

As Nellie left the shop, a dark cloud blocked the sun's warm rays. *Could this dark cloud be a sign of Laurence's guilt?* Nellie shook her head and resolved to let hard evidence, and only hard evidence, form her conclusions.

*You have made us for yourself,
and our heart is restless until it rests in you.
—Augustine—*

Chapter 8

A meandering path off the main road led Maggie to the Presbyterian Kirk. The sun's warmth penetrated the tall trees and chased the chill from the air. Childhood memories returned.

An aged fir tree in her childhood backyard had grown so tall Maggie had imagined a brave explorer could ascend to the top and touch the sky. The immense tree filled the yard. A handmade swing hung from a lower branch.

Her father had built a playhouse with a shuttered opening on three sides and a Dutch door. She'd placed a small table, two tiny chairs, a doll's highchair with her only doll, and her favorite stuffed animal inside to complete the child's world. Maggie would open the top section of the Dutch door and survey the woods at the edge of their property where her imagination took root.

Now in Scotland, this wooded region conjured up images of her quiet neighborhood that lured children into make-believe adventures. She stopped for a moment to soak it in and wished she still lived in a quaint town like Rolen.

Her life had become cluttered. Preoccupied with success, she experienced a giant void in her life. Memories of her mother as she baked bread, sewed clothes, mended socks and still made time to play games gave Maggie pause to reevaluate her choice not to have a family. Her mother gave sacrificially, and this example tugged at her heartstrings. Perhaps the greatest job in life had indeed slipped through her fingers.

Maggie refocused on the present and resumed her walk. A sign came into view, "Rolen Presbyterian Kirk, Dr. Reginald Shane, Minister, Sunday Worship: 10 am." The path crested the hill where a lovely stone building with a tall steeple and bell tower greeted her. Simple stained glass windows graced each side of the carved wooden doors. Large pots filled with red, yellow, and orange flowers were on each side. The cemetery lay across the lane from a well-maintained yard. Shade trees with benches underneath dotted the grounds.

Memories of her mother and her remarkable example of faith returned. Maggie had accompanied her to worship every Sunday. Her mother thanked the Lord before meals, played hymns on the piano, and prayed with her at bedtime. All this created a loving and safe home. A tinge of conscience rose to the surface, but she resisted. She had made her choices; education finished, then a large city in the East became her new home. Determined to succeed, her priorities would not be her mother's. Nor the faith environment. Maggie's goodbye signaled the resolution to follow her own path and broke her mother's heart. The old ways disappeared in the haze of new temptations.

Maggie ascended the kirk's steps. She placed her hand on the door latch, lifted, and pushed in. The heavy carved wooden door of the old kirk creaked. The narthex and sanctuary filled with light from the side stained glass windows. One lone candle brightened a dark corner by the altar. This must be the eternal candle. Her mother explained that it symbolized an ever-present God.

A welcome sign above a thick tattered guest book requested visitors to register. Perusing the pages, Maggie hunted for any familiar signatures. Interrupted by the sound of another creaking door close to the altar, Maggie hurried to the center aisle. A man emerged with hands clasped in front of his waist. He came down the aisle toward Maggie.

"Guid day. I'm Dr. Shane, the minister here." He extended a hand to Maggie. "Welcome to Rolen Presbyterian Kirk. Have you moved to the area or just visiting?"

"Thank you, Dr. Shane. My name is Miss Richards. I'm visiting Rolen. The sun inspired me to stroll through the countryside. Then I came upon the rugged church sign and stopped for a visit." As Maggie shook his hand, she sensed a heart of compassion and understanding. She felt confident he would have some answers.

"You must be from America. I can tell from your accent."

"Yes, I am. I rented a flat in Inverness for a month, but desired to explore some small communities for a larger perspective of Scottish life. Rolen's quaintness with such friendly residents has been a delight."

"I couldn't agree more. These people can trace their history back to the 1500s and are very proud of their independence and self-sufficiency. They have simple needs and follow the principles in the Bible, lending to neighbors and strangers alike from their bounty. I'm blessed to have served them for many years and pray I have reciprocated the blessing. I noticed you were by our guest book. Did you sign it?"

"No, I didn't. Just looking for any names I might recognize from town. Do most of the residents attend here?" Maggie longed to discuss the true reason for her visit, but some general questions would do for now.

"Yes, most of them. There are a few families whose roots are in larger neighboring towns, yet they travel back every Sunday to worship with their parents or other relatives. We also have several families living five to twenty miles from Rolen. They are a tight-knit group, but open their arms to strangers and those in need. If you attend worship for two Sundays in a row, they count you as one of them. What names were you looking for?"

Maggie felt awkward. If she didn't offer a name, Dr. Shane may discern she lied.

"My friends and I are staying at the Creag Au Tuirc. I wondered if Mr. and Mrs. Wellington were members here?"

"Yes, and what a dear couple. They've been members since their conversion many years ago. Their lives changed when the Holy Spirit revealed the love of God. They made a promise to the Lord to be in attendance every Sunday. Sometimes that meant they left the inn open for guests to come and go as they pleased. God has not failed with His protection of the inn. Anyone else you were interested in?"

Maggie felt Dr. Shane could see into her heart with that question. Oh course, she wanted to know about someone else, but she didn't know how to ask.

"Would you mind showing me the church grounds?" Maybe physical exercise would clear her mind and prepare the next question.

They stopped at the front of the sanctuary and Dr. Shane explained the kirk's history. Stained glass windows down each aisle allowed light to illuminate a masterfully hand-carved baptismal font. A rough-hewn cross hung above the altar. Dr. Shane's eyes moistened and with a quavering voice, he shared the story.

"This congregation desired to have a cross closer to the one used for Christ's crucifixion. Not one sanded smooth, but a cross with broken edges and exposed splinters adding to His already battered, broken and bleeding body. They wanted to remember the agony because of His love for them. An empty cross, instead of a crucifix, reminded them of the glory of His resurrection. No other person in all history accomplished what Jesus did, and they longed to remember that every time they walked into this house of worship." Dr. Shane paused, pondered the cross, then continued.

"When I think of their devotion to the Lord and remember His devotion to His children, I cry and smile at the same time. Think of it. The God who made heaven, earth, all we see, touch, smell, taste and hear, from the smallest microscopic entity to the unfathomable enormity of the universe, loves us with an unending, always-present and ever-calling love. Attempting to convey this in the cross, baptismal font and stained glass windows, the congregation hoped to touch the infinite with all their senses. Do you have faith in the Lord?"

Maggie did not want to hear another word. While an interesting tale, she must not listen to more. She felt as if a heavy blanket was cascading over her head and she would smother at any time. *Get out of this place.*

"No, I don't, Dr. Shane. Could we go outside now?"

She followed Dr. Shane's direction toward the side door. Once outside, Maggie filled her lungs with the fresh air, then forced her breath out as if expunging from her head everything she had seen and heard. *His words can't take root and, perhaps, the outdoors will provide an escape.*

Each bit of information heard was like those dandelion seeds she would blow as a child. Maggie attached a nugget of Dr. Shane's tale to each seed and visualized them flying away in the wind, disappearing forever in the sunshine's warmth to places unknown.

Stone benches engraved with Bible passages bordered the narrow gravel path to the cemetery. The smell of Scottish heather filled the air. Their beautiful purple flowers added color to the otherwise drab grey tombstones. The markers surprised Maggie. They were not like the gravestones in the States.

"Could you explain these markers to me? I have seen nothing like this before."

"The Scottish people bury family members together in one grave. The coffin of the first one to die rests on the bottom and they stack each subsequent member's coffin on top. It takes up less space and families appreciate knowing they'll be together, even though, as Christians, we know only our earthly bodies are in repose."

Maggie proceeded in silence and listened to the sweet chirping of nearby birds. With mixed emotions, she hoped a visitor would call on the minister, yet no one did. If anyone could answer her questions, it would be Dr. Shane.

"I might be mistaken, but I sense you're looking for a specific grave marker."

"To be truthful, I am. My friends and I were enjoying a coach ride in the countryside yesterday. The driver took a wrong turn and stopped at a place called Stuart Hall. Mr. MacLaren was gracious and invited us for a rest. He seemed a sad, lonely man. I understand his stepmother had passed a short time ago. If she's buried here, I would like to pay my respects."

"An admired and loved member of our kirk, Mrs. MacLaren had a kind word for everyone and an obvious servant heart. Her faith in the Lord shone like diamonds. Her grave is this way on the other side of that fir tree. The children think the tree is perfect for a swing. Maybe someday. Please follow me."

The path curved past several bushes of heather. He stopped, motioned to Maggie, then backed up to allow her a clear view. Maggie plodded toward the marker, afraid her hesitant gait might be noticeable to Dr. Shane. She dreaded this moment. She still hoped beyond all hope that she would find someone else's name on the marble slab. Maggie blinked her eyes several times, then focused on the letters.

"Claire Margaret MacLaren, Beloved wife of Ramsay, 1848—1899, Gone Home to her Lord."

A host of conflicting emotions invaded Maggie's body. Sorrow overwhelmed her. She wanted to cry, scream, beat the marker and caress it at the same time. With the realization Dr. Shane rested behind her, Maggie mustered every ounce of energy to pull herself together. She didn't convince him. He placed his hand on her arm and guided Maggie to the bench. She retrieved a hankie from her pocket to dry a tear.

"I must have something in my eye, or maybe allergies to the heather." Her flimsy excuse failed.

"Are you all right? Is there anything I can do to ease your grief?"

Ease my grief? What grief? I only learned about this woman yesterday.

Quiet prevailed there on that bench in the far corner of the cemetery for what seemed like an eternity. Maggie scanned the clear blue sky, the beautiful green trees, and marveled at the stillness of the countryside. Dr. Shane had found the perfect resting place for Claire, who commented how nature reminded her that God was the ultimate artist. No human being ever came close to His majesty. With one more deep breath, she prepared to confide in this servant of God.

"Dr. Shane, if my memory serves me right, clergy are like lawyers, sworn not to divulge information. They are to respect the right of privacy. Is that correct?"

"You are correct. Anything shared in private remains between myself, my parishioner, and our God. Whatever you wish to say to me will go no farther than this bench. I want you to know before you say anything that I sense you knew Claire before meeting her stepson yesterday. I would like to support you through whatever pain you're experiencing."

Maggie's eyes met his. His words astonished her. Her mom had taught her God worked in mysterious ways, but not in Maggie's life. She wrote God off years ago. Now this mystery lay right in front of her. The moment had arrived that she'd prepared for, but also dreaded. She needed to broach each question with the utmost of care. Conscious time ticked away, Maggie refocused.

"Dr. Shane, I have some questions, but I've lost track of the time. Do you have a pocket watch?"

"Yes." He pulled his watch fob. "It's a little after one."

Shocked, Maggie felt her heart beat faster. She realized her visit had ended.

"I'm so sorry. I need to return to the inn or I may miss the train. Thank you so much for your time."

She paused for a moment, then added, "I'm sorry to rush off like this. I'll be back in a week. May I impose on you to continue our conversation, then?"

He enfolded her hand in his. "I will welcome further conversation and pray for a safe trip now and on your return."

She thanked him and made her way in haste down the path and back to the road toward town. A slight drizzle from one lone cloud fell on her. Her habit was to run from the rain, but this time it soothed her. Maggie let the drops fall on her face and mix with tears. Not knowing the worth of it, she talked to God for the first time in many years. "If you're there and you care at all about me, please help me find some answers." The rain drops ceased, and the cloud blew away. A glorious sun warmed her face. Afraid she'd arrive late at the inn, she increased her pace.

Chapter 9

The clickety-clack of The Great Northern of Scotland train wheels lulled the ladies into slumberland. Max closed his notepad and soaked in the scenery. A shrill from the train whistle startled the girls awake.

"Hard to believe we're back in Inverness already." Max checked his pocket watch. "A mighty short train ride." He leaned toward the window. The smoke escaped the chimney and cloud billows skated across the platform.

"Maggie, Nellie, as soon as the train stops, I'll hop off. It can be chaotic finding our luggage." The last blast of steam and the screech of the metal wheels clued Max their journey had ended. He jumped off, hailed a carriage, and scoured the platform for their bags. Maggie and Nellie stretched their legs, then descended the stairs.

A brief carriage ride returned them to their apartment before nightfall. Once unpacked, Max crossed the hall from his room to Maggie and Nellie's. Maybe I can scrounge something together. We'll need to go shopping tomorrow."

"Thank you, Max. That sounds delightful. Will you join me, Nellie?" Maggie collapsed on the leather sofa. Nellie followed suit. They put their feet on two upholstered footstools.

Max lit the gas stove to heat the teakettle and placed a caddy of loose leaves inside the teapot.

"The water for tea is heating and I've got dinner started," he said, as he joined the ladies. "I'd like to share my adventure first, if you don't mind. After that stuffy train ride, I think we need a good laugh."

Max relayed his eventful morning in the M-G Store & Cafe'. An expert at description, Nellie and Maggie could taste Mabel's morning rolls. Ernest's fishing story was delightful, and the girls laughed over the widow Grubbs' adventure.

"Mabel had difficulty talking about Claire." The whistling of the teakettle interrupted Max's story. He rose and entered the kitchen.

Within a few minutes, Max returned carrying the tea tray and set it on a side table. Resettling in a chair, he continued.

"They must have had a close relationship. George explained that when Laurence came into the store, Mabel stayed in the kitchen. She harbored ill will toward him, but was working hard at forgiveness."

Max untied his shoes and loosened his shirt collar. "I followed the hammer sounds to the blacksmith shop and struck up a conversation with the smithy. He's a strong, congenial man, willing to share whatever he could. Apprenticed under his father, he became the town's sole blacksmith at his father's death. I inquired about the Cheshire's, but he was a young lad when they lived at Stuart Hall and he only saw them in town. Gwen was in his class at school. He found her to be a quiet, contemplative girl who loved history, music and art. The only thing he could tell me about her home life was that one day she hoped for a family and wanted to continue living at the Hall."

Max excused himself to check on the dinner, then returned and poured the tea.

"I asked him if he shoed the MacLaren's horses. He replied he would go to the Hall when their own stable hand was on holiday. Maybe once a year. I mentioned Ernest's memory of a black horse and asked if he knew anything about him. I noted his reply." Max flipped through his journal.

"'Oh, yeah, Fireball. The biggest, blackest, fastest son of a gun horse around here. I had a week's wages down on Ol' Blue at a race some time back when that horse came out of nowhere. Like watching a bolt of lightning streak across the finish line. Incredible!'"

Max closed his notebook. "The blacksmith called the horse a demon; not only huge, but an 'in-your-face' attitude. He recalled one visit to the Hall to re-shoe the stallion. He had trouble holding up a leg and feared being knocked down or worse."

Max handed Maggie and Nellie a cup of tea, then sipped from his own cup. "The blacksmith called MacLaren out to calm his steed so he could finish the job. When he finished, he told MacLaren that if he needed his services again, he would charge double. Know what MacLaren said? 'Don't know what your problem is. Walter shoes Fireball on a regular basis and has no trouble. You must have spooked him.' The blacksmith figured it was the other way around." Maggie and Nellie chuckled.

"Mind you, I had to write with speed and fill in the blanks later. He spoke like a freight train barreling down a mountainside. Hard to do, but I'm sure I got the gist of his tale," Max side. "If you'll excuse me, I see if dinner's ready."

"This powerful horse and MacLaren concern me." Maggie set her tea cup on its saucer. "Something we'll need to be wary of when we return."

Max called the ladies to dinner. His ability to create a superb meal from miss-matched left-overs made Maggie's top ten list for the day. They delighted to be back in their own space, recounting their Rolen experiences.

✳✳✳

With full stomachs, they retired to the living room with a cup of tea in hand. Nellie retrieved her journal and shared her conversation with Mary Beth. The concern Mary Beth expressed regarding Claire's safety now concerned them as well.

"I'll attempt to gain a copy of the inquest proceedings. A friend I met in Chicago moved to Inverness years ago. She told me she hoped to work in the judicial department. If she's there, we'll be in luck," Nellie said. "If Mary Beth shared her conversation with Claire and her fear for her safety with the judge, that evidence would be reliable testimony and should affect the outcome." Nellie paused.

"On a side note, Mary Beth is sewing a new dress for me. She promised to have it ready when we got back. I haven't had a new dress in a long time and never one tailor made."

Nellie reached her cup toward Max. He poured another cup of tea for both ladies.

✳✳✳

"You only need to share whatever you desire, Maggie." Max's words comforted her. "Nellie and I can wait until you are more at ease, if you prefer."

"Thank you, but no." Maggie wiped her nose. "As I mentioned at the start of this quest, there would be hard times. It's imperative we all have the same information to determine our plan of action."

Maggie sipped her tea, opened her journal and recounted the delightful stroll to the parish, the well-built stone church and surrounding cemetery. She described Dr. Shane and his gracious manner, then the inside of the sanctuary and their journey outside. She breathed a deep breath, exhaled and recounted her heavy steps to Claire's grave.

"I thought I could control myself enough to hide my relationship with Claire. All was well until I read her name on the grave stone. Then my emotions hit. I wanted to scream, cry and fall down on the grave all at the same time. Funny how a simple name on a grave marker can have that effect. Yet, the truth, the finality, stared me in the face. My Mom was gone and I could never tell her I loved her. Can't remember the last time I said those words."

She dabbed her eyes and drank more tea. "I don't know how long I stood there before the minister took my arm and led me to a bench. After a short rest, the shaking subsided. Then I realized the lateness of the hour and told Dr. Shane I needed to leave, but would welcome a chance to visit more when I returned."

Maggie paused. Her voice trembled and tears welled in her eyes. "I don't know how he knew, but he knew I lied about not knowing Claire. He knew the reason I came was to see her grave. Mom always told me God moved in mysterious ways. To see her gravestone was more than I could handle."

Nellie grasped Maggie's hand and gave her another handkerchief. "Maggie, we knew this wouldn't be easy for you. We love you and will do everything we can to see this through to the end. Whatever that end may be. Please confide in us anytime. We want to be your support and sounding board through this journey."

Maggie smiled. "You know the ironic thing? She's buried beneath an old fir tree like the one in our backyard at home. Dr. Shane said the children wanted to put a swing in it. My Dad put a swing in ours. I still remember my childhood afternoons, pumping as hard as I could to force the swing parallel to the ground. I'd lean back as far as possible, hoping my toes would touch the clouds. Mom would smile if she could see where the town laid her to rest."

With goodnights said, they headed for their own bedrooms. Three minds filled with information and questions. For Maggie, the wait would be most difficult. Time had come for her to rest and prepare for a new day.

Chapter 10

An early morning rat-a-tat on Maggie and Nellie's door signaled Max's arrival. A fragrant smell emanated from the box he held and wafted through the air when she opened the door. Her taste buds expected sweetness. She closed the door behind him and followed the aroma.

"Went to the bakery early. Blueberry scones. The apples and oranges are from a little fruit stand I passed. I'll put this on the dining room table."

Nellie waited there with her journal already opened.

"There's hot tea in the kitchen. Please, help yourself." Maggie set her plate on the table.

"I'm not very hungry this morning." He wrapped a scone in brown paper and polished an apple. "I'll take these with me and grab a bite at that cafe' down the street." Max placed his journal beside Nellie's. "Nellie, may I escort you down the stairs?"

"Thanks, Max. I'd like that." Nellie grabbed a sweater for an extra layer from the early morning Scottish chill. "I'll save my scone for dinner, but an orange to go would be nice."

"See you two later," Maggie called as they descended the stairway.

She opened all three journals and with pad and pencil, designed a schematic of the known facts. When she finished, Maggie read the list out loud to check for gaps.

"Mr. and Mrs. William Cheshire bought the manor, which had fallen in disrepair during a long vacancy. They had three sons who left home, and one daughter, Gwen.
- Gwen married Ramsay MacLaren
- Gwen died from an unknown illness
- Ramsay married Claire Ferguson

- Claire died in a horse riding accident (?)
- Ramsay seems to have disappeared
- Laurence is now master of Stuart Hall"

She paused and studied the chain of generations. Confused whether to add, change or put in parentheses "murdered" instead of "died in a horse riding accident," Maggie felt the question mark would suffice for now.

Next, she listed each person interviewed and their relationship with Claire.

"Walter, stable hand: said little, perhaps knows more
- Leach, gardener: Gwen hired him
- Harriet, cook: nothing yet
- James, butler: nothing yet
- George/Mabel: Mabel and Claire - close relationship - think it was not an accident
- Blacksmith: afraid of Fireball
- Dr. Shane: revisit later
- Ernest McIntyre: more information on return; fishing trip, Max?
- Mr and Mrs Wellington: nothing yet
- Mary Beth: concerned about Claire's safety when alone with Laurence"

The "not an accident" and "concerned for Claire's safety" flashed at her. If two people recognized the danger Claire may have been in, and if the stable hand and gardener didn't want to discuss it, Maggie felt red flags should have popped up at the inquest.

The opportunity arose for the judge to delve deeper into the relationship between her mother and Laurence. She could feel the intense emotions well up inside of her. Maggie became even more determined to prove him guilty of murder. She also recognized you need all the facts before making accusations.

Maggie entered her bedroom and opened her handkerchief sachet. While she kept some very special hankies from her mother, this embroidered case also held keepsake letters. She returned to the dining room and unfastened the case.

There they were. All the letters she had saved from her mom. One letter each week had awaited in her mailbox. Maggie responded once a month for a time, then her letters dwindled until she stopped writing.

She had read most of the letters, but several remained unopened. The last two arrived a week before word reached her of her mother's death. Again, Maggie wished for a relationship that no longer existed. She felt her mother's love and desire to remain a part of her life. Yet wishing, and hoping and thinking and, yes, even praying didn't make it so. There needed to be action on her part for reconciliation, and Maggie's prideful attitude won. Now she regretted her decision, realized how much she loved her mother and wanted to see justice done. Not only for her mom, but to redeem herself in her own eyes. She put the letters aside for now.

A knock at the door disrupted Maggie's melancholy.

"Max," Maggie flung the door wide. "Here, let me help you." She reached for a bag of groceries and the newspaper stuffed under his arm.

"Thank you, fair lassie." Max nodded. "If you'll be so kind and put the groceries in the kitchen, I'll put them away. Then, if you could fetch a vase for these flowers, I thought they would brighten this dismal apartment."

Maggie poured water into a vase, arranged the flowers and set them on the dining table with a doily underneath.

"Oh, Max, they're lovely. The room is brighter already. Thank you." Maggie stepped back to admire the bright yellow and violet blooms.

"I'll cook tonight. I'd like you and Nellie to look over my notes when she gets here. If you two could add anything of importance I may have missed, I'd appreciate it. I'm going out for a breath of fresh air. The walk will do me good. See you later."

✻✻✻

The streets were the usual hustle and bustle. The sounds of carriage wheels and horse hoofs on the cobblestone road gave Maggie a sense of belonging. Even though she had never been to Scotland, stories from her grandfather rooted her to the land of his birth. She loved his Scottish brogue, but had a hard time understanding some words, especially when he sang songs of the "old country," his term of endearment for Scotland.

Her fondest memories were of when she had arrived at his home for the Christmas holiday. Her foot hadn't touched the living room rug before he scooped her up in his arms for a grand hug. With only one arm out of her coat, her grandpa would pull her to the floor for a game of cribbage. Even though he usually won, she believed he messed up the counting on purpose so she could win a game or two. Lots of laughter, songs and warm scones with her Grandma's homemade orange marmalade created a taste of Scotland.

The late afternoon Inverness sunshine warmed her. Its brightness gave Maggie a sense of well-being, an assurance the answers she sought would surface when they returned to Stuart Hall. For now, patience was the key. She trusted that Nellie's friend still worked in Inverness and could retrieve the inquest transcript.

Reminiscing about her grandma's warm scones, the smells from a nearby quaint cafe' enticed her. Maggie found a corner table, ordered a scone with orange marmalade and Scottish Breakfast tea. No sooner had she unfolded her serviette, when Nellie rushed to her side and slid into the chair across from Maggie. Nellie caught the server's attention. "I'll have what she's having."

"Nellie, you're out of breath. What on earth have you been doing?"

"Well, my dear Maggie," she removed her sweater and laid it across her lap. "You'll never guess what luck I've had today." She leaned closer to Maggie. "I went straight to the magistrate's office and inquired whether Mrs. McGregor still worked there. I said I was an old friend over from the States. Not only did she still work there, she came out of the back office at that exact moment. She saw me, rushed over for a hug and 'Tis sure guid tae see ye.' I was thrilled. She remembered our special friendship years ago."

Maggie's heart raced. What wonderful news! A good day, for sure.

"We located a corner with empty chairs for a visit. 'Taking a wee break,' she called to the clerk. After the usual catching-up news, I said I needed a favor. I explained our mission, left out most of the details, and wondered what the chances were for a copy of the inquest proceedings."

The server brought the scones, marmalade and a pot of tea. They felt warm and smelled delicious. With marmalade spread on the scones and tea poured, Nellie continued.

"Mollie said it wouldn't be any trouble since once they settled cases, the transcripts became public record. She should locate them in a day. I'll take a note pad and copy down important testimony. She has our address and will send a messenger when they're available. Oh, Maggie, I'm so pleased."

"Great job, Nellie. I knew my confidence in you was justified." A sip of tea warmed Maggie, head to toe.

"Max arrived at the apartment an hour ago. I volunteered to fix dinner so you two could review my chart and add, or clarify, anything I missed. I feel we're getting closer to some answers, yet we have a long road ahead." Maggie bit into her biscuit. "These scones are delicious. Let's take a few back for breakfast tomorrow."

"I'll order some," Nellie volunteered. "Then one more stop before returning home. You may come with me if you like. There's an old book store around the corner. Sometimes they have copies of out of print books. Never know what I may find for a good read."

"Sounds delightful, Nellie. Let's finish and be on our way."

Maggie clutched a bag of scones and shadowed Nellie to the bookstore. The sights of old, well-used books and a noticeable musty smell filled the shop. Nellie found the section that piqued her interest.

Maggie set out to locate books on the histories of Scottish families. Not sure such a book even existed, she hoped she might learn more about the Cheshire's genealogy. The store had a small section on the history of Scotland's castles. Maggie pulled one off the shelf, scanned the table of contents and located Stuart Hall.

"Nellie," she whispered. "Come over here, by me. Look what I found." Maggie tried to contain herself until Nellie arrived. "Listen while I read this entry: 'Stuart Hall; built in the late 1600s by Mr. Donald Stuart, who secured his fortune from local coal mines and timber. At one time, it encompassed 1200 acres. Timber sale reduced the land to 500 acres. Mr. Stuart and his wife had six children. After their deaths, the Stuart's heirs squandered the revenue. Necessity caused many to seek gainful employment in western Scotland. The last generation of Stuarts vacated Stuart Hall in 1725. The bank took possession until Mr. Cheshire acquired it for back taxes. Mr. Cheshire and his bride inherited wealth and completed the renovations needed to make a cold, uninhabitable castle into a warm, inviting home.' We know more about its history now. I'll put the book back on the shelf. Did you find anything interesting?"

"I found a book filled with folk tales from small communities. I never thought there could be so many stories or small towns in Scotland. Look at the size of this volume. Think I can carry it home?"

Maggie admired Nellie's passion for books. The storekeeper wrapped Nellie's find in brown paper tied with twine, then the two ladies strolled back to their apartment.

Chapter 11

Maggie fetched her mother's letters, still bundled with a green ribbon. She nestled in an overstuffed chair with a tartan throw and a cup of tea. Maggie read each letter to Max and Nellie. She emphasized the key points.

"Falling in love with Ramsay seemed to be easy for my mom. It sounds like she was filled with apprehension at the thought of meeting Laurence, yet She still promised to build a relationship with him." Maggie set her teacup on the table by her chair.

"I wonder why Laurence didn't share her desire. Is he so self-centered there's no room in his life for anyone else?" She gulped. "Let me read you one of her comments; 'Laurence is about the same age as you, Maggie. Ramsay said his son takes long rides in the forest. I remember how you delighted in exploring the woods by our house and asked us over and over if we could buy you a horse. Perhaps if you come to Scotland, you and Laurence can ride together. Wouldn't that be wonderful?'"

"Well, Maggie, what about it?" Nellie asked. "Think you'd like to go for a ride with Lawrence?"

"I will do all I can to make sure he takes me to where my mom died. Nellie, this is so difficult to wait for Mollie."

"I understand, but she is very efficient and will do her best. Remember, I'll need to copy the testimonies. We must be patient," Nellie responded.

Maggie held her mom's last two unopened letters close to her breast. Her heart pounded as she tried to gather enough courage to read them. She slid the letter from the first envelope and unfolded the paper. The letter shook in her hand.

My dearest Maggie,

It doesn't seem possible I've been here almost two years. The time seems to fly by when Ramsay and I are together. We enjoy each other's company so much and have planned a trip to Edinburgh for next week. Ramsay insists I visit some historical places around the city and Edinburgh Castle.

I remain determined to build a relationship with Laurence, but hit a brick wall at every instance. I have never seen a young man so intent on keeping to himself. Ramsay had suggested we extend Laurence an invitation to join us, and it surprised me when he agreed. Please pray for me and for wisdom to know how to connect with this young man. Maybe this trip will be a turning point. If you will, pray for him too?

I love you so much. Please write.

All my love,
Mom

How could Laurence treat Claire that way? Everyone who knew her mom commented on her sweet, thoughtful, and generous nature. The sharp pangs of conscience and guilt bit into her soul. A trip to Stuart Hall to meet her mother's spouse and stepson may have been beneficial. Perhaps she would have sensed the danger and intervened, with the insistence that Laurence receive counseling. Maggie heaved a sigh and opened her mother's last correspondence.

My sweet Maggie,

We arrived home from Edinburgh last week. Visited several museums and I learned about John Paul Jones and portrait artists, Allan Ramsay and Henry Raeburn. Ramsay reads Robert Burns every evening. I have a greater appreciation for Scottish artists and poets.

Laurence seemed pleased with our holiday. For the first time, he smiled at me. I don't know what happened, but he may be softening.

Maggie, I am optimistic. Laurence plans to enter a local horse race and asked me to join him tomorrow as he conditions Fireball. That's the name of his horse. He suggested I ride a more spirited horse to challenge Fireball. Her name is Peggy. He must not have known I rode Peggy several times each week. When Ramsay attends conferences, I'm nervous and uncomfortable, almost suspicious that he wishes me harm. Even with Ramsay at the dinner table, Laurence sends chills down my back when he glares at me.

I'll let you know about the ride in my next letter.

I continue to pray for you daily and look forward to a letter from you. My heart aches with your absence from my life. I miss you. God's blessings.

All my love, Mother

P.S. Laurence inquired if you might come for a visit. Please think about it.

Maggie placed the letter back in the envelope. A tear spilled down her cheek and wet the paper. She remembered a plaque in her childhood home and always wondered what the proverb meant. She now knew its truthfulness; "We git tae soon auld 'n' tae late smart."

Arms of love surrounded Maggie as Nellie drew her close.

"This is from your mom, Maggie."

Emotions climaxed as she released a flood of tears. Nellie wrapped her even tighter. Maggie became a little girl embraced in arms of love.

"Maggie, we love you so much. You must not give in to regret. The past is over. We need to move forward, come what may. The hour is late and you need time alone to process your mother's words. Let's say goodnight now," Nellie said.

Maggie wiped the remaining tears from her cheek. She clasped Nellie's hand and agreed tomorrow would be better. Emotionally spent, she allowed her head to flop back on the overstuffed chair.

Max crossed the floor to Maggie and knelt beside her. "Maggie, you know I care for you and hate to see you hurting this way. I'm here whenever you need a listening ear. I'll say goodnight now. See you ladies in the morning." Max closed the hall door behind him.

"I'm going to turn in. Is there anything I can do for you first?"

"Thank you, Nellie. I think a few minutes alone will help me reclaim my senses. Have a good sleep."

Maggie ambled to the open window and gazed upon the clear blue, star-filled sky. What a beautiful, quiet night. As she grasped the window knob, a shooting star streaked the heavens. A breeze rustled the curtains. She closed and latched the window.

"Mom, I will sort this out, whatever it takes. I promise."

Chapter 12

The days dragged by while Nellie copied the transcript. She took great pains to read the document in its entirety. Her head dizzied with information, yet Nellie pushed herself to read through one more time. Important missed testimony might jeopardize their actions once they returned to Stuart Hall. The task completed, she bundled her notes, then rushed to the apartment.

"Maggie! Max!"

Maggie heard her friend call from the bottom of the stairs.

"I've got it. I'm finished."

Maggie burst into the hall. "Come on up. I've been pacing for the past hour." She grabbed Nellie's arm.

Once in the apartment, Nellie slumped down in her favorite chair. She held the inquest notes in the air. "Who wants to see it first?"

"This is no game of keep-away, Nellie." Maggie slid into the chair beside her. "Your diligence has given us a valuable gift. Perhaps now we can understand the events that led to my mother's death." She turned toward the kitchen. "Max, is the tea ready?"

"Yes, as you requested. Why don't we sit around the table? I'll pour while you two make yourself comfortable." Max brought the tea and refreshments.

Nellie laid down the stack of papers. She shuffled through them again to be sure they were in order, then she explained her choice of copied sections.

"The straightforward beginning held no new information, so I skipped to the testimonies. Many opened more speculations. You two sit back while I read my notes. I'm sorry some of them aren't full sentences."

Max scooted a cup of tea to each of the girls. A plate of left-over scones graced the table for any takers. Maggie reached for one and set it on her saucer, fortified for Nellie's report.

"Harriet, the cook, said Mrs. MacLaren was a lovely person who met a tragic end. On the day of the ride, she asked her to prepare a special lunch for their return and seemed excited Mr. Laurence invited her to ride."

Max interjected, "I find that rather telling of your mother's care and concern for others. It seems to shine through in many of her interactions with the people of Rolen as well."

Nellie underlined Harriet's comment, then continued.

"James, the butler, stated he didn't engage in conversation about the personal lives of Mr. and Mrs. MacLaren or Master Laurence. Concern regarding the relationship between Mrs. MacLaren and Master Laurence resulted from overheard conversations, which most times were rather tense. He observed that Mrs. MacLaren showed considerable restraint. James stated that when Master Laurence returned from the fatal ride, he went straight upstairs. Seemed to show a lack of concern, a bit of a smile on his face. James also observed that Master Laurence seemed more jovial than usual the day after the funeral."

Nellie cleared her throat and sipped her tea. A small bite of scone. Then she continued.

"The judge asked Harriet and James if Mrs. MacLaren showed any signs of illness the day of, or the days before, the ride. Were her eating habits normal? Drinking more water than usual? Anything that might have shown she wasn't feeling well? Harriet responded there was no difference in her eating habits in the days before or the day in question. James noticed nothing to suggest Mrs. MacLaren felt ill.

"The judge asked James if any tension between Mr. and Mrs. MacLaren might have distracted her focus. James stated they appeared happy and in love." Nellie's voice rasped. She stopped for another sip of tea.

"Could the judge not see the possibility of something other than an accident?" Maggie pushed her chair away from the table. "My mother wasn't sick. Something's not right here, especially with this — this — Master Laurence."

Maggie's face reddened. She rose from the table and paced across the room, then blurted, "These feelings of animosity toward Laurence wear at my emotions. I'm trying to maintain an open mind, but explain to me the smile on his face after the accident and James's description of a more 'jovial' appearance following the funeral. How unfeeling and insensitive. How about his father and what he must have been going through? What happened to a son's compassion? His feelings for another human being? Closeness to his father? What kind of relationship did they have? Where is Ramsay MacLaren?" She screamed.

Max reached her side and placed a firm hand on her shoulder. "Maggie, take a deep breath and slow down. We're with you all the way, but we can only study one question at a time. Nellie and I understand your frustration. We're frustrated too. Nellie spent many hours with the transcript and her expertise in detecting the relevant parts should assure you we've got the best information possible."

As Maggie gazed at Max, she noticed a depth to him she had overlooked in the past. His eyes glistened. A warmth and concern shone through and touched her heart. This seemed to be more than friendship. Perhaps empathy, sympathy. Or something more?

"You're right, Max, as always. I've trusted your judgement for as long as I've known you. I'll attempt to remain in control and not come unglued again."

Max held the chair for Maggie. She positioned herself, but couldn't get settled. The questions crashed upon her mind like the pounding of ocean waves on the shore.

Nellie poured more tea and continued. "Next up, Walter. If you remember, he's the stable hand. He recalled Laurence's excitement when Fireball galloped into the paddock for the first time. A young unridden horse, Laurence did all the breaking himself. Walter described Fireball as a very spirited horse, impossible for anyone but Laurence to control. Concerned for his own safety cleaning the paddock, Walter asked for Laurence's help. Laurence laughed off the request and told Walter to get some backbone."

"Sounds like he's an expert with horses." Maggie paused. "I wonder. Since he trained Fireball for his riding needs, could he not also train another horse for a different need?"

"You mean, could he have trained Peggy to respond in some adverse way at his command? Be it verbal or nonverbal?" Max asked. "Is that what you're hinting at?"

"Well? Could he?" Maggie pressed.

"Let's finish my notes before we get sidetracked," Nellie said.

"As a child, Walter stated, Laurence showed a compassionate and outgoing nature. As an adult, however, he became more secretive.

"I skipped over several sections and scanned down the transcript to the day in question. Walter said Laurence seemed preoccupied, brushed past him in the stable yard without responding to his greeting. Laurence then walked straight to Fireball, patted his neck, gave him a carrot, and said, 'This is your big day, boy. You won't disappoint me, will you?' Walter thought he misunderstood.

Or perhaps Master Laurence referred to the horse race in Rolen. Maybe he meant that this would be the day to discover if his training of Fireball, against Peggy, was enough to win."

Nellie passed her tea cup to Max for a refill. A few remaining drops fell into her cup.

"That's all right, Max. I prefer water. Do you mind?"

Max left the table for the kitchen and returned with three glasses. "Sounded good to me, too."

Nellie drank half the liquid, cleared her throat, then began again.

"The judge asked Walter if he noticed any hesitancy from Mrs. MacLaren before the ride. Did she seem sick, dizzy or out-of-sorts in any way? In Walter's opinion, did he feel she possessed the competence to keep up with the pace Fireball would set? Walter responded that Mrs. MacLaren had ridden Peggy and seemed to improve with confidence each day. As far as her health, Walter stated he seldom noticed her out of sorts."

"A visit with Walter when we return may be of value," Max said. "I think he knows more."

Nellie rose and sauntered around the living room. "My disappointment with the judge surfaced at this point. Even though Claire shared her safety concern while alone with Laurence, and George and Mabel said they suspected something not right between Laurence and Claire, the judge didn't recognize a red flag. Mabel had a hard time believing a snake, or something, spooked Claire's horse. She believed Claire to be a conscientious person, mindful of her surroundings and her horse's safety. She would have stayed on the trail, not gotten sidetracked into brush."

Nellie needed a break. Maggie and Max agreed. Their stomach's growling signaled dinner time. The remaining transcript could wait for tomorrow. Maggie had more than enough to consider tonight.

Chapter 13

The new day brought with it an eagerness, as well as apprehension, regarding more testimonies. Maggie left the apartment. Some fresh air to clear her head might help. The Inverness Castle intrigued her. Perhaps she would find portraits of Scotland's clan patriarchs, including the MacLarens or Cheshires.

When she didn't find any, Maggie headed for the Cathedral Church for St. Andrew. On a grass covered knoll by the banks of the River Ness, the cathedral shone like a gem even in Scotland's sometimes dreary weather.

The majestic structure beckoned her. She entered the sanctuary greeted with a coolness that chilled her. Maggie rubbed her arms while she meandered through each alcove, amazed by the beautiful stained glass windows. A sense of both calm and distress flowed through Maggie at the same time. She searched for an exit and found the way out.

Outside, Maggie spotted a lone bench close to the crystal blue river. She reached into her bag and pulled out her notepad. The gentle sounds of lapping waves on the bank calmed Maggie. Children's voices rekindled memories of her childhood as they chased each other around their mothers' skirts. Those were carefree days filled with laughter. The clock on a city building chimed five. Maggie shoved her notebook into her bag, brushed her skirt, and hastened back to the apartment.

The room smelled of burnt toast and fried onions; the result of hurried cooking from chief Max. Maggie unlatched the window and shoved it up. A cleansing breeze blew through the apartment.

Heavy footsteps in the hallway, then a bang on the door startled her. She hurried across the living room.

"Who's there?"

"It's us, Max and Nellie. We've brought gifts for her royal majesty." Max sounded in good humor. She unfastened the latch.

"We thought when we returned, you would still be engrossed in the transcript, so we brought dinner." Max carried a large box to the kitchen counter.

"A cute shop four blocks from here uses local ingredients and cooks every order fresh." Nellie puffed as she lugged another box. "The sights and smells were incredible. A hard decision had to be made with home grown Angus beef at the top of our list. Followed with tatties, greens, fresh fruit, and chocolate fudge for dessert. Thought we might be scone-saturated. Made my mouth water just thinking about it." She washed her hands and removed the containers from the boxes. "I was a good girl, though — no sampling."

Maggie grabbed utensils and set the table, while Max portioned the food on each plate. Their desire to finish the inquest transcript moved to second place. Dinner first. Maggie added more water to the teakettle.

"Nellie, you were right," Maggie said. "I reviewed your notes from last night and still wonder why Inverness has such a thick-headed judge. He listened to testimony that would cause any ordinary person to conclude, well at least question, the true nature of this incident. Too many people shared concern over my mother's safety, hinted at Laurence's instability and no one knows what happened to the senior Mr. MacLaren.

"I was so annoyed, I couldn't sit still. So I headed outside to find the judge's house and give him a piece of my mind. I realized, however, our top priority is to arm ourselves to confront Laurence with clarity and calmness. Then we can bring the facts to the judge. I'm confident he can make a wiser decision and put Laurence in his proper place." Maggie inhaled the enticing aromas. "For now, let's eat!"

Refreshed in body and spirit from the delicious dinner, Maggie awaited to hear the rest of the transcript.

"Nellie, thank you again for your diligent work. I can't imagine how you sat for so many hours sifting through and copying the testimony. This has been very helpful."

"You're welcome. I loved using my detective skills. Narrowing the volume of pages down was a challenge. An enjoyable experience all the same, yet not one I want to repeat soon. Are we ready for Dr. Shane and then Laurence's testimony?"

"As ready as I'll ever be." Maggie shoved away from the table and moved to the sofa. Nellie joined her.

Max handed each a cup of tea, then nestled into his favorite chair.

Mixed feelings consumed Maggie. On one hand, she wanted to hear Dr. Shane's insights. On the other, jitters invaded, fearful of what she may hear. After her father died, her mother's trust in God for strength increased. Maggie didn't understand why anyone relied on someone else for personal strength.

Nellie flattened the papers, then began.

"Dr. Shane's testimony compelled me to copy every word including, the judge's questions. His examination was longer than others, but I believe worth the effort. The judge began;

"Dr., can you tell us what knowledge you have of the events on the day of the fateful horse ride?"

The events. How could he know anything about the events? What reason did he have to be there? Why not ask about conversations with Claire? About her misgivings regarding Laurence? Why not probe into sessions when Claire poured her heart out over her uneasiness and diminishing sense of safety? Why not, why not, why not? These words raced through Maggie's mind. She felt herself more agitated. Her heart pounded. She rose from the sofa and paced, then peered out the open window. Below, men, women, and children milled about. Some stopped for a chat.

"Look at those people down there." Maggie pointed toward the street. "For them, this is another ordinary evening in this ordinary town of Inverness in an ordinary country called Scotland."

"Hold up there, Maggie. Why are you coming unglued again? I only read the judge's question. What's going on?" Nellie asked. "Why are you in such a tizzy?"

Maggie bowed her head. "I don't know. I haven't talked with my mom for over five years, yet I feel so close to her. Maybe I feel guilty about the way I treated her. It's impossible to ask for her forgiveness, but I would sure love to hug her one more time."

Nellie wrapped an arm around Maggie's shoulders. "I love you, Maggie, and I believe that for the first time you're feeling remorse over your actions. Perhaps through this process, you can redeem your own conscience. This may be an ordinary day for all the people on the streets, but it's no ordinary day for us. We've made progress to unravel this mystery. Now, how about we continue with the transcript?" Nellie guided Maggie back to the sofa.

"I'll begin again;

"Dr., can you tell us what knowledge you have of the events on the day of the fateful horse ride?"

"Well, Your Honor, Mrs. MacLaren came for a visit two days earlier and asked if I might come to Stuart Hall for a time of prayer on the day of the ride."

"Did she give you a reason for this request?"

"Yes, Your Honor. Mrs. MacLaren shared her ambivalent feelings over her relationship with her stepson Laurence MacLaren. Inviting her to ride with him encouraged her. However, still apprehensive, she asked if I would come to pray with her for safety and the start of a positive relationship. We asked God to guide her words during the ride in the hopes Mr. Laurence MacLaren might soften and communicate more openly with her. She longed for this, not just for Mr. MacLaren, or herself, but for her husband's sake."

"Did Mr. Ramsay MacLaren join you and his wife for the prayer time?"

"No. However, he knew I would be there."

"Following your prayer time, did you leave right away?"

"No. I accompanied Mrs. MacLaren to the paddock and spoke with Laurence. I wished them a safe and pleasant ride, then watched as the horses trotted toward the woods. Ramsay and I had a brief conversation."

"What did your conversation comprise?"

"General pleasantries as we walked back to my carriage, and I took my leave."

"Did Mr. MacLaren ever share with you a concern regarding the relationship between his wife and son?"

"Only that he knew of the strain and hoped this ride would be the first step toward reconciliation. He was grateful I came and thanked me for the prayer."

"When did you hear about the accident?"

"At the M-G Store when Harriet burst in. She hoped to find the doctor. Harriet told us of the accident at Stuart Hall. I thought my presence could be helpful, so I left right away."

Nellie sipped her tea and repositioned herself.

"This ended Dr. Shane's testimony. Only one person left. Yet this one person would be the most significant of all: Laurence MacLaren. I took great pains to read and copy with accuracy. Are you ready?"

Maggie imagined Laurence would strut to the witness chair, cool as an icicle. He would appear a suave, in-charge type of man who controlled situations for his own purpose. She pictured him with the "bit of a smile on this face." The same attitude James had mentioned.

"Yes, Nellie. I'm ready. And are you ready to calm this lady down again, Max, should I come unglued one more time?"

"I'm ready as always." Max refilled Nellie and Maggie's tea cups before Nellie continued.

"Mr. Laurence MacLaren, you are the principal witness to the events in question. Your testimony will shed light on the untimely death of Mrs. Claire MacLaren. I would advise you to consider your answers and speak the truth. Do you have questions?"

"No, Your Honor. I understand."

Nellie excused herself. "Time for a fresh pot of tea."

Maggie appreciated the break to brace herself and wondered if Max had bought a bottle of wine while they were shopping. Something stronger than a cup of tea may calm her.

"Break time." Max opened the hall door. "I'll be right back."

Alone in the room, Maggie ambled over to the window and poked her head outside. A deep breath of fresh air cleared her mind. The evening breeze cooled her skin. Carriages and pedestrians hustled down streets and sidewalks. Maggie recommitted herself to her goal—find Laurence guilty.

The apartment door slammed. Maggie turned around and saw Max with a bottle of wine in hand. He lifted it high. "Not to be opened until we've finished."

Nellie handed a cup of hot tea to Maggie and Max. She returned to the kitchen and scurried back with her cup, then settled in her chair.

"Mr. MacLaren, before we question you regarding the events of the fateful day, would you explain to the court why your father is not here? I find no record in the police report of his whereabouts. Would you be so kind as to enlighten us?"

"My father has had a hard life; first losing my mother when she was so young, and then his second wife in this tragic accident. I tried to console him following the funeral, but his heart had broken. He said he needed a change of scenery. Stuart Hall held too many memories of his beloved spouses. He packed his chackie, said he would send for his personal items later. He added he would let me know when he found a place suitable to put down roots. I have not heard from him since."

"Have you not made inquiries as to his whereabouts?"

"Yes, but with no success."

"Thank you, Mr. MacLaren. Now, if you will give us a detailed description of the day in question."

"I went to the stables early in the morning to warm-up Fireball. I asked Walter to saddle Peggy. About an hour later, my father joined me. Dr. Shane and Mrs. Ferguson approached from the house together."

"Mrs. Ferguson?" the judge interrupted.

"Oh, I'm sorry, Your Honor. Mrs. MacLaren."

"Continue please."

"We exchanged greetings, then Claire, Mrs. MacLaren, and I mounted and rode toward the woods. She seemed a little uneasy in the saddle. I asked if she would rather postpone to another day. She admitted being nervous, but assured me all would be fine. By this time, we were in the woods and entered a clearing where the horses could run free. I noticed Mrs. MacLaren's pallor appearance and asked if she was all right, or would she rather wait while I let Fireball loose. She said I should go ahead and she would follow at a more reasonable pace.

"Fireball ran like a champ across the meadow. I stopped to observe Peggy. Seemed like Mrs. MacLaren had lost all control. Peggy ran headlong into the woods. I urged Fireball in the same direction and called to Mrs. MacLaren to pull back on the reins. She must not have heard me.

"With one hand she grasped her hat. Her other hand flew out of control, barely holding Peggy's reins. I didn't know if she was aware a steep gully lay inside the woods, so I prodded Fireball to catch Peggy. There's a sharp bend in the path you have to navigate or you end up right over the edge.

"I reached her as Peggy reared up and tossed Mrs. MacLaren from the saddle. She hurtled into the gully. At first, I thought a wild animal must have startled Peggy, but it could have been Mrs. MacLaren's lack of riding ability which confused the horse.

"I halted Fireball, dismounted, and shoved Peggy aside. Leaning over the edge, I called to Mrs. MacLaren. Then I saw her caught in some branches protruding from the side of the cliff only a few feet from the bottom. Her legs were in such a strange position, they had to be broken. When I called again, she emitted a slight moan. I told her to stay quiet and as still as possible, then I checked Peggy for injuries. Finding a few minor scratches, I took her reins, mounted Fireball and went back to the Hall. Walter met me and cared for Peggy. I went inside to find my father and told him what had happened. He sent Harriet into town for the doctor, then called for James and Leach to join us.

"Walter had the team harnessed to the wagon and ready when we returned and I mounted Fireball to lead the way. When we got there, father called, but we heard no response. Walter tied a rope around my father's waist and secured the other end to the wagon. Then father made his descent. I realized she was dead, but father hoped she was only unconscious.

"He reached her, got no response, and asked Walter to let down a blanket. Leach joined father to secure the blanket around her body with the rope. Then we hoisted her to the surface. Once we laid her body in the wagon, we examined her more closely and determined she was indeed dead. Then we went back to Stuart Hall where the doctor and the Reverend were waiting. The rest, you know."

Maggie wrung her hands and wiped them on her skirt. Tears flowed down her cheeks. She reached for a hankie, dabbed her eyes, and blew her nose.

"I can't believe it. I won't believe it. Mom was an expert horsewoman. He's lying."

Nellie placed her hand on Maggie's. "This is his side of the story, Maggie. We kind of knew what he would say already. Remember, we need to hear from everyone and explore the evidence ourselves."

"I suggest we call it a night and start fresh in the morning," Max uncorked the bottle of wine. "But first one glass for relaxation." He poured wine into three glasses, then raised his wine glass and said, "A toast to finding the truth."

"Here, here," Nellie chimed in.

"To the truth." Maggie clinked her friend's glasses.

What a calculated, precise speech. Maggie imagined Laurence practiced at the Hall until his words were fluid. She counted the days until their return.

Chapter 14

Maggie awoke to the delightful sounds of children playing in the park across from the apartment house. She opened the window and smiled at their laughter. Fresh air blew inside and allowed last night's staleness an escape route. Maggie filled the coffeepot and prepared scrambled eggs to accompany their breakfast scones. A knock at the door summoned Maggie. Max entered, the morning paper clutched under his arm.

"Do we have questions or insights from yesterday's readings that need to be clarified?" Maggie bit into a blueberry scone.

"Only a comment," Max said. "I'm curious why no one has questioned the condition of Peggy or Fireball when they returned to the stable. Were they hot? Lathered from running hard, or were they cool to the touch? It seems like Walter should have noticed and commented. If Laurence took his time to get help, the horses may not have even warmed.

"I'm also curious if anyone checked around the accident site for animal tracks. From Laurence's testimony, Peggy reared up, throwing Claire into the gully. He concluded an animal scared the horse, which caused it to react in such a manner. Yet there was no mention of tracks other than the two horses." Max seemed to be on to something significant, and Maggie hoped they would address it in the rest of the testimony.

Nellie perused her notepad while she finished her eggs and scone.

"Ah, here it is," she said.

"Mr. MacLaren, you said a wild animal might have caused the accident. Yet in reading the police inspector's report, they found only hoof prints. They noted it appeared to be several horses, perhaps yours, Mrs. MacLaren's, the wagon team and the rescuers, all in the same area. They are required to scour the location for several hundred feet in every direction, but found no other tracks. The police were thorough as they looked for broken branches, crumbled leaves or bedding spots showing animals frequented the area, but found nothing. Do you still believe a wild animal may have frightened Peggy?"

"Well, it's possible, Your Honor. I've been riding in those woods since I was a young lad and have sighted tracks and the animals. Perhaps your inspectors found nothing because the hoof prints and the footsteps of Walter, Leach, my father and myself, might have obliterated them beyond recognition. Then again, it might have been a snake and they don't leave footprints."

"Oh, he thinks he's so smart," Maggie said. "He only responds to footprints in the immediate area while the inspectors looked beyond for several hundred feet. He's so smug. I can't wait to get back there and put him in his place."

"Now Maggie, we all want to know the truth. Don't let your emotions get the better of you."

Maggie pushed her coffee cup toward Max for a refill. "Continue please, Nellie."

"Mr. MacLaren, describe your relationship with your mother. Then your father, and with your stepmother."

"I loved my mother. We had a wonderful relationship. She encouraged me to follow my dreams. When she played the piano, I sat on the floor beside her, lost in the music. My father was more stern than my mother. He wanted me to become a solicitor like himself or maybe teach at a university. That wasn't for me and when I told him, he was upset. We argued once or twice.

"As for my father's second wife, I had no love for her. I accepted her because I could see how much my father loved her. The only thing we had in common was a love for my father. She had no desire to build a relationship, so I kept my distance. I agreed to the horse ride because it made my father happy."

"Did you ever wish her harm, or perhaps try to cause problems between her and your father, hoping to end the marriage?"

"Certainly not! My father was happy, and that's all that mattered."

"You attended college for a short time and told your father you did not want to follow in his footsteps. Which of your dreams has become a reality? How are you supporting yourself and Stuart Hall?"

"I'm living my only dream, being lord of the mansion. Choosing what I do with each day, how I occupy my time, what I eat, where I travel, or even if I should travel. The family legacy and investments which I manage fund all of this."

"This ended the testimony." Nellie sipped her tea. "They did a competent job interrogating Laurence. There didn't seem to be anything else relevant to the case. The only section left was the judge's closing statement, if you'd like me to read that."

Maggie already knew what she would hear. Conflicting emotions struggled inside her. What would it be like to spend a week at Stuart Hall with the very self-occupied Mr. Laurence MacLaren?

"Please go ahead, Nellie. May as well finish."

"In closing this hearing, the court finds unanswered questions, which will remain unanswered for now. It finds a young man who dreamed dreams at a very young age and never seemed to break from childhood to the adult world of responsibility. A grown man who finds himself unable to handle difficult situations which are part of the growing and maturing process. As a result, he's manipulated his life events in such a way that the father he seemed devoted to, left. The mother whom he loved died early, and the final adult influence, who only wanted her love reciprocated, met her death under questionable circumstances. Mr. MacLaren's testimony would leave us to believe the relationship between Claire MacLaren and himself was not amiable, and she may have feared for her safety. However, we do not find conclusive evidence of negligence by Mr. MacLaren. Until fresh evidence comes forward, the court is forced to conclude that Mrs. Claire MacLaren met her death by an unfortunate accident at Stuart Hall. This inquest is concluded."

Maggie's haggard appearance said it all. She finished her coffee, then scanned her 'Facts Board.'

"Anything we missed the first time through?" Nellie closed her notes and tapped her pencil on the table.

"No. We seem to have caught every piece of information." Maggie rubbed her forehead, then folded her hands. "There were a few new bits from the transcript, but nothing of any earth shattering value. I appreciated the closing remarks and understand why the only logical verdict was accidental death. Yet the judge left it open for speculation that Laurence had a hand in causing the 'accident.'

"I'm confident if we work together and stick to our plan, we'll be able to uncover the 'new evidence' needed to reopen the case and try him for murder. He's a very 'smart cookie', as my mom would say, but the three of us are smarter. We must keep our guard up and focus on the mission. Are you ready, Max?"

"Absolutely, let's get this rogue and bring him to justice." Max paused. "That is, if he's guilty of murder."

Chapter 15

Dear Miss Richards,

My staff and I look forward to your stay at Stuart Hall. We have three rooms ready, and Harriet plans a traditional Scots dinner on your first evening. I left word at the Creag an Tuirc to bring us a message upon your arrival. Walter will bring the coach to fetch you. We expect a delightful and profitable visit.

With fondest regards,
Laurence MacLaren

Maggie refolded the letter and laid it on her lap. She scrutinized Nellie and Max for any reaction or comments.

"I'm so thankful Laurence doesn't expect us to stay with him for an entire two weeks. I tremble at the thought of spending more time than we need with that man. On the train ride back to Rolen, let's check for any gaps in our plans. We can't accept any more inconclusive judgements."

Maggie blamed her nervousness on the inevitable. Face-to-face with Laurence while maintaining her composure would be a formidable challenge.

She noticed that the warmth of the morning sun and the rhythm of the train's wheels had lulled Nellie to sleep, while Max busied himself with the morning paper. For Maggie, the travel time allowed her to delve deep into her thoughts.

While the scenery whizzed by, Maggie remembered her mom had prepared a new breakfast cereal. It had promised children an extra boost of energy. Certain she could run like a train and fly like a bird, she'd eaten two servings and run outside to find the perfect strip of grass. Focused on the ideal mark for liftoff, Maggie had run as fast as she could, flapped her arms and jumped at just the right moment. To her amazement she had attained liftoff, flew into the sky, touched the clouds and floated back to earth.

Surveying the flight distance, disenchantment had overtaken Maggie. Her off the ground experience covered only a foot or so. Upset with false promises adults make to children, she vowed to be wiser in the future. From that point on, she would live in reality, not fantasy.

This impending confrontation, however, would not squelch the many fanciful childhood adventures that filled her creative brain. She wondered about writing children's books and illustrating them using her artistic talents. At the end of this train ride, she'd be enmeshed in an adventure that would not make a delightful children's story. She gazed out the window, recognized the landscape, and nudged Nellie awake.

"Nellie, Max, we're nearing Rolen. While you're meeting with Mary Beth, Nellie, and you Max, are meeting with Ernest, I'll set up a time with Dr. Shane. Laurence insisted we inform him when we arrive at the Creag an Tuirc. I would rather wait a few days before sending a message." Maggie stretched back her shoulders.

"Max, I'm curious." She picked up the newspaper. "You buy a copy of the local paper wherever we are and digest it from cover to cover. I know you're interested in history, but this is current news. Can you tell me if you're looking for something specific?"

"You're correct on both counts," Max said. "I am, at the moment, most interested in the history of Stuart Hall and one missing Mr. MacLaren. These newspapers may provide a clue as to his whereabouts. Since we've discovered very little from the locals, and it only seems minor conjecture for him to be taken to an institution, I keep hoping something will show itself.

"For example, a photo in the Edinburgh paper of a local men's club a few days ago had no names in the caption. Since I remember his portrait at Stuart Hall, I expect something might surface. Either a photo or notice of his death. It's a long shot, but I'm willing to try."

The train conductor announced Rolen as the next stop. Maggie put on her wraps. Late August afforded some lingering warm days, but a slight breeze lingered in Rolen. This extra layer helped insulate her from the chill.

"A walk to town will feel good after that three-hour ride." Maggie stretched tall. "Didn't realize how numb my hind end had become." She rubbed her backside and stretched again. "Max, can you find someone to take our bags to the Creag an Tuirc?"

They walked together toward town and commented on the quaintness of Rolen. A cart flew past them. Bags jostled and a small cloud of dust swirled. A brawny lad gripped the cart handle with one hand and tipped his hat to Maggie with the other.

"Aren't those our bags?" Maggie exclaimed.

"Why, they are indeed." Max smiled. "The boy said he'd have them at the inn before we arrived. Looks like he's going to make it."

"I love this town." Maggie waved back to the lad. "Perhaps we should stay a few more days once this ordeal with Mr. MacLaren is over. Any thoughts?"

"I'd like to see more of the country, but my editor is waiting for another submission," Max said.

"Sounds like my agenda. I never seem to get ahead." Nellie said. "Scotland has such a pleasant aroma everywhere we go. Must be the heather."

Maggie glanced at her reflection in the window as they passed Mary Beth's Dress Shop. "Want to stop in, Nellie?"

"No, I'll wait until I have more time to visit. That was thoughtful of you to remember I have a new dress." Nellie peeked in the window.

"Speaking of tantalizing aromas, get a whiff of that smell," Maggie said, as Nellie joined her.

"Smells like cinnamon rolls." Nellie's eyes widened. "I didn't know they were a Scottish pastry. Let's follow our noses, Maggie."

"I'll check our accommodations at the Creag an Tuirc. That young lad traveled so fast, he may have passed it right by." Max stopped in front of the M-G Store & Cafe'. "Will you order for me as well?" He left the girls for the inn.

"Guid afternoon, Lassies. If I can get anything for you, please let me know. Otherwise, if you're here because Mabel's cinnamon rolls tempted you, have a seat anywhere and I'll be right with you." The man in blue pants, white shirt and black apron, tied around his waist, scooted behind the counter for a paying customer.

Maggie found a corner table by the front window.

"For Max." Nellie laid two newspapers on the table, one local and the other from Edinburgh, then slid a chair close to Maggie.

"Very well stocked for a small store," Nellie said. "Looks like you could find almost anything you needed. That's another thing I like about small towns, Maggie. You don't know what you're missing 'cause you don't even know it's available and since you don't know it's available, you don't know what you're missing, and never needed it, anyway."

After a brief pause, Nellie's face scrunched. "Did that make any sense? It sounded right in my head until I spoke the words out loud. Too long sitting on one end has caused the other to go to sleep." The two chuckled as George walked over to take their order.

"Haven't seen you two here before." He riveted his attention on Maggie. "You remind me of someone. Have we met before?"

"No. This is my first time in your cafe'," Maggie said.

"My name's George. My wife Mabel and I own this fine establishment, the only one like it in town. That's why it's so fine. No competition at all."

George glanced down at the newspapers. "I see you're interested in our local news. We've got lots happening this month, if you're able to stay awhile. Our annual fall festival is one of the nicest ones around. I can say that, 'cause it's a long way to the next town where they celebrate their version of the Highland Games."

George laid two serviettes on the girl's table.

"In case you don't know about the Highland Games, it began in the 11th century. The agreed on conjecture is that young laddies who wanted to show the lassies how brawnie they were started the competition."

George drew out a pad and pencil from his apron pocket.

"Oh my, I'm rambling on about something you might not be interested in, and you came to taste Mabel's great cooking. Now, what can I get you?" He wet his pencil lead in his mouth and flipped the top page of his order pad.

Maggie liked George. He was eager to share his love for the community, make friends, and keep the customer happy.

"I'm Miss Richards and this is Miss Cox. Another friend will join us soon. We arrived on the afternoon train and a small refreshment would be delightful. Could you please bring each of us one of those delicious smelling pastries and a cup of tea? I'm curious though. I didn't know you Scots baked cinnamon rolls. At all our stops in Scotland, this is the first cafe' to offer them."

"Well, Lassie, me missus, and I went for a trip to Sweden several years ago. Those rolls were melting in our mouth before we ever tried them. My Mabel raved about them and one cook shared the recipe. Ever since we came home, Mabel has been baking them. It sort of became a tradition here. We have piping hot rolls ready by six o'clock every morning. All but Sunday, when we're closed in honor of the Lord's day. We still have traditional scones, marmalade and black pudding, but the locals seem to love these rolls. They can always make porridge at home."

"Sweden, huh? That's a country I'd like to visit one day," Maggie said.

Max entered the cafe' and made a beeline for Maggie and Nellie. George startled as he turned and faced Max.

"Well, look who's here. Our old friend, Max. We haven't seen you for quite some time now. Where ye been? Getting horse riding lessons for that fishing trip with Ernest? You know, he asks about you every time he comes in. Figures you may have gotten too afraid to take him up on his offer."

Max received a hearty handshake and a slap on the back.

"Max, I'd like you to meet our newest arrivals in Rolen. Miss Richards and Miss Cox. Lassies, Max. Sorry, I forgot your last name. Age, I'm told."

"How do you do, Lassies? Mind if I join you for a cinnamon roll and a cup of tea? You have ordered, haven't you?"

George's mouth gaped, then all became clear. "Why, Max? You're the third person they said would join them. Well, I'll let Mabel know you're back and bring your order right out."

George shook his head, laughed and muttered to himself as he headed for the kitchen.

Max glanced at the newspapers. "For me, I presume."

✺✺✺

A sudden shout from the kitchen resonated throughout the cafe'. Mabel ran into the room, wiping her hands on her apron. George followed close behind. Max sprung to his feet and received a warm Scottish welcome.

"Praise the Lord! I told old Ernest if you said you'd be back, you'd be back. Just wait 'til he comes in tomorrow. He's in for a surprise. We even made a small wager. If he won, I would fix his lunches for an entire week at no charge. If I won, he owed me a week of work. Well, we shook on it. Now I can make the list of repairs I've needed done for so long. Hallelujah!"

Mabel focused on Maggie and Nellie, then faced Max.

"So you got two lassies by your side. Isn't one trouble enough?" She glanced back at Maggie and gasped. With her hand over her heart, her foot faltered. George put his arm around her waist to steady her.

"Are you all right, Mabel?" Max pushed a chair behind her.

"Lord, Almighty. I'm sorry, Max. This beautiful young lass is a striking resemblance to someone we once knew." George fanned her with his apron. "I'm all right now."

"Yes, dear, I agree with you," George whispered.

"A Rolen resident?" Maggie asked.

"No, Lassie. She lived on the outskirts of town, but is no longer with us. A terrible accident took her in the prime of life."

George rubbed his wife's back.

"You remember, Max. The lady we talked about after Ernest left the cafe' the first time you were here? Well, this lass could be her twin, only much younger."

"Yes, I remember, George. If there is a resemblance, your friend was exquisite."

Maggie's cheeks redden. "I've heard it said that we all have a twin somewhere in the world."

"These are my friends." Max motioned toward Maggie and Nellie. "Miss Richards and Miss Cox. We'll be in town for a few days, so you'll get another chance to visit with them. Now, where are those cinnamon rolls you were tantalizing us with all the way from the station?" Max asked.

Mabel and George rushed back to the kitchen. George returned with a tray that held cups, saucers and a pot of tea. He placed it on the table. Mabel came next. She balanced a tray with three plates, each holding one of the largest rolls the trio had ever seen. Melting frosting oozed over the edges of the roll and a pat of softened butter covered the top. "Hope you enjoy this 'small refreshment.'"

"These look incredible, Mabel." Maggie broke off a corner with her fork and ingested her first bite. "They melt in my mouth. And the sweetness is not overpowering."

"We'll be back for more, Mabel. These are incredible," Nellie agreed.

"But not too many times. I can't afford a new wardrobe before leaving Scotland." Nellie tapped her hips. Laughter filled the cafe'.

Chapter 16

Maggie enjoyed this brief time of relaxation with her friends. The warm tea and Mabel's cinnamon rolls settled her nerves before the return to Stuart Hall. A few customers moseyed in and out. Some stopped at the counter to visit with George. Maggie cocked her head toward the door. Dr. Shane entered and hastened to her table.

"It's so good to see you again, Miss Richards."

Maggie received Dr. Shane's hand.

"I assume this is the vacation you mentioned, and these are the friends you spoke of."

"Yes, Dr. Shane." Maggie introduced Nellie and Max.

"Let me get another chair for you," Max said. "You will join us?"

"Oh my, those rolls look delicious." Dr. Shane removed his hat. "Well, if you don't mind. Thank you very much. Another cinnamon roll and cup of tea, please George."

"So, tell me a bit about yourselves, Miss Cox, Mr. Sullivan. What do you think of Scotland?" Dr. Shane sprinkled a spoonful of sugar into his tea.

"Rolen is a delightful piece of Scottish tradition and the area around here conjures images of homespun stories and folklore. Nellie and I depend on these historical tales for our livelihood."

"Oh, then you must meet Ernest." The aroma of the cinnamon roll reached Dr. Shane. "Yum, this smells delicious." He cut off a corner with his fork. "He's here almost every day and can tell you whoppers which may or may not be based on truth. If anyone knows the people and history of Rolen, it's Ernest."

"I met the dear man last time we were here," Max said. "I enjoyed visiting with him. He promised to take me fishing when I returned and I intend to accept the offer. I'll bring you back a fish or two, should I catch anything."

George set a fresh pot of tea on the table.

"Heard you mention Ernest. Yes, sir, I can see the surprised look on his face when he hears you're in town. He'll plan the best fishing trip you ever had. He could babble on forever about his fishing excursions. Now Max, don't you be catching Ol' Moses. Just wouldn't be fair to Ernest," George said.

"Don't you worry about that. If, by some remote possibility, I do hook Ol' Moses, I promise to release him. I'll attempt to not let Ernest see the event, either."

George returned to the kitchen with the dirty dishes.

"So you're here to investigate the MacLaren family and..." he turned toward Maggie, "... discover something more about Claire. Am I correct?" Dr. Shane asked.

The atmosphere tensed as Maggie realized this minister did indeed have a gift of discernment. She glanced at Nellie and Max. From their expressions, she knew they were of one mind. She nodded and prepared to take Dr. Shane into their confidence.

"Dr. Shane, I don't know how you knew, but you're correct. We're here for a specific reason and if you are available one day this week, I would like to come in and talk with you. We hope to not arouse suspicion and complete our investigation in Rolen in a couple of days. Mr. MacLaren invited us to spend as much time as we wished at Stuart Hall. It was more than we hoped for. I trust your professionalism that we will keep this conversation in strictest confidence. Is this agreeable?"

"I promise, Miss Richards. If I can be of any assistance, I would deem it a privilege. I have some unanswered questions for Mr. MacLaren as well, and perhaps our investigations will complement each other. I've been more than curious where the senior Mr. MacLaren disappeared to following Claire's death. He loved her so and to abandon his ancestral home, practice, and friends still seems incredible. I'm attending a conference at the end of the week, but I could meet with you tomorrow. Shall we say 10 o'clock?"

"That would be wonderful, Dr. Shane. I look forward to our visit. We're confident you will be a great asset to this weighty problem. Sometimes I'm overloaded with information, yet struggle to make any sense of it."

Confident of Dr. Shane's abilities as an intelligent and able assistant, the heavy burden Maggie carried now had a helping hand. A measure of weight lifted from her shoulders.

Dr. Shane sipped his last spot of tea. "Someone once wrote, 'Worry is an old man with a bent head, carrying a load of feathers he thinks is lead.' Let's trust together we can carry each other's load and it will indeed become like feathers flying away on the breeze of truth. Until tomorrow."

He nodded to Nellie and Max, picked up a few supplies from George, and said his goodbyes.

The three friends finished their tea. Max folded the newspapers and sauntered to the counter. George and Mabel met him there.

"You best be putting your bawbees away. These treats are on the house. It's so good to see you again and meet these fine young lassies."

✻✻✻

Back at Creag an Tuirc, Maggie settled in for a few nights stay. Dr. Shane's profound quote kept churning through her head. Weighed down with worry and concern, she became anxious about their stay at Stuart Hall. How could this load of 'lead' become mere feathers blowing away in the wind? How could she rid herself of the negative thoughts she harbored toward Laurence? And how could she remain impartial during their stay and avoid giving her true motives and identity away? If George and Mabel saw the resemblance between herself and her mom, would Laurence?

The longer she dwelt on these questions, the more tense with worry she became. A few drama classes in school would not be sufficient. Only an expert actor could pull this off.

Opening a desk drawer, she found a copy of the Holy Bible. Lifting it out and running her hand over the cover, she sensed a familiar feeling; one of home, gathering around the piano to sing hymns, and images of her mom leading Maggie in prayer at bedtime. These flooded her emotions and gave her a small measure of calm. Then she did the unexpected. She opened the Bible and allowed it to flop in her lap.

Maggie glanced down. The two covers separated and lay opened to the Book of John, one of her favorites as a child. She scanned down the page. Her eyes stopped on these words: "Peace I leave with you. My peace I give to you; not as the world gives, do I give to you. Let not your heart be troubled, neither let it be afraid." This was verse 27 of chapter 14 and one she had memorized as a small child. She had repeated this verse out loud as she lay in the dark. Sure there were imaginary monsters living underneath her bed, the fear of what they may do sometimes overwhelmed her.

Now she had bigger, perhaps an actual monster to deal with and, again, this verse stood out from all the others.

Maggie closed her eyes, bowed her head, inhaled and prayed. "God, please help me through the ordeal ahead." She opened her eyes and glanced at the page, then shook her head and tried to re-connect with her reality. Namely, that God did not exist.

However, she left her options open if she was wrong. How else could she explain the events of the day? Dr. Shane's quote, a Bible in the desk drawer and a special verse from her childhood. Just a coincidence. Nothing more, she reasoned. She placed the Bible back, then shut the drawer. Time to finish unpacking.

Chapter 17

Maggie arose early, anxious about the day's events. Her upcoming meeting with Dr. Shane couldn't come soon enough. She checked the time and wished the next two hours would disappear along with the morning fog.

"Max, do you think Ernest will be around today in time for a fishing trip?"

"I hope so." Max peeked through the front window of the Creag an Tuirc. "Morning clouds fill the sky, but they should burn off later. For now, the smells of breakfast sausage, sweet rolls and coffee call to me. I'll leave a note with the Wellington's if the fishing trip is on."

"Sounds great." Maggie patted the serviette on the corners of her mouth for breakfast residue. "When we finish here, I'm going to take a slow stroll through the village, then make my way to meet with Dr. Shane. Nellie, how about wearing your new frock at dinner?"

"I'd love to." Nellie patted her stomach. "I'll need to be careful how much breakfast I eat, or Mary Beth may have to alter it on the first day."

✳✳✳

Nellie arrived at the dress shop a little after nine. She tried the door. Even with an "Open" sign in the window, the door remained locked. Nellie placed her palms beside her eyes and leaned close to the windowpane. Through the glass, she saw Mary Beth pile bolts of fabric on a table under a large 'Sale' sign. Nellie tapped on the window. Mary Beth startled, then pivoted and her face beamed. She darted to the door and lifted the latch.

"Well, I'll be. You've come back for your new frock. I know you're going to love it. Come in, come in." Mary Beth swung the door wide. "My arms were so full with a basket of coffee, scones, and tea, I just slammed the door shut with my foot and forgot to come back and unlock it."

Mary Beth tied back the window curtains, then disappeared into the back room.

Nellie strolled among the lines of new fabric. Soft and luxurious, she imagined a new skirt or jacket.

"Won't you join me for a cup of tea?" Mary Beth placed a tea tray on the side table. "Help yourself. I'll be back in a flash."

Nellie reached for the tea tray when Mary Beth returned and hung Nellie's new dress on a pole beside the table.

"Oh, Mary Beth. It's beautiful." Nellie caressed every part of the frock.

"The fitting room is right behind you. Why not slip it on while our tea steeps?"

Nellie didn't need to be prodded. She flew to the fitting room like a young girl with her first party dress.

Within a few minutes, she sashayed out of the fitting room, her face alight with joy as Mary Beth poured the tea.

"I can't believe how well it fits. And so comfortable." She stroked her sides, following her body's contours. "Oh, Mary Beth, thank you so much."

"Take a gander in that full-length mirror. I'll get a hand held so you can see the back too."

Nellie twisted from side to side and admired her new frock.

"My, my, if you don't look like a young girl. The smile tells me everything. It makes me smile too, bringing some joy to your heart. You seemed sad the last time we met, so this is delightful. Here, I've poured your tea." Mary Beth pulled out a chair from the table. "Let's sit and visit awhile."

Nellie gave Mary Beth a hug.

"You do beautiful work. Beyond my expectations. So comfortable and I feel, well, almost glamorous. All my clothes as a child were hand-me-downs. While I've been able to purchase some new items as an adult, I never imagined I would own a custom-made frock. What a treat. I must be part Scottish, as I'm a spend-thrift and use every penny with care. This dress is elegant. I can't thank you enough."

Nellie opened her purse, retrieving the remaining balance plus a bit more.

"Oh no, I don't believe you owe me that much. Let me get the receipt."

Nellie grabbed Mary Beth's hand to stop her from leaving. "I feel very honored to wear this beautiful dress and I want to thank you with a little extra. Please don't begrudge me this joy."

Mary Beth squeezed Nellie's hand. "Thank you, Nellie. Ready for some tea and conversation?"

"Mary Beth, I feel I can talk with you and whatever we say will remain here, between us. Last time, I asked you some questions about Stuart Hall and Laurence MacLaren. You seemed to have had a close relationship with Claire. She's the reason my friends and I are in Rolen. We're investigating her death, hoping to uncover the truth, if there be one different from the outcome of the inquest. Would you be willing to answer some questions?"

"So that's why you were sad the last time we met. You got a taste of young MacLaren in your craw. Well, you are a breath of fresh air. I've been praying for someone to take the case more seriously and find additional evidence to suggest it wasn't an accident. Never thought it would be an American."

Mary Beth drank from her cup. "Claire was an excellent rider. She only pretended not to be hoping to build a relationship with Laurence through lessons. Claire told me he always had some excuse about why he couldn't and if she needed lessons to talk to Walter. He's the stableman. The whole situation frustrated her. Claire loved Ramsay with all her being. She couldn't imagine causing any kind of rift between Ramsay and his son." Mary Beth warmed their tea.

"I'll tell you straightaways, that upstart young Laurence. Why, if he were my child, his sore little fanny would keep him out of the saddle for days. I would get so upset with him and the way he treated Claire, but I felt it was out of my hands. I suggested she make an appointment with Dr. Shane. Then, I prayed for her and knew she prayed for the Holy Spirit's guidance.

"Wait, let me change the sign to 'Closed.' I'll draw a couple curtains and we can have our privacy." Mary Beth closed the curtains, then returned in eager anticipation. "Now, how can I help you?"

"You mentioned during my last visit, Claire feared Laurence when they were alone. Do you have any specifics?"

"Hmm, I'll have to think on that for a minute. Maybe another sip of tea will help." She gazed at the ceiling for a moment.

"Now I remember. Claire came in for a fitting in a very agitated manner. I consoled her and said that it always helped to share your troubles with someone. Remember where two or three believers gather, the Lord promises to be in their midst. That's a promise we cling to. Anyway, she thanked me and then told a bizarre story." Mary Beth swallowed and cleared her throat.

"Ramsay had a case in Glasgow. Claire asked to accompany him, but he said he would be busy the entire time. He hoped, in his absence, Laurence and Claire would mend the problem between them. He left early the next morning and Claire spent much of the day outside in the garden.

"She remembered Leach, the gardener, telling her that Gwen, the first Mrs. MacLaren, kept a journal hidden away under the bench at the far end of the garden. Claire put her hand under that bench, found a ledge and, after more exploring, felt Gwen's journal. She was elated. Claire said the journal was wrapped in leather and closed with a buckled strap. The first few and last pages had mold spots from the dampness, but otherwise she could make out everything. Gwen had lovely handwriting, and for Claire, it was like being welcomed into the family. So many thoughts were about Gwen's brothers and their demise."

Mary Beth laid her hand over Nellie's and leaned close. "Then Claire came to a section about Laurence. Gwen expressed her concerned over his well-being. Seems he rarely left the Hall or show any interest in gainful employment. He didn't even accompany them on outings to the Highlands. He had no friends and didn't seem to want to cultivate any relationships.

"Claire realized Laurence was a troubled young man before she married Ramsay. Ramsay told her Laurence was a hard lad to get to know, but hoped they would learn to get along."

Mary Beth flung herself to the back of her chair. "Get along? Well, my goodness, anyone who spent even a short time with Laurence could see he wasn't easy to get along with." Mary Beth checked the teapot. "Shall I make more?"

"Not for me, thank you."

"Right you are. I've had enough too." She downed the final few drops from her cup and paused. Mary Beth wiped her brow and folded her hands in her lap.

"This is where Claire's story frightened me. Claire said she sat across from Laurence at breakfast one morning when Ramsay was on a trip. Laurence talked about their recent travels to Edinburgh. While she and his father explored historic sites, he said he visited the Edinburgh Lunatic Asylum. You know what that is, I'm sure."

"Not unless it's different from our hospitals in the States. For those who are mentally ill. Am I correct?"

"Sort of." Mary Beth tipped her cup. Nothing there. "You see this hospital's for those people we call insane or unbalanced. There are two sections; one for the wealthy and one for the poor. Anyway,

Claire said Laurence picked up a cutting knife, slammed the handle on the table with the point angling toward her and said, 'It's not just a place for people who kill other people. They'll admit anyone with or without their consent. They've even committed patients for depression over their efforts in the Highland Games.' Then he let out the most hideous laugh she'd ever heard. She tried to get him to talk more, but he just wielded the knife, all the time staring at her. Claire became so frightened, she excused herself from the table. Now, what do you make of that?"

"You're right. Very bizarre behavior, indeed. I can understand why it scared Claire to stay alone with him. Do you know if she told Ramsay?"

"She did. He said he would talk with Laurence, but that knave is so strong willed and determined, anything his dad may have told him would be like a chilly breeze over the moors."

Mary Beth rubbed her hands together and Nellie could tell the memory of this conversation made her new friend uneasy. She assured Mary Beth that she did the right thing to listen to Claire and she should not carry guilt over 'what she should have done.'

"No, I've given all that to the Lord, but when I think about how sweet and kind she was, the thought of her last few years on earth being so strained saddens me."

"I hope she focused her time and love on Ramsay and let Laurence stay in the background. I know that's what I would've done." Nellie rose from the table. "If you'll excuse me, I'm going to change. If you think of something more, please tell me when I return."

With that, Nellie reentered the fitting room and heard Mary Beth's footsteps enter the kitchen area. When they rejoined at the table, Nellie asked if she remembered anything more.

"Only that on one of those days when Ramsay was gone," Mary Beth said, "it was also the servants' day off. Harriet always prepared the meals the day before, so Claire only needed to warm things up.

"When she put the dinner on the table, Laurence mentioned how he reads mystery novels. He was especially interested in the variety of ways one could kill another without detection. For example, how easy for someone with devious thoughts to poison food.

"Well, let me tell you, Claire was almost sick to her stomach with that thought. She waited until Laurence had a bite of everything. That lassie had some emotional issues to deal with, but she was determined to keep trying. She was in constant prayer, not just for Laurence, but for her own safety. Claire hoped that whatever circumstances arose, it could all be used to bring Laurence to the Lord and a sound mind."

Mary Beth's brow wrinkled and her face grew tense. Retelling these memories became exhausting. Nellie folded her new dress into a bundle as the time had come for her to leave. Mary Beth wrapped the bundle in brown paper and secured the package with twine. Nellie hugged Mary Beth, thanked her again for the dress, and strolled toward the door.

"May as well open the curtains and let some of this glorious sunlight in. I pray you will find your answers. If I can be of any more help, please come by. I hope you can prove it was not an accident and Laurence gets his comeuppance."

"We'll do our best, Mary Beth. Thank you again for your time and beautiful workmanship. Please remember this conversation must remain confidential. Thanks again."

The sun warmed Nellie's face as she ambled toward the Creag an Tuirc. A small park graced the center of town. She found a bench, took a notepad from her purse, and jotted down the highlights of Mary Beth's story. So hard to believe that Claire could remain at Stuart Hall under those conditions. Perhaps she shared with Ramsay her tale and suggested they commit Laurence to the Royal Hospital, for her peace of mind, but also for Laurence to receive the medical attention he needed. Without Claire or Ramsay, these lines of query would lead nowhere.

Chapter 18

"Guid mor'ing, Laddie. What can I get you?"

"A cup of hot tea and the latest edition of the newspaper would be fine. Thanks, George." Max located an empty table, then glanced around the store. "Has Ernest come in yet?"

"Not yet. His day starts with Mabel's cinnamon rolls. I'll go fetch the paper and bring you that tea."

George swung around and beheld Ernest in the doorway. He wore a downcast, haggard expression. George blocked Ernest's view of Max.

"What's the matter Ernest? You look kind a worn out. Where've you been this morning?"

"I'll tell you, George. I tossed and turned all night. Max said he'd return in a few weeks. And, by my calculations, time has run out. The fishing season's almost ended, so I wonder if he fibbed or just forgot. He seemed like an upstanding young lad. I can't imagine him going back on his word unless something happened."

"Oh, I wouldn't be too concerned. I'm sure Max would let you know if he couldn't make it. He wouldn't miss the chance to go fishing up Elk Mountain for Ol' Moses."

George stepped aside and exposed a full view of Max. "You want to go fishing with Ernest, don't you, Max?"

"Hoot mon!" Ernest slapped his thigh. "You came back. Great day in the morning. It's good to see you again." Ernest extended his hand. A broad smile evaporated the gloominess.

"Have a seat, Ernest."

Mabel bounded out of the kitchen like a puppy eager to play fetch and said her guid mor'ings to Ernest.

"Remember our wager? I've got my list ready. You can start anytime. Shall we say Monday next?"

"Ah Mabel, I hoped we could forget the whole thing. Yet I'm a man of my word. Are you still making my lunches on those days?"

"My goodness, Ernest. You like to butter both sides of your bread, don't you? Yes, I'll make your lunches with the condition you do a good job with every task. Is that agreeable?"

"Sure thing, Mabel. I'll be ready early Monday morning." Ernest turned back to Max. "Now, what about that fishing trip?"

"How about today? I'll have to round up some gear first."

With another shake of Max's hand, Ernest hurried to the door. "I'll be back in a half-hour with my fishing poles and tackle box. And a couple of excellent horses."

Max turned to Mabel. "I'm going to need a hat, a warm shirt, and a pair of gloves." Max wandered to the clothing section. They displayed hats on the shelves above the gloves. "I wonder, would you make a sack lunch for us?" Max called to Mabel. "Oh, I almost forgot. Is there someone who could take a note to the Creag an Tuirc? It's for Nellie and Maggie."

Max wrote: "Gone Fishing, Max," on an order pad on the counter.

"George will leave it at the front desk." Mabel received the note from Max and headed back to the kitchen. "Pick out what you need and I'll get busy fixing your lunch."

Max tried on several pairs of gloves and a couple of hats before deciding. Finding the right shirt was easier as the store only carried one style, but at least the customer had a choice of either blue or green. He piled his purchases on the counter and waited for Mabel to add them up. A whinny outside caught his attention.

"I'm back, Max," Ernest yelled from the street.

Max squinted in the sunlight. Seems like the clouds disappeared in a hurry. He strode down the steps. Ernest sat atop his mount with fishing poles strapped to the side of the saddle, the tackle box and another container for fish secured to the back.

Ernest motioned to the riderless horse. "What do you think? Look tame enough for you?"

Max sized up his horse and concluded that they would get along just fine.

Mabel jostled down the steps, lunch bag in hand. "Here you go, Max. Now, don't ye be catching anything small, you hear? We only want you to come back with Ol' Moses." She winked at Max. Ernest glared at her with a stern expression.

"Don't you worry none. I think you're going to see Ol' Moses in person. Then you and the rest of the townsfolk will have a lot of backpedalling to do." Ernest wiped his brow and plopped his hat on his head.

Max slipped his hands in his new gloves, settled his hat on his head, and tied his shirt behind the saddle. He placed his foot in the left stirrup and swung himself up with ease. His horse remained stationary, which calmed him. He had no desire to meet the ground anyway but feet first.

Max and Ernest waved goodbye to Mabel and headed toward the tree-covered mountains a few miles ahead. Ernest led the way, winding through the beautiful Scottish landscape. White and pinkish-purple heather blanketed the hillside.

"This is a breathtaking view, Ernest. The crisp mountain air reminds me of my cottage back on Eden Lake. I forgot to tell you I've got an Ol' Moses there as well."

Ernest didn't respond. Max wondered if he was hard-of-hearing or the distance was the issue. He enjoyed the scenery and left a conversation for the lake.

When they entered the dense forest, the air chilled as the sun hid behind the trees. A covey of red grouse scurried across the path between the two horses. Neither one seemed to mind.

As they waded into a shallow stream, a loud splash diverted Max's attention. He marveled as a beaver added another stick to his well-engineered dam. Nothing better than a ride in the woods. However, his goal remained to inquire about Laurence; although catching a fish or two would be a real plus.

Two hours passed during the steady, gradual climb. The trees seemed to move apart, the sun grew warmer and a glorious clear blue lake loomed on the horizon.

The men dismounted and untied their fishing gear. Max was eager to cast a line into the mirror blueness of the water. He followed Ernest up a steep hill to a cluster of rocks that hung over the lake; a perfect perch for fishing.

"We may be a little late this morning, but you never know about these Scottish fish. I know they can't tell time, but if they're like me, they're always hungry."

"Ernest, I can't believe how beautiful this is. If I didn't know better, I would say your lake and my lake were twins. Does this lake have a name?"

"Yep, Loch Morlich. It's about at the center of these here forested mountains called the Cairngorms, which in Gaelic means Blue Mountain. See that tallest peak over there?" Ernest pointed. "That's Ben Macdui. It's a mite over 4,000 feet. Lots of snow in the winter, but I prefer the summer days of fishing myself. Never liked to be cold for very long."

"Where are the anglers? I don't see anyone here but us."

"Most of them prefer the rivers, looking to hook a big salmon or trout. They're easy to find in the Tay, Dee and Spey rivers. The lads who hunger for a challenge head to Loch Awe up near Argyl or Loch Lomond. This loch here suits me just fine."

Ernest placed one foot in front of the other, avoiding any loose rocks. He reached his favorite spot and directed Max to another excellent place.

"I stand to cast off, then pick a smooth rock for sitting. Here's my rule. We visit until the nibbles begin." Ernest lifted his tackle box lid and rummaged through a wide assortment of lures and hooks. He appeared to dig for buried treasure.

"Never can find anything in here. On every fishing trip, I tell myself it's time to clean this mess out and get organized. Nothing ever changes, so I figure this is the way I organize. Now somewhere in here are the lures we want to use. I'm sure I've got two of those big spoons."

"Spoons? We're using spoons? I thought we were fishing for trout, not bottom fish. What are we after?"

"Why, Ol' Moses. I thought you knew that. He's the only reason I come to this loch," Ernest said, then a corner of his mouth raised. "Oh, I forgot to tell ye. Ol' Moses is a pike."

"Pike? I thought you said they were in other lochs, not here."

"Sure they're in those other lochs, but those pikes are puny. They're maybe thirty to fifty pounds, but I'm sure Ol' Moses will weigh in at more than that."

Ernest chuckled, situated his gear, cast off and positioned himself at the edge of the rock. His feet dangled over the ledge. Max followed his example, but chose a spot in the sun's warmth.

"Ernest, I need to be honest with you. My intent is two-fold. First off, to spend the day fishing. And second, I believe you may be a wealth of information. I request, though, that our conversation remain confidential."

"I love an air of mystery, Max. Makes me feel like an investigative reporter again. Fire away."

Max explained the purpose of his journey to Rolen and Stuart Hall. Ernest listened to the detailed information and became interested in participating. Max left out the connection between Maggie and Claire.

"Ernest, can you tell me your impression of Laurence Mac-Laren?"

"I'll tell you, Max, being on the newspaper staff for thirty years, I've known MacLaren from the time of his birth. He came to town with his kin as a wee lad until his maw passed. He seldom came in with his father, nor with his stepmother. After his stepmother's funeral, I don't think he came to town at all." Ernest repositioned his hat. "He's a queer one, Max. Keeps to himself. The last time I remember him coming to Rolen was for the Highland Games horse race. I told you about that last time you were here. Sounds like he's still got Fireball. Wonder if he plans to race in the games this year. It would be nice to know and make a little wager."

"Did you have any dealings with him as a youngster?"

"Only one time. Laurence wrote a story and submitted it to a publisher. A rejection noticed arrived. He was very disappointed. I offered to print it in Rolen's paper, but his folks declined. I thought it might cheer him up a wee bit."

"Ernest, nobody seems to know anything about Ramsay Mac-Laren. What about you?"

Ernest tugged his line, but there was no tug back.

"Ramsay MacLaren. Such a caring gentleman, devoted to both his wives and his son. He had a successful practice in Covenshire and often received notoriety in the papers as far as Glasgow and Edinburgh. It seems strange that he just up and left everything.

"As a journalist, I did some searching, but found no leads. He seems to have vanished. If you hear anything, I would appreciate being notified. I considered Ramsay a close friend, a friend that I admired."

Ernest grew silent. Neither pole bent. They reeled in their lines and unpacked Mabel's lunch.

"Max, I always thank the Lord before meals." Ernest bowed his head, quieted his hands and prayed. "Lord, thanks for this food, for a friend to share it with, and for the sweet woman who made it. Bless them all. Amen. One more thing, Lord. Could you send Ol' Moses our way? I'd be so grateful. Amen."

"You know, Ernest, I don't mind not having any nibbles. I'm enjoying spending time with you in this beautiful country." Max bit into his sandwich. "This lunch is delicious. I must remember to thank Mabel again."

"Yer right about our beautiful country. When I was a young lad and caught nothing, I would tell myself, 'There's always tomorrow.' At my age, though, there may not be a tomorrow. Now I'm not complaining or anything. I've had a good life here in God's country, meeting some wonderful people and, of course, catching some big fish." Ernest sipped from his cup of water.

"I figure the Lord has us all on a time card, like the one I kept as a reporter. We punch in at our birth and when He's ready to take us home, He punches us out. I trust the Lord Jesus knows what's best for me, but I keep asking for some over-time to catch Ol' Moses."

Max chuckled, paused, and considered the seriousness of the moment. Amid the beauties of Cairngorm, with an intriguing man, trying to catch the world record fish, and they're talking about the end of life. He programed his internal clock on his own time schedule, doing whatever he thought best. Max almost never pondered there could be a Creator, especially one interested in him.

The finality of life and death hit Max hard. Nothing spiritual ever enters his life. An ache deep inside surfaced for the first time. Ernest seemed so content with just being and allowing God to mastermind the events. Not that he was a puppet that the Almighty could pull his strings, but as a participant in the grand life-play; to fulfill his part in whatever act or scene his life had entered.

In his mind, Max reviewed his bookshelves at home and saw the Holy Bible he had received as a child. He had wedged it between two literary books, which he had read several times, but never cracked the Bible open. He vowed to read this book when he got home. Then a quiet inner voice pierced his heart. "You may not have tomorrow."

The Bible recognizes no faith that does not lead to obedience, nor does it recognize any obedience that does not spring from faith. The two are at opposite sides of the same coin.
—A.W. Tozer—

Chapter 19

The sun glistened off Loch Morlich and ricocheted into Max's eyes. Closing his lids to slits, Max wondered if his intention was to keep his spiritual side at bay. He rationalized that if he didn't acknowledge there was a spiritual dimension to man, he wouldn't have to contemplate what happens upon death.

"So, Max, what ya been thinking about? You seem far away and it doesn't look like you've hardly touched Mabel's lunch." Ernest settled alongside his fishing partner.

Max blinked, then shook his head.

"I've been thinking how flippant my view of life is. I've never thought about the hereafter the way you have. My philosophy is to live and let live and when we die, it's all over. You said your faith in God is the center of your life. If you asked me that question, the center of my life is me and what's mine, especially my cabin at Eden Lake. It all seemed so fulfilling until now."

A battle raged within Max. He fought off the urge to explore the inner depths of his soul. *Ask more questions.* No, let it go. *I've got to do it now.* Not now, wait. *If not now, when?* Relinquish the center of my life. *Don't give in.* I've got it good. Why change?

The two sides were in a spiritual tug-of-war. He didn't want either to win. At least, not now. Not when fishing seemed of paramount importance. He could always decide later.

"I know what you mean." Ernest munched into a sandwich. "I thought little about the Lord until I was well into my reporting years. When I first started writing obituaries, I realized how short some of those lives were. Then I accepted the job to investigate and report on unexpected deaths, like Mrs. MacLaren. It made me stop and think about my own death." He guzzled some water and washed his bite down. "I opened the Bible one night and saw a verse that said something like 'You don't know the hour nor the day of your death. Now is the time of salvation.' I'm not great at quoting, but something like that.

"I realized we have no promise of tomorrow, so I vowed to trust the Lord with everything until I left this earth." Ernest reached for a dill pickle. "He's been my best friend ever since and we go fishing together almost every day. Oh, not for fish, but for helping people, sharing His love with them. Like with you now. We're fishing, and yet, I'm casting my faith line out to you in the hopes you will latch on to the bait and follow Jesus, too."

Max bit into his sandwich. He sensed Ernest's eyes fixed on him. Was Ernest praying for him? Time to change the subject and stick to fishing.

"Ernest, I'd like to ask another question about Ramsay Mac-Laren. You said he seemed to just disappear. Can you elaborate?"

Ernest rubbed his chin. "I could tell something was wrong at Stuart Hall, but I'm not sure what. My assignment was to report on the social events given by both Mrs. MacLarens many times. Gwen pulled out all the stops, so to speak. Just about the entire town came, and the cook put out a spread that topped Mabel's and the Creag an Tuirc. No one had seen anything like it. She hired musicians from nearby Aviemore and everyone danced. Gwen played the piano. Oh, how beautifully she played. Laurence sat close by with his eyes closed. The smile on his face told me he was dreaming of faraway places." Ernest moistened his mouth with a drink of water.

"When Claire came, things weren't as elaborate. She preferred a more intimate gathering of about twenty guests. The decorations were seasonal, and she hired a quartet for music. I attended each one, but left after an hour. There were other things to do and social gatherings weren't my cup of tea." He nibbled a cookie. "At one of these, I noticed Laurence off by himself with an unusual expression on his face. Not the far away, semi-happy, but more of 'I'm working things out,' if you know what I mean."

"Did he see you?"

"Yes. I greeted him, and he nodded. Nothing verbal. I thought that kind of strange, since he had always been very cordial. The last social was about a month before Claire died. Ramsay accompanied me to the door and suggested we get together soon. His voice seemed strained and his handshake felt like a dead fish; all stiff and clammy. He glanced toward the music room and made eye contact with Laurence.

"Maybe me, but I'm sure Laurence's expression changed to contempt. I asked if everything was all right. He hesitated, then replied, 'Yes, just the strain of a recent case and some investigation to be done.' Then he asked how I gather truthful information. I thought, my goodness, Ramsay, you do that all the time as a solicitor. His eyes, and the tone of his voice, told me this investigation was something out of his normal avenue of pursuit and of a different nature."

"Did you meet with him?"

"No. I told him to contact me at the paper when he was ready. He shook my hand with many 'thank you's.' Then it seemed like he turned away from Laurence on purpose and returned to the dining room. As I put on my hat and coat, I saw Laurence rise and leave the music room. He looked my way with an unnerving expression and went upstairs. I'll always remember that look. Very unsettling. Felt like his eyes were shooting arrows into my heart."

"So, Ramsay never contacted you? What did you think happened to him?"

"Laurence claimed Ramsay was too distraught over Claire's death and packed a chackie. I believe that's what you call a trunk. But I don't believe it. Ramsay wouldn't have left Stuart Hall." He reached for another cookie.

"Ramsay's intention was to see me, and he always ran on an even keel. I knew it depressed him when Gwen died, but he didn't run off. Why should he when Claire died? He had a strong faith in the Lord and understood the unexpected circumstances of life. We need to rest on God's mercy and grace to get through. No sir. I believe Laurence had planned all the events that led up to Claire's death. He somehow got his father out of the Hall, into a carriage and took Ramsay some out of the way place. Laurence may have drugged his father, so the servants wouldn't hear any protests."

"Did you investigate further? Did you question Laurence?"

"I would never question Laurence. He can look right at you, tell you what you want to hear, and be lying with every word. But I went back to Stuart Hall maybe a week after the funeral. I knew Laurence wouldn't be there. The excuse I used was that I lent some books to Ramsay and would like to retrieve them. James couldn't find the books in the library, so I asked if I could check Ramsay's bedroom." Ernest brushed food fragments off his shirt.

"Laurence had given explicit orders that no one should go in his father's room. He wanted nothing disturbed. I promised I wouldn't touch a thing, just look for the books. James gave his permission, so up I went."

Ernest finished his cookie. Another gulp of water, a sleeve wipe across his face, and any remaining crumbs disappeared.

"A rope lay draped across the bedroom door. I made a mental picture of its position, then laid it on a chair and turned the knob. I don't know what I was expecting. Maybe Laurence would jump out at me, or perhaps, Ramsay laying on the bed. Either alive or dead, entered my mind.

"The room was dark. I parted the curtains to let the sunlight in. A musty smell permeated the area, and a thick layer of dust covered everything.

"The armoire seemed full of clothes for a man on an extended trip. A single gap between suits suggested Ramsay may have worn one when he left. The hats sat on the top shelf. No gaps between them. Ramsay's favorite hat was still there. He never came to town without it. The bottom shelf had room for one more pair of shoes. Ramsay's walking stick still leaned in the corner."

"What did you do next?" Max leaned closer to Ernest.

"Closing the doors of the armoire, I stepped to his bureau and inspected each drawer. They were all full. Oh, you could squeeze in a pair of pajamas, some underwear and socks. But not enough clothes were missing to warrant packing a chackie. His personal items lay on top of the bureau, including a hair brush, tonic and some ointment. Wouldn't you take those things if you left on an extended trip? I know I would."

Max finished his sandwich and followed with more water.

"I felt the pinch of time, so I scanned the room for any other clues. Several photos of Gwen were in ornate frames. But are you ready for this? The glass covering Claire's photo had been broken beyond repair. There were so many scratches it was difficult to recognize her face." He paused. "A freestanding screen in one corner enticed me. My hands shook and my knees wobbled. I feared Laurence would come back any time and find me there. My feeble legs got me to the screen, and I peeked behind. I couldn't believe my eyes. What do you think I found? Right there, behind that screen? Not very well hidden either, but maybe the best that demented lad could do. Ramsay's chackie!"

"Did you open it?"

"No. By this time, the shaking had taken over my entire body. I knew I had to get out. There were three books on Ramsay's night table. I took two to verify my story and held them under one arm while I closed the curtains. Back in the hall, I replaced the rope, inspecting it several times for accuracy, then almost ran down the stairs. James came from the dining room. I bid him adieu, showed him the books, and thanked him for any inconvenience I may have caused.

"Outside, I wondered if James had noticed the quivering in my voice. With great restraint, I guided my horse down the drive. I felt like a jaybird over water and out of steam with no land in sight. I prodded my horse into a gallop once out of eyesight."

"Weren't you afraid James would let Laurence know you were there and in his father's room?"

"James assured me he would say nothing. He might lose his situation if he went against Laurence's instructions."

"I don't understand why you weren't called as a witness."

"Max, they weren't interested in Ramsay, only the events surrounding Claire's death. My testimony wouldn't have added anything. I didn't know Claire as well as I did Ramsay. There's not much else I can add. What say we go down to the beach now and try our luck?"

Max packed their lunch leftovers while Ernest carried the fishing gear to the beach. Tiny pebbles blanketed the shore, a stark contrast to the sand beaches on the Oregon coast. Casting their lines out, Ernest looked at the sun.

"This will be our last attempt. The sun's putting down for the day. We need to be back in town before nightfall."

At peace standing there, Max replayed all Ernest had told him. He became concerned for Maggie alone with Laurence and decided some self-defense lessons would be necessary.

A racket in the woods broke the silence. Sounded like hammering to Max. Then, a conversation in a foreign language followed.

"Is Gaelic spoken around this area of Scotland?" Max asked.

"Gaelic? Oh, some still know it, but it's not spoken this close to Rolen. Why do you ask?"

"Thought I heard hammering and then words I've never heard before. Very faint. In the woods there, at the far end of the beach."

Ernest closed his eyes, grinned, and let out a soft chuckle.

"That's a capercaillie sounding his mating call." Ernest reeled in his line and cast it farther from the shore. "I've seen pictures of your wild turkeys and a capercaillie looks something like it. We have a short hunting season for those birds. I'm told they're mighty tasty."

Max listened again to this strange sound and hoped to get a view of one on their ride back.

"Ernest, I forgot to ask. How did you get the books off the night table without disturbing the dust? And what were they?"

"I found three books stacked together and retrieved the bottom two. The top book sheltered the other two from the dust, so I left it behind. I had a scraping knife with me and slid the blade under the top book. Then I removed the two underneath and replaced the top book in its same spot without leaving fingerprints anywhere. The names of the books gave me even more certain something was amiss. One was *Recognizing Abnormal Behavior*, a second, *Schizophrenia: Signs, Symptoms, Cures*, and the last was *Loving Back to Reality*. I left *Loving Back to Reality* on the table. Ramsay must have tried to help Laurence on his own."

"Why do you think Ramsay wanted to see you?"

"I assumed he was looking for any knowledge I had about treatment centers, specialists or just as a friend. As a reporter, I know a lot about a lot."

A break in the water, 100 feet off shore, startled the men. A large fish soared above the surface. The pike twisted and splashed back in the loch.

"Ol' Moses," Max yelled. "Look at that fish jump! Must be a twenty pounder."

"Relax, Max, just a grandson of the great granddaddy. Time to reel in our lines."

Disappointed their afternoon together had ended, Max appreciated the wealth of information Ernest shared. The urgency to find Ramsay became another priority.

"Thanks for coming with me, Max. Even though we didn't hook Ol' Moses, I enjoyed our conversation. If you need my help, just let me know. I'm still looking for clues about Ramsay. I fear something dreadful has happened."

"All my pleasure, Ernest. I'm sure we'll be talking again."

Max reeled in his line. The large spoon glistened under the water about twelve feet from shore. At that moment, they both noticed a fish following the lure. The closer to shore, the bigger the fish appeared. Ernest whispered to Max, "Slower, slower, let the fish take the lure."

Engrossed in the fish's actions, Max's thoughts were on the fish. He didn't hear Ernest, and kept reeling at the same pace. The fish reached shallower water, its mouth open to catch the spoon. The pike's belly must have touched the bottom of the lake. It wiggled extra hard and scurried back into the loch, exploding water in its path.

"That was Ol' Moses!" Ernest couldn't contain himself. "You almost caught Ol' Moses! Why didn't you listen to me? You could have all the bragging rights in Rolen. Maybe all of Scotland."

Ernest fell back on the beach trying to catch his breath from the excitement.

Max's mouth hung open, amazed at the size of the pike and grateful to have seen the famous fish.

"Did you see him look me in the eye? Like he was saying, 'I fooled you one more time.'" Ernest cupped his hands around his mouth and yelled across the loch, "Ol' Moses, I'll get you next time." A soft echo reverberated across the water. Then, one more time, Ol' Moses showed himself. He jumped several feet out of the water, twisting and glistening in the late afternoon sun.

Yes, sir, now Max could corroborate Ernest's story about Ol' Moses when they returned to town. If he saw an elk on the way back, it would seal the day as perfect.

Chapter 20

Maggie enjoyed a glorious walk to the kirk. The early morning clouds had burned off, and the sun warmed her cold arms. She had made appropriate notations in her notepad and tucked it in her handbag. Afraid she may forget a question or two, it seemed like a good precaution. The sunlight shone on the pathway like a lamp to guide her footsteps. Birds sang their morning song and the fragrance of heather filled the air. A glorious day indeed.

At the last bend to the kirk, Maggie stopped to collect her thoughts. Her body quivered, like a swarm of butterflies had just taken up residence. Comfortable talking with Dr. Shane earlier, Maggie wondered what made her so jittery now. Her pace slowed.

She spied the kirk sign. Her first visit brought a sense of trepidation. This second visit seemed more relaxed. Maggie glanced up the path and spotted Dr. Shane as he trimmed shrubbery. Her pace increased, as did the butterfly dance.

"Good morning, Dr. Shane." Maggie waved.

"Guid day to you, Miss Richards. A fine day for a stroll among the heather. Those wee birds are singing their morning song. And did you breathe in the lovely scent of the flowers?" Dr. Shane stretched his back and removed a glove to greet Maggie.

"Many of my sermon illustrations come from my love of nature. Take these wayward branches of this elder shrub. It spreads in every direction. The birds love its fruit, but the scent can be overpowering. Every so often, I trim these untidy branches back. Reminds me how the Lord, in His love, also needs to prune us wayward souls. Would you like to go to my office or stay out here in the sun's warmth?"

"Oh, outside would be wonderful. I can't get enough of these dwindling summer days. I see a bench over there by the side of the kirk." Maggie pointed. "Would that be all right?"

"Of course. Why don't you make your way there? I'll deposit these clippings and be right with you."

Maggie's eyes followed Dr. Shane as he hiked to a small shed, placed the clippings in a large basket, and put his clippers away. Thankful he didn't suggest the bench at the back of the kirk. Too close to Claire's grave. At this distance, she could keep her emotions in check. She reviewed the questions on her notepad. Didn't want to overlook anything. Dr. Shane smiled as he drew close.

"Now, you can ask all the questions you want, but I believe I know what you're going to ask and why you're here. Since our first meeting, I've been reviewing all I know about the MacLaren's, Claire, and Laurence specifically. You may begin when ready."

"Thank you for your time." Maggie glanced at her notepad. "My friends, Nellie and Max, were impressed with you yesterday at the cafe' and appreciate your willingness to help us.

"First, let me tell you how we came to be in Scotland. Max, being a curiosity seeker, read about this case and thought Nellie and I might be interested in pursuing it to a different conclusion. All three of us have a thirst to right wrongs and see justice prevail. After we read through the inquest transcript, we felt the testimonies seemed to point to a strained relationship between Laurence and his stepmother.

"With that information, we concluded perhaps her death might not have been an accident, but premeditated murder instead. My first question then, could you tell me what you know about Laurence? His childhood, friends, interests and any conversations you may have had with him that were noteworthy."

"Miss Richards, or may I call you Margaret?"

"Margaret would be fine, but my friends call me Maggie."

"If you will permit me, I will call you Margaret. It has an air of dignity. Now I'm going to be honest with you and I would appreciate it if you would also be with me. I'd like to make some corrections. If I'm off base, let me know. If not, then I think we can move on to the crux of the issue." Dr. Shane cleared his throat and faced Maggie.

"I believe, that while Max may be a curiosity seeker and he, Nellie and yourself thought this would be an interesting case to pursue, I cannot imagine how this one in a thousand cases in Scotland would have been newsworthy in the States. While getting to the 'truth of the matter' and 'righting any wrongs' is admirable, again you live in the States. We're in Scotland and your interest in news from the small town of Rolen makes no sense. It makes no sense unless you, or one of your friends, have a personal interest in the MacLaren family."

Maggie squirmed on the bench.

"I believe that not only did you know Claire, but that you are her daughter. That you were receiving letters from her up to the day, or days, before her death. That you are now here out of a compulsion to get to the truth, locate Ramsay, find Laurence guilty of murder, if indeed he is, and relieve your sense of guilt over a lost relationship with your mum, who loved you."

Maggie buried her face in her hands. She released a flood of tears and sobbed, heart-wrenching sobs from the depths of her soul. The flood of tears she had dammed up for so many years burst forth. Not a minor break, but an effluence that knocked the complete edifice into crumbling rock.

"I'm right then," he said. "You cry as much as you need. God gave us tears for two reasons; one for times of joy and one for times of sorrow. I believe you have held onto your sorrow for far too long. Time to let go, Margaret. Healing can come after sorrow and repentance. God will heal you when you are ready to ask Him."

Overcome with emotion, Maggie imagined her mother's loving arms surrounding and supporting her through every event in her life. The tears subsided. She accepted a handkerchief from Dr. Shane, wiped her eyes and composed herself.

"Oh, Dr. Shane, I've made a muddle of everything. I had a wonderful mother, but I never gave her credit for half the things she did. Rebellious as a child, in my young adult years, I thought I knew more about life. After all, I received advanced training after high school and had a promising, successful career. I recently discovered success in her eyes and mine were opposite.

"Mine was about prestige, respect from my peers and a lucrative career as a free-lance artist in a man's world. Success for mom was helping others, loving the unlovable and serving whenever she had the means. We were opposites.

"While we've been in Scotland, I've come to know my mother for the first time. Even with Laurence, who must have terrified her, she seemed determined to win him over, seeking his best. How could I have missed that at home? How could I have judged her as a simple woman who didn't understand the world? I've got a lot to learn from her." Maggie paused. She lifted her tear-stained face and glanced at Dr. Shane. "How did you know?"

"I noticed on your first visit how uncomfortable you were in the kirk and talking with me. Only visitors sign the guest book, yet you said you were looking for names of members. At Claire's grave, your obvious demeanor gave you away. In the sunlight, the striking resemblance to your mother became clear. Claire mentioned she had a daughter, about your age, with golden red hair of her Scottish heritage. She also mentioned that her daughter hadn't responded to the letters she'd sent. I soon realized who I was talking to and perhaps the reason for you and your friends' trip." Dr. Shane repositioned himself on the bench.

"You've been on a journey for quite some time and I believe Claire would be proud of you right now, Margaret. Just as horses wear blinders to keep focused on what's straight ahead, you too have had blinders on, but I believe they are falling off. Once your world view broadens, the true Light of the world will show you the truth. I pray I will be there when that transformation occurs. You still have some roadblocks to overcome and if I can assist, I would be honored."

Maggie slid to the back of the bench and bowed her head. She waited until her breathing returned to normal.

"Thank you. There are some things I need to work through by myself, but I appreciate your counsel and friendship. My list of questions seems rather moot now." She closed her notepad and slipped it back into her handbag. "We're here to find some overlooked evidence to convict Laurence of murder. Ramsay is also a missing piece of the puzzle, so anything you have to share would be of great help."

"While I think Laurence is a disturbed young man who needs professional care, I'm not sure there is any evidence that even suggests he murdered your mum." Dr. Shane folded his hands in his lap.

"At the inquest I heard testimony that intimated Claire felt threatened when alone with him. Without corroboration from others, for example, the servants, it is only her word. While a delightful woman of faith and integrity, we need someone else to make the same statement. I believe you know who I mean."

"Laurence. Somehow, we need to get his statement in front of others."

"You seem to have him tried and convicted, Margaret. What if it is as he said? What if an animal bolted from the woods and scared Peggy, which caused her to rear and throw Claire over the embankment? What if it truly was an accident? Are you ready to accept that as the end of your quest? Even if you find Ramsay, what light do you think he will shed on the event? He waited at Stuart Hall and took his son's word for what happened. Will you relinquish your guilty verdict and judge Laurence innocent?"

Those were hard questions. Maggie's trip to Scotland had the sole purpose of convicting Laurence. Nellie and Max had warned her the outcome may not be what she wanted and now Dr. Shane echoed their words. How could anyone who knew so much about Laurence and his strange behavior think anything but guilt? She became even more determined to find the evidence, get him to confess, locate Ramsay, and take all the facts to the judge in Inverness to reopen the case. Maggie would not veer from this course.

Dr. Shane shared that Ramsay and Claire came to worship every Sunday, unless sickness or out-of-town responsibilities prevented. Not so with Laurence. Dr. Shane had spoken with him about it, but Laurence sloughed it off as one of those nonessentials he might get around to someday.

"My biggest concern, is for your safety and clarity of thought. I assume you're going to Stuart Hall, Margaret. Laurence can be a very persuasive young man and may entice you from your intended course. Know that I will pray for you every day. My other great concern is for Ramsay. Have you, Nellie or Max, been able to find out anything?"

"Not yet. We seem to have reached a dead end. I don't want to abandon the search, although I'm not sure where else to look. Perhaps we could trick Laurence into divulging his father's whereabouts. Max reads the local papers along with the newspaper from Edinburgh, hunting for any clues. We're assuming Laurence took his father someplace, but we have no evidence. Other than those assumptions, we have nothing."

"Margaret," Dr. Shane sat up straight. "I have a brilliant thought, and I don't get them too often. The conference I'm attending is in Edinburgh. I don't need to leave for another day or so, but what if I left this afternoon instead? That would give me two days on my own. I can check church records for new members and visitors alike. The Edinburgh Registrar office would have a record of deaths for all of Scotland. If I find anything at all, I'll telegram you at the Creag an Tuirc. How does that sound?"

"Oh, Dr. Shane, that sounds wonderful. What a help you would be! Max will be very excited to learn you are on the case as well. He's sure that one day when he looks in the paper, there will be a photo of Ramsay. Dreaming maybe, but at this point, our dreaming is about all we have when the path grows cold."

"Fine. I'll plan on that. At one time, I thought I would like to work for Scotland Yard as a detective. Short-lived as this investigation may be, I can still fulfill that dream in a small way." Dr. Shane clutched Maggie's hand, then rose from the bench. "So, unless there's anything else you wish to discuss, I must excuse myself. Lots to do before I catch the east-bound train."

"I can't think of anything else. We'll expect a message each day with some news. I believe we'll delay our stay at Stuart Hall until your return. On my walk here this morning, I felt like a hundred cocoons had opened and butterflies took flight in my stomach. They've all left now, and I'm calm and confident that progress is being made.

"Thank you again for changing your plans on this quest for the truth. Oh, one last request. Please don't tell anyone about Claire being my mother. And you can call me Maggie. All my friends do. Thank you again."

Maggie remained on the bench while Dr. Shane disappeared into the church. She couldn't leave without a visit to her mother's grave.

She spotted the fir standing as majestic as ever, pointing straight to the sky. What a magnificent tree. The branches pointed toward God and the roots in the ground cradled her mother. A wave of emotions overwhelmed her. She brushed some fallen needles off the gravestone, then related her discoveries to her mom and her fear encountering Laurence face-to-face. She whispered, "I love you, Mom," wiped tears from her face, and wandered toward the path that led back to Rolen.

A soft cool breeze brushed her cheek, like the sweet kisses her mom gave when she tucked Maggie into bed for the night. Her memory then flooded with her mom's prayer by her bedside. It began, "Now I lay me down to sleep." The rest flowed away from her memory. Invigorated from her visit with Dr. Shane, she hurried back to share the news with Max and Nellie.

Our greatest weakness lies in giving up. The most certain way to succeed is always to try just one more time.
—Thomas A. Edison—

Chapter 21

A mere two days had passed since Dr. Shane left for Edinburgh, when Maggie received a telegram. Simple and to the point. Three words, then brief directions; "Found Ramsay Alive, Morningside Road Station." Maggie's legs gave way. She found a chair nearby, plopped down, and read the message again. What a gift Dr. Shane had become to the group. She located Max, who responded to Dr. Shane's telegram; "Leaving on the noon train."

✳✳✳

Max spied Ernest chatting with a group of men on the other side of the road. He headed straight for his friend, bumping a filled lumber cart. The driver yelled at him. Max waved and shouted, "I'm sorry."

"Ernest, am I glad to see you! A message from Dr. Shane arrived. He found the man we're looking for. There's a train leaving at noon. You will need an overnight case. Can you be ready?"

Max calmed his heavy breathing and noticed the men's stares.

"Oh, I'm so sorry to have interrupted your conversation. I have urgent business with Ernest and lost my sense of manners."

"Gentlemen, this is my friend Max Sullivan. He's a Yank, so some leniency, if you please." Ernest wrapped his arm around Max's shoulders. "Excuse us, gentlemen."

Max accompanied Ernest to the shade of a nearby tree.

"Now, Max, tell me again. Slower this time so I can catch every word."

"Dr. Shane found Ramsay. Here's the telegram he sent. We need to take the noon train. Can you be ready?"

"Ready? Max, I'm overwhelmed!" Ernest grabbed his chest. "My good friend has been found and you ask if I can be ready? I can pack in ten minutes. Our 'finding Ramsay' adventure has begun in full force. Did Dr. Shane say where he found him? What condition he's in?"

"Dr. Shane only said he found Ramsay, and we were to get off at the Morningside Road Station."

"Morningside, huh? That means he's at the Edinburgh Lunatic Asylum. Concerned, I am, but rejoicing at the same time. I'll meet you at the station in ten minutes or less."

※※※

The train traveled at a snail's pace for Ernest. He volunteered to help shovel coal, but the conductor reassured him the train ran at full speed.

The large stone structure of Edinburgh Castle came into view. As the train slowed, Max and Ernest stepped toward the exit door, waited for the conductor to place the steps on the platform, and disembarked. Dr. Shane waved to them from the far end of the platform. They saw the excitement in his face, but also concern. A carriage waited to take them to Ramsay.

"Dr. Shane, can you tell us how you found him? How is he? Did he remember you?" Ernest spouted, breathless with excitement.

"Set your bags in the carriage. Then I'll answer your questions on the way." Dr. Shane waited for Ernest and Max to climb into the carriage, then gave directions to the driver and joined his friends.

"First, I went to the kirks and made inquiries. The ministers didn't know him or have any record of a visit, which didn't mean he hadn't gone to worship, just not signed the guest book. Then, I searched the tenements and boarding houses. After a prayer for guidance, the Lord urged me toward the hospitals. There's one institution here for long-term residents; the Edinburgh Lunatic Asylum.

"To give you some background, Max, they built the hospital in 1813. Most residents have had a hard time functioning in society, so they're admitted by family, but sometimes they admit themselves. While most need the professional care these doctors can give, others just need some rest and relaxation."

Ernest removed his hat and placed it on his lap. With all the jostling of the carriage, he worried the wind may catch his hat and blow it out the open window.

"I didn't know what to expect when I entered the institution," Dr. Shane continued. "Rather than speak to the receptionist, I asked for the Chief of Staff. Being a man of the cloth allows me some privileges." He grinned and touched his clerical collar.

"They directed me to an office down the hall. There I met Dr. Alec McDonald. After we greeted, he offered a cup of tea, which I never turn down. Once the general pleasantries were complete, I told him I'd been searching for a friend and wondered if he might be at the hospital. I brought a photo of Ramsay with me. When I handed the photo to him, his eyes glistened with recognition.

"Since they did not know his true name, they called him Robert Gregory. Dr. McDonald hoped I could give him the missing details for his file. I told him I would be glad to and would appreciate knowing how Ramsay came to be at this hospital and his physical, as well as mental condition.

"Dr. McDonald told me a carriage brought him in the wee hours of the morning, driven by a well-dressed young man. He dragged Ramsay up the steps and through the front door. Dirt caked Ramsay's skin, his clothes old, ragged and torn. The staff thought he might be under the influence of drink or drugs. After evaluation, they found no evidence of either." Dr. Shane stuck his head out of the window. "We're coming to the hospital now. I told Dr. McDonald you were taking the noon train from Rolen. He's eager to meet you."

"Is Ramsay all right, Dr.? Did he know you? Can we take him home?" Ernest couldn't contain his excitement.

Dr. Shane responded, "Be patient. You will know soon enough."

The enormous and imposing stone building had a tall wrought-iron fence surrounding the grounds. Dr. Shane showed a pass from Dr. McDonald at the doorway and they were admitted.

Inside the hospital, they were directed to Dr. McDonald's office. Ernest grew more concerned over Dr. Shane's comment. Could Ramsay be insane? Would he recognize Ernest and regain his senses? Could they take him home? Would he be able to testify against Laurence? His agitation with Laurence increased. How could he do this to his own father?

Dr. McDonald greeted them with an outstretched hand. His office appeared professional and comfortable. Padded chairs, arranged in a living room-like setting, created a relaxed atmosphere.

"I'm sure Dr. Shane gave you the basic information regarding your friend. I can't tell you how glad I am to clear up our missing pieces." Dr. McDonald motioned to several chairs for the men. "My staff and I have had a difficult time believing the man's story, but without identification papers and our fruitless background checks of missing persons, we had no choice."

"Dr. Shane shared a little on the ride here. Could you tell us the entire story?" Ernest asked.

"I'd be glad to. A young man brought him in the wee hours of the morning and told my admitting staff the man had been living in the woods on his property for several days." Dr. McDonald slid into the stuffed leather chair behind his desk.

"The vagrant, what the young man called him, was told he would have to leave and not return or they would summon the local constable. We were told the vagrant claimed to be owner of the manor, Ramsay MacLaren, but carried no papers to prove it. The man wandered off when requested, but always returned the next day, still insistent about his claim to the manor. The next evening, the servants found the transient in a makeshift camp, carried him to the stables, dumped him in a wagon and the young man brought him here. I asked the young man to fill out the paperwork, which he did in a hurry. He signed his name Ramsay MacLaren, lord of Stuart Hall. The vagrant appeared incoherent and persisted in *his* claim to be Ramsay MacLaren. You can see our confusion."

"So that's how Laurence got him here. What a conniving son." Ernest's agitation grew.

"To satisfy myself, I would appreciate a photo of Ramsay MacLaren and his son together. That would be a real clincher, and then we could go forward with legal proceedings."

Ernest couldn't move fast enough. His hand thrust into his coat pocket. He had brought a newspaper photo of Ramsay, Claire, and Laurence during a social gathering at Stuart Hall. Unfolding the paper with care, he handed the clipping to Dr. McDonald, who studied the photo images, read the caption, and asked if he could keep the clipping for evidence. Ernest agreed.

"Yes, this could be the young man who brought Robert here. We had the evening lights on, so the entry was dim. He also had his hat pulled low over his face. I was called back to the hospital to check on a patient and the staff asked me to intervene. I will never forget his brisk manner. He seemed rather antsy to be leaving, and after what you've told me, I understand why."

Dr. McDonald withdrew a magnifying glass from his desk and studied the photo even more carefully. He seemed to look for something else. His eyes opened wide and mouth gaped.

"This is incredible." He studied the photo. "The young man in the photo is the same gentleman who came to the hospital several months ago. He asked the usual questions, but also inquired if we accepted homeless men. I told him that if they were a threat to themselves or society, then yes. He seemed very inquisitive regarding the policies and asked if we would keep anyone for the rest of their lives. I thought some questions odd, but answered as best I could. That young man and this man in the photo are the same. Since the stranger who brought Robert here is the same person in the photo, we have one disturbed son on our hands."

Ernest remembered Ramsay and Claire's trip to Edinburgh and how stunned they were that Laurence agreed to go with them. Laurence must have planned this for quite some time.

"Now as to the details of Robert's, or Ramsay's, condition before you see him."

Dr. McDonald offered tea around and cleared his throat. Divulging a few details with Dr. Shane, the time had come for the entire story. The three men listened, intent on every word.

"We've been treating Ramsay as if he were a delusional, reclusive, sometimes violent, homeless man. He is in the West House, a place for those whose families, or themselves, are without financial means. Sometimes the residents can be difficult. Because we only had Laurence's story, we gave Ramsay a sedative and started therapy the next day. Ramsay continued insisting that he was Ramsay MacLaren and became belligerent and violent at times. He has attempted to leave the hospital, one time during the middle of the night. Several weeks passed before he resigned to accept his fate. We've lessened his restraint, but maintained a vigilant watch as a precaution. I'm afraid the accumulation of medications and confinement may have done some damage."

Ernest paced. He couldn't bear to think that Ramsay might be a permanent resident and never venture outside the hospital's walls or return to his beloved Stuart Hall. As Dr. McDonald detailed accounts of Ramsay's behavior, Ernest became more distressed.

"There's been a change the last few weeks. I can't elaborate, but he seems to accept the hospital as his last home. Yet many afternoons he plods toward the iron barred wall and gazes out at the world beyond. Almost as though he felt he would be on the other side soon. Please expect little on your first visit. He may not even recognize you. I also request you call him Robert, not Ramsay, and keep the conversation in simple sentences."

"We'll do our best. Right, Dr. Shane? Ramsay doesn't know Max, so the two of us will be careful and follow your directive."

"Thank you, Ernest. At this time of day, I'm sure we'll find him on his favorite bench in the shade of a large fir tree. I'll stay with you. Please greet him as a stranger, begin a conversation, and we'll follow Ramsay's lead."

Ernest prayed Ramsay would recognize himself and Dr. Shane, that there would be a joyous reunion and they could make plans for his departure. Always the optimist.

Chapter 22

Down the hallway from Dr. McDonald's office, they saw French doors open into the bright sunshine. The three men followed the doctor through the opening and into a manicured courtyard. Hospital residents sat at wooden tables: some played checkers, while others played cribbage. Lawn bowlers competed in a shady section of the park-like setting. Ernest's heart sank as he noticed a group of residents that appeared to be in a stupor. *Would this be Ramsay's condition?*

The path wound toward a large fir tree where a lone man hunched over on a bench. With a firm grip on Ernest's arm, Dr. Shane held him back. "We don't want you to startle Ramsay. We need to be cautious."

Ernest nodded in agreement and slowed his pace.

"I suggest you walk past Ramsay, keep visiting as a group, then return and greet him." Dr. McDonald directed the men. "I'll find a couple more chairs for us."

Ernest shut his eyes and held his breath at the first glimpse of this 'lost' man. Ramsay's gaunt face and sunken eyes replaced his once-vibrant friend. Ramsay appeared in a stupor similar to the other residents. Ernest glanced at Dr. Shane and realized he shared the concern. They may not reach him after all.

"Excuse me, would you mind if I sit beside you?" Ernest asked Ramsay.

Ramsay glimpsed him. "No. That'd be all right."

Max, Dr. Shane, and Dr. McDonald placed chairs opposite the bench.

"Robert, these three men are visiting today. I saw you out here and wondered if you would mind a brief chat with them. Would you, Robert?"

Ramsay slowly raised his head. Ernest gazed into his eyes and shuddered. They seemed vacant, disconnected from the world.

"No, I guess not." He wiped saliva from the corner of his mouth.

"Fine. Let me introduce these visitors to you. First is Max Sullivan, next to him is Dr. Shane and beside you, Ernest McIntyre."

Ramsay fixed his eyes on each man and studied them. He hesitated with Dr. Shane, then placed his full attention on Ernest. Ernest prayed he would remember something from their friendship to ignite a spark in his buried memories. Then Ramsay's eyes returned to Max.

"Do I know you?" His speech was quiet and hesitant.

"No, Robert. We've never met. I'm from the United States and visiting Scotland for the first time."

Next, he faced Dr. Shane and studied his features and clothes.

"You're a minister. I knew a minister once. Do I know you?" Ramsay stretched his shoulders back.

"You are right, Robert. I'm the minister of a small congregation northwest of here. And yes, we've met before."

Ramsay's forehead wrinkled. "How did we meet?"

"You came to my kirk for worship."

Ernest sympathized with Dr. Shane. He sensed the minister longed to tell Ramsay about Gwen, her beautiful piano playing and singing in the choir, that he had baptized their infant son and officiated for the marriage to his second wife. Then Ramsay turned toward Ernest.

"Do I know you?" He pressed his eyes closed, then opened them again.

Ernest had prepared for that question since Ramsay had asked Max. How would he answer the second? How can he remain objective when he wants to give his 'lost' friend a big hug, welcome him back to the living and take him home? He prayed another quick prayer, *"Lord, please give me the right words when needed."*

"Yes, you know me." Ernest's stomach churned as he waited for the next question.

"How do I know you?"

Okay, Lord, I need those words right now!

"We've been friends for many years."

Ramsay peered straight into Ernest's eyes. Ernest imagined Ramsay could see into that part of his brain where he'd stored all his friendship memories. Perhaps Ramsay saw the day they went fishing and caught so many trout they had a hard time packing them home. He longed to tell him about the many social events at the Hall with beautiful music, fantastic food, and, of course, the Highland Games celebration in Rolen.

Ramsay studied Ernest, then glanced at Dr. McDonald, then back to Ernest.

"If we've been friends, you know my name. Can you tell me my name?"

Ernest checked for approval from Dr. McDonald. Should he say Robert or tell him his real name: Ramsay William MacLaren, lord of Stuart Hall, Rolen, Scotland? Dr. McDonald nodded approval.

"Your name is Ramsay MacLaren."

Ramsay's mouth gaped. One minute Robert and now Ramsay.

He inhaled a slow, deliberate breath. "Ramsay," and again, "Ramsay," with more conviction.

Ernest waited for an immediate transformation. Would the truth take hold? Could he dismiss the lie the hospital led him to believe? He recognized the hurt in Ramsay's eyes. The expression was like a child promised a chocolate chip cookie for good behavior, only to find the cookie jar empty.

"Do I have a family?" Ramsay continued to question Ernest.

"Yes, Ramsay. You have one son named Laurence."

"And a wife?"

"I'm sorry. Your first wife died many years ago. Your second wife a short time ago."

"Where's my home?"

"At Stuart Hall, near Rolen."

Edinburgh and the barred wall became Ramsay's focus. The castle on the hilltop bathed with the glow of the late afternoon sun. Ramsay's face lit up as well. Then he turned straight on and faced Dr. McDonald. From a bent-over, defeated man, Ramsay stretched tall and transformed into one who appeared confident, strong and determined.

Ernest felt he had witnessed a miracle. Ramsay appeared liberated.

"So, Dr. McDonald," Ramsay said, "I have a home out there. Outside of these walls, I have an identity. I am who I said I was from the very beginning."

"Yes, Ramsay. Without these gentlemen's persistence, we would have never known. So now we have more pieces of your puzzle."

Ramsay leaned against the back of the bench and relaxed every muscle as tears trickled down his face. Ernest handed him a handkerchief. Quiet prevailed.

"It's the dinner hour now," said Dr. McDonald. "Come Ramsay. We'll accompany you to the dining hall."

They wandered back to the hospital building. Dr. McDonald and Max led, then Ernest and Dr. Shane on each side of Ramsay. Nothing more needed to be said.

"I'd like to speak with all of you in private." Dr. McDonald directed them back to his office, leaving Ramsay in the dining room.

Ernest caught sight of Ramsay one last time in a far corner of the room, head held high.

"What happened this afternoon was a genuine breakthrough." Dr. McDonald motioned the men to chairs and closed his office door behind them. "That was an unexpected reaction from Ramsay. My hope was for a polite conversation with three strangers. Ramsay's more alert and engaged than I had expected. My staff will monitor him tonight. Depending on how things progress, we can look for some clarity in the next few weeks. Whom shall I contact with updates?"

"You can send information to me, Ernest McIntyre, in care of the Rolen Times. I have a box there and stop in several times a week. I'll relay the news to Max and Dr. Shane. How soon, or should I say, do you see Ramsay able to return to Stuart Hall?"

"I believe in time Ramsay may return to his former self. We'll monitor him for at least another week for any unusual behavior. During that time, we'll introduce Ramsay to his true self. This photo you brought, Ernest, may rekindle buried memories. I fear for his reaction if, or when, he understands his son brought him here."

Dr. McDonald seated himself behind his desk and flipped a manilla folder open. He placed a notepad on top of the papers inside and jotted some notations.

"As for returning to Stuart Hall, that all depends on Ramsay and how quickly he reverts to himself. I would expect maybe several weeks to months. However, based on what happened this afternoon, the transition may be faster. He's set his sights on the outside world and is eager to leave the hospital. You gentlemen gave him the impetus.

"If there is nothing else, I need to make a few notes on what transpired and then return to my duties. I appreciate your devotion to Ramsay and your time to make the trip to clear up this mystery. A friend of mine is an investigator for Scotland Yard. I'll give him the details of this case to find out what charges they can bring against the son."

The three men thanked Dr. McDonald for his compassion and expertise. Ernest glanced toward the dining hall as they prepared to exit the hospital, but didn't see Ramsay.

The streets of Edinburgh were crowded as the work day ended. Ernest spotted a quaint pub and suggested they partake in a meal and a special drink.

"We need to celebrate the end of our finding Ramsay journey and the progress we made today!"

Ernest led the way into the pub and straight for the bar. "Ales for three."

With glasses raised and a resounding clink, in unison, they let out a hearty, "Cheers!"

Chapter 23

"Oh, Max, Ernest, I can't tell you how excited I am over your news about Ramsay." When they finished relating the news from their trip to Edinburgh, Maggie hugged both men, then blushed. "I'm sorry for my forwardness. I get so excited. Ramsay has a fighting chance to regain his memory and return to Stuart Hall."

Maggie closed her eyes and inhaled deeply, then exhaled. "Let's invite our dear friends to join us at a mini-celebration party. But first, I'll meet with George and Mabel. Maybe we can use their cafe'. And, Max, will you share the good news with them?"

"I'd be happy to," Max said.

✳✳✳

Mary Beth arrived first, followed by Nellie, Dr. Shane, Ernest, and Max. Maggie and Mabel carried trays with cups, saucers, and two teapots. George celebrated with warm Caramel Shortbread. Once Mabel served each guest, the cafe' became quiet with anticipation.

"We've invited you here today to share some good news," Maggie said. "Ramsay has been found because of the efforts of our good friend Dr. Shane. He, Max, and Ernest traveled to Edinburgh Lunatic Asylum. I'll let Max share their findings."

Max waited for the jubilation to subside. "Our first impression led us to believe, with help and time, Ramsay may return to his former state of mind. However, Dr. McDonald explained the medical protocol and cautioned us not to get our hopes up. The transition may take months before his return to Stuart Hall. Ernest, would you read the recent letter from Dr. McDonald?"

Ernest reached into his coat pocket.

"We've all been concerned about Ramsay since his disappearance. Even though we did everything possible, it took these three Yanks to get us off our duffs and back on the trail. We owe them a huge thanks." They raised their teacups with hearty cheers.

"Now for the letter, which arrived this morning."

Dear Ernest,

I trust this finds you well. With this unseasonably warm weather, our residents stay outside during the day and well into the evening, including Ramsay. He spends much of his time pacing the perimeter fence and gazing at the outside world. Ramsay's memory continues to improve. I showed him the newspaper clipping you brought, Ernest. He cried. Ramsay misses Claire and remembers a terrible horse-riding accident. Then he gazed at Laurence and became very agitated. Finally, Ramsay peered at me and exclaimed, "My son brought me here, didn't he?"

Ernest sipped his tea and cleared his throat.

When I confirmed his words, Ramsay dropped his head. Sorrow overtook him. He speculated that he must have been a bad parent to rear such an uncaring son. I assured him that sometimes children are out of our control, and guilt was not warranted.

Ramsay asked if I knew of any legal action he could take against Laurence. I reminded him that he might recall similar cases with his solicitor's education. At this point, his demeanor changed. Ramsay appeared to lose any emotional attachment to Laurence. He suggested we admit Laurence here to the hospital. We'll discuss these feelings later.

"I don't want him committed," Maggie interrupted. "I want him convicted."

Ernest continued.

If this rate of progress continues, I'm confident Ramsay will be ready for release in another few weeks. Something will have to be done about his son. However, I will leave that in your capable hands. I'm concerned about Ramsay's safety if he returns to the old situation.

Sincerely,

Dr. Alec McDonald, Head of Staff

Edinburgh Lunatic Asylum

Edinburgh, Scotland

Silence filled the room. Mary Beth and Mabel wiped tears from their eyes. Each one waited for a response from the other and hoped for a resolution to the now "Laurence Problem."

Ernest placed the letter on the table. "My friends. I must say this is more than I expected. Ramsay seems to have made rapid progress toward recovery, which both excites and frightens me. Do any of you feel the same?"

"Margaret," said Dr. Shane, "I would like to hear your response to Ernest. Without you, Nellie, and Max, our quest for Ramsay would have ended."

Maggie paused and gathered her thoughts to make her purpose clear.

"I'm beside myself with joy. However, I need to ask all of you to maintain secrecy no matter how excited you are about the news. My friends and I came here not to find Ramsay but to find the truth about Mrs. MacLaren's death. Locating Ramsay adds more evidence to our case, but again, I must ask for your silence. If word gets out prematurely, it may ruin everything. Do I have everyone's promise you will say nothing until the right time?"

They all agreed.

"Thank you. Then we can continue. At Laurence's invitation, Nellie, Max, and I plan to go to Stuart Hall in a few days."

Maggie wiped her sweating hands on her serviette.

"As to Ernest's question, yes, I'm excited about the possibility this wronged man may be able to return home. Yet, I'm fearful of what he will come home to; a son who doesn't want him. I understood Dr. McDonald would contact a friend at Scotland Yard. Perhaps he can find legal grounds to remove Laurence from Stuart Hall." Maggie sipped her tea.

"Last, I request your prayers for us. I feel we're about to enter a lion's den and need the wisdom of a sage, the cunning of a fox, and protection from many soldiers. Thank you so much for coming this afternoon and to Mabel for her tea and shortbread."

"Margaret, I'd like to pray for the three of you with your permission."

Maggie's heart warmed, pleased with Dr. Shane's offer.

"Our Father in heaven, we praise you for who you are. Not only a God of the entire universe but a God who is very much involved and interested in each of us. We thank you that Ramsay's been found and may be returning home. We ask for your special protection for Nellie, Margaret, and Max. May your Holy Spirit surround them and give wisdom and direction as they continue to search for answers. We also ask for a blanket of protection as they may be facing dangers they hadn't anticipated. We ask this in the name of our Lord and Savior, who redeemed us with His precious blood and loves us beyond our imagination. Amen."

***

Footsteps thundered up the porch steps. George and Mabel stared at the cafe' door. The stunned expression on their faces caused Maggie and the others to pivot in their chairs. Laurence stood with the sun on his back, a striking silhouette. He appeared more like a western cowboy than a Scottish lad with his riding hat and boots. He strode toward the group, removed his hat, and greeted everyone. Maggie drew a quick breath.

"I feel like I've interrupted something, Miss Richards."

Ernest nonchalantly moved the letter out of eyesight.

"Oh, no. We were enjoying afternoon tea together. Sort of a goodbye party. We planned to contact you tomorrow about coming to Stuart Hall." Those pesky butterflies assaulted Maggie's stomach again. She hoped her voice sounded natural and didn't shake. *How long had Laurence been outside? Could he hear Dr. Shane's prayer? Did he have any idea why they were meeting together?* She tried not to let her nerves show and extended her hand in greeting.

"I believe you know everyone."

"Yes, I do, except the lassie next to Dr. Shane."

"I'm Mary Beth McGregor. I own the dress shop about two blocks from here."

Laurence circled the table and shook her hand. Mary Beth's face tensed as she frantically wiped the sweat from her hands on her skirt. She made a great effort to be pleasant, look him in the eye, and respond to his "nice to meet you" greeting. Laurence returned to Maggie.

"You have arrived in Rolen and are ready to accept my invitation. Splendid. When can I send Walter to fetch you and your friends?"

"Would the day after tomorrow be convenient?"

"Day after tomorrow would be fine." He turned to George. "Now, the reason I'm here. I want to buy an entry ticket for the Highland Games Race next week. Fireball won't let me skip it again this year."

Nellie clasped Maggie's hand under the table and squeezed. Maggie kept her eyes on Laurence, who followed George to the counter. Ernest trailed behind him.

"Now, that's the best news I've heard all week." Ernest patted Laurence's shoulder. "The boys and I talked about whether you would enter this year. We're ready to place our wagers. Now we'll have a real horse race." Ernest said his goodbyes to all and left the cafe'.

The group moved to the porch and chatted about trivial matters. They kept the conversation light-hearted for Laurence's benefit, said their good evenings, and went separate ways.

Laurence caught up with Maggie.

"I'm so glad you returned in time for the Highland Games. It's a day filled with fun, incredible food, and immersion in Scottish culture. I'll send Walter with the carriage. Shall we say 10 am, the day after tomorrow?"

"That sounds fine. We look forward to our time at your beautiful manor. Thank you again for your kind invitation."

"It's truly my pleasure." He gently kissed her hand. "Until then."

She instinctively pulled her hand from his grasp. *How bold of him!* Warmth filled her cheeks as she turned and rushed to Nellie and Max. They finished their walk to the Creag an Tuirc arm in arm. Their mission was now underway.

❊❊❊

Max carried the luggage to the lobby of the Creag an Tuirc and thanked Mr. and Mrs. Wellington for their kind hospitality. He reserved rooms for one more night after their return from Stuart Hall unless their plans changed. *Could their plans change?* They had their course planned out, and unless Laurence threw the proverbial monkey wrench into it, they should solve the mystery in two weeks. He had prepped Maggie in self-defense tactics, confident she could defend herself. Max opened his valise one last time and checked his supply of writing tablets and sharpened pencils. Then made a mental note not to leave anything lying around for Laurence to find.

Maggie and Nellie descended the stairs and joined Max.

"What do you think, Max?" Maggie spun around. "We thought we'd wear the same outfits when we first met Laurence. I want a reminder of our tourist status and 'accidental stop' at Stuart Hall. Make sense?"

"It's perfect, girls. You seem a bit tense, Maggie."

"Tense? Yes, overly tense. I'm so nervous. I can't remember if we've had breakfast yet, maybe because my stomach is all in knots. My mom always gave me a cup of tea to settle my stomach. Nellie, would you mind? Without you two faithful friends to support me, I would be a basket case."

A corner table afforded an excellent vantage point to watch for Walter and the carriage. Nellie brought tea on a tray for Max, Maggie, and herself as well. The friends sat in silence.

The front door flew open. Ernest burst in, found his friends, and hurried to their table.

"Oh, thank the Lord. I was afraid you might have already left." Then, out of breath, he withdrew an envelope from his coat pocket and waved it at them.

"Look, another letter from Dr. McDonald. I haven't opened it yet. I hoped you'd still be here, and we could read it together." He tore the envelope open, then glanced around for any eaves-droppers. None in sight, he continued.

Dear Ernest,

I just wanted to give you a quick update. Ramsay is doing wonderfully. He has immersed himself in researching cases in the law books I brought him. We've had several counseling sessions regarding his son's behavior. He accepted that they did their best to raise Laurence. As hard as it is to let his only child go, Ramsay understands Laurence needs professional help. He has expressed concern that being heirless will force him to sell the Hall. I remind him to take one day at a time. Please greet Max and Dr. Shane for me. With your continued prayers, Ramsay may return within the month.

Sincerely,

Dr. Alec McDonald

Maggie couldn't believe what she heard. "Within the month? Do you realize Nellie, Max, I can call him stepfather? How wonderful if we could extend our stay and meet Ramsay."

The sounds of a horse and carriage on the street caught their attention. Max watched through the window as Walter brought the carriage to a stop in front of the inn.

The moment they had prepared for had arrived. They were ready. Ernest helped Max hand the luggage to Walter, then whispered to the lassies, "I'll pray for you each day."

With a flick of the reins, the horse pulled the carriage north toward Stuart Hall.

Max noticed Dr. Shane hurry down the sidewalk and stop beside Ernest. He waved goodbye.

"I wanted to be here earlier to pray with them, but an urgent matter required my attention. I hope our friends are as confident as I that the Lord goes with them and the Holy Spirit will protect and guide them."

"They do, Dr. Shane. They do," Ernest said.

Once the carriage disappeared, Ernest pulled the letter from his pocket, waved the envelope at Dr. Shane, and announced, "More good news."

Chapter 24

The carriage bogged down in the mud from recent rains, jarring it in the ruts. The conversation inside the carriage remained superficial, not knowing how much Walter could hear. A weightiness pressed on Maggie. No birds sang. The early fall colors spotted the trees as leaves drifted to the ground. *A sign of defeat before a beginning?*

The horses' hooves sloshed, and the carriage slipped as it veered off the main road on the last turn to the manor.

Stuart Hall looked majestic in the light mist. For the first time, Maggie felt a kinship with the old dwelling; charming on the outside, but needed cleansing on the inside. She recognized a purification had begun inside her. Now, she carried a load on her shoulders for Stuart.

James, Stuart Hall's butler, waited on the front steps. He assisted Maggie and Nellie with one hand and held an umbrella above their heads with his other.

"Fàilte to Stuart Hall, Miss Richards, Miss Cox, and Mr. Sullivan. Ah trust ye hud a pleasant journey. Laurence waits fur ye at th' side porch. Walter 'n' ah wull care fur yer luggage."

Maggie appreciated James as an excellent butler. His position trumped the other servants. Stooped over like many men his age, he still kept a sweet disposition.

"Thank you, James. It was a pleasant ride, even with the cooling mist." Maggie ascended the porch steps and waited while James shook the rain from his umbrella.

Maggie liked James the first time they met and even though formal in manner, she sensed a tender side. She hoped to break that shell and learn more about her mother and Laurence. She determined to see him smile just once before they left.

They followed James to the side porch. A beautifully set table awaited with a lace tablecloth and fresh-cut flowers.

Laurence greeted them.

"What an honor to have you back at Stuart Hall. Somehow, it seems like you were never gone. Perhaps the anticipation of your visit bridged the gap in time. Please have a seat. Harriet fixed a small lunch and outdid herself for dinner tonight. A true Scottish feast awaits."

Harriet carried a large salad bowl filled with lettuce and vegetables to the table. James followed with a bowl of freshly grated cheese and another with warm rolls. A large decorative platter graced a side table laiden with pears, peaches, apples and assorted sliced cheeses. Homemade marmalade, salad dressings, and hand-churned butter completed the meal.

"This is lovely. My compliments, Harriet," Maggie said. "If I remember correctly, you tend a garden. Is that correct?"

"Yes, Miss Richards. Everything you see is grown right here at Stuart Hall, except the rolls and cheese. Our milk is delivered twice a week, so I churn butter as well. What you see is the last of the lettuce as growing season has ended. Please excuse me and enjoy your meal. James will be out with the coffee and tea."

A jolly soul, Harriet appeared in her sixties and on the rotund side. Maggie expected an excellent meal since friends had told her first to scrutinize the cook at any restaurant. If the cook was robust, then you could expect ample portions. Harriet had a weathered complexion. Yet, her entire face lit up when she smiled, and her eyes sparkled.

James brought a tray with coffee and tea things and placed it on a small table near Laurence.

"Thank you, James. May I offer coffee or tea to any of you? Miss Richards? Miss Cox? How about you, Mr. Sullivan? Coffee? Tea?" Laurence poured a cup of tea and passed it to Maggie's outstretched hand.

Laurence exhibited the behavior of a consummate host. He provided not only warm hospitality on the first day, but also service. Maggie hadn't expected this. She assumed he would be more of a dictator. Instead, Harriet and James seemed very relaxed around Laurence. He didn't fit the stereotype she had conjured up of him. A gentleman and a rogue didn't seem to mesh together in the same body.

"I would like to suggest an itinerary for the next few days."

My goodness, he's even planned our activities.

"First, a tour of the grounds and manor after lunch. The drizzle might end soon, but we have umbrellas if necessary. I reserved the remaining time until dinner to settle in, unpack and relax. After dinner, we should get to know each other with conversation in the parlor. Is that all right?"

"Sounds fine to me," Max said. "We would all enjoy a tour of Stuart Hall."

"After breakfast tomorrow, I would like to show you the vast grounds, into the forest and down to a delightful stream. Harriet will pack us a lunch. Mr. Sullivan and Miss Cox, this tour will give you a better sense of the surrounding countryside and my neighbors' homes, should you wish to meet them. They might provide you with interesting stories. Miss Richards, I hope the surroundings will provide inspiration for your drawings. Oh, I forgot to mention we'll be on horseback."

Laurence seemed like a perfect gentleman; hospitable and accommodating. Had she been wrong? The question kept repeating in Maggie's mind. *Was any good going to come of this?* Then she remembered Ramsay. His coming home would be "the good."

"Do you all agree with my plans? I want you to be familiar with the grounds before venturing out on your own. Please also know that I've instructed Walter to have my horses and carriages at your disposal whenever you require them. I should qualify that statement, however. All the horses except Fireball. I'm conditioning him for the race next week in Rolen. Did I mention I'm escorting you to our local Highland Games? I know you'll all enjoy the day."

"Mr. MacLaren, we wouldn't miss it." Maggie sipped her tea. "It sounds like the highlight of the year. Mrs. Wellington raved about Harriet's winning marmalades and pies. Miss Cox and I would like to assist Harriet in the kitchen with her permission. As to your plans for today and tomorrow, they sound wonderful."

She placed her cup back in the saucer. "Now for myself, I have not ridden in many years, so please, a gentle horse. One that sort of walks along and isn't excited about a faster pace."

They all laughed.

"That includes me as well," Nellie said. "Anything more than a slow walk will get my heart racing."

"Don't worry. We have several horses that like to mosey along and another one that I think will be perfect for you, Mr. Sullivan. If you don't have suitable riding attire, I'm sure James can find something in the trunks upstairs. Now I don't want to rush you, but the drizzle has let up. We never know in Scotland when the next rainfall will start. I love our weather, just very unpredictable."

As they rose from the table, James offered umbrellas. Laurence extended Maggie his arm, and Nellie and Max followed.

The rose trellis provided a gateway into the formal garden. Maggie marveled at the care of this area.

"I admire your gardener's work. The flowers, trees, and manicured hedges create a relaxed place for a stroll. My shrubs never looked this healthy. I must learn his secret."

"His name is Leach. I'll introduce you."

They reached the end of the path when Maggie recognized Gwen's bench. The marble bench looked neglected. Moss grew on its legs, and tall grass tips tickled the seat's underside. Maggie thought it strange that the gardener would keep the rest of the grounds immaculate yet had allowed this bench to become so forlorn.

"Now, I'll take you to Harriet's vegetable garden. Harriet has been harvesting everything she can before the frost sets in."

"What a great idea to grow flowers between the vegetable rows. Not only visually appealing, but they must draw a plethora of pollinating bees each spring." Maggie bent to inhale the fragrant flowers.

"Harriet considered a few bee hives, but her day is already full," Laurence responded. "Now, for the stable."

Maggie draped her arm back in Laurence's while Nellie and Max lingered behind.

"There's Walter, the best stable hand I've ever known. His expertise with horses beats anyone within 100 miles, if not all of Scotland."

Walter hammered nails into a loose board. He saw them coming and stopped work to greet them.

Maggie supposed Walter was younger than Harriet and James. He'd rolled his shirt sleeves above the elbow and used a handkerchief tied around his neck to catch sweat drips.

"Walter keeps a well-organized stable. Everything hung in its place. Saddles, halters, blankets, and harnesses are all in rows."

Laurence seemed proud of Walter and his organized stable.

The threesome trailed Laurence to the paddock.

"Mr. Sullivan, the bay over there will be for you tomorrow. He's gentle, yet he can display a mischievous nature without warning. This beautiful equine specimen prancing our way is yours, Miss Cox. She suspects me of hiding a carrot or two whenever I'm here. She's one of the older mares, but still keeps up." Laurence placed a boot on the bottom rail and leaned his arms on the top railing. "Miss Richards, the roan in the corner, is for you. Her name is Peggy. She's been with us about four years and enjoys the forest rather than the paddock. My stepmother rode this horse, and it's the only one I own you have to prod to come back to the stables. With the others, once you turn their heads this way, it's homeward bound. Peggy is an explorer."

Peggy? The same horse my mother rode the day of her "accident"?

"Thank you, Mr. MacLaren. Your horses appear in wonderful shape. I wish I could say the same for myself." Maggie rubbed her backside. "I'm afraid I may not walk after the ride tomorrow. Are there plenty of cushions available?"

"It may be awhile before either of us can sit again." Nellie rubbed her rump in agreement.

"Let's return to the foyer, and I'll introduce you to my family." Laurence motioned toward the veranda.

They placed their umbrellas into the oak and wrought iron stand by the door and found the best vantage point to admire the portraits.

"This is my family." Laurence displayed pride in his heritage.

Maggie again questioned her judgment of this young man.

"The painting on the left is of my grandparents, three uncles, and mother with her dog, Smokey. My father, mother, me and my favorite dog Lancelot are in the middle painting. The painting on the right is of my father and his second wife. I attended university and could not be home for the sitting. I felt a bit snubbed, but I plan to have a portrait of myself painted soon. Perhaps I'll wait for the right woman who would like to share my life at the manor and marry me. That would complete the gallery."

Maggie noticed Laurence in her peripheral vision glance her way, but she remained focused on the portraits.

"I assume you've scoured all the right places for a lady of the manor." Nellie couldn't resist the opportunity to comment. "It will take someone who appreciates this beautiful home, grounds, and your love for horses. Maybe the right woman will be at the festival next week in Rolen. She might even win the horse race."

"That would be impossible, Miss Cox," Laurence responded in a monotone. "There is no horse faster than Fireball. He's unbeaten in every race we've entered. As for a lassie, it couldn't be someone from around here since there are few young lassies my age in Rolen, if you hadn't noticed. Most residents go to the bigger cities to find spouses. They come back to Rolen when they're ready for a family. So no, it would have to be someone from outside the area. Maybe even someone who is not from Scotland. I am open to all possibilities."

Maggie blushed as she caught Nellie's eye. He couldn't be referring to her. Or, if he were, she would have to dispel that thought at once.

Laurence led his guests to the library. The smell of pipe tobacco hung heavy in the air.

"Please, read any of my books. If you wish, take them to your room, or on the veranda."

The music room across from the library had a comfy, warm feeling. Late afternoon sunlight cast shadows from the weeping willow tree on the grand piano. A piece of opened sheet music rested on the piano and beckoned Maggie to play. Her mother had been an accomplished pianist, but Maggie played for her own pleasure.

Laurence rang his fingers along the length of the keyboard sending tingles up Maggie's arms.

"When we had concerts or parties, we'd open these pocket doors dividing this room from the parlor. Doing so enabled the guests to mingle easier. Both my mother and stepmother enjoyed entertaining. The parlor remains one of my favorite rooms, especially with the pocket doors closed. Come, I'll show you."

After they left the music room, Laurence closed the doors to the parlor. The overstuffed and straight-backed chairs, tables for refreshments, and a large fireplace with a hand-carved oak mantel made the parlor another delightful room. Maggie noticed the pear, peach, apple, and rose motifs repeated on the sides of the mantle.

"My mother entertained small and large groups in these rooms. She had a gift for organizing. If she didn't play the piano, she made sure music from a quartet or soloist filled the Hall. One of my favorite pastimes was to sit at her feet while she played and allow the music to carry me away to distant lands. Must be an adventurous spirit hidden within."

Laurence showed his admiration for his mother but did not mention Claire, the events she organized, or that she also played beautifully. If he felt snubbed when not included in the family portrait with her mother, Maggie now felt snubbed that Claire received no recognition.

Opposite the parlor, they entered the dining room, with a table large enough to seat twenty. Maggie admired the crystal chandelier which hung above the table. French doors opened to the patio, where they had enjoyed their lunch. Again, everywhere were images of pears, peaches, and apples. A beautiful bouquet of roses sat on a corner table, and a silver coffee service graced the sideboard. A full-length mirror above the sideboard reflected crystal candlesticks that sat in front of it. Maggie glimpsed Harriet as a door swung open at the back of the dining room.

Max sniffed. "Something smells delicious. My olfactory senses are soaring with pleasure. May we watch the master chef at work?"

"Of course," Laurence replied, and held the door as they entered the kitchen. Maggie smiled as Max scooted close to Harriet.

"The smells in this kitchen are incredible. My taste buds are doing flip-flops in anticipation." Max licked his lips.

Maggie chuckled. She knew how much he loved good food.

"Thank you for the compliment. I hope you enjoy our native dishes as much as I enjoy preparing them." Harriet smiled, pleased with the appreciation.

"Now, Mr. Sullivan, if you can put your appetite on hold for a few more minutes, I'd like to move upstairs to your rooms."

Laurence led them through the foyer and ascended the grand staircase.

"The sitting room is in the back corner — a wonderful place to relax. Mr. Sullivan, Miss Cox, this may be an excellent room to write. The room at the top of the stairs is my father's. I placed the cord across the double door as I wanted his room left untouched for his return. I forbid even the servants to go in. Nothing is to be disturbed. The room next to my father's, on the right, will be yours, Miss Richards. And the room next to hers is yours, Miss Cox. Mr. Sullivan, the last room on that side will be your room. My room is at the far end of the North hallway."

Maggie studied the rope over Ramsay's door and visualized ways to bypass the obstacle.

"Each room has a pocket door to the adjacent room," Laurence instructed. "The keys are in the locks if you wish to open them. If there is nothing else, I'll excuse myself and allow you time to unpack and relax. Harriet will serve dinner in two hours. I expect a delightful evening getting better acquainted."

Maggie waited to speak until Laurence reached the bottom of the staircase.

"Once you're settled and changed for dinner, let's meet in the sitting room." Nellie and Max nodded approval, then entered their separate chambers.

Chapter 25

Maggie unpacked and changed clothes in record time. She stared at the pocket door between her and Ramsay's rooms. Maggie half expected to walk over, turn the knob, and magically Ramsay's room would appear. Instead, she made her way in slow steps to the obstacle that kept her from more of the truth. Maggie placed her hand on the knob. She held a deep breath, then twisted her wrist to open the door. There was no movement. Locked. *Max would have some ideas. He always does.*

The thought bolstered Maggie's confidence that she would find Gwen's journal once they entered Ramsay's room. Perhaps Claire kept a journal as well. She muttered, "If I were Ramsay, where would I keep both my wives' journals?"

Time to consult Nellie. The key to Nellie's adjoining room rested in the lock. She knocked, waited for Nellie's response, then turned the key and slid the door aside.

"Hi, Nellie. I want to experiment." Maggie turned around and grabbed the door handle.

She closed the pocket door and saw there was no key.

"Did you remove the key, Nellie? Maybe it fell out when I pushed it open."

"No. I noticed a key in the door between my room and Max's, but none for yours. So I assumed there was a single key that would open the door from either side of the bedrooms. Let me knock on Max's room."

Max answered, and Nellie unlocked his door and shoved it into the wall.

Maggie explained her dilemma, and they all agreed they should try something different.

"Here, Max. You take Nellie's key and try to lock and unlock your door." Maggie held her breath.

Max closed his room's pocket door. Maggie pressed her ear on the wood and listened for him to insert the key. The key locked and unlocked the door. Her face beamed with delight when he pushed the door open.

"Now, Nellie, let's use my key to do the same thing between our rooms." Maggie locked Nellie's door using her key, then unlocked and opened the door to her room.

"The moment of truth has arrived, my friends." Maggie held the key to Nellie's room high in the air. "If my key opens the door to Nellie's room, just as Max's key opened the one to Nellie's, shouldn't my key also open Ramsay's?"

"You may have something there." Nellie's face scrunched with her detective, all-knowing expression.

They tiptoed to Ramsay's door. Maggie inserted the key while Nellie crossed her fingers. She turned the key to the right and then to the left. Nothing happened. She tried one more time and still nothing.

Maggie plopped into a nearby chair. "I guess my hopes were too high. Now what?"

Max rubbed his chin. "Laurence must have either changed this lock or has it jammed on the other side. It doesn't work the same as ours. Let me think this through, Maggie."

"Thanks, Max. I knew if anyone could solve this, it would be you. But wait. Let's try one more door."

Maggie led the way to the sitting room on the opposite side of Ramsay's bedroom. Inserting the key in the door that led to Ramsay's room, Maggie eyed her two friends. She pivoted the key in both directions. Nothing. She tried one more time, but still nothing. These doors remained locked as well.

"Here, Maggie, allow me to investigate." Max removed the key and knelt to peek through the keyhole. No light shone from the other side.

"Something's wedged in the lock. But don't worry. I'll figure something out, and perhaps tomorrow we'll be able to explore Ramsay's room." He paused, then smiled. "Just a minute." Max snapped his fingers. "Remember Ernest's story about going into Ramsay's room on a pretense to retrieve some loaned books? Remember he didn't use a key. He just removed the rope over the doors in the hallway, turned the doorknob, and walked right in. What do you think, ladies?"

"Max, you're wonderful." Maggie's heart pounded in anticipation. "Shall we try now?"

"Just me, Maggie. You two stay here. I'll be right back."

Maggie and Nellie gazed out the window. A full view of the paddock lay below. Laurence stood in the stable yard brushing Fireball. A perfect uninterrupted opportunity for Max. Laurence glanced up and waved to the ladies.

"Wave back, dear, and smile." Maggie elbowed Nellie. "No hint on our faces that something sneaky's going on." Maggie grinned at Laurence and responded with a wave.

"I can't stand this waiting for Max." Nellie explored the bookshelves while Maggie paced. It seemed like an eternity.

When Max reentered the room, disappointment covered his face.

"The door's locked." Max flopped into a leather chair. "I'm wondering if Laurence suspected someone had been in the room. Perhaps the rope on the door wasn't quite right, or he went in and found the books by the bedside no longer numbered three. Laurence must be a real detail man, and any little change set off alarms. Of course, this is just conjecture, but I bet he felt he needed more precautions. It would be better to go into Ramsay's room from your side, Maggie. I'll come up with something by tomorrow."

"Thanks for trying, Max. I'm sure your genius brain will create a solution."

The three friends found the sitting room charming. Perfect for lazy afternoons to read or write.

"This will be my hide-a-way for journal entries. I can hear if anyone ascends the stairs should I need to conceal my writing." Nellie rose. "Harriet must have almost finished dinner. I'll go down and offer my help. It's time to start relationship building."

"I'll walk down with you. I'd like to explore the library," Max said. "Seems like Ramsay should have some reference books there for his practice. What about you, Maggie?"

"I'd like to sit and think for a while."

Maggie perched herself in a chair close to the window and watched Laurence as he groomed Fireball. What a complicated and contradictory man.

✳✳✳

An excellent dinner, Harriet did indeed create a feast for royalty. The appetizer; a sampler of fresh vegetables, haggis, and slices of assorted bread. The first course was cock-a-leekie soup composed of fowl, leeks, and prunes. The strange combination of ingredients surprised Maggie, but she enjoyed sampling new dishes. A fresh garden salad followed, then the main course of tatties and Angus beef. A platter of fresh fruit, cheese, and crackers comprised the dessert. The conversation remained light-hearted and jovial as Max shared his fishing trip with Ernest.

"Is there any good fishing around Stuart Hall?" Max inquired.

"Believe it or not, I've never been fishing. I don't even own a fishing pole. There are several excellent streams nearby, but you should ask James whether there are fish for catching." Laurence pushed his chair away from the table.

After dinner, they retired to the parlor for a glass of wine and conversation.

"Since we're going to be together for some time, I would deem it an honor if you would call me Laurence instead of Mr. Mac-Laren. When I'm called Mr. MacLaren, I feel you're referring to my father instead of me. So with your permission, I would like to call you by your first names, Margaret, Nellie, and Max."

"I use my formal name, Margaret, for professional reasons. My friends call me Maggie."

"Then Maggie it is."

"Laurence, you mentioned your father this afternoon and again tonight," Nellie said. "We'd be interested to know when we'll be able to meet him? Your father's recollection of his brothers-in-law and what he remembers about the residents who lived in the area would be of great interest."

"I'm sorry, Nellie. My father doesn't live here. I have been distraught since he left. We were very close and confided in each other about everything. If we had a problem, we were always there for each other. He was, is a kind man who would do anything for anyone. All I can tell you is that following my stepmother's death, he became very depressed. He lost his appetite even though Harriet would cook his favorite dishes. We became concerned about his health and suggested he see our family doctor. He no longer confided in me and seemed to not care about anything."

Laurence slid one hand into a side jacket pocket; his other elbow rested on the mantel ledge.

"When we gathered for dinner, he often arrived with dirty clothes, face, and hands. Almost like he had dug in the dirt like a dog. His nails became dirty and unkept, cracked and sometimes his fingers bled. I could tell he needed professional care and suggested we contact the Edinburgh Lunatic Asylum. He seemed to not care about anything. It concerned me that, sometimes, he didn't even remember his name."

Maggie noticed his furrowed brow. He rubbed his hands together, then continued.

"I would take him to the foyer to study the portraits. His face would brighten as he returned to his usual engaged self. One morning he came downstairs with his chackie and heavy overcoat. I asked him what this meant. He said he needed to get away from everything that reminded him of his wife. He didn't know where he would settle, but promised to send a card.

"That was so many months ago that I've lost track." Laurence added more wine to Max's glass. "We've had no word from him. I went to Edinburgh a couple of months after he left and checked at the hospital, but they did not know him. All the letters I sent to friends and relatives came back without any word as to his whereabouts. I've considered contacting Scotland Yard, but I doubt they would act on conjecture. We have such little information."

"I'm so sorry to hear your sad tale," Maggie's forehead creased. "It must be hard losing your stepmother and then your father's disappearance. I have lost both my parents and feel such a void. When I revisit our family vacation spots, memories overwhelm me. Emotions rise to the surface at the most inopportune time."

"With your permission, we could talk with residents in this area and at the Highland Games, perhaps learn something of your father," Max suggested.

"Thank you for the offer, but I have talked with anybody I felt might have some knowledge of my father's whereabouts. It always led to a dead end." Laurence slumped into a chair close to Maggie. "Now, how about changing this subject? Would each of you tell me something about yourselves? Max, why don't you begin?"

Maggie knew they needed to be careful when they shared their lives. They would mix some fabrication in with the truth to keep Laurence from the real reason for their trip to Scotland. Laurence seemed interested in learning about his guests.

"I see the sun has gone to bed, and if you will excuse me, so must I." Maggie rose and placed her wine glass on a tray. "It has been a delightful day, but this body must rest before our morning ride."

Maggie, Nellie, and Max picked up riding pants, jackets, and even boots from a pile James laid in the parlor. Then, they said their good nights, and headed upstairs with riding gear in hand.

"Goodnight to all of you," Laurence said. "I expect a hearty breakfast and an invigorating ride. May you all sleep well."

Chapter 26

A stream of warm sunlight danced on Maggie's closed eyelids. Cozy under her eiderdown comforter, she turned her back to the bright light when a rap on her pocket door pulled her from the world of sleep into the reality of Stuart Hall.

"Are you awake, Maggie? May I come in?" Nellie's muffled voice sounded chipper.

"Certainly." The click of a key announced her friend's entrance.

"Maggie, my dear, if you slept as well as I did, you've got energy galore this morning." Nellie thrust the window curtains to one side. Light filled the bedroom. *No more sleeping.*

"I can't remember when I've eaten such a satisfying dinner as last night. I slept like a little child without a care in the world." Nellie gathered Maggie's riding clothes and laid them on a chair close to the bed. "When I woke, however, I realized I was not in Chicago but Scotland. Laurence came to my mind. I don't know about you, but I like Laurence. He seems like a gentleman and is conscientious about our every need. Maybe we're wrong, and it was an accident after all."

"I know what you mean, Nellie." Maggie flung her feet over the edge of the bed and nestled them into her slippers. She stretched her arms toward the ceiling and shuffled her way to the washstand. "The whole time we visited last night, I felt sorry for this man. He doesn't seem to have a friend in the world, and yet, even though isolated by choice, he has an engaging personality. I, too, find myself drawn to him."

She splashed the tepid water on her face, blotted the moisture with a towel, and examined her image in the mirror. "Look at these bags under my eyes. Maybe it wasn't as good a sleep as I thought."

Maggie hung the damp towel on the side rod of the washstand. "I think they call it magnetism. Whatever it is, I'm trying hard to separate my feelings from the facts. I don't want to be fooled."

"I'll check on Max while you dress. Be back in a minute." Nellie strode back through her room to Max's bedroom door.

❋❋❋

Maggie dressed as she listened to Nellie trying to rouse Max. The riding clothes James had given her were a perfect fit. She admired herself in the mirror. Even her ample backside filled the riding skirt. *No more sweets for a while.*

Maggie picked up her hairbrush and returned to the mirror. Her hair responded to each stroke; a clip here, a hair comb there, and her tresses were under control for the day. She stepped back for a full view and noticed Max's reflection.

He stood motionless, with an approving grin on his face. Maggie's heart skipped as if she had seen him for the first time. Not as a stranger, but more than that. Her cheeks reddened. Time to compose herself.

"Good morning, Max. Whatever have you got there?"

"Maggie, Max has something to show us." Nellie closed the door behind her.

"Good morning, Maggie. You look lovely today." His eyes fixed on hers as the words flowed from his mouth.

"Thank you." Warmth ran down her body. "I can't believe how well all our riding habits fit. It's as if we went to the store and picked them out ourselves. But what is that you're holding?"

Max laid his invention on a table. "I've fabricated a device that might open Ramsay's bedroom door. Last night, after you two went to bed, I snuck out and found a piece of wire by the stable. It slipped up my coat sleeve with ease, then I tiptoed back upstairs. I've formed one end of this wire into a kind of plunger. On the other end, I bent it over itself to create a strong shaft for pushing strength. Are you girls ready?"

Maggie grabbed Nellie's hand and pulled her across the room.

"Wait, Max. Let me stand by the hall door and listen for Laurence." Nellie posted herself as a sentry.

Max peeked into the keyhole. "I see a faint glimmer of sunlight. We may be in luck today. Yet something's blocking the opening."

Maggie's forehead scrunched. She held her breath as Max inserted the wire.

"There's resistance here. I'll apply more force." The wire disappeared farther into the keyhole, then stopped. Max applied more pressure toward Ramsay's room. Maggie saw the disappointment in his face.

"Please keep trying, Max." Moisture covered her palms.

He exerted more force.

"There was a slight give that time. I'll push harder. I feel sure we're making headway." His face wrinkled with concentration as he shoved on the wire. His hand hit the door as the object in the keyhole gave way.

"It worked." Surprise filled his voice. "The wire moved through the opening."

Maggie dashed for her key as Nellie raised her arms and crossed her fingers. With her key in Max's hand, Maggie wrapped her arms around herself and closed her eyes. She heard the scrap of metal upon metal as Max inserted Maggie's key into the lock.

Her attention was diverted as Nellie frantically waved her arms. "Someone's coming up the stairs." Like a little boy caught with his hand in the cookie jar, Max leaped to his feet and shoved the key into his pocket. Maggie rushed to Nellie and clutched her hands.

"Shh. The person's walking to your room, Max," whispered Maggie, her ear pressed tight to the door. She heard two light knocks.

"Coming this way now." Maggie pressed a finger over her lips.

Two more knocks down the hall. Then the footsteps stopped outside Maggie's room. Two raps.

"Yes?"

"Good morning, Maggie. It's Laurence. I wanted to let you know Harriet has breakfast ready. There were no answers when I knocked on Max's and Nellie's doors. I trust you slept well."

"Thank you, Laurence. Max and Nellie are here with me. We're admiring how well our riding clothes fit. We'll be down in a few minutes."

They held their breaths until Laurence's footsteps reached the bottom of the staircase, then sighed with relief.

"We better wait for another time," Maggie said. "I know it'll be hard, but I don't want Laurence wondering why we're so slow to breakfast."

Max returned the key to Maggie and hid his wire opener in the bookshelf.

A hearty Scottish breakfast awaited. Everything looked and smelled delicious. A bowl of porridge topped with golden raisins and honey warmed Maggie's stomach. Then she partitioned her plate to make room for black pudding, a poached egg, a sausage patty she shared with Nellie, and toast with Harriet's delicious marmalade. Maggie hoped the horse ride would jostle off the added pounds. The conversation centered on who would stay on their horse the longest and who would not be able to walk after the ride. Light-hearted and cheerful, Maggie noticed Laurence joined with the gaiety.

"We're greeted with blue skies and a warm sun," Laurence said, as they journeyed to the paddock. "It may not last. Our weather is so unpredictable this time of year. We try to take advantage of any nice day we can get."

"I must compliment James regarding our riding habits. They seem to fit each of us like they were our own. I'm amazed you had them available." Maggie pulled her coat across her chest.

"I must take credit for that, Maggie. I sized the three of you up when you first arrived. Max looked to be my father's size, Nellie, my mother's, and your habit was my mother-in-law's."

Maggie stopped short as her knees wobbled. Max grabbed her arm.

"Are you all right?" Laurence hurried to her side. "It looked like you were going to faint."

"Yes, I'm fine. A short, dizzy spell. I may have overeaten and need to let my belt out a notch." Maggie loosened her belt and inhaled the morning air. "That's better." She leaned close to Max. "Thank you for staying close by me."

The horses were saddled, bridled, and tethered to a paddock rail. Walter held a carrot for each horse. Some pieces fell to the ground as they munched the orange treat.

A conversation with Peggy would be necessary before Maggie mounted. She whispered in Peggy's ear, "Now, Peggy dear, I wish you could talk. I need to know what happened to my mother. Do you think you could learn to speak my language before I leave? That would be so kind of you."

Peggy whinnied and jostled her head as if to respond in the affirmative. Maggie hugged Peggy.

Laurence asked, "What did you say to her?"

"Oh, nothing much. I asked if she would be ever so gentle as to not make a fool out of this city girl who has forgotten so much about riding a horse."

Laughter filled the air while Walter helped Maggie into the saddle.

Laurence came alongside Maggie. Max and Nellie followed. The horses walked toward the front of the Hall, which unsettled Maggie. She desired to go straight into the forest and see the place of the accident.

"I would like to show Max and Nellie the easiest way to reach my neighbors should they wish to interview them. And Maggie, I remembered an ideal setting for your drawings. An old, dilapidated building stands on the edge of the property, and may have been used as a guest house. It has a sense of mystery. I've asked Walter and James if they knew the building's history, but they only remember it as always in a state of disrepair. The ivy vines have covered most of the structure. Still, it would make a great subject for drawing or painting. Perhaps Nellie could write a story about the old place."

They rode on until they reached a clearing. Laurence pointed to a farmhouse in the distance and gave Max the historical details and names of the present residents. From there, they rode west and came to the decaying building; what Laurence called the old ruins. The roof had disappeared, three partial sides remained, and ivy had taken over what was still standing. Indeed, a wonderful setting for artistic inspiration.

Nellie amazed Maggie as she fabricated a story on the spot. "I see Gwen's three brothers. Before us, their fort. Fallen branches became swords when they practiced defense techniques on a marauding gang of looters. Imaginary, of course. No one ever sustained an injury as they drove the looters off. Perhaps magical animals were living in the forest who came to their aid should the need arise."

"Those are the makings of a great children's story, Nellie. You must write your thoughts down when we return." Laurence smiled.

They left the ruins behind and rode southward to another clearing. The manor in the distance appeared larger than Stuart Hall. Still not in the direction Maggie hoped for.

"Such wonderful subject matter. I'll have to remember this place for a future drawing." Maggie sat tall in her saddle for a better look.

"I now challenge all of you to a race. Fireball needs a good workout. Are you ready?"

"No!" the women yelled in unison.

"Where are we headed, and what happens if we can't keep up? You will come back to get us, yes?" Maggie's pulse raced.

"Maggie, you stay close to your old friend Nellie. If we become separated from these strapping lads, we'll return to the old ruins and wait for our valiant knights to rescue us." Nellie winked.

Now accustomed to the saddle, Maggie preferred the gentleness of meandering to a full-out gallop. Peggy's quiet demeanor calmed any apprehension she once entertained. No wonder her mother had a simpatico relationship with this magnificent animal.

"I'm eager and ready." Max jostled in the saddle.

"Nellie and I will follow you two. At least, as best we can," Maggie assured the men.

Laurence gave Fireball a nudge with his boots, then a click in his ear. Fireball broke away from the group like an entire hornet's nest had stung him. Max prodded his horse to catch Fireball, and the race was on. Both riders and horses were out of sight in an instant, throwing dirt clods into the air. Maggie didn't mind being left behind. She enjoyed a leisurely ride with her good friend as they followed the trail. While they rode, they discussed a second attempt at the bedroom door.

"Maggie, I suggest you keep Laurence busy outside, maybe in the paddock where I can keep a watch on him from the window. Max knows where your key is and can try again."

"Not on your life. I want to be there. We need to wait for a more suitable time."

Distracted by the beauty of the woods, they came upon Max and Laurence unawares. The men rested by a babbling brook while their horses drank the refreshing water.

"What a delightful place." Maggie soaked in the beauty of the surrounding woods. "Where does this stream start and end? Max, maybe you could fish here."

"This stream begins high in the mountains. I've followed it as best I could, but the vegetation grows so thick just a short distance north, I couldn't continue," Laurence said. "I'm not sure which loch it joins or where, but I have a hunch it might be Loch Morlich, just east of Rolen. As for fishing, well, Max, you can try. I believe there may be some gear at the Hall. You'll have to ask James. How about you, Maggie? Would this be another pastoral setting for a painting?"

Maggie cocked her head and squeezed her brows together. "Let me think. Between this setting and the old ruins, I'm not sure which one should be first."

Laurence seemed pleased, then excused himself. He fetched the lunch from Peggy's satchel Harriet had prepared. A plaid cloth spread on the ground created their meal table.

"This reminds me of my home on Eden Lake." Max scanned the wooded area. "On my excursions around the lake and in the surrounding forest, I've spotted small herds of elk and deer. You should come to visit me sometime, Laurence."

Come to visit me sometime? What? Max, are you crazy? Maggie cast Max an icy stare. *How could he even think about inviting Laurence as a house guest? He's going to jail.*

Maggie studied Laurence. He seemed at ease with the threesome. Here they came again, those recurring thoughts she could be wrong and this entire trip was a waste of time and expense. Laurence pivoted her way and caught her eye. He smiled.

Maggie gritted her teeth, then stuffed her hands in her pockets with clenched her fists. She forced her mind off him and onto something else to maintain her equilibrium.

"Nellie, we must remember this spot for another day trip. What do you think?"

"It's embedded in my memory already."

Chapter 27

Dark clouds in a threatening sky signaled it was time to return to Stuart Hall. Maggie hoped Laurence agreed.

"My new friends, it appears to be time to load up and head back to Stuart." Laurence knelt to gather the leftovers. "Before we leave, I have a thought, and I'd like to hear your comments. How about we have a grand party like my mother hosted? I will find a local music group, and you may invite your friends from Rolen. Harriet loves to create fancy hors d'oeuvres and prepare special meals. James relishes a large group at the Hall. Filled with guests, music, and dancing, he feels Stuart come alive. Sweet James." Laurence rolled the silverware inside the serviettes.

"Even in the short time you've been here, I've felt some life and vitality return to Stuart Hall's gloomy rooms. What if we plan the gathering for the day after the Rolen games? A kind of closure and celebration for the townsfolk. What do you think?"

"That would be wonderful, Laurence." Maggie's excitement filled her entire body. "I'm sure our new friends would love another social. Many of them commented on how much they missed the grand parties."

Maggie thought about Mary Beth. Others also expressed concern regarding their feelings for Laurence. They feared their negativity toward him might rise to the surface and reinforce an already daunting barrier between them.

"If you'd provide James a list of names, he'll have the invitations in town by tomorrow afternoon. Would that be convenient?"

Maggie noticed Nellie's excitement join hers. Being raised in an orphanage and then Nellie's hard life on the streets of Chicago never included a fancy ball with all the flourishes.

The orphanage where Nellie was raised and then her hard life on the streets of Chicago, never included a fancy ball with all the flourishes.

"I'll make a list the moment we return, and with Maggie's help, we'll have it ready by dinnertime," Nellie said. "This is very thoughtful. I can already imagine women in beautiful dresses and men in their best suits. I can't wait."

A frown and furrowed brow covered Maggie's face. "I just realized neither Nellie nor I have an evening gown. We'll look out of place with our traveling clothes."

"Don't worry," Laurence touched her arm. "I'm sure James can find some suitable evening attire."

Maggie bristled at the touch of his hand. Taking his arm while they toured Stuart Hall yesterday was polite. But this was an unwanted advance. She glared at Laurence, but he had returned to packing lunch things and hadn't noticed.

With the picnic supplies repacked, they mounted their horses and headed back to the Hall. Laurence led them into the beautiful, quiet woods. Squirrels ran up the tree trunks. Birds appeared everywhere, and their delightful songs pulled Maggie back to her childhood.

"You look far away, Maggie." Laurence steered Fireball closer to Peggy.

"I'm remembering afternoons my father would take me to a local park. He'd bundle me up and grab some bread crumbs for the mallards. Our favorite bench was under an immense oak tree. We listened to the enchanting songs of robins, bluebirds, and sparrows. I could have stayed there all day and listened to the bird's serenade."

As they rounded another bend, Stuart Hall came into view. Peggy quickened her pace. "Must be eager to get under cover." Laurence clicked to Fireball. "Horses seem to know when the weather changes. They like to keep dry, like us."

"Peggy's been so gentle, I'd like to find a treat for her. A thank her for not bucking me off. Hopefully, Harriet will have a surplus apple or two. I'll be right back." Maggie dismounted.

"If you'll excuse me," Nellie said as her foot touched the ground. "I'm going to change and write about my impressions of the vistas around Stuart Hall. I should have that guest list before dinner, Laurence."

Max and Laurence removed the saddles and harnesses, then brushed down their mounts.

Maggie returned with a basket that held four apples, just enough, one for each horse.

"Laurence, I've never given a horse an apple. Those big teeth frighten me. Would you mind doing it?"

"Here, let me show you how. Hold your hand flat, fingers bent slightly backward, rest the apple in your palm and extend your arm." Laurence demonstrated.

Maggie's hand shook. Laurence placed his hand under hers for added support. Together, they stretched their arms to reach Peggy, who eagerly accepted the apple and munched away. Maggie's eyes met Laurence's. She had that tingling, butterflies inside sensation again.

"There, that wasn't so bad." Laurence's voice calmed and comforted her.

"No, it wasn't bad with you helping me."

"Now, let's see if you can do it alone."

Max's mount waited beside Peggy. His nostrils sniffed out the apple and grabbed it from the basket before Maggie could cradle it in her hand.

Maggie walked to where Max curried Nellie's horse. She placed another apple in her palm and stretched out her arm. Standing close to Max, she noticed a disturbing look in his eye. Maggie hadn't seen this gaze before. After the mirror encounter this morning, she wondered if Max was jealous. She felt their relationship was as friends and nothing more.

"Hey, what about Fireball?" Laurence interrupted.

"Fireball scares me. He seems to prefer you to all others. I'm reluctant to have my hand so close to his mouth. Would you mind?" Maggie handed an apple to Laurence, her eyes begging, "Please, sir, I don't want to do this."

"Here, we'll do it together. First, pat Fireball and talk to him in a soothing voice."

Maggie hesitated. Laurence put his arm around her waist and guided her toward Fireball. She had felt uncomfortable with his hand on hers feeding Peggy, and again with his touch at the picnic. But now, with his arm around her waist, she quivered from head to toe, and knew she should pull away, saying, *"Thank you very much, but I think I'll forgo this one,"* to Laurence, yet something inside her allowed him to take control. The gap closed to the black stallion.

"If you'll excuse me, I'll go change now." Max dropped the curry brush on a bench. Maggie's heart had saddened at the abruptness of Max's departure. She didn't want to be left alone with Laurence. Her eyes followed him as he hurried to the Hall, head lowered.

"There, there, boy, I want to introduce you to Maggie." Fireball whinnied, tossed his head from side to side, and pawed the ground.

"She finds you overpowering. With your permission, she would like to stroke your neck." Laurence's voice had a calming effect on his horse.

Maggie mimicked Laurence as her hand reached for the big horse's neck. A whiff of the sweet apple was all it took. Fireball's nostrils twitched as he followed the aroma to the apple on her flattened, outstretched hand. Fireball enveloped the tasty reward with his lips and crunched down, breaking the fruit into pieces, leaving traces of saliva on her fingers.

"What a handsome horse you are." Maggie patted his neck with her dry hand. Fireball shook his head in agreement, whinnied, and ran into the paddock to join the other horses.

"Thank you for your help." Maggie wiped her hand on a cloth Laurence offered. "As a child, I didn't have many opportunities to ride horses. My family lived in the city. I was about fourteen years old when I had some lessons. At the end of the session, we practiced jumping over logs which, was great fun. The final ride of the session was my favorite. I inquired about riding bareback. By this time, the instructor felt confident in my abilities. With a boost up, I mounted my favorite buckskin and trotted off into the woods."

Maggie realized Laurence still had his arm around her waist. Embarrassed she hadn't rectified the situation, she removed his arm with her hand and took a few steps away from him.

"When we reached a meadow, the horse stopped. I stretched out on the horse's back, hugging his neck, with my legs stretched over his rump. It was such a delightful moment, I believe I could have stayed in that position all afternoon. My mind wandered then, imagining this horse belonged to me. Since then, I haven't ridden."

Laurence offered her his arm, and together they proceeded toward the patio.

"Maybe before your time here ends, you'll feel confident enough to take Peggy for a ride bareback and off toward a beautiful meadow just south of here. I always believe it's a good idea to regain some of our childhood, which we tend to lose as we get older. If you like, I'll take you there after our evening meal. It might be a grand end to a perfect day."

"While that sounds wonderful, this body of mine may not appreciate more riding this evening. I already sense some sore and stiff muscles. Would you be agreeable to saving that offer until morning? That is, if I can still walk."

"Consider it saved until tomorrow. When you go by the kitchen, ask Harriet if she has anything for sore muscles. Seems like she has a remedy for every ailment."

Laurence held the door for Maggie to enter the Hall.

"I'll see you at dinner. I need to speak with Walter."

Maggie trudged toward the kitchen, rubbing her derriere.

"I would say, have a seat, lassie, but that may be the last thing you need from the way you're walking. Let me get you some liniment. I make it myself and it sure relaxes sore muscles." Harriet disappeared into the pantry and came back with a large jar.

"Here you are, lassie. Take this to your room and rub some on all those sore spots." Harriet laughed. "Share that salve with your two friends. Remember that nursery rhyme, 'There was a crooked man who had a crooked house'? Well, their strides weren't bad, but I bet in the morning they'll be telling a different tale."

"Thank you so much, Harriet." Maggie handed Harriet the empty apple basket. "If you don't mind, I'll come down later and help you with dinner."

"No need. Miss Cox already offered, and she looked in a mite better condition than you. You just rub that on and rest a bit. Try not to lie down too long. Keep those muscles in motion so they don't tighten up even more."

Maggie ascended the stairs at her usual pace for the first few steps. Then things slowed down as her muscles cried for rest. She counted the stairs as she forced her legs to climb each one. When she reached the top, she let out a faint moan, placed her hands on her hips, and arched backward to complete one long stretch.

She peered through her opened door. The sight of her bed spurred her on the last few feet. Once inside, she noticed the door between her and Nellie's room was ajar. Then, she remembered their quest from earlier this morning awaited.

Maggie scanned her room for any signs of Nellie or Max.

"Nellie, are you there?" Maggie whispered.

"Yes, Maggie. Max and I changed, and we've been waiting for you. I even had time to make a guest list. I placed it on the small table by your bed. Add anyone I may have missed. Where have you been?"

"Learning how to feed apples to horses, getting a jar of liniment from Harriet, and climbing what seemed to be Mt. Hood back in Oregon. I have a potential date with Laurence for a bareback ride in the morning if I can walk. Harriet said this ointment would help sore muscles. I'm counting on it. How about you two? Are you able to get around?"

Max joined Nellie in Maggie's room. He retrieved his door-opening tool from the bookshelf.

"I'm doing fine, Maggie," he said, "but I may sing a different tune in the morning. It might be a good idea for all of us to use some of that salve before bed. However, right now, I want to know if your key will open Ramsay's door. I saw Laurence still outside by the stable, so this might be an excellent opportunity."

Max excelled in efficiency: make good use of your time; never lose a moment; time is precious and will never come again. These were some of Max's axioms.

As he slipped the wire into the keyhole one more time, Maggie crossed her fingers. His hand glided toward the door and touched the cold metal. He pulled the wire out and glanced at Maggie.

"It's clear now. Do you have your key?"

She handed him her key, and Max inserted it in the keyhole. He turned it to the right and then the left. All three heard a click. Max grabbed the door handle, shot Maggie and Nellie a reassuring glance, then turned the knob. A door emitted a soft creaking sound as Max widened the gap.

Time seemed to stop in that instant. Max opened the door farther, allowing the light from Maggie's room to seep into Ramsay's. He placed his foot over the threshold while Maggie grabbed Nellie's hand. As they tiptoed farther into the room, Maggie heard footsteps coming up the stairs. They backed out, and Max closed the door after them. He handed the key to Maggie and pranced to his room. Nellie opened Maggie's door to the hallway. Maggie froze.

"I'll see you later, Maggie." Nellie stopped in the hall. "I promised Harriet I'd help her with dinner. After you've changed, why not join us in the kitchen?" Nellie closed the door, turned, and bumped into Laurence.

"Oh, please excuse me. I must look where I'm going more often."

"It could happen to anyone, Nellie." Laurence said. "You seem to be doing well after the ride. I heard you say you were going to help Harriet. She'll love some company, but don't be surprised if she won't let you help. She takes pride in doing all the preparation and cooking herself."

Laurence continued toward his room, then paused, leaned over the railing, and called to Nellie.

"Have you seen Max? I spoke with James about the fishing equipment. He's sure he could find some."

"I imagine he's still in his room. He mentioned he would like to lie down for a bit."

Once Maggie heard Laurence's door close, she breathed easier. The key lay in her hand. She weighed the pros and cons of going in alone or waiting for her friends, then decided that with Laurence close by, he may hear her. One obstacle had been conquered: entrance into Ramsay's room. Her mother had told her that patience was a virtue. She needed all the patience she could muster to wait a bit longer.

Chapter 28

Nellie bounded into the kitchen. "Harriet, here I am, cleaned, changed and eager to learn the secrets of your exquisite dishes. Well, at least, some pleasant conversation while I watch a master at work."

"My, lassie, you don't look the worse for wear. Wonder though if your gait will be as smooth in the morning." Harriet placed her wooden spoon on the counter. "I'm putting the finishing touches on this evening's meal. How about a hot cup of tea? I would love to get off my feet for a bit. Old age sure creeps up on a body."

As the teakettle boiled, Nellie found cups and saucers. Harriet spooned tea leaves into a tea caddy, placed it in the pot and poured hot water over it. The two ladies made themselves comfy at the small wooden table.

"Harriet, could you share your experiences with the Cheshires and MacLarens?"

"Let's see now. I'll have to think for a minute. So many years have gone by." Harriet scratched her head.

"I came to Stuart Hall when Gwen was a mere teen. I hardly knew the boys. You probably know they left home, and poor Mrs. Cheshire waited for some word. The strain showed. Thankfully, Gwen lit up the Hall, easing the months that passed into years for the Mrs.. More sadness came with Mr. Cheshire's death. Then Gwen married, and oh, Mrs. Cheshire, why her happiness returned. She loved Gwen's husband, Ramsay, as no other mother-in-law could and thrilled when baby Laurence came along. Laughter, music and grand parties returned to the Hall."

Harriet poured the Scottish tea into their cups and slid Nellie's across the table.

"I noticed melancholy times returning when I brought tea to Mrs. Cheshire. She sat in her favorite chair in the music room for hours each day. Just stared out the window. I know she expected one or more of her sons to come through the front door.

"With her passing came a quietness again, but Gwen wouldn't allow gloominess. She planned wonderful evening socials for all the neighbors and a few residents from Rolen."

"Did Mr. MacLaren join Gwen's enthusiasm for the socials?" Nellie asked.

"Oh my, yes. Such a supportive gentleman. He wanted to fit right in to Gwen's group of friends. A real keeper, as my mum used to say. Then a wee bawbee came along. Gwen doted on master Laurence. Anyone could see that the lad was the apple of his parents' eyes. They made sure that Laurence didn't lack for anything." Harriet sipped her tea and closed her eyes for a moment.

"I remember a time when the whole Hall was aflutter. An opportunity came for young Laurence to publish a story. His parents spared no expense for tutors and would have sent him off to a private boarding school if Laurence was agreeable. But in the end, his work was rejected for publication and the young lad became depressed and withdrawn. The Mr. and Mrs. did everything they could. About a year went by before he returned to his normal self. That was a relief to everyone."

Nellie wanted to get to the crux of the matter. This might be her prime opportunity with Harriet and she didn't want to waste it.

"I understand Laurence's stepmother died on a horse ride. That must have been very hard for Laurence since his own mother had passed away young as well. Did he become depressed and withdrawn again?"

"Well, now that you ask," Harriet scooted her chair closer to Nellie, "and I know Mr. Laurence is still in his room, I'll answer your question. I can hear footsteps upstairs and I know his well enough." Harriet paused for a moment, poured another cup of tea, then continued in hushed tones.

"That's the strangest thing. When he arrived at the stables to let senior Mr. MacLaren know about the accident, he wasn't shouting, nor did he seem very agitated. He told his tale in almost a matter-of-fact sort of way. After they brought poor Mrs. MacLaren back home, Master Laurence passed through here on his way upstairs, asked if I had baked his favorite cookies, snatched one from the plate and went on his merry way."

"Maybe he was in shock," Nellie suggested. "Sometimes a person's emotions don't surface right after such a horrific accident. I'm sure the funeral must have been difficult for him."

"Now that's another queer thing. As long as I've known Master Laurence, he hasn't seemed happy or smiled. One of those times was when you all came to stay for a while. It lightened his spirits. Yet when they returned home after the funeral, he had a smile on his face. Like he enjoyed the whole doings.

"I would have attended, but the senior Mr. MacLaren invited some friends over for afternoon tea and comfort, I'm sure, so I was busy preparing the food trays and drinks. Walter drove the carriage for the men and attended the service as well. He told me later that he noticed a sort of contented look on Master Laurence's face. It unnerved Walter. He couldn't understand why Master Laurence showed no signs of mourning, or at the very least, comforted his father. Mrs. MacLaren tried her very best to get acquainted with the master, but he shunned her every time. I felt so sorry for the Mrs.."

Nellie studied Harriet's expression and mannerisms. She hoped Harriet would give a visible cue if she did not want to continue the conversation.

"I hear footsteps on the stairs, but they're not Laurence's. Maybe James," Harriet said.

"I'm curious about one more thing, Harriet. Was there enough evidence to question Laurence's version of the story?"

Harriet's eyes squinted, her lips pursed. She removed a hankie from her apron pocket and wiped her brow.

"Now Miss Cox, those are waters not easily crossed. I don't intend to be the first one to wade in. Between you and me, however, I believe there was some foul play afoot," Harriet whispered. "None of the staff want to give damaging witness against our master, but we have been praying for someone outside the Hall to take more of an interest in the case. Even at the inquest, nobody questioned his story. Yet you could tell many of the people did not believe he told the whole truth."

"I hope I'm not interrupting." Maggie sniffed the air. "Smells like tea time. Any left?"

"Sure thing, Miss Richards. Have a seat and I'll fetch a cup and saucer."

"You made it downstairs, Maggie. Harriet insisted we have tea and conversation instead of my helping with dinner. We were discussing Mrs. MacLaren's horse riding accident and how little it bothered Laurence."

"That's what I understood from the people I spoke with in Rolen, Harriet. Maybe he's not an emotional person." Maggie chose a cookie off the plate.

"I'll share the information later," Nellie whispered in Maggie's ear.

Harriet returned with the cup and saucer, then poured Maggie a cup of tea. She pointed toward the ceiling. "Master Laurence is on his way down." Harriet refilled hers and Nellie's cups.

"How are you feeling after your ride, Miss Richards? Think you'll be ready to ride again soon?" Harriet changed the tone of the conversation as Laurence reached the bottom of the stairs.

"Not for a while, I'm sure. I loved the ride, but this body will need more time to adjust. I spend most of my time at a drawing table and my chair doesn't teeter like Peggy."

"Smells delicious, Harriet." Laurence entered the kitchen. "I'm assuming there may be time before dinner for a stroll in the garden?" Laurence stopped beside Maggie. "Always good to keep your muscles moving following a horse ride."

Maggie extended a piece of paper toward Laurence.

"Ah, the guest list. Harriet, see that James gets this list. Now, Miss Richards," he extended an arm to Maggie. "How about that stroll?"

As the two left the kitchen arm in arm, Nellie closed her eyes for a moment, then opened them to see Max standing in the doorway.

"The kitchen is always the nicest place to congregate," Harriet chuckled. "My mum used to say the kitchen was pleasant for conversation and a chocolate cookie." Harriet excused herself and returned to the stove.

"So, are there chocolate cookies?" Max asked. "I'll take one for myself and another for Walter. Thought I'd chat with him before dinner."

"Right there in the tin. Help yourself. And Nellie, if you're still willing, how about setting the table?" Harriet asked.

Chapter 29

Max found Walter behind the stable, cleaning one of the smaller carriages. The stable hand appeared aloof on their first visit to Stuart Hall. Max hoped for a better conversation this time.

"Hi, Walter. You're working hard. That rig looks brand new. Special event coming up?"

Walter arched his back for a long stretch.

"I see you're still standing straight after that horse ride. You seem to move easier than Miss Richards, anyway. She swayed going into the house. I laughed to myself and sure hope she didn't hear."

"Oh, Walter, I'm sure she didn't. Her eyes focused on the Hall. Once inside, she stumbled up the stairs and collapsed on her bed. She wouldn't have heard anything. So, are you getting the rig ready for something special, or is this part of your normal routine?"

"You're partly right there, Mr. Sullivan. Part of my routine, but Master Laurence asked for everything to be in tip-top shape if Miss Richards or Miss Cox wanted to venture out on their own."

Max inspected the carriage and admired the shine on the decorative silver buttons. Never had he seen a carriage this beautiful and complimented Walter on his attention to detail.

"Walter, did Mr. Ramsay MacLaren use this carriage every day?"

"No, siree, Mr. Sullivan. He used the larger one over there." Walter pointed behind Max. "Mr. MacLaren liked this one to be available for the Mrs. to drive when she needed. That second Mrs. MacLaren enjoyed rides in the late afternoon. A real horsewoman, that one. She brought treats out to the horses every time. Those horses could always sense when they were going to be needed. They have a sixth sense; I guess you could say. So if the Mrs. went into the paddock to brush one or bring treats, they'd all follow her back to the gate. They loved her if that's possible for horses." Walter tucked the rag into his back pocket.

"That is, all except Fireball. He's Master Laurence's horse, and no one else gets near him. If I'm gone, and he needs shoeing, the Master has to pay the blacksmith from Rolen double. That's what's called a one-man horse. You might have noticed even the other horses stay away from him. They know their place, and if they forget, Fireball will remind them."

"This morning, Laurence challenged me to a race. It didn't take long before Fireball took the lead and held it to the finish."

"Oh, that Fireball." Walter shook his head. "It wouldn't shock me if your mount held back. He was probably afraid of the chewing out he'd receive from that stallion once back in the paddock. Yes, sir, laddie, those other horses quake in their horseshoes when the black trots their way. Head held high and fire coming from his nostrils." Max chuckled at the picture Walter's words painted.

"Walter, could I ask you a couple of questions?"

"Sure, Mr. Sullivan. When you came the first time, you seemed to have something on your mind. I heard you and your friends were coming back for a visit, so I knew eventually you'd get to me. Go ahead. Ask away. I'll do my best."

"Thank you. Miss Cox enjoys a good mystery. She and I have been discussing the events surrounding Mrs. MacLaren's accident. We have a question and believe you are the one who may know the answer. If Laurence raced back to the hall, I think Fireball might have a layer of lather and exhibited labored breathing."

Walter removed his cap and rubbed his head. Then he cupped his chin in one hand and blinked a few times. Walter sighed and took a deep breath.

"You know, now that you mention it, I found it rather curious. Fireball wasn't breathing hard at all. I noticed a little sweat on the horse's neck when I grabbed the reins, but no lather. The more I think about it, Peggy was just as cool. No sir, if Master Laurence were in such an all-fired hurry, like he said, both horses would have lathered up. Instead, Peggy felt as if she had picked up her pace from the woods to the Hall. I've taken care of enough horses to know what signs to look for from running extra hard. No, sir. Peggy and Fireball possibly walked to the edge of the forest, then galloped the rest of the way."

"Do you think it's possible that Laurence was not in a hurry but thought it best to ride harder once anyone around the stables could see him?"

"Now, Mr. Sullivan, don't be putting words in my mouth. I gave you an honest answer to your question, and I'm not adding anymore."

Max found Walter's breaking point, yet sensed the man also believed something was amiss in the woods that day. One more question remained. It must be now or never, so Max surged ahead.

"I'm curious about one more thing. Laurence mentioned his father. When we spoke with the people in town, it sounded like Mr. MacLaren had disappeared. Do you know what happened?"

Max waited while Walter dumped the dirty water, rinsed the bucket, then returned with clean rags for the final rub. Max wasn't sure if this long wait meant Walter would not answer him or was mulling over his response.

Tossing a rag to Max, Walter continued, "You may as well use more muscles than your mouth. With both of us working, it won't take as long. But you mind yourself now, I'm fussy about doing not just an adequate job, but doing the best job of anyone in all of Scotland."

Max figured this meant Walter had accepted him as a confidant and rubbed the carriage. Neither spoke. Max feared that Walter would remain silent and not answer queries about Ramsay. He didn't mind helping Walter, and used the quiet time to think of a way to rephrase his question. Max watched as Walter worked on the far end of the carriage and edged closer to him. When they were almost side by side, Walter spoke in a low voice, keeping his head bent toward the ground.

"Mr. Sullivan, I'm going to keep my head down in case Master Laurence spots us. I think you and your friends are here with ulterior motives. I'm not the prying kind, so I won't ask questions. I like to observe people and their surroundings. I sensed there was more to your first trip than just getting off the beaten track. Harriet, Leach, and I have been praying that someone would take a personal interest in these happenings." Walter snapped his rag. Dust blew in the air.

"We know that Master Laurence portrays a gentleman, but we fear underneath, he's not what he seems. I'll tell you what I know, and then ask that we don't talk of it anymore unless we're sure Master Laurence canna see us. I like my situation, and at my age, I couldn't find another as good. If he thought I was talking behind his back, he would have my things packed and waiting by the door faster than I could saddle a horse."

Walter's intuition surprised Max. His admiration for this man increased.

"I appreciate your honesty. We may be the answer to your prayers, but let's wait for a while. I don't want to be thought of as a divine messenger if things don't come to a head as we're hoping. Now, back to my question. What do you know about Ramsay's disappearance?"

Walter glanced toward the Hall and behind his back as well. He was still taking extra precautions.

"Mr. MacLaren was as kind a man as you could know. He was always supportive and encouraging to Master Laurence. He loved the second Mrs. MacLaren as much as the first. A few days after the funeral, he became depressed and told me he might take a trip, perhaps to the coast for some fresh sea air. I could tell things weren't the same between him and Master Laurence. And Master Laurence, well, I saw a definite change in him. He seemed to take over as head of the Hall and almost forced his father into servitude." Walter peeked toward the Hall.

"Anyway, a couple of months after the funeral, Mr. MacLaren seemed to just up and disappear. I live in that small flat over there at the edge of the lawn by the stables. One night I wasn't able to sleep very well and got up around midnight to make a cup of herbal tea to settle me down. I saw Master Laurence ride toward the front door in the carriage we use for supplies. It was mighty strange, so I watched as best I could out the side window. Master Laurence stopped the carriage at the front door and went inside. When he came out again, he carried something over his shoulder. It appeared to be Mr. MacLaren. Master Laurence placed him in the back of the carriage, then got in the driver's seat and headed toward the road. I puzzled for a long time but finally went back to bed."

Walter handed Max a clean rag and continued buffing the carriage.

"I slept a little but decided it was useless and got up at 5 am to feed the horses. While I measured grain at the back of the stable, the sound of a carriage grew closer. Master Laurence brought the carriage to the front, unhitched the team, took their tack off, and put them back in their stalls. Then he took a rag, wiped the dust and some mud off the carriage, threw the rag away and went into the Hall. Mr. MacLaren was not with him, and we haven't seen or heard anything since.

"The next morning, Harriet asked Master Laurence if his father was coming down for breakfast. He responded that there was no answer when he knocked on his father's bedroom door. He opened the door and found a note. Mr. MacLaren wrote he was going to take an extended trip and would write when he got settled."

"Did he show any of you the note?"

"No, he didn't. I hoped he would, since I know Mr. MacLaren's handwriting. So that was the end of that. We have asked from time to time if there had been any word, but Master Laurence seemed to tire of us and said that when he knew something, he would share it, but until that time, we were not to speak of it again."

Max glimpsed Laurence and Maggie as they left the garden toward the Hall. He knew it was time to part ways with Walter.

"Here's your rag, Walter. Thank you for the information."

"Thanks for your help polishing the rig and listening. If anyone can find out the truth, I believe you and your friends will. Remember, Harriet, Leach, and I are praying for you."

Max turned his gaze to the Hall and mulled over Walter's words as he entered the kitchen.

The delicious smells filled the dining room. Soon, all had gathered around the table and enjoyed another delightful offering from Harriet. Max patted his stomach. "I could get used to this."

"I feel the need for liniment and a long rest this evening." Maggie rubbed her arms. "I also need to gather my drawing supplies for tomorrow. That is, if this body will endure another horse ride in the morning."

"Maggie, I'd be glad to go with you," Laurence interjected. "Or if you want to be alone, you could take the small carriage. I asked Walter to be sure it was ready for you or Nellie."

"That's very thoughtful of you. I'll wait to make that decision in the morning. Nellie and Max, I'm heading upstairs. If you're not retiring early, I'll say my good night and see you at breakfast."

Max noticed Maggie's stiffness as she rose from the table and exited the dining room. He thought maybe Nellie would join her, but she cleared the table.

"Harriet agreed to show me some of her secrets for marmalade. I'll be in the kitchen if you gentlemen need me."

Laurence invited Max to the parlor for a brandy.

"We need to discuss what event you might enter at the festivities in Rolen. After all," Laurence urged, "the games are only a few days away."

Chapter 30

Maggie raced upstairs as fast as her saddle-sore legs would carry her and flung the door wide. Panic set in for a moment until she remembered Ramsay's room key nestled inside her dress pocket. She clutched the key in her fist and pulled it out.

This tiny object became crucial regarding the mystery of Claire's death and Ramsay's disappearance. She tiptoed to the stair banister and listened for Nellie. She could hear her friend's faint voice in the kitchen and couldn't wait for her to come upstairs.

Max and Laurence stayed engaged in conversation. Maggie knew Max would come to her room when he could, but the pacing and fingering of the key made her more agitated. How long would she have to wait for him? The opportune moment had arrived, and she wouldn't waste it.

As she faced Ramsay's door, her hand shook. She inserted the key and rotated it to the right, held her breath, and closed her eyes. A click, and the door unlocked. She pushed the door into the wall, then her nostrils filled with a musty smell. The dim evening light from her room filtered into Ramsay's. Maggie entered and blinked to allow her eyes to adjust. The curtains were half closed, yet allowed some light to shine through. Using footsteps as light as a kitten's, she tiptoed from one side of the room to another and scanned where Claire might have placed Gwen's journal. She wiped her blouse sleeve across her forehead as frustration took hold, recognizing she had a limited amount of time. With a deep breath, she quieted herself. "Mom, I need your help. Where did you place Gwen's journal?"

Half expecting to hear an audible voice, but not surprised at none, Maggie released all her breath. *What would Mother do if she were in my situation?* The answer came instantly: pray. So Maggie did what she hadn't done in many years. She prayed.

"Lord, I know I haven't talked to you in a long time, but I trust my mother's example. Please help me find Gwen's journal. Time is running out. So if you don't mind, could you tell me, like, right now?" She hoped God had a sense of humor.

Maggie squeezed her eyes closed. *Maybe the answer will be right in front of me when I open them.*

She opened her eyes and concentrated on the only object in view. In a step of faith, she approached the bed and sensed a powerful urge to check underneath.

She dropped to her knees, lifted the bedspread that hung on the rug, and peeked at the dimly lit floor: nothing but dust balls.

Maggie scanned every inch, then concluded that her prayer didn't reach God. Or perhaps it did, and He didn't have a sense of humor after all.

Time ticked away as fast as her heartbeat. Her search would have to wait for another day. Her eyes noticed a bump under the mattress as she rose from her bent position. She slipped her hand into the crevice and lifted the mattress a few inches — a brown book. Maggie clasped the book and carefully pulled on it. Gwen's journal. She marveled it appeared the way her mother had described it to Mary Beth.

Maggie clutched the journal to her breast, glanced toward the ceiling, and mouthed, "Thank You." After she straightened the bedspread to its original position, she tiptoed out of Ramsay's room. With the door now closed and locked, she hurried back to her bed and slid the journal under her pillow.

Nellie and Max had not returned to their rooms and Maggie lacked any energy to continue. She prepared for bed, extinguished the lantern, and pulled the blankets to her waist.

Eager to open the journal, Maggie tossed and turned under the covers. Light from her room might cause suspicion when Laurence retired for the night. Perhaps she could wait until he passed to go to his room. That sounded better than enduring a night of nagging questions.

Time crept by like that last drop of honey from the honey pot. *What can Laurence be doing? He must require sleep!* Footsteps ascended the stairs. Maggie's heart raced.

"Good night, sweet Maggie." Nellie voiced as she passed Maggie's room.

The wait continued.

Maggie heard Max and Laurence talk as they ascended the stairs and said their good nights. When all three doors closed, she retrieved the journal, lit the lantern, and unlatched Gwen's book.

Some mold showed on a few pages at the front and back of the journal. Amazed the middle section remained intact, she flipped through the journal and noticed something out of place. Someone had slipped another paper inside.

She skimmed through a second time and stopped at the insertion. Maggie removed this one added sheet and recognized her mother's handwriting. Then she read the several short cryptic entries:

"Trying hard to build a relationship with Laurence: a brick wall.
Lots of prayer with little progress: the brick wall grows.
Concerned for my safety when Ramsay is gone:
there's a bomb on the brick wall.
Laurence may be softening but unsure of motives: brick wall could be crumbling.
He took a trip with us to Edinburgh: delightful travel time.
Invited for a horse ride: the brick wall seems to grow smaller.
Perhaps my prayers are being answered in the affirmative: patience is a virtue.
Tomorrow is a decisive horse ride: crumbling brick wall?
I pray so."

Maggie thumbed through the journal again, frantic for any other entry by her mom. She found none, closed the journal, and placed it under her pillow.

With the flame extinguished, Maggie planned to have a good night's sleep. However, her mind still raced. Ill feelings toward Laurence magnified. Conscience that this may hinder her acting ability to eject a confession, she did it again: she prayed. "Lord, thank you for answering my prayer to find the journal. Now I'm asking if you could turn off my mind and allow me to get a good rest. Tomorrow may be a full day. Thank you."

***

Maggie rose early and opened the curtains. A thick fog covered the trees and blanketed the paddock. She hoped that the fog did not foretell a gloomy day. Once dressed, she knocked on Nellie's door.

"Yes, Maggie, I'm up and dressed. Come on in."

"Nellie, I found Gwen's journal last night." Maggie flashed the book at Nellie. "Mom placed a sheet of paper inside with short notations about Laurence. Here, read for yourself." She handed her mother's notes to Nellie.

"I hear voices in there." Max knocked on Nellie's door. "Are you both up and dressed?"

Maggie hurried to open it and greeted him with a smile.

"Good morning, you two lovely lassies. I sense some excitement in the air. What's up?"

"Nellie, if you've finished, could you show Max the paper?" Maggie had a hard time curtailing her excitement as she paced from the bedroom window to the dresser and back again. "Thanks to you, Max. I opened Ramsay's door last night. Neither of you will guess how I found Gwen's journal. Once I entered Ramsay's room, I scoured the entire area. I grew frustrated as I knew I had limited time. Then the thought: What would my mother do?"

Nellie answered, "Pray."

"You're right. And when I opened my eyes, all I saw was the bed. I crept over and peered underneath. Nothing. Please understand I have not become religious, but my mother seemed to connect with the Lord. So, I didn't see any harm. Anyway, a bulge under the mattress caught my attention. Voilà, the journal. My mom wrote a few thoughts about Laurence and placed the paper inside Gwen's book."

They heard Laurence's footsteps in the hallway. The three friends stared at each other and held their breath until he reached the bottom of the stairs.

"Maggie, this is immensely important," Max said when he finished reading the notes Claire had jotted down. "Your poor mother's hopes raised, only to have them dashed again."

"I'd like to read Gwen's notes, but another time. Where are you hiding the journal?" Nellie asked.

"Under my pillow. You and Max may come in anytime to read more. But remember, we need to keep up appearances. If we stick to our plan, we'll persuade Laurence that we're here to write, gather history, and draw." Maggie paused as she heard a voice from downstairs.

"That's James calling us for breakfast. Let's go down now," Maggie said.

"Before we join Laurence," Max drew near Maggie. "I must tell you, Walter knows the basics of why we are here. He said that he, Harriet, and Leach were praying for someone to solve this mystery and shared that he saw Laurence take his father off the estate in the wagon. But he had no information beyond that. So we have an eyewitness to Laurence taking his father to Edinburgh. I believe I can get him to show me where the accident happened and explore it today."

"That would be wonderful, Max. I suppose that means I, or Nellie, will need to keep Laurence occupied."

"Let's wait until we see him. He may have plans of his own." Max held the bedroom door open for Nellie.

Maggie replaced her mother's notes in Gwen's journal and slid it under her pillow. She closed her door and joined the others in the dining room.

"Guid morning. How are you all feeling today? Anyone up for another horse ride?" Laurence sounded upbeat and eager to know if Walter should saddle any horses.

"I'd like to explore the estate grounds and then over to your neighbors. Curious about any history they might share." Max pulled chairs out for Nellie and Maggie.

"Wonderful. And how about you lassies?" Laurence asked.

"Nellie mentioned she planned to compile notes from conversations in Rolen all day. If I may, I'd like to take advantage of your carriage offer and make some drawings of the ruins." Maggie laid her serviette in her lap.

Maggie hoped Laurence had duties that would occupy his time this morning. Some quiet was what she required to sort the chaos out of her feelings. Despite her suspicions, she melted every time he looked at her. His handsome face portrayed a gentleman like no other she'd known.

Compassion for Laurence filled her heart, even though she felt he was a scoundrel deep inside. Her emotions stirred, thinking about all he's gone through; his childhood struggles, losing his mother and stepmother, and his father's disappearance. Feelings she dare not call love. To entertain such a notion was unthinkable at this point. She needed to muster all her resolve to remain objective. Falling in love didn't rank very high on her list of potential outcomes. She scolded herself; love shouldn't even be on the list.

Harriet offered another masterful mix of warm, cool, hearty, filling, and delicious dishes for breakfast. Maggie observed Harriet give Laurence an extra portion.

"Harriet," Nellie inquired, "could you use my assistance this afternoon? I'd love to watch the master at work creating your entries for the festivities in Rolen?"

"That would be delightful, Miss Cox, and I may put you to work. My plan is to make two different marmalades this year, a mincemeat pie and blueberry scones. The fruit needs to be prepared today, but I won't bake until tomorrow. Everything needs to be fresh."

Harriet glanced around the dining table. "Oh, I see long faces. Don't worry your heads now. We'll make extras to leave here in the Hall."

Maggie accompanied Max to the stables, her handmade bag filled with drawing supplies.

"Good morning, you two," Walter greeted them. "I must say, Miss Richards, you seem to manage just fine on those two legs. Peggy lived up to her word and gave you a gentle ride yesterday." Walter swatted a speck of dust from the seat. "Here's the carriage all ready for you. This mare is as docile as a kitten with a tummy full of warm milk. No need to worry at all. If you become nervous or unsure, give her her head, and the love of dry quarters and hay will bring her back to the stables."

Walter assisted Maggie into the carriage, waited until she settled, then gave the mare a swat on the rump. "She's kind of like a homing pigeon."

The fog lifted as Maggie left the yard and headed toward the ruins.

※※※

"Good morning, Walter. I wonder if we could saddle the same horse I rode yesterday. I'll retrieve him from the paddock if you don't mind getting his saddle." Max went to the paddock with a lead and attached it to the horse's halter.

Busy nibbling from a pile of hay, the horse didn't notice Max come alongside. Max stroked his neck, attached the rope, and led him back to the stable.

He slid the bridle in place while Walter threw the blanket and saddle on the horse's back.

"Walter, could you give me a detailed description of where Mrs. MacLaren's accident happened? I want to ride that way and look over the site."

"It happened right on the main path, south of the hall. There are lots of places that look alike, so maybe I should draw you a map. Can you finish this?"

Max cinched the girth strap while Walter found a scrap of paper and drew a crude map.

He folded the paper small enough to fit in the palm of his hand. Walter searched the area for any signs of Laurence, then passed the map to Max.

Max slipped the map in his pocket and mounted. "Thanks, Walter. I thought I'd ride over to some of the neighbors' then return by the back road." He glanced at the sky. "The sun may come out yet. Wish me luck."

Chapter 31

Nellie hurried to her room, gathered her writing materials, then scurried to Maggie's bed and retrieved the journal. She stuffed the writing supplies and leather-bound book into her heavy fabric bag. A clasp made of metal and stone secured the satchel.

"Good morning, James." Nellie met him at the bottom of the stairs. "Thought I'd sit on the veranda to write. I remember a small table in the corner. Seems like the fog has lifted and the sun may grace us with a warm day."

Nellie expected a smile from James, but received a polite nod instead. *We need to work on that one.*

The fog had indeed lifted. The corner table and chair sparkled in the mid-morning sun.

Nellie gathered her thoughts as she arranged her paper and pencils. The rose trellis appeared forlorn. A few dappled flowers were all that remained. *Could be the majestic Stuart Hall that once was, is dying as well.*

She would start two different stories in case Laurence chanced her way and asked to read her work. A fanciful tale of Gwen's brothers and their adventures with imaginary battles at the ruins would be first.

"Ah, Nellie. I see you found a sunny spot." Laurence said, as he came out the front door. "How are you doing? If you need anything, please ask."

He seemed to not be interested in her, only a passing remark as he glided down the steps before she could answer. As he headed toward the stables, Nellie noticed he had a spring in his step. *What's he so happy about?*

Retrieving Gwen's journal, Nellie thumbed through the pages. Ready to do some in-depth detective work, she made notes of important clues. Anything that would bring light to the chain of events that led to the accident and Laurence's behavior.

✳✳✳

Maggie reached her destination. The sun touched the corner of the uppermost point of the crumbling structure. The ruins were beautiful even in their decayed state.

As she climbed out of the carriage, Maggie noticed a small stool with a note attached. "Thought you might need this. Walter." *What a considerate man.*

With her art bag flung over her shoulder, Maggie carried the stool inside the ruins. She marveled at how beautifully the sun reflected on the stone surfaces. The wild grass blew in the gentle breeze and invited her to sit a spell and imagine the years past.

Wild rose vines clung to the walls and showed their last blooms of summer. Large orange rose hips dotted the green foliage. The trailing plant brought a kind of elegance to the place. Maggie found a comfortable corner, leveled the stool, and opened her sketch pad. All she needed to complete this scene would be her mother playing Bach on a harpsichord.

As Maggie sketched, her mind wandered to Gwen's brothers, as they may have played here. She added three warriors to the composition.

With the background and one warrior sketched in, Maggie rested her pencil. She leaned back against the stone wall and closed her eyes. The sun warmed her face and melted away the cares and concerns she carried with her.

First, the walk with Laurence through the garden. Then the time Laurence taught her to feed apples to the horses. Lately, whenever she stopped activity, her mind brought Laurence's image into view. He had been a gentleman these past two days and his eyes seemed to absorb her.

Maggie recognized her challenge: keep his image in the character of a ne'er-do-well rather than a knight in shining armor. She continually reviewed the evidence against Laurence. Perhaps not enough to convict him, but at least to reopen the case. She trusted Nellie to discover clues from Gwen's journal.

The thunder of horse hoofs interrupted her thoughts. She turned toward the sound and received the full blast of the sun in her face. With hand raised above her eyes as a shield, she squinted and recognized Fireball standing next to the carriage.

"Hello there, Maggie," Laurence called. "Fireball needed a morning jaunt, so thought I would stop by. Everything all right? I brought a light snack for you." He dismounted and untied a satchel.

So, her knight in shining armor had come to her aid, even though she needed none. Especially not Laurence.

"May I offer my hand?" Gentleman Laurence, always thoughtful at the appropriate time.

"Why, yes, thank you."

He brought her to her feet and gazed into her eyes. Face to face now, she inhaled the smell of his leather jacket. An aroma filled with strength and comfort. *What's wrong with me? This is the man I've accused of killing my mother. I've got to keep my distance and remain objective.*

"I brought some fresh blueberries and Harriet's biscuits, plus some water. May I see your drawing?"

Maggie handed him her drawing pad after he sat the satchel on the ground.

"Such a treat. Thank you very much for thinking of me."

Laurence's attention shifted from her drawing to her face.

"You're very welcome, Maggie." His deep-set eyes captivated her. "I must be honest with you. You seem to be on my mind more each day. I must also be honest about your drawing."

Maggie focused on her work while he shared his impressions.

"I see a sensitive and imaginative artist who has created a very romantic scene. I foresee a beautiful finished piece. Perhaps you will allow me to keep this as a reminder of your time spent at Stuart Hall."

"Laurence, I'm very flattered. While I've done many drawings and paintings, I've never had such compliments from a few sketchy lines. I'd feel honored to gift you my finished work as a thank you for your kind hospitality to myself and my friends."

A green and red tartan blanket unfurled as Laurence prepared to cover a spot of grass. With hand outstretched, he assisted Maggie to the ground. Laurence joined her and placed the biscuits and fruit on a serviette.

Maggie gazed off into the forest that surrounded them. Lost for words, Laurence's actions and statements caught Maggie off guard. Oh, how she wished Max or Nellie would come and break up this uncomfortable state of affairs.

"Sometimes thoughts come to me that there is a hidden depth to you, Maggie. I would like to get to know the inner you. What goes on in your mind on a day-to-day basis? I understand, and can see, you're a talented artist, but what activities keep you busy when you're not creating?"

"I live in a small, but comfortable apartment back in the States," Maggie said. "Since there is no yard, I have dear friends with ten acres of pasture land. They have allotted me enough space for a garden. I enjoy growing lettuce, tomatoes, cucumbers, chives and a few herbs that I dry myself. From spring to early fall, I spend most of my spare time outdoors.

"There's a local art community that meets twice a month. I volunteer to set up the exhibits and teach classes to children. Other than that, I love to read biographies and mysteries are my favorite. Nellie has me edit her manuscripts before she sends them off to a publisher. Sometimes I create the illustrations for her stories and poster art for plays and musical performances."

"What about trips, holidays? What made you come to Scotland?" Laurence said.

"I've never been abroad and mentioned to Nellie that we needed to expand our horizons. While we were very enthusiastic about the idea, we felt a little uneasy traveling by ourselves. Then, almost in unison, we suggested Max might come. We contacted him and he was most eager to join us." She reached for a biscuit.

"We considered other countries as well and made a list of requirements. An English speaking country topped the list. Nellie and I struggle with French and Max learned German, but none of us felt competent to converse with native speakers. The trip also needed to be within our budgets and of interest for all three of us.

"Scotland came to our minds at the same time. We researched what we would like to see, both historically and culturally, and settled on Scotland. So here we are. Max is having a wonderful time meeting people, learning about your history and folklore, while Nellie has lots of notes to compile into another book."

Maggie munched on a mouthful of blueberries and drank some water.

"For myself, my drawing portfolio continues to grow and I plan to complete several paintings when we return. Did that answer your question?" Maggie became more uneasy and afraid she might divulge too much information. *Oh, if only Nellie or Max would come. Rescue needed here.*

Laurence reached for her hand and smiled. His steel-blue eyes seemed to peer into her soul.

"Maggie, your home and life sound serene. I have never been abroad. Perhaps you would do me the kindness to show me your country should I venture that way. Maybe there is a residence close by where I might lodge. You would like that, wouldn't you?"

Trapped. She never felt so trapped. Like a wild bird jailed in a small cage and flitting in all directions, desperate for an avenue of escape. She wanted to say that he would be most welcome anytime and lodging could be arranged. She wanted to say that she would be delighted to show him her country. She wanted to say she would expect his arrival and to stay as long as possible. Her throat tightened at the thought of speaking the next words. Foremost, she wanted to say that she would not look forward to his visit because, after all, he would be in jail for a very long time or at the end of a hangman's noose.

A drink of water gave her a reprieve to collect her thoughts. A silent prayer calmed her nerves. She glanced at Lawrence and smiled while she calculated a response.

The sound of horse hoofs in the distance broke her concentration. Her heart thumped to match the hoof beats as the horse drew closer. The pounding slowed, and the horse stopped at the entrance to the ruins.

"Ah, I thought I might find you here, Maggie. And Laurence as well. Must be my lucky day." Max dismounted. "When I returned from my ride, Harriet had lunch ready. She asked if I might find out if Maggie would join us. She didn't know where you went, Laurence, so I'm glad I found you both."

Maggie saw Max as her knight in shining armor come to save her from the fire-breathing dragon. He seemed to always be there whenever she needed him. The warm spot in her heart grew a little each time they were together.

"That sounds wonderful, Max. Laurence brought some fruit, but my stomach tells me I need more nourishment. I have enough completed on this sketch to finish at the Hall."

As Maggie untangled her dress from her boot heels, Laurence leapt up to assist her.

With the blanket, stool, basket, and Maggie loaded in the carriage, Laurence pulled on Fireball's reins. "I'll tie Fireball back here and accompany you to Stuart Hall, Maggie. If you don't mind."

Maggie fired a glance at Max with a "Help me" expression.

"Nothing doing," Max interrupted. "You suggested I take part in the Highland Games. After a lot of thought, I've decided to enter the horse race. This horse needs a bit more training, so I challenge you to a race back to the Hall. What do you say?"

"Oh, I couldn't leave Maggie by herself. No, I think I should accompany her back."

Maggie heard this as a demand, rather than a request. Whichever it was, it was the exact opposite of what she wanted. Time to demand something for herself.

"Why Master Laurence, if I got here by myself, I can just as surely get myself back. You and Max have your race and I'll see you at the Hall."

"If you insist, Maggie. And you, Max, get ready for the ride of your life."

Maggie waited for Laurence to mount Fireball and then gave the "Go" signal. Both riders disappeared in a cloud of flying grass and dirt.

Once they were out of sight, she heaved a sigh of relief. Maggie cupped her hands around her mouth and shouted, "Thank you, Max, for coming." With a fair distance between her, Max, and Laurence, she felt safe that neither one heard her.

Maggie clicked to the horses, then realized she forgot something. She pulled back on the reins, gazed skyward and said, "Thanks to you as well."

Chapter 32

"Nellie, gaze upon these elegant gowns from James." Maggie spread the frocks on her bed. "I'm astounded. The seed pearls on this bodice must have taken hours, if not days, to finish."

She ran her hand gently over the delicate, luminescent gems. "I've never seen such expert detail work. James mentioned that Master Laurence chose these especially for us. They're both gorgeous. You will glow in this electric blue gown, Nellie. I prefer the soft peach. Let's try them on."

A full-length mirror inside the armoire afforded the girls a complete view for admiring themselves. They swished and swayed for the complete effect of the full skirts. Maggie gathered the side seams, eliminating a half-inch on each side of the gown.

"My goodness, some altering needs to be done, but not much. Do you think Mary Beth would consent?" Maggie asked.

"I'm sure she'd be glad to, but there's not enough time to take them into Rolen. Harriet won't have time either. She's absorbed with her culinary treats. Remember, the Highland Games are tomorrow. We'll have to alter the gowns ourselves. I promised to help Harriet, so once we're finished pinning I'm off downstairs. Hope you don't mind."

"No, that's fine. With a cup of tea and the sun brightening the sitting room, I'll be content. You go ahead. I understand from Max that Laurence had challenged him to another conditioning race, so they're off in the countryside somewhere. Uninterrupted quiet will be lovely."

Maggie, confident they had assimilated into life at Stuart Hall, knew their information gathering time had ended. Now, thanks to Max and Walter, she had a map of the accident site. She placed this treasure in Gwen's journal for safe keeping.

She had no further communication from Ernest about the state of Ramsay's health. Perhaps he took a turn for the worse. She counted on Ernest's presence at the Highland Games tomorrow with any latest news. Her major concern, at present, centered on Laurence's attentiveness. His actions were not flirtatious. However, his concern and care for her every comfort led her to believe he thought of himself as more than her host. She tried to receive his advances as graciously as possible while she struggled to keep her own emotions in check.

Maggie was not new to the experience of men's attentiveness. She had even entertained marriage once or twice. Laurence, however, needed to be kept at bay. Her quandary peeked whenever they were together. Her mind questioned whether he could kill another human being. This forced her emotions into a game of tug-of-war and she feared the not guilty side gained strength.

Now she needed to confront Laurence about the conflicting stories regarding his father's disappearance: his, and the version Walter related. After all, Laurence may have a logical explanation and she felt he deserved an opportunity to tell his side.

Hoof beats grew louder outdoors. Maggie leaned toward the window and saw Laurence and Max return from their ride. She hung the gowns in the wardrobe and joined Nellie in the kitchen.

✳✳✳

"I finished the gowns, Nellie." Maggie said. "After dinner, we should try them on in case I missed something. Everything smells wonderful."

Max and Laurence entered the kitchen, out of breath and filled with laughter.

"Welcome back." Maggie greeted the men. "From the expression on your faces, you must have had an exhilarating ride."

"The best yet, my dear, Maggie." Max removed his gloves. "What is that tantalizing aroma emanating from this kitchen? Now let me guess. Blueberry pie?"

"Why, our brave knight returns from his conquest of that fire-breathing dragon in yonder ruins. Sir Maxwell, I believe." Nellie curtsied. "Indeed, your olfactory senses serve you well. This beautiful, talented culinary chef has prepared a blueberry pie for dinner and a mincemeat to wallop the competition in tomorrow's contest. If ye and your noble companion will perform your ablutions, a meal fit for kings awaits your return." Nellie smiled at the two men. Max shook his head and laughed, but had no comeback for her clever rhetoric.

Maggie tossed them a towel as they hurried to the washroom.

"Here, Harriet, let me set the table." Maggie lifted dinner plates from a shelf. "You and Nellie seem to be consumed with dinner preparations."

"Harriet, I wonder, could the staff sit with us tonight?" Nellie asked.

"My no, Nellie. We servants know our place. The kitchen is fine. You are most kind to ask though and I thank you." Harriet removed the rolls from the oven and placed them in a basket. She laid an embroidered cloth on top to keep them warm.

Maggie folded the serviettes and placed one by each plate. As Max and Laurence brought the hot dishes from the kitchen, Maggie arranged holding stands for the bowls to protect the table.

"Our ride today astounded me." Max drew two chairs out from the table for the ladies. "Laurence led me over every hill and dale around here. I'm positive that minus the hilling and dale-ing, my horse would have beaten Fireball."

"I doubt that very much, Max. Fireball is the better horse. We shall see tomorrow which horse is the fastest and who's the better rider." Laurence winked at Maggie.

"Max, you're entering the horse race?" Maggie's eyes widened.

"To be sure, my dear. And mark my words, Max didn't come here to lose," Max said.

The pleasant company calmed Maggie. She hoped Laurence would share more deeply as they became better acquainted. Maybe tonight.

"Oh, worthy opponent, I have a query to put to you. Are you ready?" Max laid his fork on his plate and leaned back in his chair.

"Max, any query you put toward this capable brain which lives in this most handsome head, I shall answer to the best of my ability." Laurence seemed to enjoy the banter.

"Here is my question then, good sir. I've been riding the same mount for the past six days of our visit and still don't know his name. Walter never mentioned it and I forgot to ask. Could you enlighten me?" Max asked.

Maggie placed her wine glass on the table, eager for Laurence's response.

"Diablo."

Laughter filled the room.

"Diablo and Fireball head to head in the greatest horse race ever to come upon Rolen, Scotland. This will be quite a match," Max said.

Maggie reached for the bowl of tatties. "I'm not sure which one to cheer for. I've always been for the underdog, so I guess whichever one is behind will be the one for me. How about you, Nellie?"

"I'm going to support whichever horse is in last place," Nellie answered. "Whether Fireball or Diablo or another horse, I always felt sorry for the one who brought up the rear. He tries so hard to stay with the pack, eats their dust, but his legs just can't maintain the pace. Sometimes I'm like that as well. When I feel out-of-sorts in a group, I like to sit by myself and watch the rest interact."

In came Harriet with slices of blueberry pie and hand-churned ice cream.

Maggie patted her stomach. "Oh, Harriet, I forgot. There's no room left. But I can't pass your delicious dessert by. A long stroll after dinner is on this girl's agenda."

"How did the gowns fit? Are they all right for the party?" Laurence asked.

"I completed some minor alterations before dinner, Laurence." Maggie scooped a bite of pie on her fork. "But perhaps after this meal, we may need to let them out again. They're so beautiful. Nellie and I have never worn such elegant gowns. Thank you again."

"You're most welcome and I believe you'll be the belles of the ball," Laurence said. "I do hope James gave you the peach gown, Maggie, and you, Nellie, the blue one?"

"Yes, James mentioned your request."

Maggie received a glance from Max. His eyes looked for approval from her to ask a question. She gave him a go-ahead nod.

"Laurence, mind if I ask you a serious and personal question? You don't have to answer if you'd rather not."

"Since Harriet will need to clear the table and wash dishes, we may find the parlor quieter. Shall we?" Laurence said. Maggie, Nellie, and Max followed Laurence into the parlor.

"This is much nicer. You can go ahead with your question now, Max." Laurence found his pipe and stuffed tobacco into the bowl.

Maggie prepared herself, expecting a safe answer from Laurence. He had slithered his way around questions before. She wondered what he would do this time.

"I believe the first evening we were here, you told us your father had left for some rest and recuperation." Max leaned against a bookshelf. "I don't doubt your word, but wonder if you and Walter have discussed this matter. I hope I'm not divulging a confidence here, but Walter seems to remember you left late one evening in the carriage and placed someone in the back. Yet when you returned early, the next morning, you were by yourself. He said he noticed this because he couldn't sleep that night, stayed up late and started early with his chores. I wonder if you transported your father somewhere. Perhaps a hospital. And if he was sick."

The silence, so thick it suffocated Maggie. She hoped Walter received no reprimand, yet they needed to challenge Laurence to tell the truth. He rose and closed the door.

"My friends, I suspected Walter was awake that evening, and hoped he would come and talk to me about the incident. But he didn't." Laurence paused for a moment. "Yes, he's right. I took my father in the carriage very late that evening. My father wasn't himself and appeared to be getting worse almost daily. I didn't want the servants to become concerned about him. All of them have known my father since he married my mother, or at least almost all of them. Anyway, my concern over their attachment to my father brought me to that course of action." Laurence struck a match and inhaled the flame into his pipe.

"On one of my trips to Edinburgh, I visited the hospital for people in distress. The Edinburgh Lunatic Asylum. There I spoke with the doctor in charge, who encouraged me to bring my father in as soon as possible. I told them money would be no object, as I wanted him to get the very best care." He exhaled a few puffs of smoke.

"We agreed I should bring him in during the night. I know, sneaky and underhanded, but I wanted the staff, his friends and neighbors, to believe he had packed his bag and left on an extended trip. My father is a proud man and couldn't face his friends in Rolen, and the staff here, knowing he wasn't in his right mind anymore." Laurence gently swirled the wine in his glass.

"He begged me to give him something that would remove him from this world permanently. I couldn't do that. So I felt that taking him to the hospital in Edinburgh was the best option. I waited until I thought everyone was asleep.

"I requested that Dr. McDonald, the head of the hospital, send me a letter in an unmarked envelope whenever he thought my father could return home. It was to remain a secret that my father was in a facility for the mentally ill."

Maggie sipped her wine and waited for Laurence to finish.

"I ask, now that I have told you my deepest, heart-breaking secret, that you will remain silent. I feel I know you well enough that I can trust you."

Laurence appeared drawn and downcast when he finished. Maggie wanted to put her arms around him in comfort, but Nellie placed her hand on Maggie and restrained her.

"You had great courage to tell us your tale," Max said. "We have no intention of prying into your personal matters. A discrepancy that needed clarification. We've been eager for your father's return. Everything we've heard about him has created anticipation for that moment when you, and he, are together again. We mean no ill will, Laurence. Your secret will remain with us. We won't speak of this matter again."

"Thank you, Max." Laurence smoked his pipe for a moment. "You three have become my dear friends whom I value and respect. Please ask me anything that may trouble you. I feel that Stuart Hall needs to have the roof lifted off and all the dust and dirt of secrecy swept away and brushed into the clouds never to fall back. Life has returned since your arrival, and I look forward to each new day."

"If you will excuse Nellie and I, the alterations on the gowns need to be checked one last time." Maggie placed her wine glass on a silver tray. Nellie followed her out the door.

"Think I'll choose a book from the library, take it to my room and read for a while. What about you, Laurence?" Max asked.

"The outdoors beckons me. A long walk in the fresh air will help clear my head. I'll see you in the morning." Laurence trod to the front door.

Maggie and Nellie waited for Max to ascend the stairs. Maggie held Nellie's bedroom door open as Max entered. She listened for Laurence's footsteps. Hearing nothing, she closed the door.

"His story sounds very plausible, don't you think?" Maggie began. "I mean, if I was in his position, I would have done the same thing. I wouldn't want my father disgraced or paraded in front of his staff and friends. The train would not be right. I believe Laurence made a wise decision and I applaud him for his courage."

"Maggie, I can't believe what I just heard," Nellie exclaimed. "Are you siding with Laurence?"

"Don't you remember what Dr. McDonald said about Ramsay?" Max interrupted. "The way he arrived at the hospital?"

"Has Laurence's rugged good looks and steel-blue eyes deceived you? Has he has succeeded to worm his way into your heart?" asked Nellie. "I've encountered some pretty slippery cads working with the police, but Laurence would win the grand prize. Can't you see that?"

"Nellie dear," Maggie responded. "You haven't had the conversations I've had with him. Laurence has opened up and I'm getting to know him better each day. He's not the man I thought he would be. I had a preconceived idea that we would meet a lunatic and murderer. Yet now I see him in a different light. I believe perhaps we have all misjudged him. After all, every man deserves a fair trial and I don't believe we gave him that option."

"Maggie, this charlatan has clouded over your mind in a few days by this charlatan. He's lying to get you to take his side. And he's doing a masterful job, I might add." Max's cheeks reddened and his voice grew stronger.

Maggie hung her head to avoid eye contact with her friends.

"It's late and we have a busy day ahead of us." Max settled down. "Let's get a good night's rest. We can revisit this conversation when our minds are clearer."

Maggie left Nellie's room with a cool, "Good night."

After she closed the bedroom door she remained within earshot of any further conversation between Max and Nellie.

✳✳✳

"Max, can you believe that? Our Maggie, sweet, level-headed Maggie, is falling in love with the terror of Stuart Hall. How is that possible in so short a time?"

"I don't know, but I know if something doesn't snap her out of this dream world, we may lose her forever. She needs to reconnect with Claire's friends: George, Mabel, Mary Beth, Dr. Shane and, of course, Ernest. I pray Ernest will have some word from Dr. McDonald tomorrow in Rolen. We must re-instill the urgency of our original mission and get her back on track. Are you with me?"

"I agree with you. But did you say you would pray? When did you get religion?"

"I didn't 'get religion.' I just remember a conversation with Ernest on our fishing trip and decided prayer couldn't hurt. Now, off to bed with you. We need all the energy we can muster for tomorrow."

✳✳✳

Maggie dragged her sluggish body to bed. All her energy had evaporated. With weak arms and exhausted legs, she was like a wet, limp rag. She felt abandoned by her friends. Perhaps at Rolen tomorrow, she might persuade someone to take her side. For now, mental fatigue overcame her. She laid her head on her pillow and remembered Max's words. Time for prayer. Indeed, time for prayer.

Chapter 33

The sun's rays warmed Maggie's room, but not her disposition. She dressed and trudged down the stairs. A hot cup of tea might put her in a better frame of mind. The night before, she felt accosted by her friends and wanted to avoid Nellie as long as possible. Max's eyes had pierced through her, so snubbing her two traveling companions seemed imperative.

Laurence smiled as she entered the dining room, his plate heaped with eggs and sausage. Maggie perused Harriet's delicious spread on the sideboard. A light breakfast eater, she chose a scone, scrambled eggs and fresh fruit.

"Good morning, Maggie. I trust you had a restful sleep and are ready for a full day of activities."

"I slept well. Thank you, Laurence. Explaining your father's absence lifted an enormous weight off my shoulders." Maggie set her plate on the dining table and walked back to the sideboard for a cup of tea. "Are you ready for the horse race?"

"I'm always up for a challenge, whether a race or a life experience. Rolen hasn't seen Fireball for several years. They think I put him out to pasture. I can't wait to see the expression on their vile faces when I bring him across the finish line this afternoon."

Maggie thought the tone of his comment vindictive, yet didn't know why. The people they met respected the MacLaren's. They held the highest admiration for Claire. Maybe Laurence felt they harbored ill feelings toward him. Much closer to the truth.

"I'm sure your name on the docket will assure the residents that Fireball can still go the distance." Maggie blew on her hot tea. "But then any younger horse might give Fireball a run to the finish line."

"Good morning, Laurence, Maggie." Max rubbed his hands together. "Hmm, something smells delicious." He scanned the breakfast choices.

"Dish your plate and join us." Laurence scooted the salt and pepper to the middle of the table.

Maggie focused on her breakfast and refused to make eye contact with Max. He didn't respond to her demeanor, which irritated her even more. *Please sit at the far end of the table,* she repeated over and over.

"Max, do you think Diablo has a chance against Fireball? After all, every race we've run, whether through forest or open meadow, Fireball overtook Diablo and maintained the lead to the very end," Laurence bragged.

Maggie studied his expression, then consoled herself. Laurence had every reason to boast. According to rumors in Rolen, he owned the fastest horse in the township.

"Laurence, my able adversary, for all you know, I may have held Diablo back. Perhaps he has speed in reserve." Max sprinkled salt over his eggs. "I believe that even if he doesn't defeat your shiny black steed, he will give your horse a run today. You may indeed have to put Fireball out to pasture."

"Now, boys," Nellie entered the dining room, "even though you may ride fast horses, and even though there may be some young stallions against you, I believe the most important contest will not be the horse race. Nor the caber toss. Nor the hammer throw. Nor the Scottish dancing. My, no. The most important contest will determine the winner in these three categories: mincemeat pie, blueberry scones and orange marmalade. And we all know the clear winner of those events: Harriet."

"Why, Nellie, thank you very much for your vote of confidence." Harriet placed a dish of warm applesauce on the table. "I do indeed hope to come home with at least one blue ribbon. Walter left the carriage by the side door, so when you brawny lads are through, I would appreciate some help loading my wares. You'll find extra scones and marmalades I'm donating to the auction."

Max and Laurence arranged Harriet's baked goods in baskets and placed them in the carriage. Maggie had no intention of receiving a verbal reprimand left alone with Nellie.

"Excuse me," Maggie pushed her chair away from the table. "I forgot my drawing pad.

As Maggie marched upstairs, she heard Nellie follow, matching step for step.

✳✳✳

"Maggie, should I read this again?" Nellie pulled Gwen's journal from under Maggie's pillow. "Here, read for yourself, in your mother's own handwriting. Her deep concern for Laurence should be yours as well."

"Enough," Maggie interrupted. "I know what you're trying to do. You want me to believe Laurence is a cold-blooded murderer. Well, I can't. You don't know him like I do. He's a considerate, kind gentleman that I don't believe could even conceive a plan to kill someone." She hunted for her drawing supplies.

"Maggie, my best friend in all the world, I love and care about you way too much to allow you to fall in love with him." Nellie's voice escalated. "Remember why we came to Scotland. Today is a significant day. Once more, we'll be with all the people who hold the same conviction that your mother's death wasn't an accident. Remember Maggie! Remember your mom! Remember Ernest! Remember Dr. Shane! Remember George and Mabel and Mary Beth!" Nellie pulled a window curtain back and peeked out. Laurence and Max were loading the carriage.

"And above all else, remember how Dr. McDonald recounted Ramsay's arrival at the hospital. Dr. McDonald didn't receive a clean shaven, well-dressed gentleman. No. Remember what Max said, how Dr. McDonald described Ramsay, 'He was dirty, his clothes were old, ragged and torn and he seemed to be drugged or passed out from drinking, although there was no smell of alcohol.'"

Maggie's nerves quivered as she misinterpreted Nellie's concern as animosity.

"Yet Laurence shared with us he transported his father to the hospital. He said nothing about a homeless, filthy man. Remember Maggie, before it's too late. Laurence has lied to everyone; his servants, people in Rolen, but most importantly, he's lied to you. He's a master of deception and determined to lure you down into a mire of confusion."

Nellie barred the door with her body. "Every moment of each day we have left in Scotland, Max and I will be like bloodhounds on this case. We will be relentless in pursuing the goal we set months ago. And as for you, we will do everything in our power to reveal the truth about Laurence, to remove the scales from your eyes that he has so cleverly crafted."

Max called up the stairs, interrupting their conversation. "Ladies, all's ready. We'll wait for you by the carriage."

Nellie cracked the door open. "We'll be right down, Max. Just needed to get Maggie's drawing pad and my hat."

Tears filled Maggie's eyes. Nellie knew it would take more than a hug to restore their friendship. She gave it anyway. Wrapped in Nellie's arms, Maggie responded to the hug like a shirt fresh off a frozen clothesline: stiff and cold.

Chapter 34

Residents and visitors alike scurried through the streets of Rolen. In carriages, on foot or horseback, all headed toward an enormous field with banners that swayed in the breeze. Many of the stores had signs in the windows: "Closed for the Games."

How easily Walter guided the carriage through the crowded streets. The throng seemed to sense the horses behind them and moved apart to make a path. They closed the gap as soon as the carriage passed.

Laurence offered his hand and assisted Maggie to the ground. Once on level turf, their eyes met. Her cheeks flushed.

"Max and I need to check-in for the horse race. Then I'm taking him to watch the He-Man competitions. I hear the crowd cheering over by the stands. Will you come with us?"

Laurence's voice was like melting butter and seeped into her soul. Dressed in his best riding habit, handsome beyond belief, Maggie's legs weakened. Her chest pounded. And those blue eyes captivated her.

Maggie cleared her throat. "I promised Nellie and Harriet I'd help them deliver the baked goods to the judging tent." She straightened her skirt. "Perhaps we'll find you later."

"I truly hope so." His beguiling smile unsettled her.

Maggie, Nellie and Harriet set the baked delicacies amongst entries that already graced the tables. Harriet signed in at the competitor's table and placed a number by each of her items. As they carried Harriet's wares to the auction tent, Maggie bumped into Mabel.

"Good afternoon, Mabel," Maggie said. "Have you met Harriet? She makes the most wonderful meals at Stuart Hall."

"It's so nice to meet you, Harriet. Do you have pastries entered today?"

"Yes, I brought several items to be judged."

Mabel faced Maggie. "We miss these two lassies in Rolen. But from their rosy cheeks, the change of scenery and your good cooking, Harriet, Stuart Hall must suit them perfectly."

"There has been little gaiety at the Hall for many a month," Harriet smiled. "But these two lassies, and their friend Max, are a breath of fresh air. The entire atmosphere has changed, and for the better, I might add. We're afraid the sadness may return when they leave." Harriet noticed a group of women. "If you will excuse me. I see some friends I'd like to visit with."

"Look, there's an empty table." Maggie led the way while Mabel and Nellie followed. "We can sit and chat." As they reached the table, Maggie saw Ernest and Dr. Shane approach.

"It's so good to see you two again." Ernest lifted his legs over the bench and sat across from Maggie. "I pray you are making progress in your investigation."

"Yes, some. But I'm eager to hear about Ramsay. Have you had any news?" Maggie unbuttoned her coat.

Ernest leaned closer to the table. "We received one letter from Dr. McDonald. He was cautiously optimistic and wrote that Ramsay appeared well enough to shop in Edinburgh for some new clothes. Didn't want him to arrive home in his hospital shirt and pants. Everything seemed fine until they entered a small cafe' for lunch. Ramsay, without warning, wept like a child.

"Dr. McDonald said he's worked with Ramsay and they've made progress. He felt sure Ramsay would be ready to come home in another week or two. Dr. McDonald agreed to accompany him to Stuart Hall. The doctor thought this might be wise, as the father and son reunion could be rather tense. Especially if an arrest for kidnapping was forthcoming."

"That sounds wonderful, Ernest," Nellie said. "Laurence doesn't venture far from Stuart Hall. Dr. McDonald will be invaluable for the home-coming."

"So you're not making much progress in discovering the truth?" Ernest's brow furrowed.

"We're doing all we can to extract a confession from Laurence." Maggie squirmed in her seat.

Nellie rolled her eyes toward Maggie. "Well, not everything."

Maggie's friends turned their attention to Nellie. She could almost hear them thinking: *What has happened to Maggie since they went to the Hall? Had she changed her mind about the accident?*

"Would anyone like something to drink? Margaret, would you assist me?" Dr. Shane slid off the bench and listened to their requests.

Maggie rose to her feet. Her muscles tensed. Dr. Shane had a keen gift of discernment. She knew this gift had nudged him to remove her from the group. Once they were out of ear-shot, Maggie knew Nellie would relate all that had happened at Stuart Hall.

✳✳✳

The smells from the food booth were tantalizing.

"Before we order, Margaret, I'd like a detailed update on your progress."

Maggie shared with Dr. Shane the information they had gathered. Her monotone voice contained no emotion. Her sentences were short and to the point.

"I feel you don't want to talk about this, Margaret. I'm wondering if you're still serious in your quest to discover the truth about your mother's death. Laurence is very handsome and you're a beautiful young lassie. I would be blind if I didn't think it might be possible that you're falling in love with him. But, I must caution you, I don't believe he can love anyone but himself." Dr. Shane motioned her farther from the crowd.

"Your friends in Rolen are counting on you to find out the truth. You must, at all costs, keep your emotions in check. Unless you're willing to do that, everything you've done to this point will be for naught. The residents of Rolen will continue life as usual, but the doubts will remain. If Laurence is guilty of murder, and gets away with it, he will gloat the rest of his life. And what of his father? What will the relationship be like when Ramsay returns and finds his son still there? Will Laurence have to murder Ramsay as well?"

"How right you are, Dr. Shane. His rugged good looks, his charming ways have softened my heart. I've a hard time keeping my emotions under control when I'm with him. I've been vulnerable the past few months and thought I needed a man's attention. He's filled a void. What's that saying: I go weak in the knees? Falling in love was not my intention. Perhaps I judged him guilty too soon?"

Maggie watched the slow moving clouds, lips pursed, and tucked her hands inside her skirt pockets. "I appreciate what you're saying, Dr. Shane. I'm in a sort of muddle today. Almost like entering a dense fog and not knowing which way to turn. Seeing Ernest and all the others reminded me I came to Scotland for a specific purpose and I've allowed Laurence to mesmerize me.

"You know, Dr. Shane, my mother's wisest counsel in choosing my friends? 'It's not the outside, my dear, but the inside that makes a genuine friend.' I discovered many times we chose friends because they were nice looking, with nice clothes, and came from a nice family. Yet, they were the ones who were self-centered. They wanted a friendship for what they could get out of it. My closest friends wore hand-me-down clothes from siblings, but had a heart of gold." Moisture pooled in Maggie's eyes.

"I may have judged Laurence by his outward appearance, yet it seems there is a genuine person who lives inside. Also there are two sides to every coin and I forgot to turn the coin over. Dr. Shane, all of my judgements before I spent time with Laurence were very one sided. However, I feel I've let my friends down.

"Nellie spoke to me rather harshly before we came today and I've been very resentful. While they think I've made a mistake, I'm not convinced I have. I'll ask for their forgiveness, but until I can say, without a doubt, that Laurence is guilty, I'll maintain his innocence. Dr. Shane, I'll try to get back on track and remain focused on the reason we came. But until we can prove Laurence caused the accident that killed my mother, I must judge him as innocent."

"There's a story in the Bible about a man who wanted to know the truth about Jesus' resurrection." Dr. Shane directed Maggie toward the refreshment stand. "He needed to know without a doubt that Jesus was not dead. His name was Thomas. He's referred to as Doubting Thomas, but became a believing Thomas after Jesus confronted him face to face. You're still a doubter, Margaret, but I'm convinced that with the resolve you now have, you'll be able to meet the challenge and Laurence head-on and stand your ground."

With cool beverages for all, Maggie and Dr. Shane rejoined their friends.

"First," Maggie set the drinks on the table, "I'm sure Nellie filled you in about what we learned from the staff at Stuart Hall and also my doubts regarding Laurence's guilt. Nellie, I need to apologize to you, and later to Max. My combative nature came forth and took control.

"I'm not convinced Laurence is guilty of murder, but, thanks to Dr. Shane, I understand my emotions may have clouded my judgement. You are all people of faith, so I would like to request that you pray for me more fervently than ever. I want to know without a doubt whether my mother's death was an accident or murder."

Maggie's hand warmed as Mabel's hand clutched hers.

"You have been under quite a strain since you learned of your mother's death," Ernest said. "I understand how Laurence could win you over to his side. He's handsome and can be very persuasive. We've been praying for you, Nellie, and Max, but we'll turn up the intensity. I don't know about the others, but I pray for Laurence as well. This has been hard for me, since like others, I judged him guilty and didn't even consider it may have indeed been an accident."

"I agree," Mabel said. "We must know for sure. Either he is guilty or innocent. We all received invitations to the gathering at Stuart Hall tomorrow and are overjoyed. It's been a long time. But please know we're committed to do whatever's necessary to keep you on track to the original goal. I know Claire would be proud of you, and in her place, I'll give you a hug and say, I love you, Maggie."

Maggie tried to hold the emotions back, but she hadn't had a mother's hug for many years. Tears gushed down her cheeks. Nellie hurried round the table and embraced Maggie as well. A dear and trusted friend.

"I know the strain you've been under and I forgive you, Maggie."

Dr. Shane prayed, "Lord, we know you are the giver of all good gifts. This group of friends is one of those good gifts. We ask now that you will make us like-minded in our quest for truth. Let all the evidence prove either guilt or innocence, without a doubt. Thank you for your grace and love. May we be mindful of these gifts as we live in community here in Rolen. In Jesus' Name, Amen."

Chapter 35

The sights and sounds of the Highland Games filled the air. Brightly colored banners swayed in the breeze as the field filled with kilts and tartan skirts. Even the children sported their clan colors as they darted around adult legs.

"Harriet and I are eager to size-up the pastry contestants," Mabel rose from the table. "Maybe they'll hand out samples. You gents, I bet you're heading for the heavy sporting events. Am I right?"

"Right you are, Mabel. George bragged about his muscle tone when he entered the caber toss as a young lad. I'm sure none of us could throw that pole end over end today. The laddies here toss the pole as if it weighed a fraction of its 175 pounds. The way they heave it in the air, you'd think it was bamboo instead of a larch tree trunk." Ernest finished his drink.

Dr. Shane chuckled. "I tried to toss a small log end over end when a wee laddie. Almost killed myself."

Maggie watched the men proceed to another field. The high-pitched tone of a tin whistle caught her attention. Lined with rows of whistles, the booth gathered a crowd as the seller played a jig.

"What do you think, Nellie? Should I try my luck with a tin whistle?"

"Why not! I know musical abilities never came my way. Why, I couldn't even pucker enough to whistle with my mouth. If it's something you want, I'll buy it for you." Nellie fingered the hand-made instrument, fascinated as the shopkeeper's fingers moved over the holes. While Maggie mulled over the idea, she spotted Max and Laurence. Laurence parted company with Max and marched to her. She grabbed Nellie's arm and headed toward the dance competition.

"Maggie, what on earth are you doing?" Nellie caught herself before she tumbled to the ground.

"It's Laurence. I don't want to talk to him just now." Maggie forced her way through the crowd to the grandstand. Nellie stumbled behind her.

"Oh, Nellie, we missed the dancers. They're preparing for the bagpipe competition. Sorry if I'm talking too loud. Hard to be heard over so many pipers warming up at one time."

Maggie scanned the spectators for two empty seats. Then she spotted Laurence, who stood in front of her a few rows away. She could see Laurence's mouth move, but couldn't hear him over the bagpipe jig. Laurence wormed his way through the crowd and reached the ladies.

"Nellie," Laurence said as he hooked Maggie's arm. "I'm kidnapping Maggie. We'll be in the picnic area if anyone needs to find us." Maggie, dragged out of the crowd, mouthed a plea to Nellie, but to no avail.

"How about a cup of tea? Then we can sit and talk. I have something serious I would like to discuss with you."

"Thank you, Laurence." Maggie forced her anger down. "I would prefer a cup of coffee if it's available." Maggie plopped down at a table Laurence had secured. Gone for a minute, he returned with two cups of coffee and sat across from Maggie.

Maggie blew into the hot liquid, then glanced at Laurence.

"Nellie and I saw the dancers from a distance. Those girls were so graceful and the kilts were so colorful. I understand each clan has their own kilt pattern. Do you know them all?" Laurence's words "something serious," had frightened her, so she felt compelled to try to control the conversation.

"No Maggie, I don't. I was never much for family history. I know I'm a member of the MacLaren Clan. Our tartan is blue and green with yellow, red and black accent stripes create the plaid. Perhaps you noticed the tie my father wore in the portrait at Stuart Hall. That's the clan tartan. But I never had much interest in clans, tartans, folk lore nor the Highland Games. All rather boring to me. And the crowd sometimes gets on my nerves. I prefer smaller groups, like ours at Stuart Hall. You, Nellie and Max. That's just the right number." He sipped his coffee.

Maggie considered his statement. "I'm sorry. I didn't know you were uncomfortable in crowds. Perhaps we should call off the gathering tomorrow."

Laurence's brow furrowed. "If you remember, the gathering was my idea, not yours. I look forward to reacquainting myself with our guests. Besides, I can't wait to see you in that beautiful gown. You'll win everyone's hearts."

Maggie blushed at his flattery, but wondered if Laurence had an ulterior motive. She knew there remained a strained relationship between Laurence and the people in the village. To wait for tomorrow would be hard, so Maggie allowed the Games to distract her.

A clanging bell signaled thirty minutes before the start of the horse race.

"I've lost track of time. Fireball needs a warm-up before his big race. Please accompany me to the stables. I want to ask you something and you can wish Fireball a successful run."

Maggie tried to think of an excuse not to, when Nellie appeared.

"Time for the pastry judging. Harriet needs our support. I told her I would find you. Would you like to come, Maggie?"

Would I like to come? What kind of question was that? Of course, I'd like to come.

"Be right with you, Nellie. Laurence was heading to the stables to prepare Fireball, anyway. If you'll excuse us, Laurence." Maggie grasped Nellie's elbow and thanked her. "You came to my rescue one more time."

The judge's arena overflowed with contestants and on-lookers. Maggie spotted Harriet. Her hat was askew, and she paced in the little area between other women. Maggie never thought of Harriet as a nervous person.

"Harriet, how are things going? Have the judges announced the winners in your categories?" Maggie wrapped her arm around Harriet's waist.

"They have announced all the winners except the three I entered. I'm so nervous. I never bite my nails, but take a gander at my manicure now." Harriet held up her hands.

"Oh, Harriet," Maggie said. "We all get nervous from time to time. Why, one day I became so nervous I didn't know whether I should tie my neck scarf or lace my shoe."

The announcer cleared his throat and tapped a wooden mallet on the table.

"May I have your attention, please? We would like to announce the winners for marmalades."

They awarded second and third place. Maggie leaned back and spotted Harriet's crossed fingers. She grinned at Nellie.

"Nellie, you hold one arm and I'll grab the other. Support may be necessary." Maggie pushed Harriet's hat back on top of her head.

"First place for marmalades: Effie Rigby of Covenshire."

Maggie and Nellie caught Harriet as she lost her balance. When Harriet regained her footing, she tapped the lady in front of them on the shoulder.

"Congratulations, Effie," Harriet said.

The announcer spoke again. "I'm sorry. I forgot to announce we have a tie this year. Two lassies outdid themselves. Tied for first place with Mrs. Rigby, Harriet McNeal of Stuart Hall."

Maggie covered her ears as Harriet shrieked.

"I can't believe I won!" Harriet bounced in place and hugged Maggie.

"Wait, Harriet, they're not through," Maggie calmed her with a hand on each shoulder. "Time for the winners in the pie category."

Maggie crossed her fingers. She peeked at Nellie, who had crossed all four fingers on each hand. Nellie winked.

Maggie and Nellie sandwiched Harriet between them for support as they announced the third and second place winners.

"I don't know about you and Nellie," said Maggie, "but this is one of those times we talked about. My shoes are laced and I'm not wearing a neck scarf, but tension mounts while we wait."

Maggie's crossed fingers throbbed.

"First place for the best mincemeat pie goes to, Harriet McNeal of Stuart Hall." The three lassies danced with excitement.

Maggie whispered in Harriet's ear. "Harriet, if you get a blue ribbon for your scones, it will be a clean sweep. How exciting that would be?"

Third place, then second place, was announced. Harriet and Nellie had crossed their fingers and ankles, so Maggie joined them. The announcer unfolded a paper containing the winner's name. Maggie held her breath.

"The judges had a difficult time choosing a winner, so once again, laddies and lassies, we have a tie. The winners of the first place blue ribbons go to Effie Rigby and Harriet McNeal. Congratulations, lassies." Harriet linked arms with Effie and walked to the judges to receive their ribbons.

"We've ended right on time," the announcer's voice rose over the crowd. "So all of you now head to the grandstands for our last event of the games. The most spectacular and much anticipated horse race. I see by the clock we have ten minutes before the start, so will someone lead the way? You all go now and cheer on your favorite horse. I understand Master MacLaren has entered Fireball. If it is anything like the last time, it should be a race for the history books."

Maggie, Nellie and Harriet felt like salmon heading for the family spawning ground as they were pushed and shoved through the crowd to find the best seat for the race. Maggie spied three empty seats in the grandstand, high enough for a good vantage point.

"There's Fireball," Harriet said. The ladies followed the direction she pointed.

How dapper Laurence appeared. He sat straight and tall. Maggie watched as he strutted Fireball in front of the crowd. He tipped his hat, grinned, and bowed toward her. She smiled back, but felt uncomfortable with the attention. Laurence reminded Maggie of a proud peacock who paraded himself for his own amusement.

"Harriet, Maggie, over there," yelled Nellie. "Max on Diablo. Doesn't he look professional? Maybe he should've been a jockey. I hope Max wins and takes some of the starch out of Laurence's collar."

"He's too tall for a jockey. Max is perfect as he is. I wouldn't change a thing. Besides, if he were a jockey, we would have never met in Portland." Maggie frowned. "I feel a void in my life thinking about it."

"I haven't heard you speak about Max like that. Is there something you're not telling me?"

"Oh, Nellie, you're a dreamer. I value his friendship as much as yours and couldn't imagine my life without either of you. But I concur; I hope he takes the starch out of Laurence's collar." All three ladies giggled at the thought.

So involved with their chatter, Maggie didn't notice Ernest and Dr. Shane slip into the seats behind them. She heard men's voices, but hard to distinguish over the din of the crowd.

"So what de ya think, laddie? I widna be surprised if that nag, Whirlwind, flew outta nowhere and mowed down all the rest." Ernest disguised his voice. "Sae Fireball's here again. That horse has gotta be too auld to keep up with the pack."

The heavy brogue behind Maggie intrigued her. She listened intently.

"Fireball canna win this race," Dr. Shane forced a bass voice.

"Looka here, Laddie. Diablo's on the ticket." Ernest covered his mouth as he spoke. "I ken they're frae the same stable. My bawbee's on Diablo. He'll run circles around auld Fireball. He may be king of the stables at his hoose, but this is Diablo's race. I hope he shows Fireball a thing or twa."

Maggie clinched her fists. These two men don't know what they're talking about. They don't know Fireball and Diablo like she does. Possibly they were correct about Diablo. Maybe this was his race.

"Oh, don't be tae sure," Ernest's voice cracked. "If Diablo occupy's the same paddock as Fireball, he may be intimidated to beat him. And besides, his jockey is some no name Yank. They're both losers in my book."

Maggie reached her limit. She spun around, ready to defend Max.

"Ernest? I might expect some comments like that from you. But, Dr. Shane? Why, I am surprised." A jovial laugh followed. "While you watched the heavy-man sports, Harriet, once again, emerged as master of pastries and baked goods. Blue ribbons all around. I think we should celebrate somehow."

Nellie interjected, "For sure. Harriet shouldn't need to cook the rest of the day, and maybe even tomorrow. Or perhaps a cruise to some foreign shore. What say you?"

"Congratulations, Harriet." Ernest grabbed her hand. "I think we should leave the reward decision until later or we'll miss the race. I've got forty farthings on Ol' Blue, so my eyes will be glued to him. This is his chance to redeem himself from his last race against Fireball. No more talk. They're ready to begin."

Maggie admired the beautiful horses as they pranced toward the starting line. Two laddies climbed wooden platforms on opposite sides of the track. Each held the end of a rope that marked the starting point. They stretched it tight until the rope was a foot or two above the jockey's heads.

For a split second, Maggie returned to those happier days and the tug-of-war games she played at school. It was extra fun when the ground felt like a sponge from a recent downpour and the winners left the field, gloating over their trophy of mud. A gun blast brought her back to the situation at hand.

"And they're off!"

The horses moved together as one, almost floating toward the first turn. One pack of horse muscle, bits of mud flying. During the first lap, the subdued crowd kept their eyes fixed on the track.

Maggie heard Nellie cheer for Max. She didn't know who to cheer for. What if Laurence heard her voice shouting, "Max" or "Come on, Diablo." *Should I be loyal to my host? Or loyal a best friends? Would cheering for Laurence improve our relationship where he might confide more? Maybe I should yell for Ol' Blue. Then again, maybe I should keep quiet.*

As the horses thundered past the crowd which ended the first lap, the pack dispersed. Four horses were in the lead, while the others stayed close behind.

Maggie's heart beat faster. Fireball led the way. Ol' Blue paced him hoof beat for hoof beat. She glimpsed Diablo on their heels.

The horses were on the back side of the track and the noise grew in the grandstands. Maggie covered her ears, but still heard cheers for Ol' Blue and MaGinty, another sleek horse from a farm closer to Covenshire. MaGinty closed the gap between the leaders and came head-to-head with Fireball. Maggie knew this would challenge the black horse. Another bolt of energy left MaGinty behind. Ol' Blue's jockey nudged an extra shot of speed from his horse. Ol' Blue surged up even with Fireball again. Maggie cupped her hands even tighter over her ears as the crowd's cheers became deafening.

Her pulse raced. She decided that from this far away, Laurence would never recognize her one small voice buried in the sea of so many. She inhaled and expelled the loudest cheer of her entire life. In fact, so loud and heartfelt, she even scared herself. "Come on, Ol' Blue!"

Nellie smiled and agreed with her.

This became a race between Ol' Blue and Fireball. Maggie smiled as she watched Nellie cup her hands around her mouth, then roared, "Come on, Ol' Blue, move your bloomin' ___." Nellie's eyes darted toward Maggie. Relieved Nellie had stopped before completing the sentence, Maggie grabbed her friend's hands and laughter released any lingering animosity. Maggie knew they reconnected and relaxed in Nellie's faithfulness.

As the horses raced down the back stretch for the last time, two laddies scurried onto the track, averting Maggie's focus. They climbed the platforms again and stretched the rope across the track. To catch the jockey's attention, a blue cloth ribbon dangled from the rope.

Rounding the last turn, Maggie recognized Fireball still in the lead. Ol' Blue seemed to run out of steam and faded back. A heavy covering of mud on the horses behind the leaders created difficulty in recognizing who held the third and fourth places.

Then out of nowhere, Maggie glimpsed another horse closing the gap to the front runners. He galloped past Ol' Blue and inched his way forward until neck and neck with Fireball.

Shocked and surprised, Maggie's eyes bulged. Diablo and Max were making their move. Max bent low over Diablo's neck. Maggie grabbed Nellie and Harriet's hands. With a nod of agreement, the three yelled, "Come on, Diablo! Come on, Max!"

The crowd leapt to its feet. The bleachers shook as if an earth quake rumbled beneath them. From the raised rope, the blue ribbon dangled, ready to be pulled by the winning jockey. Hoof beats grew louder and louder competing with the noise from the crowd.

Maggie covered her ears, eyes riveted to the horse's powerful strides. Fireball and Diablo were neck and neck in the homestretch. It was all or nothing for both horse and rider. Laurence kicked

Fireball, spurring him to go faster, while Max leaned closer to Diablo's neck. Maggie loved how the horse and rider became one.

Little by little, Diablo pulled away. Then, with one last burst of speed, he passed Fireball. Max stretched to grab the blue ribbon. Diablo won by a length.

The excitement escalated. Maggie jumped and shouted for joy along with the crowd. Her heart burst with pride as Max and Diablo walked to the winner's circle. A wreath of purple and white heather graced Diablo's neck. When the roar of the crowd subsided, the chairman made his announcement.

"It is with pleasure that I present this Highland Game Horse Race trophy to Max Sullivan and Diablo. Diablo is from Stuart Hall and, believe it or not, Mr. Sullivan here is from the United States. It took a Yank to ride a Scottish horse and beat the past Stuart Hall champ, Fireball. Congratulations, Mr. Sullivan."

Max shook the chairman's hand, raised the winner's cup over his head and received a standing ovation fit for a monarch.

Maggie grabbed Nellie's hand and fought their way through the crowd. When they reached the winner's circle, the ladies threw their arms around Max, mud and all.

Caught up in the moment's excitement, Maggie kissed Max. Shivers ran down her arms. Their eyes locked and Maggie felt transported to another place and time. A quiet day on the beach. A hike in the mountains around Mt. Hood. Just the two of them lost in time and space. Not in a winner's circle in Rolen, Scotland with hundreds of on-lookers.

Something bumped Maggie's side. The trophy dangled from Max's hand. A beautiful shiny silver cup. Max won the race and with the heavy beats in her breast, Max had won her heart as well.

"Max, you did it. You and Diablo beat Fireball. We're so proud of you," Nellie yelled.

From the corner of her eye, Maggie glimpsed an outstretched hand as it reached for Max.

"Well done, Max, old boy." Laurence shook Max's hand. "You ran a calculated race and knew when to give Diablo his head. An expert ride, dear friend."

Maggie's face beamed as she gazed at Max.

"Thank you, my dear friends." Max held the cup high. "Quite a race. Diablo ran by himself. I went along for the ride. Laurence, would you join Diablo and myself for a cool-down lap?"

"Be glad to, Max."

Maggie followed the men with her eyes and wondered if this marked the start of a closer bond with Laurence. Once again, unsure of her feelings toward him, she recognized the need for impartial truth. She would have to trust her friends' wisdom.

"Maggie, there you are." Ernest rushed to her side. "The crowd blocked our way to congratulate Max. Dr. Shane and I would like to treat you good friends to a pint of Scottish Ale in celebration."

"Ernest, speaking for myself, I'd be delighted." Maggie clasped Ernest's arm, and they led the group to the nearest refreshment center.

"Well, who would have thought that a Yank could get a Scottish horse to gather enough courage to beat his own stablemate?" Dr. Shane lifted his pint in the air. "Why, it wouldn't surprise me if old Fireball gives Diablo a good thrashing once they get home. Walter may have to keep them separated for a time. He may even have to sleep in the stables to be sure Diablo is safe."

Maggie smiled with delight that Dr. Shane couldn't get over how Diablo came from behind, dashed to the front, took the lead, and won the race. Her feelings for Max seemed to bubble over. Filled with a genuine sense of pride for her dear friend. Or was it more?

"Maybe Diablo lived up to his namesake." Dr. Shane shared his insight. "Satan uses his diabolical cunning to slither his way into our lives and keep us from the Lord. This horse unleashed his cunning and showed Fireball that when he, like us, let down his guard for an instant, another horse will slide in to take the winning trophy."

Maggie studied Ernest's face. He seemed forlorn. "Are you all right, Ernest? You seem to enjoy your pint, but you appear distant. Is there anything I can do?"

Silent for a few seconds, his gaze was trance-like. He shook his head and responded in a slow, monotone voice.

"No, Lassie, I'm fine. But I thank ye for asking. It's just that for two races now with Ol' Blue up against Fireball, I wished and hoped that for once Ol' Blue would beat the hoofs off that horse. Fireball seems so full of himself and maybe the sharpness of a loss would let the air out. I'm glad he was beaten, though. And imagine, a paddock buddy did it, ridden by a Yank."

Ernest lifted his pint in the air. "To Diablo and Max."

The clinking glasses assured Maggie that these wonderful people had become close friends. A moment of sadness filled her with the knowledge they had a limited time left in Scotland. She valued and loved each one in a short time they'd been there.

"Ernest, I'm so sorry. I just remembered. You put a wager on Ol' Blue. Does third place garner any winnings for you?"

"No, Maggie. In these races, the winner's pot is a shared pot. The rest of the money goes into a fund to help Rolen residents who find themselves in a needy spot during the year. Thanks for asking though. I'm fine and I celebrate with you, Nellie, and Max. I feel you're coming to the end of your quest and we'll be losing you back to the States. That'll be a sad day for all of us."

Maggie saw a tear form in Ernest's eyes. She patted his shoulder.

The tents came down, then the vendors repacked their wares. Horse carts carefully made their way through the crowd. The Lord had given them a pleasant sunny day, and by the smiles on their faces, Maggie knew everyone had a wonderful time.

"Do you think we might have some of your delicious pie when we get back, Harriet?" Maggie asked.

"You will have a choice. There's blueberry, mincemeat, and a pumpkin I baked last night while you all slept."

"You have piqued my appetite." Maggie settled on the carriage seat. "Oh, yes, and a nice cup of tea, if you please."

Scottish songs filled the air during the ride back to Stuart Hall. Maggie recognized one as a favorite of her grandfather and sang along.

Chapter 36

The staff scurried like mice as they prepared for the gala event. Maggie busied herself in the kitchen with Nellie and Harriet as they cooked the evening's delicacies.

She glanced out a window. Max, James, and Walter set up tables and chairs under the shade of a large oak tree. Beyond, she noticed Leach clip dead blossoms from flowering bushes and shrubs. A basket of freshly cut flowers lay on the grass beside him. How beautiful the blooms would be as they graced the tables for the social.

"Harriet," Maggie said. "I haven't seen Laurence all day. Do you know where he is?"

"I believe he saddled Fireball for a jaunt earlier this afternoon. Can't say if he arrived back or not. I can hear him when he goes upstairs, but we've been so busy, I haven't noticed. Don't worry though, lassie. Master Laurence has counted down the days to this evening. He'll be here and he'll be ready on time. One thing I can say for certain about Master Laurence: he's always punctual."

Maggie placed a rolled serviette on each plate at the dining room table. Then she retrieved the silverware from the kitchen and completed the place settings.

With a silver candelabra at each end of the table, the dining room looked elegant. Maggie admired her handiwork. *This evening will be the climax of my Scotland trip.* Maggie jostled her brain to re-think that statement. *This evening will be the social climax of my Scotland trip. There, that sounded better.* She returned to the kitchen.

"It's about time you two lassies get all fancied up before the guests arrive." Harriet nudged Maggie and Nellie out. "I can finish by myself. Thank you for your help. I enjoyed the company and conversation."

Maggie beamed. She skipped up the stairs and beat Nellie to the top.

"I don't know about you, Nellie, but I feel like a teenager again, getting ready for the graduation dance."

"I'll come to your room when I've changed, Maggie. We can do each other's hair. I can hardly wait to see you in that beautiful gown. Remember, though, if Laurence's eyes fall out and his tongue dangles to his waist when he sees you, move back at least an arm's length away. On second thought, the other side of the room would be better. If Max reacts the same way, well, that's just fine."

A knock on Maggie's door came sooner than expected.

"Oh, Nellie. You look lovely. I'm having a bit of a problem with some of these buttons. Could you help?"

Maggie heard footsteps in the hall as Nellie fastened a button.

"Sounds like Max," Maggie said. "More steps. Must be Laurence."

A gentle knock on Maggie's door interrupted the buttoning.

"I'll be downstairs," Laurence said, "and wait in anticipation for two gorgeous ladies. Stuart Hall will again be alive with dancing, music and much laughter. Your last evening here will be one to remember."

Maggie felt her emotions swell again as Laurence continued down the stairs. She glanced at Nellie with questioning eyes.

"I'm afraid of what this evening holds for me. While I've tried to keep my distance, sanity and sense of purpose toward Laurence, I find myself drawn into his world. Just the sound of his voice sends shivers up my back. I try to keep my mother's image in front of my eyes at all times. Then his rugged good looks and gentlemanly ways steal me away. What can I do, Nellie?"

The buttoning completed, Maggie sat straight on a chair for Nellie to comb through her long tresses. The pace had been so hectic the past few days, she'd had little time to give her hair a thorough brushing.

"Do you remember the thoughts you had when you first received the news of your mother's death?" Nellie removed more hair pins. "Do you remember what you said to me and how determined you were that we come to Scotland? And what about Max? Your persistence was enough for him to put his work on the shelf for an indefinite period. Because you were so unyielding in your determination to follow this course of action, we agreed to leave the States and help you."

Her friend's words both comforted and challenged Maggie as Nellie styled her hair.

"We believed in you and what you had to do. I think now is the time, Maggie, for you to believe in yourself and your resolve to see this investigation to its end. Perhaps this evening, whenever you feel your resolve weakening, find me. I will watch you always. If you give me any kind of sign that you need to be rescued, I'll come to your aid.

"If that's not possible, look at the weeping willow. While they planted it for Gwen's mother, claim it now as a symbol of your mom and how proud she would be to know you are on a path to the truth. Uncover that resolve within. Remember, we have little time left to find Laurence guilty or innocent."

Maggie squeezed Nellie's hand. Tears welled up not only for her mother, but more for this dear friend and the confidence she inspired. As she gazed into Nellie's eyes, Maggie regained a sense of commitment and determination to complete their mission.

They finished each other's hair in silence. Nothing more needed to be said. Their time in Scotland had ended. Maggie felt determined that when Ramsay came home to Stuart Hall, he would not find it occupied by Laurence. She recommitted herself to unlock the truth, even if she had to ask him flat out.

A knock at Maggie's door startled both ladies and brought them out of their contemplations.

"I wondered if you two lovelies are ready?" Max cleared his throat. "If so, might I have the honor of escorting you downstairs? Our guests may arrive and I fear it wouldn't be proper to find us absent to greet them."

Maggie opened her door. Max placed a foot behind him to catch his faltering step. He scanned her entire body from head to toe, then back up. His eyes sparkled as he gazed at her.

"I'm overwhelmed with your beauty, Maggie. I'm reserving the first dance, here and now."

Nellie waltzed to the door and interrupted the moment. "Good evening, Max. You, if I may say so, are quite handsome."

Max extended his arms for the ladies. Maggie gratefully accepted, thankful for the extra support.

"May I say, ladies, I have never had two more ravishing beauties on my arms. You are both a picture of elegance and grace. I pray this evening will be a delight to all and one giant step closer to the truth. Are you ready, my dears?"

Maggie felt secure and safe on Max's arm. This man's presence warmed her from the inside-out. At that moment, she knew it was Max she loved. More than anything else in the world.

Voices from the foyer floated up the staircase. Maggie and Nellie strengthened their grip on Max's arms as the three friends descended.

A pleasant breeze from the open front door wafted up the stairs to greet Maggie. Her eyes fixed on Laurence as he held Mary Beth's hand to welcome her inside. Mary Beth's attention switched from Laurence to Maggie. Both ladies' faces lit up when their eyes met.

"Who is that beautiful lady standing next to Laurence?" Max asked.

"Why that's Mary Beth," Maggie said. "You met her at the Merc when we gathered as a group. Don't you remember?"

"Oh, yes, now I do. What a difference elegant clothes make. I thought her rather plain at Mabel's, but not now."

Max hadn't verbalized interest in Mary Beth. Maggie reassured herself if Max had a fling with Mary Beth, it wouldn't last long since they lived on different continents. Mary Beth exemplified a delightful woman, but Maggie was confident she would not leave Rolen and her livelihood. The more she pondered the idea that Max may have his eyes on someone else, the more deeply she felt an attachment to him.

Maggie gasped as Laurence faltered backwards. He excused himself from Mary Beth, as his attention was now focused on her. He held out his hand to Maggie and fumbled for words.

"I — I am speechless. That dress looks stunning on you. You are a vision of loveliness, Maggie."

He tenderly kissed her hand, then placed it on his arm.

"Nellie, you are enchanting, and Max, do I dare say it? You are indeed handsome, my friend."

Maggie accompanied Laurence to the door to welcome guests. She hoped Max and Nellie would join her, but Max entered into a conversation with Mary Beth. Nellie disappeared into the parlor where a sampling of Harriet's appetizers had already begun.

An uncomfortable feeling came over Maggie with Laurence's hand on hers. When she tried to remove it from his arm, he applied more pressure. She scanned the group in the parlor to catch Nellie's eye. Instead, Ernest burst into the foyer and went straight for Maggie. She hoped he would be her rescuer.

"With your permission, Mr. MacLaren, might we venture to the stables for a closer look at Diablo and Fireball? I'm dying to see these magnificent animals up close."

"By all means. I want Maggie's guests to enjoy and explore all of Stuart Hall tonight. Walter should be in the stables if you need any assistance."

Maggie's hopes dashed as Ernest, followed by George and Dr. Shane, sprinted through the parlor and out to the stables.

"Now that everyone has arrived, Laurence," Maggie brushed the front of her dress, "would you like to go out to the stables and join the conversation?"

"Thanks, but no. They should have their speculations and observations without me. Excuse me, please. I remembered something upstairs that would be outstanding with your gown. Why don't you join your friends while I'm gone? Only remember, when I return, you will again be on my arm."

Maggie felt some relief as Laurence ascended the stairs. She joined her friends at the stables and a sense of well-being calmed her. Dr. Shane, Ernest, Mary Beth, Max, George and Mabel, and Nellie had gathered close to the paddock. All her friends, assembled together for a final evening at Stuart Hall.

Ernest retrieved an envelope from his pocket. "I've been waiting for the right moment to read you Dr. McDonald's recent letter. Maggie, do you have any idea where Laurence is?"

"He went upstairs for something. He may be down any moment. Go ahead and read it, Ernest. George, could you keep your eyes on the hall? Alert us if you see him coming. Thank you."

"You can imagine my excitement when I received this letter today." Ernest ripped the paper from the envelope. "A short message, so this won't take long."

Dear Ernest and friends of Ramsay,

I have good news for you. Ramsay has made great strides in recovery and is ready to go home. We will plan for early next week. I am confident you will prepare Stuart Hall for his homecoming, including Laurence. Scotland Yard responded to my query. They may charge him with emotional abuse, if the staff corroborates.

I'll come with Ramsay as per his request. Unless you see any further need of my services, I send you my regards.

Dr. Alec McDonald

"This seems incredible. We've been here for such a short time, it doesn't seem real that he will come home next week. Such exciting news." Maggie smiled.

George signaled, so the conversation ended.

"Mary Beth, with your permission, I would like to show you the beauty of the leisure garden." Max offered Mary Beth his arm. Maggie wished she held his other arm and strolled away with them.

Maggie led the group back into the parlor and spoke of the architectural marvel of Stuart Hall.

"Ye micht persuade Lassy Richards 'n' Lassy Cox tae tak' ye oan a tour." James offered beverages on a silver tray. "Micht share thair knowledge o' th' Hall's history."

"An excellent idea, James," George agreed. "Speaking for Mabel and myself, we haven't been here for many years. How about we begin in the kitchen? Since we're kitchen dwellers at the cafe', I would relish an opportunity to view first hand where Harriet creates her award winning pastries."

Maggie guided the guests toward the kitchen, then she noticed Laurence motioning to her.

She excused herself from the group, but not before she caught Nellie's eye. The two exchanged reaffirming looks and head nods, then Maggie joined Laurence.

Maggie accompanied him to the patio. His hand rested in a side pocket. Laurence withdrew his hand and revealed a beautiful diamond and ruby necklace. The necklace gleamed and glistened in front of Maggie's eyes as Laurence stretched the strand between his two hands. She had seen nothing so beautiful.

"This has been in my family for several generations. My stepmother, my mother, my grandmother and my great-grandmother wore it. Beyond that, I'm not sure how many matriarchs. I know each lady wore this treasure with dignity and grace, proud to be a member of the Cheshire-MacLaren family clan. I'd be honored if you would accept this small token of thanks for the joy you have returned to these dusty old halls."

Maggie quivered as Laurence placed the family heirloom around her neck. His hands touched her skin while fastening the clasp. One more tingle bolted up her back.

"Oh, Laurence," Maggie said as she placed her hand on the jewels. "I can't accept this. This needs to remain in your family. My time in Scotland will end soon and I would not feel right to keep this beautiful necklace. No, Laurence. I can't accept this."

"Then, at least do me the honor of allowing these diamonds to grace your lovely neck this evening. Who knows, it may grow on you."

Laurence guided her to the window to view her reflection. As she placed her hand on the necklace, she admired its incredible beauty and realized Laurence spoke the truth. This heirloom paired perfectly with the gown.

James interrupted the quiet moment. "Th' musical folk hae arrived 'n' wondered whaur ye wid lik' thaim tae assemble fur th' forenicht."

"Please excuse me, my dear. One minor duty to perform and then I'll return."

Maggie strolled into the hall and heard her guests laughter. She followed the sound and rejoined them in the foyer. They were admiring the family portraits.

"Maggie, there is a glow about you I didn't notice earlier. Has something happened we don't know about?"

Dear Mabel. Always the inquisitive and observant one. A skill she gained serving her many patrons. Maggie smiled as Mabel followed the group upstairs, but said nothing.

Her cheeks warmed. Was this happening again? Why was Laurence so beguiling, always invading her mind?

She closed her eyes and squinted for a few seconds, as if to force herself to refocus. Laurence's words about the necklace replayed in her head. She studied each of the family portraits, concentrating on the matriarchs. Sweet Gwen as a child. Her mother was behind her. The portrait with Gwen, Ramsay and Laurence, as a young boy. And last, the painting of her mother with Ramsay. They were all beautifully and stunningly dressed.

Wait. Maggie saw something similar about these women.

She backed up a little to scan them with one sweep of her head. Once. Twice. Then, as if the ceiling caved in, the similarities came into focus. All the ladies wore a diamond and ruby necklace. The same necklace that now graced her neck. Yet, something more. She looked again, as if with a magnifying glass. Yes, they all wore the same necklace, but something else emerged in the last two portraits.

Gwen, Laurence's mother, wore the dress that Nellie now wore.

No. It couldn't be. Claire wore the dress Laurence had given Maggie.

Maggie stared at her mother, who seemed to look back at her. Almost a mirror image. Even with the age difference, the resemblance was striking.

Could Laurence see it also? Did he know Claire was my mother? How could he? We've been so careful. Our scheme has worked so far. Would we lose all tonight?

Chapter 37

Maggie heard the musicians tune their instruments in the distance and knew Laurence would return in a few minutes. A rat-a-tat-tat at the window startled her. Max tapped on the glass and peeked in. Confident he would rescue her, she dashed out of the Hall and joined Mary Beth and Max on the veranda.

"Hurry, say something, Max. As if I've always been with you," Maggie said as she spied Laurence. Desperation covered her face and spurred Max to action.

"What a beautiful evening," Max tilted his head. "At an exquisite manor, with the best company one could imagine." He noticed Laurence draw closer and understood Maggie's panic attack.

"Master Laurence, you have added sublime music to set just the right atmosphere."

"You, and Mary Beth, create a lovely ambiance here on the porch. So I don't believe you'll mind if I steal Maggie away from you." Laurence reached for Maggie's hand.

"When you were here before," he said, "I mentioned that the garden was the best place to learn about my family history. With your permission, I would like to do that now. Max, if you and Mary Beth will excuse us." Maggie accepted his invitation and the two strolled across the drive.

✳✳✳

Max's envious heart swelled and wished Maggie had strolled with him instead of Laurence. He tried to keep his emotions in check, but realized with another man in the picture, his feelings for Maggie intensified. Suppress his emotions for now? Yes, he must! There was no need to complicate the situation.

"If I didn't know any better," Mary Beth said, "I would say Maggie is smitten with Laurence. I trust my assumptions are as flimsy as a rotten shutter hanging by one screw in a windstorm. I do believe we must pray for her. Judging from the way Laurence looks at Maggie, the feeling seems to be mutual. What do you think, Max?"

The fear and concern in Mary Beth's voice echoed Max's own feelings. If prayers were answered, Max knew this would be a good time. He remembered his afternoon with Ernest and wished his friend would join them on the veranda. Ernest's simple trust in God and heartfelt prayer remained with Max. God would listen and answer Ernest's prayer for Maggie.

"Max, don't you think we need to pray for Maggie right now?" Mary Beth stared at Max.

Does she expect me to take the lead? He wasn't on speaking terms with God. He'd gone through life on his own steam. She must have assumed otherwise and seemed to lose patience with him.

Max glanced at her, then a quick, silent *"Help me."* Footsteps inside the Hall grew louder. His mouth dropped as Ernest and the tour group came through the front door.

"What's the matter, Max? You look as if you've seen an angel." Ernest said.

"It worked." Max's jaw dropped. He came to his senses and gazed straight at Ernest.

"What did you say?"

"I asked you what the matter was."

"No, the part after that."

"I said you looked as though you'd seen an angel."

"That's the part. Explain yourself. Shouldn't it be 'You look as though you've seen a ghost'?"

"Not in my faith world. I'd be much more surprised to see an angel than a ghost. I know both demons and angels are with us every day. Yet to see an angel, wouldn't that be something? I mean, to see one of God's angelic beings. Why, if that happened, I wouldn't care about Ol' Moses. I'd be ready to go home."

"Oh, Ernest," Mary Beth frowned. "Please be serious. We need to pray for Maggie. Max and I are afraid she's falling in love with Laurence and he with her."

Max scoured the group and found Nellie. Her expression changed from lightheartedness to obvious deep concern for their friend after what she heard from Mary Beth.

"They've gone to the garden and may return at any moment," Mary Beth said. "The urgency of prayer is upon us and our time is brief. We need to pray. I was about to ask Max if he would take the lead, but maybe, Nellie, since you're close friends, you would like to lead us in prayer."

Relieved the prayer burden changed from his shoulders to Nellie's, Max averted his eyes away from her and bowed his head. All eyes now rested on Nellie. One by one, they joined Max's example and waited in silence. *Would she take the lead and pray?*

Max remembered recent conversations with Nellie in which she'd shared her hesitancy to believe in God, especially during difficult investigations. When the crime scenes were gruesome, she puzzled over why God hadn't intervened to change the outcome. Max wondered if their time in Scotland among people of faith had helped answer her question. Nellie had responded that her faith journey had not only begun in earnest, but she had the answer to that distressing question.

She'd decided there was a God, and He cared deeply for all of creation. However, if He not only intervened, but altered every evil action, thought, or desire, humankind would be mere puppets on a stage, acting in a play for all of history. Instead, He allowed free-choice to permeate His creations, desiring we love Him with a genuine love from the innermost part of our beings.

Max had observed this mindset in those closest to Claire and the MacLaren family. While they were heartbroken over the turn of events that involved Claire and Ramsay, they were also in deep sorrow for Laurence and his choices.

Their show of love for the entire family was an example of God's unconditional love. Yet, they also knew that right must prevail over wrong. Maggie's mission had been to expose Laurence's guilt in the death of her mother, and Max knew they were at a critical juncture in that mission.

The sweet voice of Max's dear friend broke the silence.

"Almighty God," Nellie whispered. "We have nothing in ourselves to bring to you but our broken and repentant hearts. I'm sorry for all my sins and ask, in front of my dear friends, for your forgiveness. We humbly come before you to ask that you touch Maggie's heart and mind. Remind her why she is here. We believe Laurence is guilty of Claire's death, but need help to prove it. While we want Laurence to be punished, we also pray that he would turn to you in repentance and seek forgiveness. Thank you for listening to your children. In the name of Jesus, our Lord and Savior, Amen."

Each person spoke the "amen" after Nellie. Max opened his eyes. Nellie's face glowed. *Had she experienced a spiritual moment?*

"I feel warm all over." Nellie hugged herself. "As if a blanket of love covered the entire length of my body. I feel so joyful and at peace. My self-centeredness seems to have evaporated. What just happened?"

Something spiritual had indeed happened. Max remembered childhood hymns that described beatific visions, but doubted those visions occurred in the present day. Yet he knew Nellie's face brightened and an aura of peace surrounded her.

"Nellie," Dr. Shane held her hand, "you have received a touch from the Lord and will never be the same. Welcome to His forever family."

Max stepped back as Nellie received a hug from each friend. He absorbed an overwhelming sense of calm from that small gathering and pondered how different this moment felt compared to time spent with Laurence. There must be a spiritual dimension to life, and Max suspected he had received a small taste of a world much greater than the reality he knew.

Chapter 38

The sky, flooded with early evening stars, reminded Maggie of the heirloom that graced her neck. She caressed the gems and thought about the ladies who preceded her. If this necklace could speak, she would hear the whole truth. No more wondering if Laurence fabricated his tales. All would be laid bare. Another step closer to the answers she sought.

"You've already heard the story behind why these trees and the rose trellis were planted." Laurence plucked a rose and handed it to Maggie. She inhaled the sweet scent. "I'm sure you also noticed that they filled the Hall with these motifs in the rugs, lace tablecloths and even some carvings. My grandmother requested images of apples, pears, and peaches could be seen throughout the Hall as a visual reminder of her wayward sons. I loved to listen as my mother reminisced about her childhood and her wandering brothers. Irritated by the many times she had to scour the woods to find them for dinner. 'Playful rascals,' she called them."

"Didn't they hear your mother from the Hall?"

"Impossible for them to hear anything. My mother said she found them in the woods with my grandmother's best serviettes either as scarves or covering one eye. They whittled branches into swords, created make-shift caves from downed limbs, and were involved in terrific battles against fierce dragons defending their true loves. Such imagination and energy."

"Sounds like they lived in a fantasy world."

"Oh, yes, as most boys do. I admired them and often thought an adventure was just what I needed. That dream never materialized. Since I'm the only heir of the manor, I felt the responsibility of ownership.

"As a young child, I read books like Homer's *The Iliad and the Odyssey* and Robert Louis Stevenson's *Treasure Island.* I placed my uncles in similar adventures and wished for one of my own someday. In my mind, they lounged under an old oak tree as they read Robert Burns' poems to their fair lassies."

"Every child needs to dream of faraway lands, sometimes in their own backyard. Did you read those books in school? Did you ever write about your adventures?" Maggie's curiosity piqued over his upbringing. She wondered if an occurrence from his childhood had had a negative impact on his adult life.

"Raised as a member of the privileged class, my mother and father hired a tutor. He came three times a week, carried armloads of books. Math, science, art, music, but my favorite subject was the classics. I couldn't get enough. While my mother played the piano, and played beautifully, I might add, I sat at her feet. With my eyes closed, my imagination drifted away to distant lands. Sometimes I felt I lived those adventures.

"Once I related a tale to mother and father. I think they became concerned that I could not distinguish between imagination and reality." Laurence cradled her elbow. "Let's walk down to my mother's bench. I'm sure you might like to rest awhile."

"That sounds lovely. Do continue while we walk. I enjoy hearing about your childhood."

"My parents said nothing to me, but I'm sure they had a talk with their pastor. What could he do? Pray? I never put much stock in spiritual things. My mother and father were confident they'd find answers for their perplexing son. For me, I found solace riding Fireball through the woods for hours at a time. Harriet packed a lunch wrapped in a serviette to place in my saddle bag. She called it 'caring for a growing laddie.'"

"Did you ever write your stories?" Maggie asked.

"My tutor suggested that very thing. So I followed his suggestion. He edited my work and sent a story to a publisher in London. Publishers, huh! What do they know about a child's imaginative stories? They're only interested in adult stuff and what sells to make a few pounds. They don't care about young writers. At least not enough to offer even an ounce of encouragement." Laurence's voice grew stern. He picked a stick off the ground and threw it into the brush.

"I take it that your manuscript wasn't well received?"

"Well received? Not on your life. A few comments were scribbled on the last page. My tutor thought they were helpful. To me, they were rejection with a capital R. From then on I wrote for myself."

"Do you still have some of your stories? I'd love to read them," Maggie said.

"My sweet, Maggie. How kind you are. I decided when I became an adult to leave those childhood dreams behind. One evening, when the air was more than a bit chilly, I asked James to build a small fire outside the paddock. I took my manuscript and page by page, let the flames carry them up to the heavens."

Maggie's disappointment must have shown as Laurence patted her shoulder. She walked faster and changed the subject. "What about college? I'm assuming you followed your love of learning."

"Devonshire College beckoned me with their emphasis on literature. I discovered an increasing interest in medicine, especially psychiatry. The mind is a fascinating organ, and I hungered to learn everything about it. They often included Scotland Yard cases in the curriculum. I tried to put myself in the mind of a murderer. Tried to understand what would cause a man to go over the edge. Even tried to devise the ideal murder. You know, one they could never prove. It was a monumental challenge, but I thrive on challenges."

A turmoil erupted inside Maggie. Something chilled her, and she knew it wasn't butterflies this time. She found him fascinating, yet dangerous as well. Her friends remained on the front porch, but at quite a distance away. She felt sure that even if she yelled as loud as she could, they wouldn't hear. Keep the conversation on an even keel, she told herself.

"Did you complete your degree? Did you become a licensed psychiatrist?"

"Again, Maggie, my dreams ended before they came to fruition. I returned home on Christmas holiday to find my father had re-married." Laurence's voice changed from calm and accepting to harsh and forceful.

"Such a short period since my sweet mother's death. I'm sure if he had taken more time, he wouldn't have married the dowager." His eyes bulged and mouth tightened.

As they sat down on the bench, Laurence took a deep breath. Maggie thought she heard a groan, but didn't call attention to it.

"Your father must have loved her. Perhaps she had some of the same qualities as your mother. Don't you think they loved each other?"

"I'm not sure. Well, now that I think about it, yes, I believe so. She tried hard to ease into life at Stuart. The staff welcomed her, and I tried hard to include her whenever possible. But she was an outsider. Knew nothing of Scottish customs."

"So, she didn't grow up here?"

"No. She was an import, like you, from the States."

"You must have found some endearing qualities."

"She played the piano, almost as well as my mother, and appreciated the arts and classic literature. I can still see her in the library, contemplating which book to read next. Father had so many of the classics. She strolled in this garden, admired the flowers and sometimes helped Leach with the trimming. Yet, to me, she remained distant."

"I'm curious about your statement that you tried to welcome her. Was she unresponsive to you as her stepson?" Maggie felt concern that his temper might flair again.

"More than unresponsive. She didn't seem to care about anything I was interested in. Except how soon I would return to the university. She seemed eager to have me gone. Down deep, I suspected her real goal was to own Stuart. She cared nothing for my father. After his wealth. Thoughts of rejection entered my mind, but I was determined to not let them get a foothold. I needed to stay and do whatever I could to protect my father."

Laurence's irritation seemed to reach additional levels. Maggie wondered how long before the inner turmoil might become outward aggression. Yet, she knew she must persist in finding the answers to her mother's death. Oh, that her friends would come her way.

"Your father must have grieved for her after the riding accident. Do you mind telling me about that day?" *Has it come to this? Last night at Stuart Hall and I almost have to ask him, point blank, did you kill my mother?*

"I will never forget that day, Maggie." Laurence rubbed his hands together. "My father sensed his wife showed no interest in me and this rested like a great weight on his shoulders. He had enough stress with the cases he represented and didn't need an unresponsive, dour wife.

"Frequently, I overheard them talk in their bedroom. He encouraged, no almost demanded, that she include me in some activity and attempt to build a relationship." He scrubbed his moist hands on his legs, flattening the sharp pant crease.

"One day, to my surprise, she asked to accompany me on my daily horse ride; the day of the fateful accident. She assured me she was a skilled rider. I led the way to one of my favorite trails. We were only a short distance into the woods when I heard a scream, pivoted and watched her fly over the ravine, her horse still bucking.

"I hurried back, dismounted, grabbed her horse's reins and peered over the edge. She dangled from some large tree branches about half way down the side. I climbed down as close as I could get. Her legs were bent in a most awkward position. They must have broken. I assured her I would be right back, climbed to the top, mounted Fireball and galloped to the stables, pulling Peggy behind me. You know the rest of the story, I'm sure. I felt sorry for her. She wanted to build a relationship after all, but my hopes were dashed in that ravine." Laurence cupped his face in his hands.

Maggie didn't know how to respond. Laurence expressed such negativity toward her mother. This version contradicted the hearing transcript as well. She couldn't imagine Claire would treat anyone the way he described.

She readied her next question, but Laurence waylaid her.

"Maggie, I've done all the talking. You know much more about me then I do about you. Tell me about your childhood, your parents and your aspirations for the future. I hope it includes Stuart Hall."

Tension rose again as Maggie was put on the spot. She knew she would have to fabricate a superficial story. Maggie formulated her response, separating benign incidents from others that could lead Laurence into suspicious speculation.

A loud bell ring diverted their attention. "Dinner is served." James called. He stood on the front porch, bell in hand.

The strength of this elderly man's voice startled Maggie. Relieved of any continued conversation, she rose to her feet. "Shall we?" She turned away from Laurence and briskly sauntered to the Hall.

As they joined their guests in the dining room, Laurence placed Maggie at one end of the table while he sat at the opposite end. The other guests found name cards beside the wine glasses and slid into their seats.

"Dr. Shane," Laurence said, "would you mind asking the blessing?"

"I would be honored, Laurence. Thank you." Dr. Shane waited until each guest had bowed their head.

"O Lord, wha blessed the loaves and fishes, Look doon upon these twa bit dishes. And tho' the tatties be but sma', Lord, mak' them plenty for us a'. But if our stomachs they do fill, 'Twill be another miracle. Amen."

Chapter 39

The guests rose from the dinner table and followed the sounds of music into the courtyard. A cool breeze was a gentle reminder that summer drew to a close and fall pressed in. James meandered among the visitors and offered after-dinner tea and coffee.

"I'd like to take this opportunity to thank Laurence for his kind hospitality," Maggie said. "Tomorrow is our last day at Stuart Hall. Then one more day in Rolen before our train leaves for Glasgow and a long boat ride back across the Atlantic. We've forged lasting relationships and would consider it an honor to repay your kindness if any of you ever venture our way."

"You're so welcome, Maggie." Laurence kissed the back of her hand. "Speaking for myself and my staff, you have warmed Stuart Hall with your kindness, congenial personalities and always laughter. I will miss each of you and invite you to return whenever you're able."

Maggie's heart skipped a beat as Laurence approached Nellie and opened his arms for a hug. Nellie's quick thinking staved off this unwanted familiarity. She reached her arm out and clasped his hand. No more body contact than that from their adversary. Then he approached Max for a hearty handshake.

Her turn next. She tried to think of a way out. Too late.

With a smile on his face, Laurence headed straight for her like a bee to honey. She wondered if it was the same smile James saw after the accident and subsequent funeral. Intervention time.

"Laurence, if you'll excuse me a moment, I'd like a drink of water."

"Please, allow me, Maggie."

Laurence coupled her arm around his and entered the parlor. A large pitcher of water and several glasses were set out for the guests. Laurence poured water into two glasses and handed one to Maggie.

"Thank you very much." Maggie swallowed, the refreshing liquid soothed her throat. "Listen. The ensemble is playing Bach's Gavotte from the Fifth French Suite. It's one of my favorite Bach compositions. When I took piano lessons, I persevered until I played it without a flaw. Let's go back before it ends. It's such a short piece." She took a step, only to be halted by Laurence's hand on her arm.

"Maggie, since this is our last evening together, I would like you to accompany me. There remains a section of Stuart Hall you haven't seen and I would hate to think of you going home missing it. Please?"

Laurence extended his arm. Maggie hesitated a moment, then agreed. She felt like a lamb to the slaughter. As far as she could remember, there wasn't any section of Stuart Hall she hadn't explored. Unless a dungeon awaited underneath. *That's it. There is a dungeon, and he intends to chain me in shackles, leave me there and make up a story to tell my friends.*

Her mind floundered in a sea of possibilities. She scanned the area to find Max or Nellie or any liberator. Alas, they were all out of eyesight. Off she went, to an unforeseeable end.

"You've seen the surrounding forest, the gardens, the stables, and the neighboring farms, but never the way I wish to show you tonight. We must climb the stairs to the next level and then more stairs to the very top."

We're going up, not down? With each step, Maggie counted her moments left on this earth. She conjured up images of Laurence as he might throw her off the roof, then announce to all an unfortunate accident had occurred. That mind of hers, bound to cause trouble.

Maggie couldn't remember any moment at Stuart Hall that wasn't pleasant or even gave her even an inkling that he might wish her harm. Since nothing rose to the surface, she needed to be congenial, even while tremors rumbled inside.

They reached the attic. She spied one more set of stairs with a door at the top. Laurence unlocked the door. A forceful, cool breeze blew a few strands of hair into her eyes. She brushed them aside and rubbed her arms for a bit of warmth. Four more steps led into the cupola, which graced the top of the Hall.

"You're right, I've not been here, and you can see everything from this vantage point. The forest, and beyond your neighbors. Over there, a bird's-eye view of the gardens. My, they appear small from this vantage point. Look, down there." She leaned against the railing and held the top board for balance. "That's Max dancing with Mary Beth. Over there, Nellie and Dr. Shane. What a difference perspective makes." Max had promised the first dance would be hers. Mary Beth is in his arms instead. Time to go back down.

"Yes, Maggie. Perspective is everything. Too often we get so close to the subject we can't see the bigger picture. Like a painter who sits within inches of the canvas. She has a limited view. Only when we step back can we see the vastness of the situation. I come here often to sort things out. I love Stuart Hall, but have always felt there was something missing in my life."

Laurence leaned into the railing beside her and pointed toward the ground. "Observe your friends and the music group below. They look like mere ants trying to find a direction home." He paused, then sighed. "So many people. So little purpose."

He faced Maggie and stepped close. "Do you have a purpose, Maggie? I've pondered this over and over since you've been here. I thought sure I knew my purpose, until you came. Now I believe I have another purpose. What about you?"

"I'm not sure what you mean, Laurence. My purpose was to do exactly what I'm doing. I have a wonderful job back home that I love, and endearing friends who support and encourage me. I've been privileged to meet incredible people.

"Since I've met the residents of Rolen, I've discovered I also have a purpose, or responsibility, to develop a relationship with God. This is a new area for me, but I now see how important it is. I've glimpsed my life from God's perspective. If that makes sense."

"You have an inquisitive mind and I admire that." He brushed a loose strand of hair off her face. "What I want to know is the true purpose behind your trip to Scotland. Oh, I know what you told me, but I believe there's more. Just as I have been missing a piece in my life, I feel you've been missing something, too. Together, I know we can find the answers."

Maggie's uneasiness grew with every sentence Laurence uttered. Her tremors shot emotional lava in all directions. She knit her fingers together to calm herself.

Laurence placed his hands on Maggie's cheeks and brought his lips to hers. Such a tender kiss. He gazed into her eyes. Then the words she never imagined she would hear.

"Maggie, I love you. Will you do me the great honor of becoming my wife? Those jewels sparkling around your neck are right where they belong, on the next Mrs. MacLaren."

Her legs crumbled under her. Without his arms for support, she might have toppled out of the cupola. Her heart beat faster than ever. *Get a hold of yourself.* She tried to fortify her resolve. *What did he just say? Will I marry him? He's got to be kidding. I came here to convict him of murder.*

"My dearest Maggie. I know this is a shock for you. I'm also in a state of disbelief. Never in my wildest imagination did I envision myself as the marrying kind. Yet, you astonished me with your beauty, kind heart, generosity and loving ways. I couldn't help myself. I love you, Maggie, and want to spend the rest of my life with you." He grasped her hands in his and shifted his weight.

"Don't feel you need to give me an answer tonight. Mull it over. Talk with your friends. Consider how this would affect your life. Consider this marriage as being your life's purpose. I'm bursting inside with the thought of your saying yes. I considered myself a contented man until I met you. Now I see how shallow my life has been. You have a piece of my heart, and if you say no, you'll take that piece with you when you leave."

"I'm beside myself, Laurence." Maggie closed her eyes for a second. "Your proposal is touching and the thought of staying at Stuart Hall would be a dream come true for any princess from a faraway country. But I'm not a princess. I'm a mere homebody who loves where I live and what I do. This would be a drastic change. My time spent with you and your staff will always be part of my memories, but must remain that, a memory."

She glanced toward her friends so far below. "I'm content being single and it's hard to imagine how marriage could bring a purpose to my life that I lack at present. I thank you for your kind words," Maggie faced Laurence, "but I don't love you, Laurence."

Rejection left its mark on his face. With head lowered, eyes closed and slumped posture, Maggie realized disappointment shattered him one more time. Unless it was an act. He seemed pretty good at bluffing the masses.

"Thank you for your honesty," Laurence said. "Please though, for both our sakes, consider my proposal until you stand by the carriage with bags packed, ready to leave. Even at that very last moment, you may consent. I'll hope for a change of heart right up to the last second."

Maggie reached the stairs that led out of the cupola. Laurence followed. She could sense his forlorn and rejected persona with each step. Unless, again, it was only an act.

Maggie entered the courtyard and inhaled the fresh evening air deep into her lungs. She envisioned this breath as a cleansing tool to force her experience in the cupola out of her mind. A dungeon, no, but just as terrifying.

"Maggie, where have you been?" Nellie approached Maggie at the bottom of the staircase. "Our guests are about to leave and wanted to say good night to you and Laurence."

Maggie gazed into Nellie's eyes. The spark that once radiated from Maggie's face had gone.

"I'll tell you later," she whispered in Nellie's ear.

"Please forgive us, dear friends. Laurence took me to see the view from the cupola. It is magnificent." Maggie descended the porch steps and drew close to her guests. "May we assist with your wraps?"

Maggie turned toward the Hall. She didn't see Laurence. She wondered if he was deeply hurt. Maggie coveted some much needed quiet time once the guests left.

With the carriages lined up in front of Stuart Hall, the visitors climbed in and covered their legs with lap robes. Maggie spotted Laurence speaking with the music group. She welcomed this opportunity to escort Dr. Shane to his carriage.

"Dr. Shane, I now understand there is a God, and He has a purpose for my life. Over the past few days, I've realized there is another dimension to life I had never considered. Maybe the distance between my mother and myself has always been my fault, and I never stopped to examine the facts. I always told my mother there was no god, or if there was, He wasn't interested in me. I've lived my life my way, but Laurence challenged me tonight when he asked about my purpose in life." Maggie halted, Dr. Shane by her side.

"I've never given it much thought. Dealing with the physical, emotional and survival aspects of life has been enough. Yet, when faced with the prospect that there is also a spiritual dimension, I find myself in a quandary. Any suggestions?"

"Margaret, you're asking the same questions people have asked since time began. The 'Who am I?', 'What am I here for?', 'Is there an intelligent being who cares about me?'

"When people say to me 'There is no god' or 'There is no creative being,' I respond with words such as these: 'You seem like an intelligent person who wants to be sure of every decision you make because every decision has a gigantic implication for your life. If that is true, I have something I would challenge you to consider. In saying there is no God, you espouse that nothing took nothing and made everything.'" Dr. Shane's eyes glistened.

"I believe you are on the verge of discovering for yourself, Margaret, the same truth your mother placed her faith in. I have been and will continue to be, in prayer for you. It's just possible that when you understand the spiritual dimension to your life, you'll find your purpose fulfilled in the Lord Jesus, just as your mother and your friends here in Rolen."

He dabbed his eyes with a handkerchief. "May God bless you and may you find the answers you seek."

Dr. Shane peered up at the cupola. "I also believe Laurence is up to his devious tricks again."

He placed his hands on her shoulders. "He may bait you for more information, fishing on a hunch. Be careful. The evening is not over yet. And with tomorrow being your last day here, he may have planned something. I dare not imagine what, but, please, be careful and very much aware at all times."

"Thank you, Dr. Shane. I appreciate your counsel and will take it to heart."

As the last carriage moved down the drive back to Rolen, Maggie joined Nellie and Max on the veranda. It seemed fitting that their last night at Stuart Hall was the same as their first visit, enjoying the view from the porch.

Chapter 40

"Maggie, are you up? I want to chat with you before your ride with Laurence." Nellie said through a crack in Maggie's door.

"Give me a minute to dress. You can keep talking if you wish." Nellie heard the bed covers swish, then footsteps across the room.

"I'm a bundle of nerves this morning," Nellie said. "I hardly slept a wink and paced most of the night. We're still unable to pin a murder on Laurence. And I'm furious over Laurence's marriage proposal. Maggie, are you listening?"

Nellie pressed her ear to Maggie's door and heard the rustling of clothes. "Last night I came up with two options for settling this sticky situation. I could either hit Laurence, knocking some sense into his thick-headed brain, or just find a gun and shoot him, putting everyone out of their misery. Knowing I should reject both those choices, I stopped pounding the floor and instead knelt by my bed and gave it all to the Lord." Nellie paused. "Maggie, Maggie, did you fall back asleep?"

The pocket door slid into the wall. A downcast Maggie, head bowed with no good morning on her lips, faltered before Nellie. She, too, had had a rough night. Nellie embraced her dear friend as Maggie let the floodgates of tears burst.

"Nellie, I'm so ashamed. I've let you, Max, and all our dear friends down. I came to prove that Laurence had killed my mother. Instead, no fresh evidence has turned up and instead of legally calling him a murderer, I receive a proposal of marriage. I've wasted everyone's time, not to mention the financial strain. Can you ever forgive me?"

Tears filled Maggie's eyes. Nellie pulled a hanky from her pocket and dabbed Maggie's face.

"My dear sweet, Maggie. There is nothing to forgive. We're adults. We knew what to expect. The investigation is over. We've all been through quite an ordeal these past few weeks. You, more so than the rest."

Nellie sat beside Maggie on the bed and wrapped an arm around her friend's shoulders. "We came here believing that Laurence was guilty not only of the death of your mother, but the committal of his father. Since our research has yielded nothing conclusive, we must accept it as an accident. Whoever, or whatever, caused the tragedy we may never know. Time to move on, my dear, and leave Scotland behind. There is a bright spot to all this, I might add, Ramsay's coming home. That should be a cause for celebration."

Nellie handed her hankie to Maggie, who blotted her eyes once more. The girls smiled at each other.

"Thank you. I feel better now. You are my precious confidant. After a restless night, I'm looking forward to the tranquility of the Inn this evening." Maggie handed the damp hankie back to Nellie.

"Ramsay. I almost forgot about him. My mind has been churning like my wringer washer at home and thoughts of him never entered the mix. I'm excited for Ramsay. But what about Laurence? Should we tell him?"

"Not on your life." Nellie straightened her back. "We'll trust Dr. McDonald's expertise in such matters. I'd like to be a spider on the wall and observe Laurence's reaction. Wouldn't that be something?" Nellie sighed. "Now, we must put all that aside and get you ready for your last ride with Laurence. Looks like your boots are missing." She scanned the room. A boot toe stuck out from under Maggie's bed. "Here they are. Let me help."

Nellie waited for Maggie to get comfortable in a nearby chair. She pushed the black boots on over Maggie's socks, then tied the laces at the top. Nellie had a few more thoughts.

"I'm going to finish packing. Max offered to take our bags downstairs. He'll leave them by the front door. Then, I'm going to the kitchen. Harriet has agreed to share some of her favorite recipes with me. I thought we could have a Scottish dinner for our friends once we get back to the States. Shall I pack Gwen's diary for you?"

"That's very thoughtful, Nellie. If it is possible, perhaps Max could open Ramsay's bedroom door and slip it back under the mattress. I believe it would be better to leave Stuart Hall's memories in Scotland. Besides, those are remembrances of Ramsay's sweet Gwen." Maggie sighed. "I'm not looking forward to this horse ride, but felt it was my last compulsory duty. Please pray for me. I want to leave here on a positive note."

✳✳✳

Maggie left her room for the last time and trudged down the stairs. How many times had she made this trip? Ten, twenty, thirty? Whatever the number, they were once steps filled with purpose. Now each movement was a chore. Each step, another reminder that she had missed the goal. Maggie reached the foyer and gazed at the portraits one last time.

"Mother, I came for one purpose, but failed. There is one positive. Your husband's coming home. I wish I could meet him, but we'll be gone. I'm sorry I turned my back on you and wasn't the supportive daughter I should've been. Thanks to Dr. Shane and your wonderful friends, I've begun my faith walk. One baby step at a time is all I can do now. I love you Mom, and wish with all my heart I could reclaim those lost years and feel your arms around me."

Almost in a stupor, Maggie dragged herself to the garden. The roses were at the end of their life cycle. Spotted with rose-hips, what blooms remained had turned brown. Fallen petals lay scattered on the ground. She realized that like these roses, her journey had also ended and she was worn out. Their Stuart Hall holiday began with budding roses. How fitting it should end as they perished.

"Maggie, there you are," Laurence called. "I've been looking all over for you. Walter saddled the horses and I'm ready to go. How about you?"

Laurence, dressed in his riding best, skipped down the front steps and strode toward Maggie. She had never seen his boots so shiny nor his habit so clean. It appeared as if he was going to a special event; one where he and Fireball would prance in front of a line of judges. He seemed to have taken more care of his appearance today than for the race in Rolen. This seemed strange, since she understood they were going for a brief ride on dusty trails.

Motion from the patio distracted Maggie's attention. Max and Nellie disappeared around the corner of the Hall. *Where are they going?*

"Well, Maggie, are you ready?"

Laurence's voice startled Maggie. "Yes, Laurence. I'm ready. I wanted to take one last look at Stuart Hall and impress its image in my memory, also the garden. I will remember your home and grounds with fondness."

"Did you give any more thought to our conversation last evening?"

"Laurence, you have been very gracious during our visit. We could not imagine a more accommodating host. You offered me the world of Stuart Hall and while it is tempting, I must decline. I have a life back in the States and look forward to returning to it. I shall miss your staff. They were always ready to meet our every need, giving little thought to the abundance of their own responsibilities."

Laurence's expression changed from hopefulness to despair.

"Rejection seems to be my constant companion, Maggie. This time I understand, so I'll not hold it against you. I've enjoyed our time together. Max and Nellie have been a delight. I hope they gathered enough information to write their books. As for you, Maggie, I look forward to your finished drawing of the ruins to add to my art collection." He reached for her hand. "I think we should begin. From the looks of the sky, we may be in for some rain."

A cooler breeze than usual blew across Maggie's face. Several dark clouds crept across the sky toward Stuart Hall. It reminded her of the clouds that filled the sky when she left Rolen Presbyterian Kirk for the first time. She had forgotten to bring a hat. Maggie could go back for one, then decided not to waste the time. She wanted this ride to be over with.

The paddock seemed lonely. Even the horses appeared to have lost their energy. They raised their heads, shook a few pieces of straw loose from their mouths, and continued munching. Not one of them trotted to the fence seeking a handout.

"Ah, my dear Peggy. Are you ready for one last ride?" Maggie rubbed Peggy's neck and hugged her. "You and I have had some very pleasant times together. If this one proves to be the same, I'll retrieve an extra carrot for you upon our return."

"Maggie, you're talking to the horse as if she understands."

"Don't you think animals sense when they're loved and treated with kindness? I have grown fond of Peggy. She has treated me with respect because she knows I care about her."

"We can find Walter," Laurence gazed into the stable, "if you need a leg up?"

"No, thank you. I can do it myself now."

Maggie settled into the saddle and laced the reins through her fingers. After they left the paddock, Laurence closed the gate behind them and moved Fireball beside Peggy.

"You've seen much of the forest around Stuart Hall, but if my recollection is correct, the trail ahead is new to you. I'd like to show you another meadow, filled with flowers in the spring, but now ablaze with fall colors. It's where I often rode, pretending to be a knight fighting off marauding bands of evil-doers bent on stealing

Stuart Hall." Laurence re-situated himself in the saddle. "We need to take the narrow path ahead and through the woods a short distance."

With no explanation, an uneasy feeling invaded Maggie. A gap in the trees afforded a view of where the narrow trail began. Laurence eased Fireball in front of Peggy. Single file would be the only way to traverse the path.

Something seemed familiar to Maggie. She pivoted in her saddle and observed the location of the paddock and Stuart Hall. It seemed like they were traveling due south, almost an exact straight line into the woods. She heard the faint chirps of birds. The dried leaves and branches crackled under Peggy's hoofs. It grew colder with little sun to pierce the trees. Maggie gazed at the sky. She realized the clouds were blanketing the clear blue expanse much faster than expected.

Chapter 41

The chilly breeze knifed through Maggie's clothing. She shivered not only from the stress of riding with Laurence but also from the dampness under a canopy of trees. Fall in Scotland had arrived, and she longed to return to the warmth of Stuart Hall.

"Laurence, maybe we should go back. I'm cold and those clouds look ominous."

"We're almost there, Maggie. I don't want you to leave before feasting your eyes on one last favorite spot of mine. We've got the trees for cover should it rain."

Peggy maintained a slow gait, which allowed Maggie to observe her surroundings. The woods grew denser. Something seemed familiar, though she couldn't say what. Ahead, about twenty feet, the trail curved.

Wait. She had it. The map Walter had drawn for Max. The same trail where her mother had met her death. *What was Laurence doing?* She wanted to spur Peggy into a gallop around Fireball, but Laurence's horse wove from side to side like a drunk stumbling down the steps of a pub. Not even an inch of space to squeeze through.

"I'm shivering, Laurence. Couldn't we end our ride and go back?" Maggie said.

"Calm yourself, lassie. Didn't I tell you we're almost there? You can't leave without seeing the best site at Stuart Hall. Historical, you might say, as well."

"I've seen enough sites and had enough adventures for one holiday. If you won't turn around, I'll go back by myself." Maggie seldom raised her voice in irritation, but Laurence had irked her beyond belief.

"All right, Maggie." Laurence rotated in the saddle. "There's a wider section on the trail, a few more feet ahead. We can turn the horses around there. I'm sorry you're not enjoying this. I had hoped this last ride would be the most memorable."

Well beyond the bend, Maggie stretched tall in the saddle. She saw no place ahead wider than the section they were riding on. With no warning, Laurence stopped Fireball and dismounted.

"What's wrong? Did I miss something?"

"I think Fireball picked up a stone. I want to check each hoof. Can't be too careful riding your horse if they've picked up a stone. Imagine it's like having a rock in your boot. Not very comfortable now, is it? You may as well get down and stretch your legs while I check. Can you get off by yourself?" Laurence seemed rather curt. A mixture of angry and control emanated in his voice.

"Yes. I'm fine." Maggie tried to disguise her irritation as she dismounted and patted Peggy's neck. She moved in front of her horse and stopped in the center of the path. She strained as best she could, but the path didn't seem to get any wider as far as she could see. In fact, with all the over-growth above the trail, it appeared to become narrower. Difficult for one horse, impossible for two side-by-side.

"Looking for something? Remember, I told you this ride would be the most memorable of all the rides you've taken. Just look over the edge." Laurence escorted her to the side of the path. "Here, Maggie, on this side." He motioned to his right. "It's the deepest ravine on Stuart Hall property. There's a little stream at the bottom. It runs into one of the nearby lochs. Can you hear it? Maybe you need to get closer."

Maggie inched as close as she dared. Fearing an undercut ledge, she didn't intend to take one more step. Yes, she could hear the stream, but why call attention to it? Then, from the corner of her eye, she noticed he had inched his way closer to her. She gazed at him. His eyes glazed over. Fear gripped Maggie.

"Did you look down the ravine, Maggie? Did you see the branches growing from the side of the cliff?" His voice grew raspy and stern. "They cross over each other, forming an X. I always heard that X marks the spot for buried treasure. You won't find buried treasure down there, my dear. No, it's buried somewhere else." He positioned an arm around her waist. "I can see by your expression you don't understand. Well, sweet Maggie, those crossed branches signify the highlight of your holiday." He nudged her closer to the edge.

"Laurence, you're talking nonsense. With or without you, I'm mounting Peggy and going back to Stuart Hall. Besides, it's raining." She tried to pull away from his grasp.

"Not yet." He clutched tighter. "Glance one last time down the ravine. You see, Maggie, this is where your mother died. She landed right on top of those crossed branches. They caught her, you might say. Since she had faith in God, you might say she landed on the cross and went to heaven."

Maggie's hands shook. Her dry mouth screamed for moisture. Not only frightened with the situation, his words pounded her brain like a woodpecker hammering for ants.

"What did you say?" She grabbed his arm. "My mother?"

"Yes, Maggie. Claire Ferguson was your mother." Laurence crushed her wrists in his hands. "She was a money-grabbing widow looking for a big score and found it at Stuart Hall. You don't need to give me that, 'how did you know' look? I've known almost from the first time I met you.

"There was something familiar about you and yet, I couldn't quite put my finger on. That is, not until your carriage was out of sight. When I entered the foyer, the portraits seized my attention. Like someone punched me. Your mother and you could be twins, except for the age difference, of course. There was no doubt about it."

Laurence pulled her within inches of his face. She could smell his breath and the sweat beneath his shirt collar.

"It took longer to comprehend why you came to Stuart Hall under false pretenses. I remembered your mother wrote to you almost weekly. I assumed she told you all about me. She probably wrote I was impossible."

Droplets of spit sprayed on Maggie's face.

"Maybe that I frightened her, especially when father wasn't home. That's true. I meant to frighten her. I wanted to frighten her right out of Scotland. That hag was not easy to scare, though."

Laurence released a frightening banshee wail, sending shivers through Maggie's entire body. Her heart pounded harder than ever as she realized Laurence's insanity. Maggie tried to take a step away from him, but he held her tight. Her wrists burned beneath his grip.

"The different last names threw me. You could be divorced, but I decided that was a blind. Too long in Inverness and Rolen. That was a mistake. I knew you could get copies of the inquest. Staying in Rolen, meeting those do-gooders, Claire's friends, would reinforce what you already knew." Laurence held her wrists in one hand and removed a white handkerchief from his pocket.

Maggie edged away from Laurence, but he pulled her closer. She searched for a way out. With her back to the ravine, there was no way to go but through him. She would have to muster whatever reserve strength she could find. Maggie prayed, *"Oh, God, please help me."*

Laurence's hands gripped tighter. The handkerchief dangled from one hand. She struggled to break free, but he strengthened his grip. She never imagined he could be so strong. Maggie struggled to break free before he tied her wrists together.

"Maggie, there's no use fighting me. It sealed your fate when you returned to Stuart Hall. As with your mother, I'm going to throw you off the edge too." His eyes bulged in delight. "Yes, Maggie, I killed your mother. That's what you've been waiting to hear, isn't it? You and your friends found everything you needed, but still couldn't get me to confess."

Maggie frantically searched the forest. Only the tree branches moved with the wind. There were no familiar faces anywhere. No knight in shining armor was coming to her rescue. She felt totally alone and completely out of her element.

"Last night, I asked you what your purpose was. Well, I knew the answer long before last night. Your purpose was to find me guilty of murder. Now your purpose is complete.

"The wench wouldn't go in peace, so, let's say, I gave her a nudge. Another unfortunate dilemma that plagued me: my father. I loved him, but he suspected me of killing his wife. He loved her and with every look, every day and every reminder of Claire, I knew I needed to take action.

"I don't know if you or Max found where I stashed him, but that doesn't matter. If he returns, I'm sure I can concoct something to remove him from Stuart Hall forever. I've always wanted to be the only Lord of the manor. Then you showed up. Poked around too much. I knew you'd find a way to prove me guilty of murder, and with me in jail, or worse, the manor would be yours, sweet stepsister." Laurence lost his hold on the handkerchief and it fell to the ground.

Maggie attempted to wiggle free. Laurence's grip tightened. Like a rope, once wet, now dried with the sun, his hands made imprints on her wrists. She felt his fingernails cut into her arms.

"Laurence, you're hurting me." Tears overflowed her lids and ran down her cheeks.

"Don't worry, my dear. It will all be over soon enough." Laurence's eyes squinted. "Your friends were talented actors, but you're the best. However, in this case, my performance was supreme. I've had you in the palm of my hand. I convinced you I was a gentleman in every sense of the word. By the way, getting into my father's room was brillant, but doubt you found anything of significance." Laurence kissed her cheek.

"Oh, and one more thing, even though you said you would leave today, since you lied about so many other things, I couldn't be sure you were telling the truth. I have to put an end to your snooping into my life."

Maggie's heart raced. "I can't believe you would even think about killing your father. You're sick, Laurence. My mother was a wonderful person. You destroyed a genuine lady. She wanted nothing more than to build a positive relationship with you, and you shunned her at every turn. My mind cannot even conceive of a person such as you. In all my dealings with people, I've met no one so unfeeling and callous."

Laurence dragged Maggie close to the edge of the ravine. Defense tactics were necessary. What had Max taught her? *What position do I maneuver him into? I can't move. Hit him in the neck? My arms are useless. My legs? That's it.*

"Maggie, my dear, this will be the last time I have the privilege of holding you in my arms. I have loved you, Maggie, in my own way. It's now time for your accident. You see, I have perfected this story in every detail. There's no one here to refute what's about to happen. Your friends will have a lovely funeral for you, and I, as the grieving, almost fiancé, will request that you and your mum share the grave. There, isn't that thoughtful of me? You and your mum will die the same way and I'll reunite you in death, daughter resting on mother. Now Maggie, how about one last kiss? Then I will have the pleasure of watching you plummet to your death."

Laurence's face moved closer to Maggie. Her taut leg muscles were ready. Sensing his lips on hers, she thrust her knee with all her strength into his groin.

"Help! Help!" Maggie yelled as her knee found its target.

The bushes rustled. Max, Nellie, and Ernest leapt into sight. Maggie's steps faltered. She screamed loud and long as the ground under her feet softened. Laurence released his grip and bent over in agony. Nellie flew toward Maggie and seized her arm.

Max and Ernest bolted toward Laurence.

"No, no. You're not supposed to be here!" Laurence screamed. "This is not the way it's supposed to end. I must win in all my adventures."

"Not this time, Laurence." Max grabbed Laurence's arm. "You've hung yourself for sure."

Laurence screamed and shouted obscenities as he punched Max's arm away.

Walter burst onto the scene. "Master Laurence. What have you done?"

Laurence clenched his fists. His path blocked. The only way out, the ravine. Rotating on one foot, he peered over the edge, then at Maggie's rescuers. With the snapping of breaking branches, the earth crumbled. Cascading rocks and broken limbs roared down the cliff. With a fear-stricken gaze toward Maggie, Laurence grabbed for Max, but missed. Plunging into the ravine., his screams echoed in Maggie's ears. A sickening thud. Then silence.

Maggie collapsed into Nellie's loving arms and wept uncontrollably. "Maggie, it's all right. We're here!" Nellie wrapped her arms around Maggie's shaking body.

"Give me... a minute... to catch my breath." Maggie inhaled and released the air slowly. She shook her head in disbelief as the profound significance of her friend's arrival sunk in.

Max hurried to Maggie and wrapped her in his muscular arms. Comfort and security calmed her nerves. Once again, these good friends were there for her.

"Maggie, I thought I'd lost you. I couldn't bear it if I had." Max's eyes glistened with moisture.

Maggie gazed into his eyes. Time stopped at that moment. She sensed a look of love in Max's eyes. For the first time, she longed to be alone with him. To hold him without onlookers. To rest her head on his strong shoulder. And, perhaps, experience their first kiss.

"I'm so sorry. We hoped to catch Laurence, but it all happened so fast," Max said. "We know how much you hoped for justice. Yet, we all heard his confession, and that's consolation enough." He stepped back and examined Maggie's raw and bleeding wrists. Max removed a hankie from his pocket. He tore it in half and wrapped her wounds.

Max left Maggie in Nellie's capable care and joined Ernest and Walter, who remained at the edge of the cliff. The three men leaned over. No signs of life emanated from Laurence's body. The woods were still again. Everyone and everything seemed to move in slow motion.

"I'll bring the horses," Walter said. "Ernest, I have a rope you can tie to a tree. Then, if you don't mind, Max, could you shinny down? We can go back for a wagon. Just need to have you evaluate what equipment to bring with us."

Maggie's heart ached for Walter as he plodded toward the woods. His head bent in sorrow. She pressed her lips together and closed her eyes. How hard this must be for him. He'd seen so much tragedy at Stuart Hall. Then she turned her attention back to Nellie.

"Nellie, how did you get here without us seeing you?"

"Maggie, let's move to the other side of the path, out of Ernest's way."

Maggie and Nellie stepped aside as Ernest attached the rope to a large tree. Max tied the end around his waist and climbed down over the ledge. Earth crumbled into the ravine.

A tug of the rope signaled Walter and Ernest to pull him up. Maggie was relieved when Max reached the top.

"He's dead, Maggie. It's all over now. I wish we could have gotten his confession some other way," Max said as he recoiled the rope.

"Nellie, you didn't answer my question. How did you get here without being seen?" Maggie asked.

"While you and Laurence were in the garden, Max and I hurried to the west side of Stuart Hall. Ernest, Dr. Shane and Walter hid themselves. Ernest brought horses from town. I feared you might have seen us when you were in the garden with Laurence."

"So that's what you were doing when I saw you and Max dart around the Hall!" Maggie exclaimed.

"We were afraid if Laurence noticed any missing horses from the paddock, he may become suspicious of something afoot. James kept vigil at the front window. He watched you and Laurence, then signaled Harriet, who signaled to us that the coast was clear. We rode as fast as we could toward the woods. All except Dr. Shane, that is. He stayed to join Harriet and James in prayer for your safety." Nellie pulled a leaf from Maggie's damp hair.

"Once here, Walter hid the horses. A layer of fallen leaves covered most of our tracks, but Max and Ernest used a fir branch to erase those closest to us. Then we concealed ourselves and waited. I don't mind telling you how hard it was to wait for Laurence's confession, knowing the extreme danger you were in. I wanted to jump out and thrash him several times."

"Oh, Nellie, my dearest friend. All of you are my dearest friends. How can I ever thank you?" Tears rolled down Maggie's face. Nellie retrieved her hankie and dabbed them.

"It's time to go. Dr. Shane, Harriet and James will be worried," said Max. "We'll send for help later to retrieve his body. For now, I want to get Maggie back to Stuart Hall and rest."

Maggie hugged Peggy. Fireball stood close to the edge, peering down at Laurence. Walter gathered Fireball's reins. He mounted his own horse and pulled Fireball along with him.

"I still have another question. How did you know Laurence would take me to this precise point? He could have taken me anywhere." Maggie needed more answers.

"Max, would you like to answer that?"

"I'd be glad to, Nellie." Max swallowed. "It all started when we overheard Laurence tell you he had planned one more ride before you left Stuart Hall. The keywords were, 'this will be the most memorable.' We discussed several interpretations of this statement and concluded that if he did indeed kill your mother, he planned to take you to the exact spot where she died. It seemed logical. Walter rode into town late last night and related our suspicions to Ernest and Dr. Shane. We felt they should be here."

"You see," Nellie said, "my involvement with the detectives back home paid off. Now Stuart Hall awaits. Harriet, James and Dr. Shane may be frantic waiting for the outcome. I dare say we could all use a stout cup of tea."

"Speak for yourself, Nellie," Ernest said. "As for Walter, Max, and myself, another type of stout drink would be preferable. This has been stressful for all of us." Ernest paused. "Well, maybe bittersweet would be more accurate. Maggie's quest is over. Laurence received his punishment, at his own hand, and Ramsay will return with no son to face."

For Maggie, it was a bittersweet ending. The truth had surfaced. Laurence received, in her mother's words, his "comeuppance". The goal was reached. Claire's murder, proven. For Maggie, the ache in her heart for her mother overwhelmed her. She missed her, but at the same time experienced a sense of accomplishment.

Maggie mounted Peggy for the last time.

"Look," Maggie said. "The clouds are parting and what a glorious blue sky. I can feel the warmth again. Like emerging from a clenched cocoon released into wonderful freedom."

She glanced skyward. A light mist fell upon her face from a cloudless sky. Then she said, "You're welcome, Mom. I love you— so much."

Chapter 42

The birds' chorus that had serenaded Maggie and Laurence earlier was now silent. Maggie's mind swirled with the events from which she had narrowly escaped. Shivers ran down her spine when she grasped the reality of her imminent death; a death like her mother's, at the hand of the same man. A pat on Peggy's neck helped calm her churning stomach. She longed to take this special horse back to the States. Peggy had become a link to her mother. With Nellie riding beside her, Maggie gained comfort and assurance all would be well.

She gazed at her close friends, who rode in front. Ernest and Max gave her the strength she lacked. The steady beat of hoofs behind her was a reminder that Walter led a riderless horse to the stables. Maggie prepared herself to greet Harriet, Dr. Shane and James. Fireball's empty saddle would clue them to the outcome.

As Stuart Hall came into view, salty tears stung her eyes and cascaded down her cheeks. Even though the shaking had subsided, her emotions remained raw. *Was this the end?* It wasn't the end she hoped for.

The headline in the next edition of the local paper should read, "Laurence MacLaren Charged with Murder." She wanted the announcement shouted throughout Scotland and back to her friends in the States. This would be the final resolution of the vexing problem she had clung to for far too long. He would be judged guilty and be punished. At one time, she had estimated how many copies of the paper she could fit in her suitcase. Was that what she wanted? A sense of "I told you so?"

Maggie heard their names shouted and spotted Harriet and Dr. Shane as they ran toward Max and Ernest. James followed at a slower pace.

"What happened, Max, Ernest? Where is Master Laurence?" Maggie heard Harriet's breathless voice. James stopped next to Max and clung to his saddle while he caught his breath.

Maggie, grateful Dr. Shane persevered until he reached her, knew her reddened-eyes would tell the story.

"It's over, Dr. Shane," said Maggie. "Laurence confessed. If my dear friends had lacked the premonition something dreadful was eminent, my mother's fate would now be my own."

Maggie dismounted. She allowed Dr. Shane to cradle her as she released pent-up emotions. Maggie heard the tender voices of Harriet and James as they gathered around her. She welcomed their touch of consolation. Love seemed to flood through every fiber of her limp body. A soft voice filled her ears.

"Thank you, Lord, for protecting Maggie and leading her friends to be vigilant and alert." Dr. Shane glanced at Maggie. "I feel we have now become friends and I am privileged to call you Maggie."

Maggie returned his smile. "Thank you."

In her heart, she too offered thanks and praise to the Creator of the entire universe, whom she now called Lord and Savior. Her spiritual eyes opened to the mysterious way in which He works. A mother's example had planted the seeds of faith in her young heart, and those small seeds had now taken root.

"I think some unpacking will be necessary," Harriet said as they continued the walk to the Hall. "While you men figure out the next step to retrieve Master Laurence, someone will need to ride to town for the doctor and constable. I'll ask Leach. I would estimate a couple of days before you three can begin your trip home. How about a light lunch with tea and coffee? Are there any requests?" she asked.

"Harriet, lassie, dear," said Ernest, "while tea and coffee are fine, Max and I were hoping for something a mite stronger. Any more choices?"

"Of course, Ernest. I'm sure we can find something special in the cellar. I'll check."

Maggie's eyes followed Harriet, who stopped and spoke to Leach before she disappeared into the Hall.

When they reached the stable, Maggie handed Peggy's reins to Leach, who tethered the horses to the fence. Leach then mounted Walter's horse and left for town.

She entered the dining room and flopped down beside Max. Maggie relaxed as Max wrapped his arm around her. Those carnivorous beasts metamorphosed back into pleasant butterflies. They seemed to quiet down for a much needed rest. His gaze reminded her she could trust Max to stand with her through life's trials. Exhausted, she related the events to Dr. Shane and James while Harriet listened through the opened kitchen door.

After Max and Nellie shared their stories, Maggie dragged herself upstairs. She expected to never climb this grand staircase again, but a quick nap sounded like a bit of heaven.

***

The next two days, for Maggie, moved slower than the proverbial molasses in January. With the investigation over, testimonies given, the incident declared an accident, official paperwork filed and Laurence's remains interred, the return trip loomed in front of Maggie.

"If there is anything of your mother's you would like to keep Maggie, please do so," Harriet snapped the luggage closed. "With no master of Stuart Hall at the moment, and you three leaving, it's going to be mighty lonely around here. You know, because of your mother's marriage, you are now the rightful mistress of Stuart Hall. I can speak for the entire staff you would honor us if you stayed longer."

"Thank you, but no thank you, Harriet." Maggie sipped her last spot of tea. "This Hall would only bring sadness and we need to return home. I thought about taking Gwen's journal," Maggie said, "but I'm certain her remembrances should remain here. And I considered my mother's gown, but decided against it. I believe Ramsay will return soon. You must keep the Hall in top condition. Make his homecoming a grand celebration. He needs some joy in his life after losing everything, even his son."

Maggie followed Max and Nellie as they descended the grand staircase for the last time, luggage in hand. Harriet came after them carrying Maggie's suitcase.

Maggie paused in the foyer to absorb Stuart Hall into her memory. The furnishings, paintings, Gwen's piano, and even the smells that escaped from Harriet's kitchen, would remain with her.

A new art work graced the foyer; Maggie's drawing of the three brothers, engaged in battle against forest dragons. She, too, had come prepared for battle and survived her foe.

"I feel like we've just arrived and the past events have been an unsettling dream," Maggie said. "The people in these portraits have become more than mere names and faces. Their history is now my history. Their family is now my family. While I leave their memory and Stuart Hall in Scotland, I will just as assuredly take them to the States in my heart."

Maggie held Harriet's hands and gazed into her eyes. "Mother enjoyed the love of two wonderful men during her lifetime. She also knew the love of an amazing God who has become my God. I can't undo the past, but I feel privileged to honor her in my present and future. I believe the Lord has done a work in each of us and we leave much different people than when we arrived."

Maggie turned toward Max and Nellie. "Well, my friends, are you ready?"

"We'll follow your lead, Maggie," Nellie responded.

The nip in the fall air created a contrast to what they had experienced when they stood on the veranda a few months earlier. A black steed guided the coach and stopped at the foot of the porch steps. A loud whinny bellowed from the paddock. Fireball made his dominance known, or perhaps, said his goodbyes. Maggie faced Walter, Harriet and Leach gathered on the porch.

"Our thanks to you for your kind hospitality. While our stay was not under the best of circumstances, your desire to know the truth spurred us on."

With their goodbyes said, Maggie followed her friends toward the coach.

Hurried footsteps sounded from inside the hall. Everyone's attention was now focused on the front entrance. Maggie's eyes opened wide, shocked to see James storm outside with the energy of a much younger man. He held a box in his hands and jostled down the steps.

"'ere, Lassie Maggie," James said as he caught his breath. "A wee gift fur ye 'n' we wilnae tak' na fur an answer." He extended a red velvet box to Maggie.

Maggie lifted the lid. Her eyes were dazzled by the lustrous glow from the family heirloom necklace. The rubies and diamonds sparkled even on the overcast day. Her eyes filled with tears. Then she noticed Harriet and Walter. The two were stoic, but they now wiped moisture from their eyes.

Maggie hugged James. His stuffiness and "stiff-as-a-board" demeanor vanished. He returned her hug and responded with an elfish smile. "Lang may your lum reek, lassie," James said, a tear in each eye.

Maggie shot a quizzical glance toward Harriet.

"A Scottish blessing, 'May your luck run long.'" Harriet explained.

"With the Lord's help, James. With the Lord's help." She accepted his hand and climbed into the coach.

The coachman steered his horse in a wide circle, then headed toward the road. As the coach passed the veranda, they waved their farewells. Maggie glanced one last time at the trellis. The rose hips drooped. The fruit trees wore bare branches. Brown leaves scattered on the ground. A cool wind entered the coach. Maggie covered her legs with the quilt that lay on the seat.

"Did you see that?" Nellie asked. "James smiled!"

The sound of another coach caught Maggie's attention. Max leaned out the side window as the coach came alongside. Startled at the change in Max's expression, Maggie quickly faced the passing coach. She glimpsed two figures inside.

"That's Dr. McDonald and Ramsay MacLaren." Max couldn't contain himself. "Driver!" He knocked on the coach's ceiling. "Wait! We need to wait."

Maggie and Nellie positioned themselves for a good view from the rear window while Max jumped out of the coach. Maggie's heart beat faster. She thanked God they could be here to witness the homecoming. Even though some distance separated them, she viewed both men as they disembarked from their coach. While Maggie couldn't see facial expressions, Harriet's body language told her Ramsay had received a hero's welcome. Their "lost" master had now come home.

Max climbed back into the coach and patted Maggie's hand. She felt a sense of rebirth for Stuart Hall. A new chapter had begun with Ramsay's return. Stuart Hall was no longer held captive in the darkness of Laurence's mind.

"What satisfaction. What joy." Max's feet danced in the cramped carriage space. "Renewed life just returned to Stuart Hall. Ramsay will face serious struggles over his son's actions and death. I'm so thankful Dr. McDonald can lend his wise counsel. And what a wonderful, supportive staff who will wrap him in their love." Max re-situated himself. "My sweet Maggie, what are you thinking?"

A sense of loss and sadness enveloped Maggie.

"Do you want to go back and meet your stepfather?" Nellie asked as she placed her hand on Maggie's.

Maggie paused. *Should I? Would it cause confusion, or one more trauma for Ramsay to surmount?*

"No. I don't believe I would," Maggie said. "Ramsay has enough weight on his shoulders without a stepdaughter who bears a strong resemblance to his former wife. Maybe someday, under different circumstances, I'll return to Stuart Hall if my stepfather invites me. For now, I want to go home."

Max knocked on the roof of the carriage. "On to Rolen, my good man."

Maggie rested her head against the back of the seat and closed her eyes. They did it. They came to Scotland with a mere suspicion regarding her mother's death from a three sentence communication. Three friends, one mission. They return with the mission accomplished, a "lost" husband returned home, adventures for Max, history for Nellie and lifelong friends in a quaint town called Rolen. Maggie knew the truth; the truth about her mother's death and, more important, the truth about the God she now called Lord and Savior.

The sloshing of the horses' hooves on the mucky road, the dampness in the air, and the fog covering the moors were one last reminder that Scotland was not Maggie's home. Cognizant that her life in the states would never be the same, she wondered what adventures lay ahead. She had arrived a hard, resolute unbeliever and returned with a soft and forgiven heart. A heart filled with love for others and for her Lord. Maggie couldn't wait for whatever He had in store for her future. She hoped the future included Max.

The rain's intensity increased as well as the muddy road. Maggie inhaled one more deep Scotland breath, released it as slow as possible, and gazed out the window toward the sky. "I love you, Mom."

God created the world out of nothing, and so long as we are nothing, He can make something out of us.
—Martin Luther—

A Note to my Readers,

I feel honored that you have chosen to read this, my first novel. Thank you for your time commitment. I pray that you have gleaned some helpful insights regarding the truth: the truth about life, about faith and about ourselves. As Maggie and I became better acquainted, it dawned on me that she and I bore similarities; we both grew up in Portland, Oregon, worked at Meier & Frank's, were artists, a swing hung from a large fir tree which grew in my backyard, my father built me a playhouse, I tried to fly using my arms for wings, our mothers played the piano, my Scottish grandfather from Dundee had the cribbage board ready for a game at a moment's notice. My mother said prayers with me every night before bed and taught me at an early age to be proud of my Scottish heritage: the MacLaren Clan. And we both struggled with matters of faith.

The quaint village where Maggie and her friends stayed, Rolen, is my grandmother's maiden name. The inn where the three friends stayed, the Creag an Tuirc means Boar's Rock and is named after a high knoll overlooking Balquhidder. This crag was the ancient rallying place of the Clan MacLaren with magnificent views of the valley village and Loch Voil. A drive through Scotland a number of years ago, kindled in me a greater appreciation of the rugged land and the kind, and stalwart inhabitants. This story had to be set in the land of my ancestors.

Maggie, while searching for the truth of her mother's death, entered her journey with a preconceived judgement: Laurence was guilty of murder. As the story progresses, Maggie became convinced there was no other reasonable outcome and Laurence must stand trial, be convicted and be sentenced to death. Determined to avenge her mother's death, there could be no other outcome. Yet the more time she spent with Laurence, the more she doubted her judgement. If not for her friends who lovingly, but strongly, reminded her of the truth, she too might have met her mother's fate. Finding truth, real truth, requires genuine soul searching and a willingness to exchange unsubstantiated beliefs for deeply rooted historical facts. The truth of God's Word and His Son, Jesus bored, through my shallow faith by means of a personal miracle. For Maggie, the overwhelming testimony of many Rolen residents forced her to open her mind's door and consider a Creator who loved her with a sacrificial love. It changed her life, and mine, forever.

The following is an excerpt from Book 2,
Eden Lake: Not Quite Paradise.

"There are far better things ahead than anything we left behind."

— *C.S. Lewis* —

Chapter 1

"Saying good-bye to relatives too?" asked a young man who gripped a small Scotland flag. He couldn't be more than sixteen years old. Peach fuzz blossomed on his cheeks, anticipation of adventures that beaconed him on distant shores sparkled in his eyes. Their heads are so full of romance. Young men can't see the obstacles before them. Max scrunched his eyelids together. The gravity of his previous two weeks in Rolen weighed heavy on his shoulders. How he wished the outcome had been different.

"Not really. I've been solving a mystery with a friend. Time to go home." Max knew the lad would not be interested in the daring trio who waded into the dangerous world of a murderer. He said no more.

The ocean liner's whistle screeched and sent a cloud of steam into the air. With his two companions, Nellie Cox and Maggie Richards directed to their room, Max had secured an empty spot by the rail. The workers heaved the heavy ropes off the dock and released the majestic ship from her moorage. The wide blue expanse of sea awaited.

Passengers bunched at the railing. The cacophony of voices sounded like a gaggle of geese. Max wrapped his overcoat's collar around his ears to muffle the din. Young men and women leaned over the guard rail and threw paper streamers toward their family and friends far below. How many of these passengers would ever see their loved ones again? Many Scotsmen left their homeland in search of a better life. For Max, however, his 'better life' could only be with Maggie.

He fiddled with his watch fob. The Sullivan family crest had been embossed on one side and gave him a sense of pride. He longed to make Maggie a member of his family. His parents would have loved her. Their whirlwind courtship encompassed the length of the ocean voyage from Scotland. His mother and father married in a dingy courthouse a week after they had arrived in New York.

Rolling waves gently rocked the ocean liner from side to side. Scotland's shores would soon be a distant memory. A two-week voyage lay ahead before the Statue of Liberty's burning torch guided the liner safely into the harbor and Ellis Island would welcome a new flood of immigrants.

Max's heart ached. When they docked he feared he would be separated from his dear Maggie and board a train to Oregon. Construction on a new immigrant processing building was underway when they had left New York. The original Georgia Pine structure had burnt to the ground. Max looked forward to whatever progress they'd made to the new building. But for now he was consumed with the prospect of leaving Maggie. Maybe forever.

He paced the deck. Past images of lunch with her in Portland's Meier & Frank Department Store flooded his memory. He had known her longer than his parents' pre-marital relationship. And after the harrowing experience in Scotland, his feelings had solidified. He loved her. Heartbeats raced, speech stammered and voices "timid and shy" caused the words "I love you," to stick in his craw. An experienced mystery writer, Max could always find the words to draw his readers into a story. His characters were heroes of the highest caliber. Yet, he failed miserably around Maggie.

Max closed his eyes and waited for sleep to engulf him. The ship's motion lingered even though he lay in his own bed. Eden Lake relaxed his body, but not his mind.

He reminisced about one glorious day on the ocean liner when Maggie's essence had filled his entire being. Her calming lavender scent wafted on the breeze.

The sun had warmed the deck and the waves were unusually calm. An occasional seagull squawked overhead. He had reclined in a deck chair, closed his eyes and rehearsed his proposal.

"Maggie, my dear, our experience in Scotland tore at my heart. I was gripped with a sense of emptiness at the thought of losing you to Mac-Laren, or worse, death, by his hand. His marriage proposal crushed my heart with fear that you might accept. In that instant my hopes were gone. I can't bear to lose you. Maggie, I love you. I believe I've known for some time, but never how deeply until a few weeks ago."

Max imagined her soft hands nestled in his. His eyes riveted to hers. "Maggie Richards, will you do me the honor of becoming my wife?"

A distant noise startled him. Reality sunk in that he no longer enjoyed the comfort of a deck chair on the ocean liner. His head reeled from the annoying noise that jolted him awake. Bang. Bang. His ears rang. Wait. He can't wake up and interrupt this dream. He needed to know Maggie's answer.

"Whoever's there, please go away," his voice thundered over the noise. Max fluffed the pillow, rearranged the blankets and snuggled deeper under the covers. Dream world, come back.

"Mr. Sullivan, Mr. Sullivan," someone yelled from the porch. Max plopped the pillow over his head and squeezed his eyes closed. The pounding continued.

"Mr. Sullivan. Mr. Sullivan."

"I ask that you kindly go away and leave me in peace." Max yelled louder.

"But Mr. Sullivan, I have a telegram for you. The postmistress, Miss Greene, said it's urgent I come right away." Silence followed, then more pounding.

Max gave in. Sleep would never return. He opened one eye as Jed licked his face, hind legs on the floor, front legs across Max's chest. Slobber covered his cheek.

"Yes, yes, Jed. Good morning to you, and yes, I know someone's here."

He threw the blankets aside, slid his feet into his slippers and straightened his nightshirt. With his faithful dog beside him, he trudged toward the door. The front door rattled from another bang.

"Mr. Sullivan, are you coming? I got to be getting back, but need your signature on this paper. Mr. Sullivan?"

"Yes, yes, I'm coming. Keep your boots on." Max bumped into a chair then strained to force his eyes open. He grabbed the latch and flung the door wide. A fist stopped midair short of his forehead. Jed rushed to sniff their uninvited visitor.

"Oh, Mr. Sullivan, I'm sorry. I almost hit you." The lad bent down to rub the hound's ears. "Hi there, Jed." The hound dog wagged his tail then skedaddled off the porch into the crisp morning air. He made a bee-line through the snow and into the trees.

"Mr. Sullivan, I didn't hear any movement inside and I need to get back. Miss Greene doesn't take lightly to what she calls lollygagging." Joel lowered his head in a sheepish manner.

Max knew Joel, a tall, gangly teenager, felt blessed to have a job. These were hard times for a young man who had been called "slow" as a little boy. Max hated it when people put labels on children. Those words stuck like pitch to a person's soul.

With one leg noticeably shorter than the other, Joel moved with an awkward gait which made him an easy target for ridicule. Max grieved for the young man. In a way, the two were kindred spirits. "Timid and shy" clung to Max still as an adult. How he wished he could take his Bowie knife and scrape the label off as easy as scaling a fish.

Max placed a hand on Joel's shoulder, "No, it's I who am sorry, Joel. Still having those dreams I'm on the ocean liner and rocking with the waves." He scratched his head and rubbed his eyes open. "Now, what did you need?"

"Here's a telegram for you from Scotland. I need your signature on this line."

Stunned, Max examined the telegram as he turned the envelope over in his hand. A telegram. From Scotland. Who would be sending a telegram? And why?

Joel grunted. "Mr. Sullivan. Please?"

Max wrote his name where Joel pointed and apologized for his discourteousness.

"I forgive you, Mr. Sullivan. Someday I'd like to hear about Scotland. I dream of traveling, but it's hard to save money these days. Well, gotta get back. Have a nice day."

Joel replaced his hat and tugged the ear flaps. He chose his footing carefully on the icy steps as he descended and mounted his horse.

"Fresh layer of snow last night, Mr. Sullivan." Joel saluted Max then prodded his mount toward town.

Max exhaled into the cool air. A fog cloud formed in front of his face and drifted upward. He inspected the envelope and ripped the sealed flap open. The only time he'd ever received a telegram it proclaimed dire news. To Max they seemed to bring tidings of a calamity.

He held the paper tight in his moist hands, closed his eyes and prayed, "Oh, Lord, let this be good news."

His chest rose with the crisp morning air. He unfolded the telegram and focused on the message: "Holiday your place - STOP - June - STOP - Respond please - STOP - Ernest"

Ernest McIntyre? My fishing pal from Scotland? Coming to Eden Lake? Max's eyes were now fully opened. The lake shone like a freshly washed mirror reflecting Mt. Hood and a small run-down cabin on the opposite side. The majestic trees, veiled in snow, towered toward the blue sky. The mountain reached over eleven-thousand feet. One of the tallest semi-dormant volcanoes in the Cascade Range, white, glistening snow gave it a magical appearance. By June only a fraction of the snow would remain.

His teeth chattered. Goosebumps tingled on his arms and legs. The realization he stood outside clothed in a nightshirt and floppy slippers while icicles dangled from the eaves, drove him inside in an instant. He stoked up the leftover embers in the potbelly stove and added kindling. Almost as cold indoors as out, Max grabbed his robe. He checked the fire in the cook stove. No life remained.

While crumpling paper, he thought of Maggie again. Why had he been so stupid? He had plenty of opportunities on the ocean trip. After all, two weeks is fourteen days and he only needed to get a few sentences out of his mouth. She slipped out of his life one more time as she boarded the train for Chicago while his locomotive followed the tracks to Oregon. He dumped the dregs from last night's coffee, added fresh water and placed the pot on the stove to heat. Max checked the tin can then added "coffee" to his shopping list.

He flopped on the couch and re-read the telegram while the wood crackled and spit. Already the cabin seemed warmer. With a two-week ocean crossing, then a week or so on the train and another day by coach from Portland, Max understood why Ernest would send a telegram in March. A long trip awaited.

June. That would be a good month. The fish would be biting. The days were longer and warmer. Excitement set in as Max anticipated fishing with Ernest. The boiling water and growling stomach brought him back to the urgency to cook breakfast, chop wood, finish a shopping list, make his bed and, oh yes, get dressed. His mind far outreached his actions. Time to slow down and calculate the best use of today.

Max flipped a page on his calendar and browsed for any commitments. Jolted to a halt, he had forgotten a doctor's appointment next week. Why could he not erase this notation from the page as easily as he dismissed it from his mind? He had an aversion to doctors, especially ones that seemed to know all the answers. And the long trip to Portland didn't help matters. Too much time to think. A scratch and moan from the porch reminded Max that Jed waited outside.

"Sorry, boy." Max opened the door and rubbed the black dog's cold ears. Jed nestled in the old blankets that created a bed by the fire. Max filled Jed's water dish.

"This is a special day for me, so how about a treat?" Jed wagged his tail extra hard, let his tongue dangle, and trotted to Max's side.

Bacon and eggs ready, Max ladled his breakfast to a plate, then covered Jed's dry food with the bacon grease. "Wait now, boy. Don't want to be burning yourself." Jed lay down in front of his dish setting his snout on the edge. His nose twitched with the smell of run-off grease. He kept an eye on Max and waited for the "go ahead" signal.

Max gobbled his food and charted his activities for the day. One day at a time, the doctor said. After all, no one is promised more than one day. With the premature death of his parents, Max knew all too well, no one is even promised a full day.

He revisited his morning dream. Maggie. Her vision floated through his mind. Red hair, petite body, winsome smile and adventurous spirit. How he wished she were here, in his kitchen, sharing his cabin, perhaps the mother of his children. But that may never be. What did Maggie say when they were in Scotland? "Wishing and hoping and thinking and even praying, didn't make it so." How he longed to be back among the heather and thistle. He regretted so many missed opportunities to express his love.

Voices from the past replayed in his mind, "You're so timid and shy. You'll never amount to anything." He had tried hard to rip those labels off, but succumbed and returned to his shell. He recognized the need to reverse that image, yet he lacked the power. So, once again, he foolishly let those prime moments slip through his fingers, lost forever.

Lost forever. Would she be? He knew the time had arrived for him to test the waters of his new found faith. Time to get serious with God. He remembered Ernest's comment in Scotland, "We're fishing, and yet, I'm casting my faith line out to you in the hopes you will latch on to the bait and follow Jesus." Max definitely needed to cast his faith line to the Lord and catch strength and guidance for what lay ahead. A moan interrupted his thoughts.

"Oh, Jed, I'm so sorry. That grease should be cool enough now. Go ahead."

Donna Hues

Made in the USA
Middletown, DE
16 July 2022